Rebel Pharaoh

Rebel Pharaoh

Hatshepsut Unveiled

Charlotte Kramer

Library of Congress Control Number:		2010917836
ISBN:	Hardcover	978-1-4568-2522-5
	Softcover	978-1-4568-2521-8
	Ebook	978-1-4568-2523-2

This book was printed in the United States of America.

To order additional copies of this book, contact:
Xlibris Corporation
1-888-795-4274
www.Xlibris.com
Orders@Xlibris.com
89296

CONTENTS

REBEL PHARAOH
HATSHEPSUT UNVEILED
PART II

HATSHEPSUT UNVEILED
PART III

PART IV
INRI
BY FIRE NATURE IS RENEWED WHOLE

Slip through the illusion of time and fasten wisdom firmly in her seat.

Allow my spirit to soar with you to the *place of the palaces*. Feel the wonder of eternal love as you walk the terraces of my temple. Stroll through my sweet gardens of myrrh.

Enter my world when cities of Egypt once sparkled like stars along the Nile. Travel with me to the mysterious 'Land of Punt.' See through veils of illusions on this journey of discovery.

I am a child princess. I am a chief wife. I am a queen. I am the most noblest of women.

I AM HATSHEPSUT
REBEL PHARAOH
QUEEN OF THE NILE

I would like to thank the following:

Lisa Davis, PhD: For your continual supply of research on elements of Egyptian dance and Egyptian culture.

Liz Rizollo: For information on Egyptian Belly dancing.

Peter Farrelly: For the photos of Hatshepsut's Temple and the specific notations on the backs of each photo.

Kevin Torregrosa, curator of reptiles at the St. Augustine Alligator Farm: For your expert advice on the nature of the Nile crocodile.

Fran Fala: For being my eyes on your felucca trip across the Nile to Hatshepsut's Temple.

Lou Ellen Tew: For your books on Ethiopia.

Mystery Lady: For your continual inspiration and loyalty. You inspired a character.

Gary Herrick: For your technical help.

Nicole Sarra: For your gentle prodding to complete this book.

Bob Kramer, my husband and best friend: For your unending faith in me.

I would like to dedicate this book to my dear friend, Emily Wilkerson, for sitting me firmly in my seat and giving me the set of tools for writing.

To the Reader

MUCH OF THIS fictional story, which is based on facts, takes place in the ancient city called the Place of the Palaces, also known as the beautiful Southern City. In the Ptolemaic period it was called Thebes, but now it is known as the city of Luxor.

The ancient mystical city of Ta Netjer was known as the Land of Punt, also called God's Land. To this day the location remains a subject of controversy. Some place it in Somalia and others in Ethiopia.

Tuthmosis and His Concubine

THE MIGHTY TUTHMOSIS gazed in awe at the grand palaces that embraced his world. He reached for his concubine, then pulled her close. He whispered into her ear, "Great is the power of my ancestors. I know all my gods and goddesses love me. They have surely blessed me with a mighty heritage in Egypt! But still I suffer from a troubled heart." He listened to the roaring Nile, and whispered, "At last, the waters have come."

"A troubled heart, my lord?" Mutnofre gave him a bashful look that concealed the cunning within her heart.

He stood proudly on the portico that overlooked the Nile. His gem-studded golden collar caught the reflection of the sun god Ra, shimmering translucent colors of green, red, and blue.

He gazed into his concubine's black-lined eyes and held back his sadness. He pressed his lips to hers. But the deafening roar of the Nile quelled his anxious heart. He laughed in an effort to repress his anguish, turned and pointed to the river.

"Ah, my ears long for that noisy sound! Look! The inundation has indeed come! Hapi, the god of the Nile, has blessed my Egypt once again. I shall arrange for the battling ships to entertain my people during the Feast of the Valley."

While the pharaoh muttered on about the yearly celebrations, Mutnofre silently planned her only option that would position her son into the royal house. She thought, *I am tired of waiting for the gods to favor my wishes. It is I that must create a deserving heritage for my own son.*

Tuthmosis's eyes were fixed on the bouncing feluccas being forced uncontrollably northward on the alluvial waters. For the moment his thoughts diverted to the glory of his world. He breathed in the Nile air and said, "My Southern City is a jewel. Look how the afternoon sun reflects across the water, giving the appearance of tiny gems dancing upon the surface. Ra has made this beautiful display just for me. It is your good fortune to be my favorite concubine, my little Mutnofre." Tuthmosis pressed a kiss on her lips, then breathed the breath of his greatness into her open mouth, but still his thoughts dwelled on the death of his firstborn son. The ache in his heart was overwhelming.

Mutnofre looked at her king with utter devotion and said, "Oh yes, it is my good fortune to live in such an exquisite city, and yes, I am immensely pleased to be your chief concubine, my lord." She brushed her hand across his chest and fondled the jewels on his golden collar. "You are such a great leader to your people. You are prized among all the pharaohs of your blessed Egypt. Your heart should feel privileged."

She placed a small yellow fruit inside his mouth, and kissed his lips. She thought, *I will lift his troubled heart,* then whispered, "I lust for you, my darling Tuthmosis. Do you lust for me?" She licked the juice dripping from his chin, then pressed a more sensual kiss on his lips. She pushed her warm body against his and waited for a response.

"It is true the pleasure of your touch excites me, my little Mutnofre." He fingered a string of amber stones that hung from her braided hair and thought, *I weaken to her beauty–a thing she must never know, an admission that I would deny even to the gods.* He looked impatiently at her, then turned his attention back to the reed dhows bouncing on the Nile. He mused on the word *lust.* It lingered in his heart like an echo soaring across the mountain range that fronted the King's Valley.

Tuthmosis watched the sun vanish behind the Valley of the Kings and observed the orange clouds arcing across the sky. He inhaled the Nile air, then answered, "Indeed I have a hunger for you, my little Mutnofre, but I lust for gold. My chief overseer told me to expect another shipment of gold on the first night of the full moon."

Tuthmosis turned toward the east. "And this is the night. The moon shall be rising soon, and if all goes well, I shall be visited by my gold bearers." He smiled with assurance, sipped his wine, and waited for the moon to crest above the eastern horizon.

After a while, an impatient look wrinkled his brow. "The moon is too slow for my agenda! I do not like to wait! Lingering here is making me anxious, so let's return to my apartment. My gold ship will be docking tonight. In the meantime, let us sup in my private apartment. We will await there for news from my annunciator."

Tuthmosis held Mutnofre close and silently prayed to Hathor, the mistress of heaven. *Hathor, my beloved goddess, bless me with a night of lively sex, sensual music, and more importantly, a bountiful supply of gold ingots. Hathor, remember the sadness of my heart. Grant me much peace!*

Anticipating this romantic interlude, the military king quickly guided his concubine across the private solaria, through the darkened halls of the royal complex and past the many temple guards armed with deadly bows and arrows.

While passing the wall sconces, the flames reflected onto his royal golden collar, causing the glistening jewels to sparkle like stars. The delicate scent of blue lotus whirled around the imperial complex and heightened the sensual expectations of the evening.

But at that moment, Mutnofre cared less about jewels and gold and tried to dismiss the aromatic appeal of the lotus. There was another matter that whirled like the desert wind inside her calculating heart.

She hurriedly walked the halls beside her lover and thought, *Tonight I will change his mind. I will persuade him with my words and, of course, my little secret, which is far more important than his silly gold.* A confident smile pressed her full lips while she gazed seductively at her king. She stepped inside the pharaoh's gold-glittered apartment and gathered her daring for her well-rehearsed presentment.

In the twilight hours outside the temple complex a full moon began to slowly crest above the eastern horizon. Inside the royal suite, Mutnofre began her seductive campaign to please her lord and his immense desires, but she also intended to please her own desires, which included her son's inheritance.

Meanwhile, sailing north on the Nile, the captain ordered the ingot ship to pass up the smaller ports. The strong arms of the oarsmen dipped and pulled their paddles through the water while the north flow of the annual inundation helped move the ship at a faster clip. The captain was responsible for the security of the pharaoh's gold and navigated with purpose and speed toward the illustrious port of the Southern City.

On the starboard side of the gold ship were the elegant temples glistening like jewels in the twilight. Servants began their ritual of lighting the lamps, giving the holy place a mystical appearance. The flames illuminated the hieroglyphs on the high wall with boldness, creating both fear and respect in the hearts of the Nile travelers and citizens.

On the port side of the gold ship stood the Necropolis town of Deir El-Medina spread out between the Valley of the Queens and the Valley of the Kings. This town was the home of the artisans and construction workers that supported the labor force for the eternal resting place of the royals. This Necropolis Valley, designed expressly as a burial site of the pharaohs and their queens, was a redevelopment program initiated by Tuthmosis.

In the dimming hours, stone masons continued to labor beneath a blur of rock powder. Granite, marble, and limestone were cut to a miter's edge using secret methods known only to stonecutters. The smell of burning limestone clashed with the aromas of grain beer, baking bread, garlic, and frying fish. The blend of aromas wafted through the air and drifted toward the gold ship. The ship passed through a plume of dust and angled closer to the port.

The crew on the lower deck pulled their oars through the waters, churning bolti (tilapia) to the surface. Hundreds of sea eagles shrieked their ancient sounds while following the waves. They flapped their wings and dove in a frenzy for the fish. Ninety-seven boatmen dragged their oars, slowing the speed of the gold ship.

The authorities at the harbor saw the approaching vessel, and immediately, the port workers began their practiced ritual. The ship's crew raised the imperial flag . . . a warning signal to the port authority that all activity was closed to commerce during the removal of the pharaoh's gold. Three short successive blows of the ram's horn signaled Theban's well-armed military troops to form tightly knitted columns of security. The captain's directives informed the oarsmen to ease the vessel into the assigned slip.

Within minutes, the gold bearers began hauling hundred's of heavy crates from the ship's hold across cedar planks and onto the tightly protected port docks. A third of the gold was reserved for the high priests to be later carried to the temples but only after the pharaoh's gold was delivered first.

The heavy clatter of sandaled feet pounded the Avenue of the Sphinxes during their march toward the private apartment of their great king. Ahead of the ingot bearers, running swiftly like a charging lion up the stone-covered avenue, a royal annunciator huffed and puffed the night air. His shiny imperial ring and golden collar band that identified his royal position, bounced around his neck as he ran.

The full moon slowly rose above the eastern horizon shining its brilliance over the royal complex. On the lips of those who knew about the gold shipment were these words, "Our great pharaoh and our temple priests will sleep well tonight. Their gold has arrived. Thanks be to our mighty Amun-Ra."

On the pharaoh's portico, a harpist plucked her stringed instrument and played slow syncopated beats.

Inside the royal apartment, Mutnofre teasingly crawled across the oversized bed. She slinked like a lioness creeping through a patch of lotus. Her movements matched the beat of the music. Keeping her seductive eyes fixed on her lover, she whispered, "The moon is shining just for your pleasure. You are Egypt! You champion Amun-Ra's heavenly authority, and you, my king, have told me that the word creates everything." Her eyes fixed on him like a predator ready to strike.

The king was enjoying the sensation of his lover's touch and focused only on his wants and her warm hand. He paid no attention to her prattle. He looked at her eyes and compared them to amber beetles glistening in the glow of the lamplight. She made him dizzy with desire.

Mutnofre continued her appeal. With the warmth of her sweet breathe, she whispered, "Simply tell them and the masses will behave! They will believe your words! They will listen to your voice. You are grand in the eyes of your citizens." She leaned down and said, "Remember, the word creates everything! Those are your very words, my love. After all, you are the one who educated me about the powerful seduction of the speaking stones."

Tuthmosis quickly sensed the intentions of Mutnofre and tried to ease his annoyance. He inhaled deeply, then uttered, "Mutnofre, your persistence about this matter is growing weary with me." He took a sip of wine and desired a more pleasurable encounter with his beautiful concubine. He looked up at his star-studded ceiling and studied the Sirius star system that the temple artisan had painted above his bed. "Come to me, my lustful little Suki." He grabbed her by the arm and pulled her close. "This is no time for prattle. Let us love beneath the sparkling stars."

Mutnofre winced at her undignified pet name, Suki, but her mind stayed the course. *I will create my own heritage in the House of Tuthmosis.* The jewels in her hairpiece jingled as she lowered herself to her lord pharaoh. Her amber eyes mesmerized the king, and her body expressed more sensuality compared to his other concubines.

With one long sigh, the seductress whispered, "But you, My Lord, are the Mighty Tuthmosis, the most powerful man on earth! Surely you can change the rules of succession."

The words "rules of succession" grabbed his heart like the vicious teeth of a badger. Still, in spite of his anger, he anticipated a more congenial evening with Mutnofre. After all, there was a reason why she was his favorite.

She began massaging his muscular thighs with Kyphi oil. She moved her nude body against his like a snake slithering across the desert dunes. Her heart pounded with confidence. She knew her ploy, along with her well-rehearsed poem and little secret would settle their recurring debate. She also knew poetry inspired him, and perhaps, tonight she might be able to harness his heart.

The aroma of burning frankincense drifted around the room. Her lips brushed against his sunburned cheek and whispered, "Oh magnificent one, your loins bring forth seeds from celestial gods, and my body is your earthly paradise. For the second time, I will cultivate your heavenly seed and the mighty ancients will defend our children . . . and so it is . . . Selah." *Hopefully that sealed it!*

Tuthmosis reclined in silence, enjoying the warm hands of his concubine. His mind was blurry with excitement, but somehow, the word *succession* throbbed like a painful dagger wedged inside his heart. The word "succession" was like an oyster too large to swallow.

Her soft voice was inviting and affectionate. She batted her eyes, then leaned closer to his ear and whispered, "The priestess tells me that I am with child again. Perhaps, Bes, our eminent god of children, will grant us a girl this time. She will be a fitting wife for our dear son and *future pharaoh.* Surely, you must agree."

Tuthmosis looked at her with his piercing dark eyes. "Our son and future pharaoh? Enough!" His nostrils flared in anger. He reached for his wine-filled goblet and swallowed hard. His hard set eyes stared like two flaming arrows aiming straight into the eyes of Mutnofre. His dynastic member withdrew like the sun vanishing behind a cloud.

She waited at slavish attention for Tuthmosis to answer. She blinked in anticipation and offered him a stuffed fig. Her eyes resumed the sparkle of seduction. "Eat, oh divine one. I am most favored by Bes. I am as fertile as your chief wife when she was in her prime. I feel your sacred seed leaping within me this very moment, my love. Oh, there it is again!" Mutnofre coolly gazed into the eyes of her lover like a snake eyeing its prey. "Place your hand here, my king." She forced his hand to feel the movement of his child.

She studied his squinting stare and tightly brooding lips. With a dutiful voice she asked, "My lord, are you not pleased with me?" Her eyes sparkled like the heavenly stars that twinkled above the beautiful Southern City.

Tuthmosis stared at his lesser wife and for a brief moment lost the boldness that gave him the strut used for his past military campaigns. His mind, for an instant, weakened between the sheets. He thought, *Damn! I wish she wasn't so bewitching!* With a callous tone he shouted, "Mutnofre! You are a willful little Suki! Are you trying to dull my thinking with your come-hither stare and this spiked wine? I am growing weary with your annoying plea! You know I have another son . . . Amenmose. It is he who will be the one in line to inherit my throne! His right of kingship cannot be circumvented by your . . . uh . . . our boy! It is true my one remaining royal son is becoming puny and frail by day and night, but you must remember that Amenmose is a *full* royal, a pure prince, my little saucy girl! Times like these I wish you were not such a tasty and insignificant morsel."

Mutnofre's eyes held back the insult and blinked in bold defiance. Her tight lips curved to a smile, and gazed back at her king with daring confidence.

Oh, she is a cunning woman. Tuthmosis eyed his concubine, upended the goblet, wiped his mouth, then continued, "To make certain his health improves I have instructed the high priest to administer him a daily potion of crocodile blood." Tuthmosis inhaled deeply and with bold confidence yelled, "My son will recover, you will see!"

"Do not forget, Ahmose, my chief wife, your half sister, possesses pure royal blood of the ancients! Combined with my own blood, my son Amenmose is

Egypt's choice." Thumping his chest he yelled, "Have you forgotten to use your most sacred thinking organ?"

Pharaoh's heartbeat quickened like the pounding of a drum. "So, let us put an end to this chatter! The succession of the purest blood is victorious to Egypt! And the succession will surely be Amenmose and no one else!"

His eyes reduced to slits. "If this does not please you, my little Mutnofre, I can always provide you with a minor apartment with fewer trappings if this royal life is too demanding. Perhaps you need a change." His stare fixed on her like an archer eyeing his mark.

Her eyes widened from the insult. Accustomed to extravagant quarters, the threat of economizing her lifestyle sobered her quickly because that kind of change always meant being thrust aside for a more fit and youthful wife. She feigned a saddened expression. With downcast eyes she peeped, "I shall not mention it again. Forgive me, oh divine one."

Tuthmosis sipped more of the wine mixture, then gripped Mutnofre's arm. Anger began to brew inside his heart. He swallowed hard, and with clenched teeth, he said with boldness, "I am Egypt!" He proudly thumped his bare chest. "I know the word creates everything! I have dictated many words! Words that tell my people what to love, what to hate, and what to fear! I know the word is the totality of being! Nothing exists before it has been uttered in a clear voice! I know this, and that is why I make the laws for my people! When I command terms for my beautiful Egypt and her citizens, it shall be spoken clearly from my mouth and not from the mouth of an insignificant concubine! Upon my authority my conditions shall be written into law! My mind will not be tinkered by gestures of seduction and this numbing poppy drink posing as wine! Mutnofre, it is your duty to soothe my loins, not plot the course of Egypt!"

Gulping the last of his drink, he tossed the golden goblet into the air. It bounced and rolled across the stone floor. He angrily pinned her against his cotton-stuffed bed and stared into her cold, blank eyes. He sternly reminded her, "You must not forget that you are a lesser wife, my saucy little Mutnofre! I order you to my imperial quarters for comfort not for conflict! The citizens must have a *full* royal for their pharaoh, not a half stripling! Full royals bring valor to Egypt! And not a word more on this subject should be spoken! Do you hear?"

Mutnofre gasped and surrendered to the will of her mighty king. In a breathless tone she puffed, "Amen! Amen! I agree! I agree! Forgive me, my lord. I shall not mention it again . . . Oh magnificent one . . . Blessed pharaoh of Egypt . . . my love . . . oh, my love . . . my love."

Although he anticipated a night of heavenly lovemaking, the king's anger had morphed his intentions into one of brute force. The thrust of his angry passion was so fierce that it nearly knocked the breath right out of Mutnofre. Occasionally, his chief concubine needed to be put in her place and tonight was such a night.

Exhausted, Tuthmosis fell back and sprawled onto his goose-down pillows. "Our capers are finished! Return to your quarters! I need my rest because tomorrow I must journey across the Nile to the Valley of the Kings. My master stonecutter wishes that I observe the splendor of my tomb."

He looked at a tray of honey cakes positioned close to his bed. He reached for a piece and took a bite. With his mouth filled with cake he yelled, "Out of here! You depress me with your impudence. Leave me with my favorite sweet cakes! Honey indeed is the nectar of the gods, and I am an earthly god! You are dismissed, Suki, my little wicked girl."

Downhearted and seething with anger, Mutnofre forced a smile on her lips. She crawled out of the king's lavish bed, put on her garments and tip-toed to the door.

In the darkened room Tuthmosis uttered the name of his child, "Hatshepsut!"

Mutnofre turned, looked at the pharaoh, "Hatshepsut? What about Hatshepsut?"

"Oh, it is a possibility, my dear little Mutnofre." One eyebrow raised in sureness.

"The citizens would never accept a woman for their pharaoh, my dear king."

Tuthmosis took a large bite of his honey cake and smiled at his concubine. "You are an impudent woman, Mutnofre. Time is the greatest revealer of all things."

Mutnofre's anger bloomed like yeast in heat. Jealousy and revenge tainted the very air surrounding her and drifted throughout the royal palace with her every footfall. She slammed the heavy cedar door and walked hurriedly to her apartment. *I will turn the heads of the gods, and their eyes will look favorably upon my son,* she thought as she made her way back to her quarters.

Pharaoh's mindfulness about the evening's events churned inside his heart like beer fizzing over the rim of a goblet. *Tomorrow I shall visit my tomb. My gold . . . where is my gold? The nerve of her to suggest changing the rules of succession! It is possible for my little Hatsu to become pharaoh if her brother should not survive! Yes, indeed, I have heard of such a thing!*

He finished a couple of his favorite cakes, and closed his eyes to a restless sleep. Thoughts continued to roil inside his head like a grist mill grinding grain. *The blood of the crocodile will surely improve the health of my boy, but will he be a healthy and powerful pharaoh? Hatsu, my little girl, has the blood most pure. She is smart beyond her years. It is possible for her to become king. Our history records such matter.* Those were the last thoughts before sleep closed the eyes of the mighty king.

Nut, the sky-goddess, began to stretch her long arms over Geb, the earth-god.

Within the hour an out-of-breath annunciator knocked on the heavy, sculptured door. He shouted, "Inform His Royal Majesty that his gold ship has arrived, and the ingot bearers are on their way!"

Just as the king had fallen into slumber a chamber maid leaned over the sleeping figure and with a soft but firm voice said, "Highest of men, your gold has arrived."

Up like a striking snake, Tuthmosis leaped across the floor and hurried toward the door. The annunciator stood inside the antechamber, but at the sight of the king, he dropped to his knees and huffed, "Your gold ship . . . my lord . . . it has arrived and the bearers will be here in the blink of an eye."

Tuthmosis turned to his servants and yelled, "Start your course of action! Open my vaults immediately! My gold has come at last!"

Inside the royal bed chamber, the pharaoh's loyal servants hustled to and fro activating their ritual system of unlocking the subterranean passageway to their king's personal storehouse.

Several hours later, the clatter of activity within the temple complex quieted. The moon traveled high across the western sky and fell behind the cliffs that protected the King's Valley. But, sleep did not come to Mutnofre, only anger. It simmered inside her stomach like the red-orange lava boiling inside the belly of a volcano.

She muttered aloud, "Half-royal stripling . . . bitch . . . Suki . . . insignificant one!" Mutnofre closed her eyes to a fitful sleep but only flopped around like a dying fish on the Nile shore.

Before Ra had the chance to lift his splendid rays above the eastern horizon, Mutnofre had already dressed. She closed the door to her apartment and scampered across the stone floor quicker than a panicky Nile rat.

Torches flickered, casting eerie shadows against the mural painted walls. Her sandaled feet tapped lightly across the limestone floor as she rushed beneath the canopied covered solaria. She left the safety of the luxurious temple complex, then ran along the Esplanade of the Sphinxes. She turned onto a dreary alleyway marked Canopus, the Ardu section of the city that was the residence of embalmers, diviners, and a few low-priced prostitutes.

An odor of decaying body fluids drifted from the opened doorways and high windows of the embalmers while she walked along the dark section of the city. She pressed a section of her cloak across her nose to keep from gagging.

Mutnofre's malevolent eyes narrowed and in a desperate tone sobbed, "Lata, you must make it more powerful! It has rendered him only weak and puny! I thought you said it would surely do him in like the other child! Now his father has ordered the priest to administer him a daily blend of crocodile blood! Woe to me! My heritage is fading in front of my eyes!"

A shock of disheveled white hair covered the old woman's head. Bewildered from being awakened in the middle of the night, her drowsy eyes glared beneath her pink, sagging lids. She looked up at Mutnofre and whispered, "My kind of poison takes patience! This potion is not swift like rushing waters. It is slow like a meandering stream. Bit by bit, day by day it will take its toll! I told you it will kill the same as it did his older brother! It is undetectable. You have very little patience, Mutnofre!"

A table adorned with bowls of sweet-smelling oleander petals permeated the stale air within the simple, mud-hewn house. Outside, on the porch, stood a hive of bees, some of which had begun to leave their colony in their search for floral nectar. They didn't have far to travel because their target was oleander bushes planted nearby. They swarmed in frenzy around the fragrant petals.

Lata's wizened penetrating eyes glared back at her night visitor, and with a fragile voice she assured, "However, since the child is taking the miracle drink, which is good to know, perhaps I should increase the dose. I will have a new mixture ready in three days. I will also have an incantation for you to recite when you are putting it into honey cakes. It will add power to your intentions. Now! Be patient! Return to your comfortable sanctuary and let me return to my humble cot! Remember to hide your face when you leave from here. No one must know who you are when you wind your way through the streets."

A flustered Mutnofre placed her hand on the door handle. Prepared to leave she sighed, "I shall return in three days."

However, before Mutnofre stepped from the doorway, Lata let out a pathetic groan, "Oh . . . You know I am old and a poor widow. It is hard for me to stay alive on my meager stash. Can you show me a little special kindness this evening? The gold dust on your apartment floor gathered beneath you sandals represents to me a week's larder of food."

Mutnofre reached inside her belt and pulled out a golden nugget. "I will have more for you when I return for the new potion." She placed it next to the bowl of floating oleander.

"Oh, thank you!" Lata stood at her doorway and whispered, "And may the god of Ammit be with you." She watched the shady figure of the pharaoh's favorite concubine vanish down the street.

Quickly she locked the door, then impatiently stepped toward the golden nugget. She snatched it up, placed it inside her mouth, and swallowed. *At least it will be safe for a few days, just in case someone might have been watching from the shadows.*

Lata walked toward the bee hive and observed the honey cells. She pushed out the honey from the uncapped cells and captured the liquid in a vessel.

Uncapped honey from the oleander was a deadly poisonous toxin used in the ancient world, and Lata provided it to her customers from time to time. She sat down an unrolled a papyrus scroll. She dipped a goose feather in her plant-extracted ink and wrote the following:

Flow out thou poison; come forth upon the ground. Horus conjures thee; he cuts thee off, he spits thee out, and thou risest not up but fallest down. Thou art weak and not strong, a coward who dost not fight.

She finished writing the incantation, then added the powerful name of Obbicuth to be uttered when Mutnofre planned the occasion for the young Amenmose to eat of the delicious but deadly honey cake.

Several nights later Mutnofre wrapped a hijab around her head and again tiptoed across the floor of the royal complex. Strapped around each ankle were well-hidden bags of nubs. The gold was heavy making her steps awkward. She made her way through the Ardu section passing the embalmers, diviners, and whoring section. She found this sector unpleasant. The smell of rotting intestines floated in the air. She pressed the veil against her nose, then knocked on the door of the potion maker who practiced the necessary arts.

"Ahh, it is ready for you. Come in, Mutnofre. There . . . on the table you will find your potion."

Mutnofre picked up an alabaster jar and embraced it firmly. *This will secure my son's heritage including my own!*

Lata spoke with a whisper, "There are important words that you must utter. Words that are as deadly as the potion that you are holding in your hands. Always remember when you invoke help from the spirit world it can be a very dangerous place. You are slipping through corridors of what is possible and what is not possible. It is like mercury . . . a place that blends and separates, conforms and rebels."

"You are scaring me, Lata! You will be paid well. I have your nubs right here!" She lifted her robe and showed Lata the gold. "This gold will safely guide me though the spirit world, won't it?"

"Mutnofre, it is important for you to understand that invoking the spirit world has to be done in a specific order. Wrongly spoken words have their consequence, gold or no gold! Now, listen carefully. These are the words that you must say, and you must say them in perfect order when you personally hand the cake to Amenmose!"

The lamplight flickered in the squatty quarters. Lata picked up the papyrus and quietly trained Mutnofre in the forbidden world of the mesh-man, a winged creature of half-man and half-bird.

"Remember, you must say his name correctly . . . shuuu . . . do not utter it carelessly . . . speak his name right." Lata pronounced the name quietly. "Shuuu . . . Obbicuth . . . shuuu. And you must ask him to protect you too as well as any future children that will come forth from your loins."

Several days went by and Ra radiated brightness over the beautiful Southern City.

"Here, my brother, Amenmose, eat my mother's honey cakes. She says this will make you feel much better. This cake was made with the nectar of heavenly bees. She offered me one, which I have already eaten, and she said you must eat this one." He held it up to entice Amenmose and remembered his mother instructing him to be sure not to lick his hands.

Mutnofre watched from the shadows while her son unknowingly orchestrated his heritage. She smiled evilly when Amenmose reached for the cake and hungrily devoured all of it. Within minutes the skin of Amenmose, the last of the pure prince from the male line of the great king, turned a ghastly shade of blue, and shortly thereafter, he died.

Not surprising, the impatient Mutnofre ignored the rules set forth by Lata regarding the spirit realm. She was the one who was supposed to hand the cake to Amenmose while at the same time uttering the incantation softly.

Her son should have never been involved. She failed to also end the verse by asking the powerful Obbicuth for protection for herself and her unborn.

By not following instructions, Mutnofre had carelessly opened up a corridor to the powers of otherworld.

Funerary Procession

BENEATH THE HOT Egyptian sun, military units marched protectively on both sides of the funerary procession. Dressed in metal-covered regalia, the soldiers on the left clutched their glistening pikes, keeping them gripped at the ready.

Prized Nubian archers, bearing composite bows, marched on the right side of the procession. Their fingers held their bows and were prepared to release the arrows at the slightest threatening movement.

In unison, the sharp-pointed pikes jabbed at the sky and the menacing arrow's deadly aim pointed toward the grieving citizens as the well-practiced armed forces strutted toward the port.

Inside this protective column of soldiers walked a long line of royals while the masses of citizens bowed prostrate with outstretched arms. The people picked up the dirt and flung it over their heads expressing their sorrow and grief. Theban women wailed and trilled their tongues, each louder than the next, creating a steady din along the sphinx-adorned esplanade. The death of the second full royal son crazed the masses with unbearable sorrow.

Leading the procession was an impressive gold embossed barque. Carried on the shoulders of eight strong guards, this holy barque created awe in the eyes of the onlookers. Standing on the bow was Ptah (Peh-tah), the high priest of Egypt, yelling, "Westward, westward, to the land of the just!"

Blaring from the inside of a concealed cubicle, located on the center platform, roared the shrieking sound of a ram's horn. The blast cowed the masses into submission.

Standing at the stern was a younger priest holding up for all to see, the highly venerated scrolls called the *Theban Recension* ("The Book of Coming or Going Forth by Day").

This Book of the Dead was always placed inside the royal sarcophagus to insure the deceased an easy entrance into the afterlife. It contained hymns to Ma'at and Osiris, charms, curses, and ways to avoid Ammit, the destroyer, who threatened the dead in their afterlife.

Next in the procession was a small gold and silver-covered sarcophagus. It was carried on the broad shoulders of privilege Nubians. They stepped along the palm-covered road that led to the port of Thebes.

The royal procession paraded past nine hundred ram-headed sphinxes, representing the god Amun. Their chiseled eyes, fixed in stone, blankly gazed back at the passing pageant of the somber sovereigns.

Following the golden crafted coffin was the shoulder-held royal litter of Tuthmosis and his chief wife, Ahmose, the mother of the deceased royal. Her sad eyes gazed in disbelief upon her son's sparkling sarcophagus.

She murmured, "Like his older brother, his life was but a fleeting star. He was hardly noticed by Egypt. Our two sons had no chance to leave their names in stone. They had committed no wrongdoing. Like his brother, I know goddess Ma'at will find his heart to be the exact weight as a feather." Tears welled inside Ahmose's coal-lined eyes and slide down her tear-stained cheeks.

A desperate cry erupted from her throat, "Neither son had a chance to leave their heritage in Egypt. Woe to me. I am a broken woman."

A desperate Ahmose looked at her husband and screamed, "Someone is killing off the royal blood of our ancestors! Egypt's power will suffer and be usurped yet again."

Tuthmosis listened to the cries of his chief wife and blankly stared at the moored ships bouncing upon the port waters. His lips quivered like a dying fish. His eyes filled with tears. *Ahmose is right! Amun-Ra must be displeased with me! My precious royal blood is vanishing. My heart has been rent asunder. Losing my two most royal of sons is more than my heart can bear! Woe to me!*

His thoughts turned to Hatshepsut. *She is the only one of my many children left that has the bloodline of the greats. Strength of character is in her lineage. Oh how I wish she were a boy! Mutnofre's son is only a weakened royal . . . alas . . . but fate has placed him next in line, unless I feel he cannot be groomed for the task.* Tuthmosis thought about the last encounter he had with Mutnofre. The memory of that night irritated him like an itch that he couldn't scratch.

Following in a splendidly crafted litter marked with hieroglyphs, "most royal of children," sat his daughter, the young eight-year-old Hatshepsut. A look of sadness stamped her lips. Her thin, fragile body slumped beside her handmaiden, Sitre-Re. She remembered when she used to ride inside the royal craft with her two older brothers, Wadjmose and Amenmose. She looked at the empty spaces where they would have been sitting if they were still alive. A tear slid down her cheek. Their empty seats seemed strangely sacred.

Sitre-Re spoke softly, "You must learn to smile even in the face of disaster. Someday you will be the queen, Hatshepsut. So you must sit like a princess, not like a thirsty lotus."

The citizens of Thebes bowed at the passing procession. The mournful sounds of wailing were deafening. Hatshepsut sat up and peered from the window of her ornate transport. A serene smile pressed her lips. Soft as a demure breeze she uttered, "No, Sitre-Re, someday, I will be pharaoh." But the sounds of the soldier's leather-bound sandals and the clatter of their pikes pounding the stone road muffled her hushed, yet bold, pronouncement.

The ongoing clank of the marching guards was a reminder of the grand task of protecting the royals. Near the end of the solemn procession, a less ornate litter followed.

Inside the shoulder-held craft Mutnofre clutched her son's hand. She whispered into his ear, "Your father has instructed me to tell you that now you will be next in succession. From now on you will be known as Tuthmosis II. You are in line for the throne, my most royal son."

The young boy pulled his hand from his mother's clutches and began picking off a patch of white scabs from his forearm. He paid no mind to his mother's chatter.

The cheery Mutnofre reclined inside her stuffy carriage. Among the grief-stricken citizens she suddenly spotted Lata. Their eyes locked in a knowing gaze, a look of guilt and a look of entitlement, both realizing the roles they had played in the turn of events. They broke their stares and Mutnofre exhaled and gave a maternal tap to her swollen belly, fanning her face from Egypt's desert heat. But a nagging discomfort gripped her loins.

Looking down at her stomach, she said in a grimacing tone, "In time, my dear little one, you will either become chief wife or a brother to Egypt's next pharaoh." She forced a wry smile on her lips as she kept an evil eye on the craft before her. *It is I who will direct the destiny of Egypt, not royal blood. It is the great god of Egypt, Amun-Ra who has now declared my son a pure prince.*

Mutnofre leaned back, closed her eyes, and whispered to herself, "Finally my heritage to my beloved Egypt is secure."

Cramping in her loins suddenly came upon her. She grabbed her belly and began to scream.

A Bungled Curse

"WHAT DID I do wrong? Woe is me! Tell me what is happening?" Mutnofre screamed out in pain and yelped like a wounded dog. She looked toward her door and asked, "Is she here yet? She can bring me a special drink to keep this thing from happening."

The royal physician spoke in matter-of-fact terms, "Mutnofre, sometimes a body cannot carry a child and no potion can be swallowed now because this miscarriage has already happened. You lost your child, and I cannot undo what is done. You must rest, Mutnofre."

The physician promptly left Mutnofre's apartment with the swaddled dead child and quickly took it to Imeut, the lord of the place of embalming.

Back in the birthing chamber, the maid servants could only provide simple comfort to the king's chief concubine.

A knock on the door could be heard.

"It is a lady who says she has a potion for you."

Mutnofre whimpered and screamed between offensive words and streams of tears. "Let her in now! . . . *(sob)* . . . Leave! . . . *(sob)* . . . Curses to all of you!"

The maids quickly left the room, and Lata walked toward the bed.

Mutnofre angrily whispered, "You did this to me!"

Lata stared back at the frantic woman. "Shuu . . . you stupid woman!" In a hushed tone she continued, "I gave you a perfect incantation. You must have bungled the curse. Now, tell me exactly what you did."

Mutnofre whispered between sobs. "I gave the cake to my son . . . *(sob)* . . . and he gave it to his half brother. Then I told him exactly what you said must be uttered . . . *sob.* He said your very words!"

Lata stared in disbelief. "You did what? You were supposed to do it yourself! You bungled it, Mutnofre. I warned you that the corridors of the spirit world were like mercury . . . it conforms, yet, rebels. It is important not to puzzle the spirits. You have mystified them. You confused the intention of your curse with your bungled words, and they have killed your baby. The only thing I can do now is to evoke Obbicuth to put an end to this curse that you made wobbly to the spirit's ears."

"I warn you, Mutnofre! You are in dangerous space! So now what do you want me to do?"

"Bees . . . you will teach me about bees and poisons of all kinds that can never be traced! You will teach me the necessary arts. Give me the precise words to make this curse stop. I must get back in the favor of my king. Gossips tell me he is busy with a younger courtesan. Woe to me."

Lata leaned down and whispered a string of words in precise order to make the curse find its end, then gave her three sips of a bitter drink.

Mutnofre repeated the words in a specific order and in a matter of minutes she was asleep.

Mutnofre Tries Again

"I AM IN MY fertile time, my lord. I know these things." Mutnofre looks into the eyes of Tuthmosis. "Do not be afraid of me, my king. Let us lie together. I have missed you these past months. I will make you feel blessed."

Mutnofre poured oils onto the loins of her pharaoh and began rubbing it into his skin. She embraced her king and kissed his mouth. "We both have felt the sting of death. I have love for you and wish to bring joy back to our hearts again."

"I am learning the cooking arts. You must taste this, my love." Mutnofre picked up a stuffed fig and touched it to her king's lips.

Tuthmosis opened his mouth and enjoyed Mutnofre's sweetness. He folded his arms around Mutnofre and passion flowed once more between them.

A Royal in Danger

A BRIGHT BLUE SKY arced above the city of Niwt-rst. Rays of Amun-Ra reached down and touched the golden shafts of emmer wheat fields that bordered the many miles along the Nile. Northeasterly winds rushed through a very impressive yet unfinished temple and whirled around the massive pillars.

A revered temple cat slowly slinked along the base of a colossal column pressing against the shock of brightly colored hieroglyphs. The shrill of its meow echoed eerily down the tall gallery of pillars. It prowled across the stone floor, scampered over a small foot bridge, scaled a privacy wall, then jumped inside a concealed solarium.

The young princess smiled, "There you are, my sacred cat." She leaned over and placed a warm bowl of goat milk on the floor. "This is for you, Bastet, now drink up."

Beneath the underbrush, veiled in the shade of a garden plant, slithered a deadly Black Mamba. Its black inky mouth opened wide revealing its poisonous white fangs. Its strong and slender body struck the cat several times with lightening speed! Poised with a sense of victory the snake's coffin-shaped head postured in silence. The small, black, viperous eyes of the Mamba watched its quivering prey and waited for the deadly venom to kill.

The doomed temple cat quivered briefly while his lifeless green eyes shimmered like glass beads, aiming its death-like gaze toward the terrified Princess Hatshepsut.

The Mamba began its task of consuming its kill. Its mouth opened wide, the jaw unhinged, and soon the head of the cat was being retracted inside the jaws of the snake. Slowly but surely inch by inch it completely devoured the temple cat. The tip of its tail was the last to disappear.

Within minutes chaos filled the temple complex. Pharaoh Tuthmosis, a man of renowned military might, stormed through the hypostyle that led to the apartment of his precious daughter, Hatsu (Hatshepsut.) His bodyguards, ever ready to defend their much-loved pharaoh, followed behind him like the tail of a charging lion. The king kicked the door open and entered his daughter's private apartment. Like a raging sandstorm blazing across the Necropolis he overturned and pitched open every piece of furniture. He tossed each article of clothing from her wardrobe and fingered through them like a monkey picking flees from its offspring.

Pharaoh crawled around on his hands and knees searching for the smallest of hiding places, examining every corner, crack and crevice within Hatsu's apartment. He was looking for a possible mate to the viper now lying in pieces on the cold gray floor.

Cleverly concealed beneath the fringe of an exotic rug, the mate to the Mamba lifted its smooth, coffin head, and flicked its thin, black tongue. Tuthmosis saw it! Anger boiled inside his heart like molten rock oozing from the earth.

Tuthmosis slowly rose to his feet and tactfully raised his weapon, slashing the blade downward like a military pro. His powerful driving force that controlled the blade chopped through the viper and permanently etched a crack into the floor . . . a crack that would still be visible thousands of years into the future. The Egyptians venerated and feared the serpent.

He picked up the snake with his blade and threw it on top of its dead mate. He rose to his feet and said to his guards, "Remove these deadly serpents from my house and have them mummified! Take this sacred cat to the embalmers and have it mummified!"

"Someone wants my royal blood to come to an end! The gods cannot be against me! I show respect to all my ancestors and to all the gods! I will find out who is behind this evil deed and, when I do, I will personally remove his head and feed it to the crocodiles!"

Kahn The Protector

"YOU MUST KEEP your head down," one servant instructed as the other showed the Asiatic guest the respected protocol for addressing the royal sovereign. The two Nubian guards opened the heavy wooden door to the pharaoh's private conference room. They motioned for the guest to enter. "Remember, do not look upon his face!"

The mysterious man entered the luxurious gold-glittered room. His bronze-colored muscular body, smoothed by the mountain winds, walked respectfully toward the seated pharaoh. His long black hair was bound by a string of badger hide. He knelt and reverently touched his forehead to the floor. He lifted his head to kiss the gem-studded, sandaled feet of the great Tuthmosis and remained bowed as he listened to the commanding voice of the legendary military hero.

Two green Narmer Palettes hung on the wall like powerful testaments behind the seated king. Tuthmosis leaned forward and gripped the arms of his gilded throne. An angry frown formed across his forehead. His eyebrows had been shorn clean, a religious covenant to honor the death of his favorite temple cat. He spoke in Egyptian and chose unwavering heart-felt words, "My daughter, Princess Hatshepsut, is a treasure to me and to the future of Egypt. She has the most royal bloodline of what's left of my pure children. I fear there are ever-present sinister schemes that flourish even in this holy place. I have lost two sons to a strange and uncommon sickness and recently I found two deadly Black Mambas slithering inside my daughter's apartment. I am quite certain they were meant for her."

Tuthmosis drew in a breath and stared down at the man. He thought to himself, *I hate these vile, godless Asiatics.* Emphasizing his words in a clear-cut and precise manner, he spoke. "So, I am searching for a personal bodyguard for my daughter. It has come to my ears that you are the best!"

A touch of sadness shadowed the face of the pharaoh. He exhaled, "I despise the thought that possibly my very own people are guilty of putting an end to the House of Tuthmosis. I am afraid this evil could be in my very own administration, residing within these sacred temple walls. It is a dangerous plot planned by a wicked rogue who wants my precious and most royal daughter dead. Deception gnaws at the heart of my administration like a deadly plague. You see, Hatshepsut carries the purest bloodline of all my children. Her full-royal siblings are both dead, but I know their spirits dance nightly in the temple. Now, I fear that someone is targeting my daughter, Hatshepsut. I call her my darling Hatsu. She must be protected at all cost because she is the only royal that can continue the future Tuthmosis bloodline which will maintain our continued heritage in Egypt."

Tuthmosis took a sip of wine and twisted the golden goblet between his hands. "You have come highly recommended. I understand that you are a master of a unique killing art." He shifted forward on his throne and said in a clear voice, "I promise you this, if you protect my daughter and devote your life to her for as long as you breathe, you will live richly within these palace walls." Tuthmosis rose from his golden throne and stood before the bowing figure. "Do you accept my offer?"

In a heavy accent the impressive Asiatic endeavored to answer in halted Egyptian, "Lord of greatness . . . you have chosen well. I will be a good guard for the princess, Egypt's future woman. I know how to protect Princess Hatshepsut with my eyes and hands. I will be her shield of safety for all time. My word is more precious than silver and gold!"

Relieved, Tuthmosis said, "You may rise! On your feet, great Kahn of Might! In several moons we will be celebrating the Feast of the Valley, and I want everyone to know that Hatsu is being guarded by an Asiatic." A triumphant smile pressed the lips of the great king.

Well, pleased with the outcome of the interview, Tuthmosis presented him with a belt made from hippopotamus hide, and then with a grateful sigh of relief whispered, "I shall depend on you."

Saddled within the belt was a short-handled knife. The blade was a blending of copper and tin, exhibiting the official seal of Tuthmosis, His Greatness of all the domains of Egypt.

Kahn cupped his hand around the handle. He kept his eyes focused on the floor, then back-stepped toward the door.

Celebration of Praise—The Beautiful Feast of the Valley

KAHN QUICKLY SETTLED into an apartment located just inside the luxurious quarters of the pharaoh's daughter. He blended with the shadows that lurked within the warren of temple halls. Like a well-crafted arrow, he had found his mark.

His Asiatic presence created a new sense of fear in the hearts of the temple royals. His Mongolian eyes could count the hair on a fly a stone's throw away. His night vision was masterful, and he could see shadows lurking even in the blackness of the night. His preferred killing art were small, star-shaped weapons. He could discharge them with deadly accuracy. They were sharp, obsidian glass and metal discs filed to a hair-thin edge. When thrown, they could rip clean through a man's torso. He kept them hidden within the folds of his loin skirt. Arms folded, he stood like a stone statue inside the private entrance to Hatshepsut's apartment and guarded her with his vigilant eyes.

In the background, the hypnotic blend of a harp and mizmar (high-pitched flute) resonated from the western end of the temple.

"It is absolutely essential that I surpass my devious and scheming half brother! He constantly tries to intimidate me! My father claims that I, the remarkable Princess Hatshepsut, should have been born a boy! He maintains that Egypt would flourish like living waters under my rule! He laughs, but I know he speaks the truth because I have heard that truth comes out in jest."

With pleading eyes, the princess looked at her trusted maidservant. "Sitre-Re, make me beautiful! Make me shine! I must appear as though Ra himself kissed my skin. Smooth your special blend over my body! I possess a knowing that someday I will become pharaoh."

Sitre-Re had milled gold into a powdery mixture so fine that if not careful, in its powdery form, could be inhaled through the nose. She blended it with essential oils, an exotic fragrance extracted from lotus.

Aware of eavesdropping temple spies, she cautiously whispered, "Hatsu, you will appear as a beam of light sent from our god, Ra, to shine over all of Egypt. From this day forward, both your attitude and your appearance must confirm your powerful destiny. It is wise to live like you have already received Ra's blessings."

Sitre-Re began massaging the princess with her secret blend. Hatsu reclined in submission and listened attentively to the soft but instructive voice of her well-informed confidant and handmaiden.

"Princess Hatshepsut, it is you I adore and prefer among the other young royals. This unguent will make you sparkle like the sun. You will eclipse your half brother. I too believe you are the one who was born to rule. You are the remaining full-royal daughter of Chief Wife Ahmose and your father, the great Pharaoh Tuthmosis. I heard that Amun-Ra crept into your mother's apartment and lay down with her bringing forth the sweetness of his being. Here you are sparkling like your heavenly father. Egypt's eyes will follow, admire, and report your life for all to see. It is a knowing I have had from the moment I first came to care for you when you were still a suckling baby."

A fleeting moment of self-doubt settled on Hatsu's delicate features. She whispered, "Whoa, I am reminded that I am a girl child!" She pounded her fist on the chaise. "How on earth can I gain the favor of the gods so they will make the citizens accept me?"

Sitre-Re's vigilant eyes searched through the thin veil partition. She spotted Kahn who was standing at the ready. She exhaled a sigh of relief, but at the same time a little mystified by his presence. Sitre-Re was not used to having a guard in such close proximity, especially one so impressive.

She held the hands of her royal charge. In a whisper Sitre-Re assured the young princess. "Balance! That is one way to please the gods. You must keep balance in all things! My dear, glorious child, you are on the threshold of becoming a woman. When that day comes, you must say, 'It is *because* I am a woman I will be the first female pharaoh, favored by all the gods and I will be remembered and worshiped by the citizen of all the lands belonging to Egypt.' Never forget that you are a direct and royal descendant of not only Pharaoh Tuthmosis, your royal father, but you are the granddaughter of the mighty Pharaoh Ahmose and the blood descendant of his brave son, Pharaoh Amenhotep. You carry the bloodline of strong ancestral gods, including the great and powerful Amun-Ra! These royal ancients are looking out for you. Show respect to them, and in turn they will grant you the power and favor that you will need for your service to our blessed Egypt. Remember, my dear child, it is royal blood that possesses power."

Sitre-Re's sharp eyes, probing beyond the thin drapery, were always vigilant for spying eyes. *Even Kahn should not hear this,* she thought, then bent closer to Hatshepsut's ear and whispered, "It is recorded in the ancient manuscripts that once, before the earth fractured like a broken cake, women as well as men ruled as equal deities on earth."

Sitre-Re massaged Hatsu's arms with the ointment. Ever cautious, she continued to whisper, "Unbelievable as it may sound, the greatest threat to the power of man is woman. That, my dear, is a secret that you must closely guard within your heart. Even in your afterlife! Only breathe these sensitive matters into the ear of Ma'at, the goddess of balance, truth, and justice. Learn to call on her name. She will give you wisdom!"

Hatsu smiled as she absorbed Sitre-Re's unusual, yet insightful, advice.

Oiled and clad only with Sitre-Re's golden lotion and a few properly-positioned, stringed jewels, the young princess glistened like a child of the sun. Sitre-Re walked hand in hand with her royal charge, down the long, multi-columned hypostyle toward the solaria. Kahn walked behind them keeping a respectful distance. The sounds from the flutes were like a seductive opiate, luring them ever-closer toward the sunlit doorway.

The portico was filled with excitement. Thinly clad female musicians played beguiling songs on Zebrawood flutes, lyres, and harps. Enchanting songs of the

Nile captivated the royals who were lounging in the shade beneath the widely stretched cotton tarpaulin.

The imperial servants dipped golden goblets into the beer and wine that filled the decorative pounded silver and copper kettles. Kneeling before their charge, they offered the refreshing fruit and grain drinks.

A long, polished onyx table was adorned with oysters, mussels, shrimp, bolti fish (tilapia), olives, lentil cakes, wheat breads slathered in garlic sauce, and wrapped spirals of peacock tongues soaked in oil of mint. Honey cakes, pomegranates, figs, dates, and nuts satisfied their incessant desire for sweets. Beautiful and seductive thinly-clad acrobats and dancing girls preformed in erotic motion beneath the protective canopy.

The royals were famous for enjoying grand displays of indulgence. They had a taste for pleasure and the exotic but conversely they possessed strong moral values. In their lust for life most Egyptians lived their time on earth seeking balance and harmony in all things. A constant reminder of the "weighing of the heart" kept most Egyptians in line. The eye of Horus was always watching.

The beautiful Feast of the Valley was in full swing. Honoring a bountiful harvest, which always included venerating the dead, was the most important festival during the year.

Princess Hatsu respected all of the gods including her famous ancestor, Ahmose, the revered pharaoh who drove the usurpers and deceitful Hyksos out of Egypt. Hatsu's mother, Aahmes, took the name of her magnificent bloodline, the name Ahmose, the mighty warrior king who had years earlier regained control of Egypt and the vital Nubian gold mines which brought prosperity back to the empire.

The young princess, Hatsu, paused for a moment to take in her wonderful heritage. She began the long walk down the pillar-supported grand hallway. Her anxious eyes looked at her handmaiden, then asked, "Tell me again, Sitre-Re, of all the young royals am I the one you truly love the most?"

Sitre-Re's eyes, bold and aware, concealed her own personal ambitions for the royal princess. "Oh, my dear Hatsu, you are the one most blessed among all the other children from the royal house of Tuthmosis. You are indeed my favorite. You are the one that carries the purest blood of the greats. You are a complete goddess in the form of a spring bud." She looked down and smiled at the shimmering princess. Holding onto Hatsu's delicate fingers, she proudly guided her toward the solaria.

Sitre-Re then gave her a gentle reminder. “Remember Ma’at, goddess of truth and justice? She demands universal order, and she will always expect it from you! Someday, she will weigh your heart against a feather! Now, remember to keep your chin level with the floor. Shoulders back! Stand tall like an obelisk. In doing so you will possess the confidence of the gods! You must maintain dignity and balance. Do not frown. Do not laugh too much. Keep a serene smile on your lips because someday your peaceful smile will be carved in a giant block of granite. Remember, my glorious Hatshepsut, *believe* that you *will* be next in line. Go! Step out and expose your budding beauty for all to see and admire!”

They reached the end of the long hypostyle and waited for the curtains to be drawn. Two Nubians, flanking each side of the entrance, drew back the thin transparent drapes. In a show of reverence, they dropped their foreheads to the stone floor.

The young princess stepped confidently onto the eastern end of the grand Elysium that overlooked the Nile. Her nearly nude, delicate skin, resplendent with the secret oils of her personal handmaiden, dazzled the large gathering of royals. Children splashed, giggled, and delighted in the huge lotus-studded reflection pool. The chatter stopped and everyone looked in awe and watched as the princess walked beneath the shaded portico. Sitre-Re knew her secret formula would impress the royals and their attendants. All eyes were drawn to the most royal child of the great pharaoh, Tuthmosis.

A group of maidservants sat like a gaggle of geese along the water’s edge gossiping outlandish tales of palace intrigue. Drawing in their breath, they stared in feigned admiration at the late arrival. Trusted Nubians stood in mindless attention waiving ostrich feathers over the crowd. They quickly turned their fans toward the royal princess when she entered the portico. “She is surely a child of Ra!” were the mutterings of many as they kept their eyes fixed on Hatsu’s golden skin. The lyre and harp chimed louder as the musicians, expressing their admiration, increased their plucking vigor.

“Hatsu, you are golden, like the sun,” observed her half brother. “It is official now, and everyone must call me Tuthmosis II. Come and wet thy skin!”

Hatsu hesitated but kept a composed expression on her face. A serene smile pressed her full, sensuous lips as she looked at her half brother. *I will make him fear me,* she thought to herself. “You better be careful, my brother. You know how Amun-Ra makes your skin suffer.”

The young Tuthmosis, who was still getting used to his new name, looked down and touched his red blotchy arms and for a moment became embarrassed. He jumped into the water and hid among the large floating lotus pads.

With instructive words Sitre-Re whispered, "Go to your kin. Call him by his new name. Look upon him as if he is a frail bird with a broken wing. Be always patient and gentle with him. But you must show these observing eyes that are gazing upon you today that you are indeed the one who is most royal." She leaned closer to Hatsu. Sitre-Re's final instruction that day entered her ear like a shot of steam. "Remember the goddess, Ma'at. Now, go play your games, my royal princess!"

Sitre-Re turned away from the pool's edge, walked toward a group of servants, then took her seat among a cluster of servant sisters.

Almost in unison, the children who were already splashing in the water squealed with delight. "You shine like Helios, Hatsu!"

Suppressing her anxiety, Hatsu asked calmly, "Would you like me to play with you, Tuthmosis II, my brother?"

Her half brother answered with eagerness. "Yes! Come here, Hatsu, I have two turtles on a lotus pad. One is you and the other is me!"

She stepped into the pool, gently submerged herself up to her neck and then rose like a golden sacred lotus. Most of the hair on her head was shaved, except for two long braids that were bound and dangled above each ear. Both braids were entwined and fastened with gold and lapis beads. Her slender body revealed a slight swelling around each breasts and her thinning waistline crowned a demure pelvis. Water dripped from her sparkling body and well-positioned jewels.

"Show me those turtles, Tuthmosis II, my brother. However, you must not name one of those turtles after me. I do not see myself as a turtle." She laughed and looked down at her golden arms, then placed them together.

Tuthmosis II looked at Hatsu. "Well, tell me what other creature do you perceive yourself to be, if not the turtle?"

Hatsu pushed her clamped arms toward the young and newly named half brother, Tuthmosis II. Hatshepsut opened her arms wide and yelled, "I am a crocodile! And I am going to eat you!"

A cluster of royals and their servants, arranged in a predetermined social order, lounged beneath the canopy's sprawling shadow. Keph, a young impertinent servant girl, whispered to Sitre-Re, "Where is the great wife of the king? This is a stately celebration! Ahmose (Aahmes), the eminent female offspring of the god Ahmose I should be here! We are celebrating the dead! The royal mother of our young princess should make a brief appearance at least for the memory of her dead sons."

Sitre-Re kept her watchful eyes on frolicking Hatsu, then leaned toward her servant sister. She cautiously whispered, "Indeed she is still troubled by the deaths of her beloved boys. She stays in her apartment and cries all day. She is resting with her opiates and favorite board game. The Promise Ceremony, to be held after the fasting days, is far more important to her. Then she will make her appearance. That occasion will bring her out of seclusion. She prefers the night time celebrations because darkness is easier on her eyes."

A look of insincere empathy shadowed Keph's face but was quickly replaced with a greatly emboldened expression. Keph, the maidservant to the young Tuthmosis II, followed his antics, watching him as he leaped and jumped about in the pool. However, after careful observation, she realized that the rhythm of temple gossip among the servants was back in full swing.

She moved closer to Sitre-Re and began a scorching soliloquy about the pharaoh and his concubine, Mutnofre. "It is rumored that Mutnofre is filled with hatred because she was moved to a smaller apartment. She was replaced by a younger concubine. It is reported that she is pouting like a child and probably won't attend the celebration tonight. Someone said that she is learning a new craft . . . she is becoming a keeper of bees, imagine that! After the tragic news of her second stillborn, she fell out of favor with the king. It is rumored he is cautious around her. He fears she is possessed by a demon. Now he has to tolerate her because after all, she is the mother of Egypt's future leader. It has been my experience that a spurned woman is a dangerous woman. It seems that disaster rests at the doorstep of our beloved pharaoh."

Keph finished with words of eagerness. "Although he is expected to make his appearance sometime today, he will probably wait until the evening entertainment.

Have you noticed that he is wasting away to nothing? His life force is waning. His body is definitely distressed by something. I hope it is not a deadly plague."

Sitre-Re stiffened with fright and whispered, "Oh god of Sobek, protect us."

The music muffled the gossip while the people whispered, laughed, and ate from the banquet produced by the waters of the Nile. To the south of the temple complex was a huge enclosed rectangular lake that was linked by a narrow canal to the Nile. The sacred pool was four hundred fifty yards wide and large enough to hold dueling exhibitions featuring small fighting ships. But today, it was reserved for the Egypt's budding royals. Sovereigns had lavish ways to honor life and death. Today the attention was focused on Hatsheps and her half brother and future contender, Tuthmosis II. Egypt's budding crown heads were now on display.

A safe distance from the splashing end of the pool, huddled in the shadows between two massive pillars, sat a cluster of royal scribes. One older man sat beside his young son teaching him how to draw human figures while also tutoring him in the scribal arts. Young Ramah carefully followed his father's directives.

"Your observations will give clarity and truth to your future readers, my son. Through your eyes, you will give power to your logos. Remember it is written on the stone face next to the Nile . . . 'The word creates everything . . . All that we love and hate . . . The totality of being. Nothing exists before it has been uttered in a clear voice.' Memorize that, my son."

"Yes, Father. My words will be true and clear. My glyphs will be an honest tribute." Ramah looked up and observed the youthful Hatsu, portraying a crocodile, as she pursued Tuthmosis II across the shallow end of the pool.

Ramah drew beautiful hieroglyphs describing scenes of the great celebration. He dipped his pen into the ink well. Using the blackest and most durable of pigment, he drew his stylus across the papyrus. He represented the young royals frolicking in the wading pool and the lotus blossoms in full bloom bouncing on top of the moving waters. He depicted the musicians strumming the cords of the lyre, harp, and the blaring sound of a high-pitched flute; dancing girls whipping their hips to the rhythm of the music; the servants who were knotted in their private gossip corner, and of course, the mighty Kahn with his always alert, viperous eyes watching everyone and, in particular, certain jealous royals. After the glyphs were drawn, Ramah drew a straight line from one side of the papyrus to the other.

He looked up at his beloved tutor. "Have I captured the scene well enough, my father?"

"Yes! But one last thing, my son . . . always remember to clearly mark your name after you depict each event."

"Yes, Father, I will sign them . . . according to Ramah, royal scribe to the confident Princess Hatshepsut, celebrating the Beautiful Feast of the Valley." His dark eyes looked up and observed Hatsu's captivating laughter. She was holding a sacred white lotus in her right hand and laughing at the silly antics of her half brother, and one day, future husband. "Catch the lotus, Tuthmosis!" she yelled.

Ramah tenderly studied her every move. He drew Hatshepsut in a most unusual style, completely forsaking the law of frontality. Ramah drew the young princess the way his eyes told him to draw her.

Then, beneath the explanation of the day's events, he drew the glyph for the Goddess Ma'at, goddess of truth and justice. His next set of glyphs would be drawn during the Royal Promise Celebration, scheduled to take place in several days.

At the end of the day, the masterful scribe looked at his son's glyphs and drawings. "Ramah! Look what you have done! You have abandoned the code of scribal law! You must replace this drawing with one expressing the law of frontality! Do not be persuaded to change our golden rules! You must always honor our scribal system."

"But, Father, she is so beautiful! I must capture her in truth. Her look is playful and brilliant! The reason I deviated from the traditional system is because she represents change!"

"Change? Ramah, do not abandon the truth of your craft! If you work spirals into the unknown, the administration will let you go. It is most advantageous to be a writer. Remember, as for writing, it is profitable to him who knows it . . . more pleasant than bread and beer . . . It is more precious than a heritage in Egypt, than a tomb in the West!"

Ramah set the drawing down and reluctantly replaced it with the traditional sketch using the accepted laws for scribes, the law of frontality.

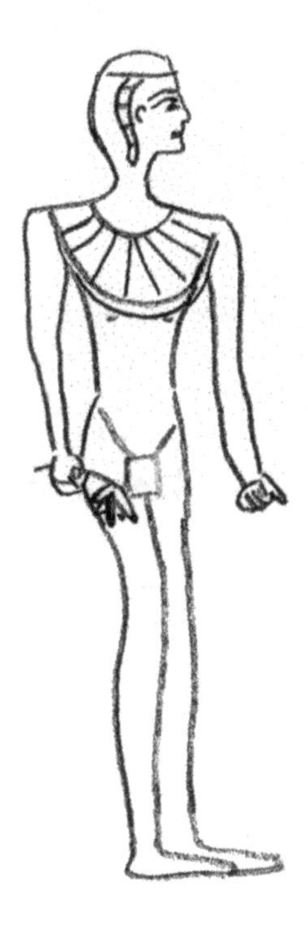

The perfume of the sacred lotus swirled around the air like an addictive drug while the royal house of Tuthmosis luxuriated in splendid seclusion, eating and drinking delectables that were offered to the sovereigns on the onyx table.

The day ended with several royal barges sailing to the western shore of the Nile, traveling to the Necropolis, the land of the dead. The great Tuthmosis dedicated an exclusive building project to become a safer, more secluded burial chamber for the pharaoh gods . . . gods that were able to affect the lives of the living.

There, at the funerary site of Ahmose and Amenhotep, Princess Hatsu placed a mummified falcon in each temple. She whispered, "Ahmose, my grandfather, I am your royal descendant. Do not forget me while I still dwell in the land of Egypt! If you grant me power and shield me from my enemies, I will protect the territories that you so bravely fought to reclaim!" She held her arms high turning the palms of her hands toward the painted stars above his sarcophagus. Repeating her plea, she placed a second mummified falcon on the tomb of the much revered Amenhotep.

Then Hatsu followed the hidden passageway to the tombs of her brothers. She brought them bundled timbers from her precious supply of frankincense. She stood between the vaults and touched the stone tombs with her hands and whispered this prayer, "May this offering sweeten your passage in paradise. Be on my side brothers, ever watchful for my safety. Grant that my bloodline surpasses that of my dim-witted half brother. Even though I am a woman, help me in my endeavors to become pharaoh of Egypt. Show the masses that I, too, can be as clever as a man."

Later that night, a brisk breeze blew across the scorched sand, wiping away the footprints of the living.

The following two days would be an absolute fasting, a purification observance in preparation for the forthcoming Promise Celebration where Princess Hatsu and Tuthmosis II would pledge to unite their royal blood in matrimony. Unfortunately, within a short span of time, Tuthmosis II would become the pharaoh king, and Princess Hatshepsut would become chief wife, the royal queen of Egypt.

The Pledge Coronation

Inside the Grand Temple of Amun
After the Fast
1523 BC

THE MIGHTY KAHN stood like a granite pillar inside the entrance, eyeing the invitees as they entered the holy temple. His eyes fixed on his royal charge like a sea eagle observing swimming shadows in the Nile.

Tuthmosis I and his chief wife, Queen Aahmes, who preferred her royal name, Ahmose, sat together inside their royal barque. Carried on the shoulders of four muscular Nubians, they ceremoniously passed through the pillar-supported halls that led to the sanctuary of Amun. Typically, they would arrive together at state celebrations, then after the event, they would leave separately.

In recent years, Hatsu's mother, Queen Ahmose, had become a recluse and found the clamor of these events too noisy for her taste. Her servants were instructed to be watchful for her hand signals whereupon they would quietly escort her back to her personal quarters. Tonight, she thought, *I will have to suffer through this miserable ceremony to the bitter end. God of the moon, help me!*

The queen looked regal in her gold and lapis headdress designed to frame her delicate but aging face. Her eyes were painted with coal black lines artfully arching along her lid, brow, and below her bottom lashes. Her royal garment was as blue as the waters of the Mediterranean and as delicate as butterfly wings.

Often, when she selected her material, she would funnel it through her golden ring. If it easily slid through, then it was given to her royal seamstress to be sewn into another splendid garment. Tapping her golden-tipped fingers on her leg, she prayed to Nephthys, the goddess of darkness, to hurry up this night's event.

The great warrior king sat nobly at her side. He always held a silver goblet filled with wine during these rides across the stone esplanade. If any wine spilled from his goblet the litter bearers were promptly replaced by standby bearers while the clumsy ones suffered under the lash of the whip.

In the last few months, the pharaoh's weight had noticeably dropped. His wide, gem-studded collar band now appeared too large and awkward. Nevertheless, the inlayed jewels sparkled beneath the flames of the wall-supported torches. The audience of priests, royals, palace officials, visiting representatives, and essential servants dropped to their knees, touching their foreheads to the stone floor. In unison, they mumbled audible prayers to the great god of Amun and Amun's earthly representative, their great pharaoh king, Tuthmosis.

Ptah, the chief temple priest, announced, "All may rise!" Then he began singing a heartfelt song to Amun-Ra: "Amun be thee inspired by Ra by day and Ra inspired by the light of the moon."

The royal barque was carefully lowered before a ceremonial table that featured two identical golden ram heads. They were affixed to the facade of the ebony altar. No one would suspect that the audience was being viewed by a young priest in training who secretly hid inside the altar, behind the hollowed-out eyes of one of the rams.

Royal servants assisted pharaoh and his queen to their gold and jewel inlayed thrones. They were positioned behind and slightly above the seemingly solid altar.

The temple of Amun was dark and eerie. The god Amun represented the male god of fertility, reproduction, and sexual power. Linked to the sun god, Ra, Amun was sometimes spoken together in the same breath . . . Amun-Ra.

The flickering flames from the pole and wall-supported lamps flooded the mural-covered walls. Shadows shifted across the paintings and hieroglyphs. This brought a breath of life into the characters that portrayed a pictorial account of Egypt's ancient past and present. The smoky mixture of pure, white frankincense and the aroma of the sacred white lotus filled the temple's interior.

The chief temple priest, Ptah, stood behind the imposing altar. The brightness from the red-orange flames spiraled upward and reflected in his dark, priestly eyes. He gazed pompously above the heads of the assembled while the rays from the afternoon sun blazed through the pillar-supported temple.

Ptah's deep voice thundered throughout the interior of the temple. He spoke these words, "In the presence of the great hall of Amun, we hold a promise of the two offspring from the loins of our majestic pharaoh Tuthmosis, ruler of Upper and Lower Egypt, the pharaoh of such military brilliance . . . The mighty one who has pushed outward the borders of our beloved Egypt . . . I bring you his son, Tuthmosis II and his royal daughter, Princess Hatshepsut. Together, they will join their royal blood and continue to build Egypt's wealth and power!"

Tuthmosis the great sat behind the altar and smiled with pride as the high priest charmed the audience with exalted accolades.

Then the high priest fumbled and mumbled a few inane words that embarrassingly at best described the minor maternal side of Tuthmosis II . . . "And his mother is, Mutnofre, well . . . uh . . . she is . . . a lesser wife, though beautiful in features." Ptah tried to find dignified descriptive words, but his voice cracked, trailed off, and disappeared into the recesses of the tall, temple ceiling.

Mutnofre stood in the front line of the audience and glared angrily at the clumsiness of the foolish priest. *I may not have the purest of royal blood, but I know how to please my lord in the darkness of the night . . . although it has been a while since he has called for me.* Her eyes glanced seductively at her king, and then smiled flauntingly at Ahmose.

Mutnofre's arms were crossed beneath her breast. A rye smile stamped her lips and camouflaged her raging internal anger about recently being moved to a smaller apartment after her second miscarriage. *When my son becomes pharaoh, he will move me to a more richly decorated apartment; even more elaborate than the one that Ahmose dwells.*

Mutnofre gloated on her shrewd machinations that steered her son to power. *No one will ever find out. That I am certain.*

In a loud booming voice, Ptah continued, "You will soon feast your eyes upon the future queen of Egypt, Hatshepsut Makare Khenemetamen. The maternal side of Hatshepsut is the glorious mother, Aahmes, known to us all as Ahmose after her great-father–god Ahmose . . . She is a magnificent earthly complement to Amun-Ra as you can all see . . . born of the moon . . . Is she not the female vessel of our deceased and celebrated Pharaoh Ahmose I, the great warrior king who drove out the Hyksos crowns? Standing here before us, she is his great and grand descendant . . . our dear Hatshepsut!"

The assembled quietly approved, nodding their heads, and then voiced aloud, "Amen! Amen! (I agree! I agree!)"

It was clear to the audience that the high priest favored the young Hatshepsut over the younger Tuthmosis. Ptah was seeing a clear vision of his future power. *Women are weak, and I will be able overpower her rule if she should ever become regent or pharaoh. My priestly coffers will grow with abundance! It will behoove me to be solicitous.* He continued his speech.

Ahmose sat confidently next to her husband-pharaoh and returned a haughty glare to Mutnofre. *Royal blood always trumps the passionate heart,* thought Ahmose. She lifted her chin and, with a look of triumph, smiled deliciously into Mutnofre's glaring, jealous eyes.

Ptah's voice resonated inside the temple like a strong wind, "It is my spiritual belief that Ra breathed the breath of the gods into the great Amose I after he victoriously regained control of Egypt. Ra was so pleased that he breathed his breath into his namesake . . . Ahhh . . . and soon he became *Ah*mose."

Ptah continued, "Yes, we have royal blood in the future treasury of our blessed Egypt. Let us gaze upon and admire this couple who will stand before us." Priest Ptah lifted his arms toward the heavens. The torches and oil lamps, bracketed along the limestone walls shimmered and flickered as the innocent and promising couple began their walk down the long hall.

The temple's high priest continued his ceremonial orations all the while using priestly altar magic that involved the use of sulfur, naphta mixed with water and quick lime. He poured the water into a cup and the audience was awed as the floating flame loomed skyward upon the altar. At the same time, a large tapestry unfolded impressively behind the reredos on the wall, which displayed a symbol of a pyramid overlapping an inverted pyramid. It was an Egyptian symbol meaning, heavenly protection coming down and blending with earth for all eternity.

Then he affixed magnetic rocks beneath a small golden box. He waved a small stylus before the box and it soon began to levitate before the audience. Their eyes grew large with wonderment as he encircled the pointed instrument over and around the floating box. He then dipped the point of the instrument into the flame and aimed it at the young couple about to make their entrance. The power of the priest was clear. Symbols and alter magic awed the masses into obedience.

Tuthmosis II and Hatshepsut slowly strolled down the corridor passing pillars painted with elaborately colored hieroglyphs that boldly stood amid the elegantly clad assemblage of the Egyptian elite.

The couple representing the promise of Egypt wore matching arm bands that displayed a symbol of the crooked cross. It was a symbol that Egypt adopted from the land of Kush (Nubia) . . . a symbol that stood for eternal life. The two golden bent crosses promised the royal couple eternal life. Eternal life for a pharaonic couple secured unparalleled power for Egypt's future.

Tuthmosis II clutched a miniature gold-and-blue pharaoh's crook. His collar band was small and studded with dazzling stones that captured the light from the flames. They sparkled like the stars that canopied across Thebes. His shorn head was adorned with a plain bronze-and-gold crown that peaked to an elevated point in the back. Around his waist he wore pleated white-linen loin skirt that draped down to his knees. His sandals were made of a wooden veneer, inlayed with pearl and ebony.

He glanced at his half-sister. "Hatsu, my little turtle, and one day, my chief wife . . . are you doing well?" He smiled with self-confidence.

Hatsu kept her head high. *Balance in all things,* she thought, and then whispered, "I am not a turtle. I am a crocodile!" Her bold words were emphasized with the most tranquil voice and the most sublime expression. She glanced at her brother and with a faint smile gave a passing look at the many royal faces that filled the interior of the temple.

She wore a black, braided wig crowned with a thinly twisted golden circlet. Her necklace of pounded gold filigree was studded with jewels from every land that Egypt ruled. Her diaphanous gown glimmered like a sparkling vapor, and her slender body shadowed like a spirit beneath it. The sandals she wore were a combination of leather and wood, inlayed with glass beads and ivory.

Her steps were unwavering and confident as she held her head high and carried herself with both dignity and authority. The radiance of her poise was spellbinding, and her oiled skin shone with the light of Ra.

The audience prized pure royal blood. All eyes were fixated on her. She was the promise . . . a future chief wife to Tuthmosis II but, most importantly, the most royal promise to the people and the future wealth of Egypt. She carried the bloodline of the greats, and everyone in the temple knew it.

The royal couple reached the front of the ceremonial dais and positioned themselves facing the elevated altar. However, Hatsu's attention suddenly was riveted on the black void behind the empty eyes of the two ram's heads that adorned the altar. She had been inside the temple for several celebrations, but she had never been this close to the reredos. Her keenly observant eyes carefully studied the architectural features of the altar that stood boldly before her.

She detected that the slits of the ram's eyes were hollow. Her mind raced. *It is quite obvious to me that there must be a secret viewing vault hidden within the altar. Perhaps it might even possess two hidden compartments behind each ram heads.* She then glanced toward her mother and father sitting on their separate thrones that were elevated behind the altar. *I wonder if my parents are aware that the dais might contain two secret chambers.*

In a shadowed corner, there was an area reserved for the royal scribes. One infatuated young scribe observed every detail of the beautiful Princess Hatshepsut. He was amazed that, at the age of nine, Hatsu appeared to understand the world that circumscribed the privately-walled borders of her world. He was also transfixed by her incredible beauty that she possessed at such an early age!

He steadied his quill and carefully placed the ink tip on the papyrus, illustrating the symbols for Hatshepsut, and Amun. He drew the symbol for ruler, completing the heading with Ra, the sun god. Artfully, he used his skill to draw certain versions of the ceremony. The code he used was a hieratic, rapid form which was usually practiced by scribes in training. He completed it with his name. (This is the observation according to Ramah, the personal scribe to the future queen of Egypt, the beautiful and sublime, Princess Hatshepsut).

At the end of the ceremony, high-pitched shrills emanated from the ram's head reredos brought the audience to their knees. Priest Ptah spoke with a commanding voice, "Amun-Ra has spoken, and he is well pleased! You may go in peace to love and serve all of Egypt's gods!"

The audience of royals left the temple and walked to the sacred lake. They reclined around the edge and watched a battling duel between two ships while the young Tuthmosis, in another part of the temple complex, was being prepared for the cutting ceremony.

Verifying Valor

Princess at the Age of Nine

AHMOSE RELAXED ON her leopard-covered chaise engrossed in her favorite board game. Suspended behind her was a colorful tapestry from the Nubian lands south of Thebes. A woven area carpet from Far East lands called Parsa warmed the cold limestone floor.

At the foot of the chaise sat a black temple cat. It reclined like a small sphinx, keeping its eyes fixed on the queen as if quietly protecting her secret world. A sacred blue lotus draped across Ahmose's lap, and a bowl of quince sweetened the room. She was unaware of her daughter's presence.

Hatsu stood silently at the doorway of her mother's bedroom and observed the elegant wooden furnishings that were gilded with gold and jewels. Hatsu observed her mother was sucking on a blue, lotus petal. She quietly walked to Ahmose's side, dropped to her knees, reached up, and plucked off a petal. She stared at Ahmose. "I didn't know one could eat a lotus. Can I taste one, Mother?"

"You're too young to dull your heart, my sweet child."

Hatsu held up a petal, "This has the power to dull one's heart?"

"It does!" Ahmose answered with diverted eyes.

"I don't want anything to dull my heart, Mother. I want to feel everything!" Hatsu looked quizzically at the beautiful petal and sniffed its intoxicating aroma.

Ahmose snatched it from Hatsu's fingers. "My child, there are other things that can deaden the heart . . . not just opiates." Ahmose spit out the old petal and inserted a fresh one.

She looked up and smiled. "I hear your half brother is undergoing the cutting ceremony today." Ahmose leaned forward and, with hallucinated eyes, whispered, "It is a maaan thing! It will render him as fearless as Sobek, our crocodile god of protection, and it will endow him with the power of Raaaa." The heat of Ahmose's intoxicated breath rushed toward Hatsu like a scorching desert wind.

"Yes, I know, Mother. It is being held inside the temple of Amun. I was told this procedure is administered by our temple priest, Ptah, and the occasion can only be attended by men. It is said that if a female is present in the room during the cutting, it will weaken the outcome of his reign. I have been told that there are many numinous rituals that power our civilization. I need to know all of these mysterious secrets, Mother!"

Hatsu sighed. "Isn't there a 'coming of age' ceremony that I can take pleasure in? After all, I am nine years old, and I am going to be a woman soon! I know that Ra and all the other gods have empowered me because I have more royal blood than my dim-witted brother! I want to know all things! It's not fair that he, my future husband, ugh, should be entitled to all the privileges! I want to know these secrets too! Secrets that have driven our past and will drive our future! It's not fair that he should have all the glory! I am strong, Mother! See?" Hatsu stood and lifted up the palms of her hands toward the heavens.

"Ha . . . but you are merely a girl, Hatsu. You will never be privileged to those matters. The ceremonies of the temple priests are conducted in a most secretive manner and are only conducted in the presence of certain select men from the House of Tuthmosis."

Ahmose drew in a breath, then continued, "Women are not allowed to be a part of such matters. I think they are afraid that women will unravel these priestly mysteries!" Ahmose leaned forward and whispered, "Men are afraid of women's potential! The temple priests are keenly aware that women cannot be deceived. That is why we are forbidden to enter into their priestly circle."

"How do you know that, Mother?"

"The pain of child birth, my dear, strips the wonder from a woman's eyes. After giving birth a woman knows what is real and what is unreal. Women hold the key to the weighing of scales. Is it any wonder that the goddess Ma'at is a woman?" Then Ahmose glared boldly into Hatsu's eyes. "Besides, how dare you question me?" She laughed cynically. "Let me add, as a child I took a trip to Dandera with my father. I mused myself among the maze of halls beneath the Temple of Light. I saw things, and I heard things that I shouldn't have."

She placed the lotus petal on her tongue. Her drug-induced eyes still harbored a long-held secret. Her hoarse voice crackled with a keen sense of knowing and a dark, sinister expression settled across her face. Ahmose at last released an internal torrent of lava-like hatred. It poured forth like ooze from a boil. She whispered into her daughter's ears what she had seen.

"Pssst . . . no one should ever hear of this . . . entered temple at Dandera into dark underground . . . I watched in the shadows . . . the priest . . . magic . . . a glowing light . . . made it look . . . a practice to take in the citizens . . . shuuu . . . you must never repeat . . . has to remain secret in order to control . . . so . . . you must go along with the priest because they are very important to society. You must allow them to do their magic. Remember, my dear Hatsu . . . this is hush-hush." Ahmose touched her finger to her lip. "And there is something else, my child."

Hatsu's eyes widened as she listened to her mother. "What, Mother?"

Finally Ahmose uttered words that would become the most important epiphany in Hatsu's life. "My grandfather, the great Ahmose, once told me that our most important sacred relic was stolen during a great wave. Egypt's holy barque containing the spirit of Amun-Ra and an amazing relic, the wonder maker, was spirited out of Egypt by interlopers. It is a secret that the priest do not want revealed to anyone because it could cause hopelessness to enter the hearts of our citizens."

She listened intently about the world her mother was privy to and the world she, herself, would soon face. Hearing about the stolen sacred relic would become a driving force that would direct Hatsu's future decisions during her lifetime. *I will find the barque and bring it back to Egypt,* was Hatsu's only thought. Her mother's enlightened but provocative words floated in the morning air like the toxic attar from the deadly, sweet-smelling oleander.

Ahmose lowered her voice to a murmur. "Shhhh . . . You must never reveal this secret about the stolen barque. Since you have been crowned the future queen at the promise ceremony it is important for you to know this thing that I am telling you. Remember . . . I cannot reveal everything, my sweet child, but I can tell you this." She paused to get a balance on her emotions, and continued, "You must know about these important matters of state."

She paused again, then let out a sigh, "Ahh, my dear, since the stolen barque that contained the spirit of Amun-Ra and the real "wonder maker" no longer dwells within our temple, our high priests must carry on this deception. Don't you see they have to?"

"Isn't deception considered immoral, Mother?"

"I suppose it could be considered immoral by some, but it is also important to uphold the illusion of hope because without hope in religious convictions, one's heart can become like dust in the wind, and when the heart crumbles then the backbone become strong like bronze and begins to revolt. Without hope in Amun-Ra and our essential gods, our kingdom will fall.

"But do not to worry, my child, another holy barque has been fashioned exactly like the original one. Hope in our god Amun-Ra is what keeps us empowered. Knowing there is one who truly steers the hearts of our people is one of the things what gives power to our beautiful Egypt."

Hatsu listened respectfully and her eyes grew large while she listened to the forbidden knowledge.

Ahmose whispered, "In order for a pharaoh to have a powerful reign, it is necessary to allow the administrative priest to demonstrate their magic. They use magical enchantments to astound us. It renders us powerless and makes us obedient as slaves. Illusion is the only way a priest can control the dignity of our ka. Keeping us always focused on our afterlife, keeps us rigid with awe and discipline. My child, in the sphere of your future administration you must allow this to happen. It is easier for a pharaoh to rule if the hearts of the masses are softened. So, pharaoh and priest must unite their powers. Although there is a silent jealousy between them, it is also an unspoken agreement. Remember, when your citizens are focused on their afterlife, they will be easier to discipline for the good of Egypt."

A knowing smile pressed Ahmose's lips. "Our priests are rich with gold. Their coffers are a third of the House of Tuthmosis. In addition, my daughter, since it is possible that you could wear the crowns of Egypt, you should know that wheat must always flow up and down the waters of the Nile! Be good to the neighboring realm even if they are your enemies! Equitable trade brings alliance and keeps peace. Egypt is the storehouse of abundance to our prized kingdom. Even our enemies that are camped outside our borders need what we have in times of draught. History reveals Egypt's benevolence, and you must make sure you continue this tradition. We must be the salvation to our enemies. That in itself is diplomacy at its best!"

Ahmose continued, "Wheat and the precious waterways of our Nile make Egypt powerful. Always remember, my child, there are two things that can throw Egypt into despair . . . draught and locusts. Thus, as a ruling head of our precious Egypt, you must keep the granaries full. Continuously replenish and never let them drop even the slightest measure! Every seven years count on either the locusts destroying crops or the Nile waters receding. Woe to your administration if both happens within the same year."

Ahmose's eyes blinked to slits. "But most importantly, my dear Hatsu, always remember that gold must intoxicate our enemies if our precious Egypt is to survive and prosper. Per stirpes, my child. You must place a family member from the royal bloodline of the House of Tuthmosis in charge of Egypt's gold mines. It has to be blood, my child! Blood protects and guards their own!"

She gazed into the eyes of her daughter. "So, my dear one, you must strive to become clever, and you must be strong, especially in these modern times. It will become a detriment to you if you do not educate yourself in every facet of Egypt's administrative functions!"

"Mother, I have been schooled from the cradle for my future service to Egypt but never have I been told of matters such as this."

Queen Ahmose leaned closer to Hatsu and stared into her eyes. She whispered, "Another thing, Hatsu . . . it has been said that a priest can utter a few words and cause great harm or . . . cause great joy. Do not directly stare into the eyes of a priest for they possess the power to make you do their will. Their eyes will render you utterly mindless. I have seen people forget their years, forget how to speak, and give away their fortune. But always remember, if you become pharaoh, it is wise to keep them on your side."

Ahmose laughed and then continued, "Lest you forget I shall remind you again. The secret about the stolen barque must remain hidden from the people. I repeat, it is most important to allow the priest to mystify because if the people become free-thinking, they will rebel, and you will have upheaval in the streets. That, my child, you do not want."

Hatsu's eyes took on a trance as if remembering past events. *All those times when I looked at the reredos inside the temple and the holy barque being paraded along the Avenue of the Sphinxes, I thought the spirit of Amun-Ra dwelled within. I shall go on a great expedition and bring back the real holy barque, Egypt's real unspeakable relic!* Hatsu's thoughts were so loud she could barely detect the sound of her mother's voice.

Ahmose leaned closer to Hatsu. Her warm inebriated breath reproached her daughter. "I know my words to you today are weighted down with secrets, but you must pay attention! Always keep in mind, Hatsu, that the priests are merely employing illusive shrouds for control for the good of Egypt. These shrouds of mystery are important to your kingdom. Most importantly, you must guard this knowledge and keep it inside your heart. After all, it is entirely possible that you could become pharaoh if your half brother, soon to be your husband should die in battle. So you see it would be essential for you to be on good terms with the high priest of your administration." She laughed and added, "I guess you could say they are a necessary evil."

Ahmose looked at her daughter with a long penetrating stare. "For your information, it is in our records that there have been females who have served first as a regent then as pharaoh." She tapped her golden tipped finger on her forehead as she tried to remember them, "Let's see, there were Nitokerty and Sobeknefru and very possibly, you and perhaps others in the future. Unfortunately, history is rather stingy when it comes to enlightening the masses of powerful females."

Hatsu's face lit up with joy. "I wonder if either one of them chose Sobek to be their god of protection. It doesn't matter. I will call on Sobek to be mine!" Then Hatsu's face took on a solemn look. "Oh yes, and every day I call upon goddess, Ma'at. She gives me balance in all things."

Hatsu looked perplexed and asked, "Do the spirits of our gods live in a box, a barque, or reredos?"

Ahmose drew in a breath and let out a warm sigh. "Oh, my child, all of our gods reside within our hearts. A box, a barque, a reredos that is inside a temple is a physical location where the masses go to pay honor to their memory, but in reality our gods should reside right here." Ahmose's eyes filled up with tears and thumped her heart. She stammered, then put a fresh petal into her mouth. "Just like the spirit of your blood brothers. The ka of each of your brothers is here within my heart! But I pay them honor when I visit their tombs. When you and Tuthmosis II marry you must have a male heir. When that time comes, I will explain to you how that can be achieved." Her eyes were downcast. "After all, you did have two older brothers." She looked at Hatsu with loving eyes, then said, "You see, it is necessary for the queen, especially one who carries the royal blood, to have boys first . . . primo genitor . . . to secure the pharaonic heritage."

Hatsu's eyes were bright with knowing. "I am sure I will figure it out in time. I do not wish to know about such matters right now, Mother, but I do know one thing."

"What is that, my child?"

Hatsu looked at her mother with knowing eyes and said, "The altar of Amun-Ra is hollow. It is an empty reredos. It is obvious that the ka of god Amun-Ra does not live inside that box. I saw eyes behind the hollowed eyes of the ram's head, eyes that are familiar to me. Ptah's son is the one that blows the ram's horn. I am sure of it."

Ahmose spit out the limp lotus petal from her mouth and chuckled, "This delightful little flower, my darling Hatsu, simply helps me to overlook these mysteries that are laid upon us like vapors of illusions." She plucked a fresh petal and placed it beneath her tongue. She peered with an eagle's coolness into Hatsu's eyes. "It pleases me to see that you are thinking clearly about the things that we discussed here today."

Hatsu stared knowingly back at Ahmose, then said to herself, "Oh, I can see clearly, Mother! That is one of the illusive shrouds. It is only Ptah's son blowing the horn, not our god, Amun-Ra."

Hatsu looked crestfallen, then said, "I will not say what I know to anyone. I will harbor these secrets in my heart. I realize what has been revealed to me is unconventional in the beliefs of our precious Egypt, but Mother, I am an unconventional girl."

A proud gaze washed across the fading beauty of Ahmose's face. "We have discussed many important issues today, and now, my darling daughter, I need to rest! Please leave me in peace! I do not wish to talk about these age-old deceptions any longer! To speak of them makes me crumble within. In order to make history you, must live in your conventional world but think with an unconventional mind! Leave me with my board game, sweet child. Find something that will make your heart sing! Enjoy yourself, my precious daughter, for life is but a blazing star that too soon fades across the night sky."

Hatsu left her mother's apartment and walked down the hall, passing intricately painted murals. The hieroglyphs depicted a queen presenting pharaoh with a goblet of wine; fields of wheat being sheared and bundled by Nubians; dancing girls mesmerizing banquet members; pharaoh in the cab of his fast-moving chariot, slaying the enemy with his composite bow; and many more images representing Egyptian life.

Hatsu walked purposefully across the stone floor. Her mind was spinning with the information that had been revealed by her mother. She reflected on her daily routine inside the temple complex. *Palace life for me is dull and limiting. It is too full of pomp and pageantry. Too much time is spent preparing for events. Painting one's eyes and primping takes too many hours . . . hours I could be learning about these age-old deceptions; learning about grand cover-ups and vapors of illusions. Sadly, they must be!* But the two things that Hatsu couldn't shake from her heart were the records stating there had once been two other female pharaohs and the stolen barque of Amun-Ra that contained an unspeakable relic called the "wonder maker."

She picked up her pace and started running past the pillars and hurried back to her private apartment.

"Sitre-Re! Sitre-Re!" Hatsu ran into opened arms and rested her small, fragile head to Sitre-Re's breast.

"What troubles you, my child? Your eyes are full of questions! I see that you are greatly mystified. What is disturbing the heart of my royal princess today?"

"Oh, Sitre-Re, you must tell me more about what life was like before the earth fractured like a broken cake!"

"Shuu! When you have a question like that you must whisper! Walls have ears."

Hatsu whispered, "Tell me what life was like when women were deities?"

"Oh, my dear Hatsu, you must speak to my father, Senenmut. He knows all the ancient oral teachings. He also claims they are written on manuscripts and are hidden somewhere in the desert!"

"Where are these manuscripts, Sitre-Re? I want to see them! I must have them!"

"Shuu! I cannot tell you that. I do not know. If I did know, I would tell you."

"In what land does your father dwell?" questioned Hatsu.

Sitre-Re answered, "The city of the sun, Heliopolis. It is the land of many mysteries. However, he grew up only a few miles south of here and went through training to become a scribe. Unfortunately, he fell out of favor with the administration because he was not honoring old traditions. He was then sent to Heliopolis where he learned the art of metallurgy. From there he went on to become an architect. My father is a man of many talents."

Hatsu gazed into her eyes and asked, "Tomorrow, will you take me to see Senenmut? We could leave when Ra rises above the eastern horizon. We can stay as long as it is necessary for me to learn about this other world. You do understand my sincerity, don't you, Sitre-Re?" Hatsu's eyes were earnest, yet, commanding.

"As you wish, princess. I will begin the preparations immediately. But first shouldn't you ask your father?" Sitre-Re's eyes watched Hatsu dash from the room.

Sitre-Re clapped her hands and was immediately surrounded by a host of lesser servants. She looked at the cluster of maidens and ordered, "Princess Hatshepsut will be going on a quest. Start packing."

The hot words of her mother still lingered inside her ears, "*Now go! Find something that will make your heart s-s-i-i-n-ng! Life is but a shooting star!* Tears welled inside Hatsu's eyes. *I will be like the indestructible stars! I will live forever on this soil! I love my city and our beautiful temples. I will never surrender my heritage to any man . . . brother, or husband. But I might to my own daughter.*"

She ran across the courtyard passing pink oleander blooms that had been planted along the garden path. White and blue lotus swirled around in the goldfish ponds.

She ran down the long hypostyle hallway and across the open courtyard. She crossed the foot bridge over the lotus-studded pool and ran westward along the narrow channel that led to the Nile.

Her delicately frail voice shouted over and over. "I am a crocodile! I am a crocodile! I will beseech Sobek, the crocodilian god, and ask him to become my protector!"

Located next to the Nile River was a major entertainment center designed to amuse the royals, the citizens, and the many boat travelers. One of Hatsu's favorite delights was watching a crocodile being subdued by the royal trainer, Aneer. She loved the sight of the instructor flipping the croc onto its back and rubbing its stomach. He straddled his legs across the underbelly of the crocodile and flipped it onto its back. He waited a few moments, then kneeled down, kissed it on the throat, stood up, and counted. With each numbered step, he distanced himself backward and away from the crocodile. Suddenly, in the blink of an eye, the reptile flipped itself and his threatening snout full of jagged teeth yawned wide to the world. The audience screamed with excitement . . . especially, Hatsu.

Under the hot Egyptian sun, at a crescent-shaped amphitheater on the eastern side of the Nile, the royal princess stood opposite Aneer, the renowned crocodile trainer. His coppery skin shone in the afternoon sunlight. His white loin skirt and knees were smudged with the Nile's black alluvial soil; around his neck hung a collection of crocodile claws. A barricaded pool, filled with slithering reptiles, was positioned in the background. The golden reptile was as still as a stone statue. His long, slender snout yawned open, exposing his conical, jagged teeth to the audience. This crocodile was Hatsu's favorite because its golden color was an oddity in the crocodilian world. *It was surely favored by Ra,* she thought.

Hatsu stood daringly before the trainer and made her desires known to him. "So, upon my return from Heliopolis and Giza, is it understood that you, Aneer, will teach me how to overpower and subdue a crocodile?"

"Oh yes, princess." Nervously, he gulped large quantities of Nile air trying desperately to swallow the large lump in his throat. His terrified, animated eyes looked back at the golden crocodile in disbelief. Sweat beaded on his shorn head. *God of Sobek,* he thought, *I could be risking the life of the pharaoh's daughter? I beseech your protection!*

Aneer knew that he had to acquiesce to the wishes of the princess. His voice trembled. Aware of the risks involved, he reluctantly agreed. "Your royal, most glorious princess, you will know all that I know. I will train you in the skills necessary to subdue the dangerous force of the much feared crocodile."

The frail princess looked up at the trainer and said, "Aneer, when I become pharaoh of all Upper and all Lower Egypt, ruler of the lands and the seas beyond Egypt's reach, I will reward you."

For a fleeting moment Aneer's eyes showed a hint of doubt. *Did she say pharaoh?* But he quickly reclaimed good judgment and humbly declared, "My training will make you invincible." He knelt down and kissed her feet.

The summer sun moved slowly over Western Thebes, and in a few hours, it would disappear over the hills that gave sanctuary and concealment to the burial chambers of ancient pharaoh kings and their queens.

Hatsu looked up at the sun. She vowed that it would not go down before she risked the destiny of her future husband/half brother, Tuthmosis II. She would hide in the altar and watch his clandestine, circumcision ceremony. It was forbidden for her to watch but that would not stop her!

She mumbled to herself as she walked purposefully toward the Temple of Amun, "I am the crocodile. He is the turtle!" She entered the sanctuary. Scurrying like a flea in fur, she hid inside the left portion of the holy chamber, the hidden compartment of the hollowed-out altar of Amun-Ra.

All the while, the mighty Kahn discretely watched Hatsu's every movement. *She is as clever as a hungry crocodile floating beneath the waterline,* he thought.

A Boy Becomes a Man

THE THUNDEROUS VOICE of the high priest echoed throughout the dark, flame-lit sanctuary. A small cluster of men stood in awe and marveled at the holy and private ritual now taking place inside the sanctum of Temple Amun.

Ptah performed a little white magic to mystify the audience of men before he began the cutting ritual. He lifted his arms, exposed his palms toward the altar, and blew into a bowl of liquid. Flames flared and brightened the room, then he announced, "On this great day you will become a man! A warrior! A great military leader! Protector of all of Egypt's boundaries! Ra will reach down and touch you with good fortune. Oh, favored son of Tuthmosis I! You, the royal son, Tuthmosis II, shall receive eternal protection by all of the gods."

The yellow flames flickered eerily on the walls inside the darkened temple.

Two male attendants held each arm of the boy. Ptah unfastened the boy's loin skirt. It fell to a heap on the cold, granite floor. Ptah placed a hallucinogenic lotus leaf under the young man's tongue. Then he applied a numbing salve to the intended organ. Ptah cautioned quietly, "He will swoon if you do not hold him firmly."

The royal artist and scribes illustrated this explicit scene by drawing their sketches and hieroglyphs onto the papyrus.

The future pharaoh stood as rigid as a wooden figure. Soon he began to feel the quieting effect of the muscle-relaxing opiate beneath his tongue, and then the numbing effect of the ointment began to work its magic. Ptah firmly held a thin, green, obsidian blade and repeated, "Hold him firmly."

Tuthmosis could feel a minor pinching effect of the priest's fingers. The blade, with edges as thin as a hair, sliced through the young boy's flesh at lightning speed. His knees collapsed, but his swooning body was quickly uplifted by the two male attendants.

Ptah announced, "Blood must flow for Ra! Arise! It is for him that you, Tuthmosis II, must now emerge as a man!" The priest then turned toward the altar and raised his arms. "Ra will sound his voice in approval!"

The sound of a ram's horn bellowed from the dark, small chamber located inside the reredos.

Ptah smiled, "Ah, yes! Amun-Ra is shouting with joy!"

In utter amazement from the hidden compartment, Hatsu peered through the slits of the ram's eyes and watched as the audience of men knelt toward the dais touching their foreheads to the floor. They rose and then the men began patting the back of Tuthmosis II, bestowing on him exaggerated compliments and flattering tributes of praise.

Hatsu had seen the entire ceremony from the hollow eyes of the altar. Throughout the entire ritual, she had been as quiet as a caterpillar on a shaft of wheat. Her breath was as noiseless as a fallen star. Amazingly, and in a very timely manner before the ceremony had begun, she had crept into the temple and had fortunately chosen to hide inside the *left* side of the altar.

Shortly after she had hidden herself inside the dark compartment, she heard a shuffling sound from the *right* side of the long, ornate altar. They were clumsy movements of a small, young priest in training. It was now obvious to Hatsu that it was he who sounded the ram's horn to cleverly create the voice of Amun-Ra! It added divine mystery to this "Egyptian" ritual! *It is a deception! Mother was right! This is one of those vapors of illusions!*

High Priests must deceive! Women must be clever and so it must be! She remembered the words of her mother.

Quietly and patiently she waited. She knew someone was still hidden on the other side. She cupped her hands around her nose and mouth in order to silence her breathing. She dared not move. Her eyes peered through the ram's eyes and followed the trailing end of the all-male entourage as they left the temple.

After the last of the male attendees left, Hatsu heard the ebony door squeak open. The young boy, who had sounded the ram's horn, crawled from his secret hiding place and ran down the aisle and out of the temple.

Hatsu watched him run from the holy place and into a building reserved for the celebration. "Ha! Just as I thought! It is Hapuseneb! Ptah's boy!" She quietly giggled inside her cupped hands.

Tuthmosis II was ushered into a splendid recovery suite. A privileged few accompanied him.

There, the future pharaoh would heal and rest for the next seven days. He would drink great amounts of beer, and wine and dine on the most favored foods: braised peacock tongues rolled and soaked in a mixture of mint oil (for sexual vigor), garlic (for health), roasted lamb (for disciplining and subduing the masses), steamed leeks (for more sexual vigor), dates, olives, pomegranates (for seeding many children), and cakes made of emmer wheat (for soaking up all the beer and wine).

Flute music could be heard coming from the luxurious quarters. A harp and stringed instruments soon chimed in and was quickly followed by the tinkling of brass symbols tied to the fingers of entertainers. The men whose attention was now being amused by the court dancers meant that it was safe for Hatsu to leave her hiding place.

She slowly opened the wooden door and cautiously stepped out of the altar's interior. From the darkened space behind the ram's eyes, she had seen it all! No one would ever know that she witnessed her brother's circumcision! Not even the high priest's son who had been hiding only a few feet away!

Could this have been one of the harmless secrets that mother held imprisoned inside her heart? The hollowed reredos? Hatsu remembered the words of her mother, "*Temple priest must deceive!*"

The mighty Kahn watched from the shadows as she ran from the temple.

Kahn's eyes had witnessed it all. *She sneaks around like a lion in high grass!* he thought then chuckled to himself. *She is much like me.*

Smiling to himself, Kahn shadow-walked behind Hatsu as they both left the temple.

In a few years Bedouins to the north would require military admonishing from the future pharaoh, Tuthmosis II.

His ambitious, future chief wife and queen, Hatshepsut would, however, become the real power behind the royal throne of Egypt. Her desire to rule would grow strong like the golden wheat springing from the black alluvial soil, raising its golden shafts to the sun.

My throne will flow up and down the Nile, and I will rule all of Upper and all of Lower Egypt. I will push the boundaries of my precious Egypt, and gold will intimidate the judgment of Egypt's enemies. These were the thoughts that dominated her will-driven heart.

Her plans were now locked firmly inside her heart. *Tomorrow, I will leave on my first royal expedition! That is, if Father allows me the privilege. Oh, but he will, for I am his favorite!*

Hatsu Visits Tuthmosis I

An attendant approached the bed holding a tray of sweets. "Mutnofre asked me to serve these to you, Lord Tuthmosis. They are more cakes she has baked for your liking. They are sweetened from the honey from her bee hives. She said they were your favorite cakes and is meant for your palate alone."

"Ahh, the little Suki is trying to gain back my favor. She knows they are my weakness. Let me have one."

"Someone knocks at your door. Shall I answer, my lord?"

Tuthmosis wiped the honey from his hands. "Yes, let them enter."

"Father, I must make a journey to Lower Egypt. It is important that I explore the regions that I will someday rule. I need to know the locations of our storehouses. I must know who the supervisors are. I must learn the value of grains, the trade stops along the Nile and the products of countries we trade with that are located inside and outside our borders. If I am Egypt's future, then I must know all of these things. If I am to lead, then I should know all of the secrets of our past! It could be possible that every mouth and belly will someday depend on me."

Tuthmosis inhaled deeply and looked into the eyes his daughter. "I am much impressed with your alertness to Egypt's kingdom. However, my daughter, I am not in the throes of death, dear child. True, my skin hangs from my bones, but I still have many years of life yet to live. These things that you feel you must know will be done according to the will of your husband-brother. It is his responsibility to make these journeys that you so enthusiastically speak of."

"Father, what if he is outside our borders on some remote warring field battling for our precious Egypt? Will he hurry home to oversee the emmer fields if our economy dries up like a thirsty lotus? My brother must concern himself with chariotry, weapons of war, training soldiers to wield their spears, and holding back the enemy." Hatsu's alert eyes looked down at her ailing father. "Can't you see that I must know everything about Egypt and that is why you must grant me this request?"

The once robust pharaoh braced his upper frame on his elbows. A trusted young Nubian servant lifted him and supported his weakened body with goose-down pillows. He looked up at Hatsu and directed her forward with his hand. "Come closer, my royal daughter, and sit here with me." His voice lowered to a whisper, "My, my Hatsu, your ancestors are surely speaking through you tonight."

Hatsu sat down and held his outreached hand. She looked at him with beseeching eyes. "Father, I must know things if I am to become a leader to my people."

Tuthmosis looked at the delicate physique of his daughter, but he was astounded by the strength of her mind. He looked at his personal scribe and yelled, "This is my daughter, Hatshepsut, female Horus of fine gold! Listen to her!"

He looked back at Hatsu and said, "You will, my child. You will go on this journey, and you will learn wonderful things about our beautiful Egypt. You amaze me, Hatsu, with your desire to know the practical aspects of our land. You are becoming such an intelligent girl." He laughed. "I have said it many times. Egypt would surely prosper under your rule," he said, then clapped his hands.

He called out to the court scribe, "Send these details to our captain. Tell him to ready the royal ship! Hatshepsut will be traveling to . . ." Tuthmosis looked at his daughter. "Where is this destination of yours?"

"Heliopolis, my father."

"Heliopolis! The ship must be prepared to spend . . ." He looked quizzically at Hatsu.

"A week, my father . . . perhaps two."

Tuthmosis yelled to the scribe, "Tell the captain to provision the ship for a complete cycle of the moon! Include plenty of guards and servants! Stock it with the finest of food preparations, our best beer and wines! Load it with wheat and stock all the storehouses along the way! Hatshepsut must know the advantages of our great land and Egypt's commercial benefits. She must know all things!"

Tuthmosis's personal scribe rapidly wrote the message on papyrus using the hieratic script. He sat at attention waiting for the rest of the message.

The pharaoh looked at Hatsu. "Your maidservant and the mighty Kahn must be at your side at all times."

"Oh yes they will, Father."

"Good!" Tuthmosis looked at the scribe and yelled, "Run off! Be swift of foot! Alert the captain! My royal daughter is in training to become a great leader of Egypt! She is going on a quest!"

Hatsu leaned down and kissed the cheek of Tuthmosis I. "Oh, thank you, Father! Thank you . . . thank you!"

After Hatsu left, he stared at the empty doorway. *I wish her brother had her insight and resolve.* His thoughts focused on the awesome responsibility of leadership. *Could this responsibility be a possibility for Hatsu? After all there are accounts in the temple hall of records that reveal such things!*

A whispering voice breathed in the ear of pharaoh, "Your Greatness, would you like me to stay the night?"

A weakened arm reached out for one of his lesser concubines. "Yes, yes. I feel sickness in my stomach, and I need your healing hands to pamper me."

The concubine slipped off her sandals and crawled to his side, then placed her head on his shoulder. A pleasing smile pressed her lips. "You are my hero, my pharaoh, my lover."

"Ahhh, my little scarab." Tuthmosis closed his eyes and began to feel a surge of strength.

The moon rose in the eastern sky and traveled high across the Nile waters and fell behind the Valley of the Queens and the Valley of the Kings.

Quest for Knowledge

RA'S EARLY MORNING glow flushed across the walls of the royal city that isolated the temple complex and the privileged from the outside world. A team of talented and well-built Nubian guards had been assigned to provide extra security for Hatsu's royal quest. They stood impressively in the chariot cabs that flanked the main chariot.

Each guard was armed with a composite bow that hung strategically behind their shoulder. Stone scepters were saddled in their belts. The charioteers held the reins of their horses, watchfully scanning the streets and darkened alleyways while the others guards kept their eyes directly on the princess.

In the cab of the well-protected chariot, Princess Hatsu and Sitre-Re stood upright on either side of the chariot master. Kahn stood boldly behind Hatsu and guarded her with his arms. In another chariot, there were a number of female attendants, clothes, and cosmetic cases. Early morning foot traffic moved aside while the royal chariots rolled along the stone-covered esplanade.

They passed the nine hundred ram-headed granite sphinxes that lined both sides of the well-traveled route that began at the royal gates. They rolled past a construction site of the future temple of Mut. Continuing south, the envoy rolled beneath the breathtaking entranceway and proceeded toward the port of Thebes. Gatemen closed the wooden portal behind them and resumed guard at their post.

In the distance, the imperial ship was anchored at the port, awaiting the arrival of Princess Hatsu and her entourage. Royalty flags of all colors adorned the docks and moored Arabian reed dhows bounced upon the waters of the falcate-shaped harbor.

Early-morning fishermen had returned with nets bulging with bolti (tilapia) fish. Their lanteen sails fluttered in the morning breeze. Fishermen used obsidian knives to slit open the bellies of the flopping fish. Hungry sea birds flocked in screaming frenzy, plunging into the water for the discarded guts. The shrill of swooping gulls could be heard across the bustling port.

The busy harbor, a crescent curve that arced into the eastern bank of the Nile, was located south and adjacent to the great Temple of Thebes. Bread stalls and mud-brick ovens lined the docks. Seductive women erected colorful tents and enticed the lonely seamen who were sailing in and sailing out. Their patrons also included sweaty dock workers, occasional "upright citizens," and a few elite men that included "shrouded" priests.

The mouth-watering aromas of baking bread, roasting lamb, and frying fish drifted across the docks and the broad deck of the royal barge. The port of Thebes was a hub of activity where many exotic and beautiful items were brought in and shipped out within the trading borders of Upper and Lower Egypt and the Mediterranean Basin.

Ramah, Hatsu's newly assigned scribe, stood at the stern of the impressive vessel. His shoulder-length straight black hair was bound beneath a white linen headdress. His sharp, brown eyes watched the royal party of chariots as they rolled safely toward the pier.

The darkly-handsome teen studied the movements of the young royal. He watched her gracefully step from the chariot's cab. She was wearing a long black braided wig interlaced with amber jewels. This hairpiece was specifically designed to capture the beauty of her dark, brown eyes.

A wide smile of anticipation pressed his lips as Ramah thought about the royal expedition to the land of mysteries . . . the great city of the sun. He was to become her shadow-walker and record her every official movement and more, if she so desired. His dark eyes took in the full spectrum of her young but provocative beauty.

The three-hundred-and-eleven-foot royal vessel was constructed from cedar harvested from Byblos, a northern country along the Mediterranean basin. It was strongly build with tightly woven grasses and wooden dowels interlocking the firmly fixed timbers. The one-hundred-foot wide deck had beams that protruded through the hull. These extension timbers provided stability to the barge that supported heavy payloads–stability that was needed to accommodate the weight of multiple chariot stalls for teams of Arabian horses, heavy blocks of stone to be carved into architectural features, many jars of wine, olive oil, and many tons of bundled wheat.

A protruding battering ram extended beneath, yet beyond the curved, falcated bow. This ornately wrapped battering ram was wrapped and tipped with a smelting of strong-blended metals that formed to a deadly point. It was designed to ram and smash into a hostile ship, leaving in its wake a disabled sinking ship.

Two golden seals representing the House of Tuthmosis adorned both sides of the battering ram and sparkled menacingly in the glow of the morning sun. The royal super ship commanded respect and awe along the Nile. The captain held out his hand to the Princess Hatshepsut and assisted her aboard the vessel.

Below the exterior deck were many individual compartments. Each one was more beautiful than the next. The largest apartment belonged to Princess Hatsu. Everyone was aboard and the vessel was set to sail.

Swarthy oarsmen sat patiently in their assigned seats that were located beneath the level of the luxurious royal apartments. Their strong calloused hands gripped the oars and readied themselves on queue to heave the barge away from its slip and head northward on the Nile.

Young male boat workers removed papyrus and flaxen ropes from the dock pilings. They tossed them onto the deck and scurried to jump onto the vessel before the wind filled the sails.

The captain ordered the super ship into the north flowing waters of the Nile and followed his course toward Lower Egypt, the land of mystery and secrets. Hatsu stood near the bow and viewed her beautiful city, passing its splendid, pillared temples.

Viewing the amphitheater, she could see Aneer struggling to subdue the golden crocodile. Chills ran down her spine. Her eyes widened when she saw Aneer lean down and kiss the reptile's throat. Every nerve inside her tingled with anticipation. *I can hardly wait for the day I kiss the throat of the golden crocodile! I wonder if Nitokerty or Sobeknefru ever kissed a crocodile.*

To the west, she saw the great Necropolis. Her grandfather Ahmose had started the village complex at Deir el-Medina and establishment these very secretive tombs to be built for Egypt's royals. And her father, Tuthmosis began the relocation project for the ancients to be surreptitiously moved to the safety of the Valley of the Kings.

About a one-hour walk from the Valley of the Kings was Deir El-Medina. It was a squatty-walled village–a city convent of dedicated workers eagerly bustling back and forth hauling large stones up ramps that led to the Valley of the Queens and the Valley of the Kings. This town was built entirely of mud and stone and housed the two hundred and eighty brilliant craftsmen and their families. Located slightly to the north was a large flat plateau that fronted the King's Valley. It captured Hatsu's attention. *I will have my personal mortuary temple, built there! I will call it Deir El-Bahri. I will consecrate it to the goddess Hathor. My temple will be in front of the Valley of the Kings.*

The Nile, the great gift to Egypt, was four thousand miles long. There was a spiritual union between Hapi, the god of the Nile, and the reigning pharaoh. This blend of intense power was thought to control the annual flooding which brought alluvial waters to the rich, black farmlands, some areas two miles wide, bordering both sides of the Nile.

The royal super ship passed long stretches of enormous emmer wheat fields that waved their golden shafts at Hatsu as she happily sailed by. Government tax collectors stretched long ropes, cording off parcels of land while calculating the tax money the wheat would bring to the treasury of Egypt. *Wheat must be abundant and grow up and down the Nile Valley for Egypt to prosper. Be the salvation to even your enemies! You will leave an illustrious heritage.* Hatsu remembered the instructive words of her mother, Ahmose.

The ship sailed past miles of agrarian land. Hatsu looked upon the vast horizon of crops and could barely take it in. "Our land is a wonder for all to see! The Kemet is black and rich. Our soil affords us two successive crops each year. Egypt is blessed to have our beloved Nile."

She closely observed the cotton, leeks, lentils, and the variety of grains that grew in abundance along many miles of alluvian borders. Past records had made Egypt wise to be prepared for the possibility of famine. She remembered her mother's advice–*two things that can throw Egypt into despair are draught and locusts. Keep the granaries full!*

Several hours into Hatsu's expedition she shared her future philosophy with her trusted handmaiden. "Sitre-Re, when I become pharaoh I will make sure that Egypt's vast agrarian wealth will keep its granaries stocked full of precious grain supplies for its citizens in case the inundation fails to appear. I will extend Egypt's arms to all people."

"When I become pharaoh" was the only thing that Sitre-Re heard. The rest of Hatsu's words drifted into the Nile air. Sitre-Re went about mindlessly doing her duties while the super ship sailed northward. Sitre-Re thought, *Hatsu certainly exhibits bold new thinking.*

The Nile and its irrigation canals also produced vast amounts of fish and shell life. Its waters accommodated lanteen rigged feluccas belonging to the poor and middle class including luxury ships and barges that belonged to the royals and wealthy traders. Many shadufs could be seen throughout the fields that were used to direct waters to the inland crops.

"Princess Hatsu! Come and eat! We will dine on the open deck and all of Egypt will speak of your beauty and glory." Sitre-Re fluffed colorful cushions for Hatsu's comfort. "Please sit, my dear princess . . . uh . . . and future pharaoh."

The sun slowly made its way across the sky, and then eventually dropped into the western horizon, the Land of the Dead. All the while an intrigued Ramah studied the beauty of Hatsu and drew ever-so-skillfully the wonder that his eyes beheld.

The yellow moon soon rose on the eastern side of the Nile and traveled across the dark, star-studded sky. Later, the passengers closed their eyes and slept while the captain guided the royal ship northward toward the city of the sun. Along the way the ship stopped while the port workers off-loaded bundles for the granaries.

In two days they would arrive in Heliopolis, a small and once religious port town that had serviced thousands of pyramid and temple workers. It was also the home of Sitre-Re's retired and very gifted father, Senenmut, the renowned metal worker, stonecutter, and architect.

This trip would become a defining experience that would fuel her unquenchable quest for knowledge and ignite future expeditions.

The City of the Sun

THE MEN BELOW deck dragged their oars slowing the ship to a stop. The passengers felt the stillness of the ship. They awoke to the sound of enthusiastic Egyptian, African, and Asiatic clatter of words gushing from the throats of boat tenders and dock workers; Jameelah! Aria! (beautiful), and guttural sounds, representing the deep southern borders of Ethiopia and Nubia, shattered the tranquility of the royal super ship.

Hatsu, on her maiden voyage and away from the security of the palace, was greatly amused by the din of excited, international jabber. All were rejoicing! The ship was docked at their port of Heliopolis. The vessel's flags flapped and popped in the wind. Hundreds of men, women, and children lifted their arms toward the vessel with their palms facing the bow.

Port workers shouted with excitement as they waited to offer their service to the royals. Brave boys dove into the Nile waters, unconcerned with the dangers that slithered below. They scooped up large shells and carried them to the surface screaming, "My gift to you! My gift to you!"

Sails were lowered. Coiled ropes were thrown onto the dock and quickly wrapped around the stone posts. The Egyptians and other port workers were respectful and displayed awe as they waited for the super ship to complete its docking procedures. The shrill of the seagulls pierced the summer morning as they soared above the port, swaying their wings and diving for food.

The Egyptian culture inspired love and respect for their gods. Navigating directly into the slip, the bow of the vessel now faced east, a tribute to sun god Ra.

Inside the state room, Sitre-Re carefully drew on cosmetic coal lines above each brow and beneath the lower lids of her royal charge while an attendant placed the black, braided wig onto the shorn head of the princess. Her wispy-thin attire clung to her delicate frame like the skin of uraeus, the sacred asp that was displayed on her headdress. Her princess diadem was then secured over her jeweled wig. Hatsu slipped into her wooden-veneer sandals. She began her stately walk down the narrow hall toward the stern of the vessel. Sitre-Re followed devotedly while the inscrutable protector, Kahn, led the way!

The early morning sun blushed at the end of the hall. Hatsu stepped onto the deck now washed by the hands of Ra. Her eyes could not believe the grandeur of what she saw. In the far stretches of desert that was located beyond the western side of the Nile, stood the sparkling pyramids. She had a great intake of breath and exhaled, "Secrets! The Giza plateau!"

City of Secrets—City of Knowledge

NEWS OF THE arrival of pharaoh's betrothed daughter spread across Heliopolis faster than an arrow could be flung from a composite bow.

Bundles of wheat were hoisted onto the shoulders of the oarsmen and transferred down the ramp onto the docks. The wheat reserves were to be transported to other boats and stockpiled inside the various storehouses that supplied Egypt's magnificent realm.

The golden litter carrying Hatsu and Sitre-Re passed through the crowded port town. It was supported on the shoulders of four strong porters who happily volunteered their service to Egypt's princess and future queen. Her bodyguards gripped their stone maces "at the ready" across their chests. Nubian guards walked on the left of the litter, while others walked on the right. Kahn followed. His eyes were always searching, and inside his hands were two sharp, star-shaped discs ready to be thrown at a split-second's warning. The small group paraded through the harbor town and down narrow streets toward the house of Senenmut. Adoring citizens of Heliopolis followed the future queen; their faces gleamed with tears of joy!

Princess Hatsu's black, jewel-flecked wig sparkled in the early morning sun. Her skin glowed with Sitre-Re's golden lotion. Her freshly coal-lined eyes and crimson painted lips gave her an older appearance. It was obvious to everyone that her future beauty had been manifested early by her perfect profile and her full, sensual lips.

To the people on the street, Hatshepsut appeared as an unfolding goddess . . . a lotus bud warmed by the Egyptian sun. Crowds of people dropped to their knees and pressed their foreheads on the dirt streets. They waited for the royal litter to pass; then, out of natural curiosity, they tagged along with the growing crowd and entertained their royal visitors with songs of joy.

Hatsu's dark, inquisitive eyes were not engaging the crowds in the street. Instead, they were fixed on the shinny golden caps of the pyramids that came into view between the mud-hewn buildings. Her eyes marveled at the magnitude of the grand monuments that could be easily seen though they were seven miles away. It appeared as if the pyramids had magically sprung up from a sea of sand. She was mesmerized by the sight of them.

"My father's house is the one that towers above the others," Sitre-Re whispered onto Hatsu's ear. "He wants a clear view of the gleaming pyramids so he can live his last days in a blissful state of wonder. My father admires the ancients and their building techniques. He started out as a metal artist who designed impermeable chest armor. Later, he designed chariots that could turn on a grain of sand. As a matter of fact, he invented many other things for your father's royal army. He even understands the sacred techniques of stonecutting. But that, of course, was in his younger and more vibrant years. Now, he reclines upon his chaise on his rooftop beneath the shade of a grape-vine arbor where he watches the sun descend behind the beloved pyramids. He has already provided for his burial, and he continues to save every piece of gold and silver for the elegant sarcophagus and tomb that he has already drawn on papyrus!"

The ever precocious Hatsu gazed at Sitre-Re with a penetrating stare and asked, "I need to understand the riddles of life, Sitre-Re. It is true that a select group of builders who are specialty stonecutters trusted with divine secrets that are known only to them? I am the future pharaoh, and I must know the secrets of the ancients! Do you think Senenmut knows secrets and would he be willing to share them with me?"

Sitre-Re was about to answer but the procession came to a sudden stop in front of her father's large, three-story home. The carriers eased the litter down to the ground and Princess Hatsu was assisted to her feet by the strong, gentle hands of her scribe, Ramah. The porters stepped back, bowed with respect, and allowed her to gracefully exit.

The impressive Nubians stood protectively on either side of the princess. Sitre-Re pounded on the wooden door of her father's home. "Father! This is your daughter the maidservant to the future queen of Egypt. Please, let us enter!"

Hatsu leaned toward Sitre-Re and confidently corrected, "Pharaoh . . . future pharaoh."

"A thousand apologies!" Sitre-Re uttered breathlessly. She immediately kneeled and placed her forehead on the dirt street. "Forgive me my glorious princess and future pharaoh . . . a thousand apologies, again! Then, she kissed the feet of the princess."

"Rise, Sitre-Re! You of all people know that it is I who will, in the future, become the ruling pharaoh! You have trained me from a child to think on these things. You even said that my face will someday be chiseled in granite." Hatsu smiled forgivingly at her now humiliated handmaiden and trusted confidant.

Hatsu remembered that, three days prior, she had secretly watched her brother's male-only circumcision ceremony. *My secret presence will surely weaken, if not doom, his future.* She smiled and thought to herself, *Ha! And no one will ever find out!*

Sitre-Re resumed pounding on her father's door and breathlessly apologized. "Obviously, I did not have the chance to inform him that we were coming here to visit." While she continued to pound, many citizens of Heliopolis began to crowd around trying to honor the princess with gifts of live geese and she-goats. The webbed and hoofed feet of the offerings had been bound with papyrus rope. Baskets of bolti fish, decorative ceramics, colorful glass, and beaded jewelry were placed before the royal visitors. Thrilled citizens hummed and chanted words of praise while the geese honked and the goats screamed like frightened children.

Kahn thoroughly examined the crowd's intentions. They all appeared to be harmless. However, he readied himself and glared menacingly at a few devotees swarming around the royal entourage.

Finally, a voice on the other side of the door could be heard. "I hear you! I had to come all the way down from the roof!" Suddenly the door swung open. Senenmut stood in amazement at the sight of his daughter, the young princess, and the growing crowd that was still gathering behind the royals.

"My Father, it is I, your daughter, Sitre-Re, who serves Princess Hatshepsut, the future queen, and one day *pharaoh* of Upper and Lower Egypt."

Senenmut reached out with opened arms to his daughter and with a smile, said, "I have missed you, my darling Sitre-Re!" *Did she say pharaoh? Certainly she did!* He adjusted his demeanor and, as natural as one could blink, he lifted up his arms and traditionally presented his palms to Princess Hatsu. *She is a delicate flower!* He dropped to his knees and placed his forehead to the stone floor. "Honorable princess-future pharaoh, you are most welcomed in my humble home. You are my most honored guest! Your unexpected visit brings me much joy!"

Hatsu was immediately smitten by Senenmut's physical appeal. *He is not old at all! His smile could calm a raging lion. His hair is the color of the night sky with rays of the sunset. His skin is tan and smooth, and his white teeth are shadowed by a dark mustache. His arms look strong and inviting . . . and oh, so tall.*

Senenmut towered above her like a majestic obelisk. She followed his every move. *He is not at all what I had expected. He's quite young . . . and wonderful to look at! My heart feels safe in his presence.*

Senenmut graciously bowed and opened the door of his home to the royal princess and her many attendants. The entourage included Senenmut's daughter, Sitre-Re, several makeup artists, many dress attendants, the wig stylist, many burly Nubian guards and selected archers, one very dangerous-looking Mongolian, Ramah the royal scribe, crates of sleek and shiny clothes, an intricately sculpted cedar box containing a selection of imperial golden jewelry; a number of wigs, many cosmetic cases, four port workers who simply refused to leave the service of the princess while she was visiting Heliopolis, twelve geese, eight she-goats, a basket full of still flopping bolti fish, an array of beautiful ceramic bowls, many core-formed necklaces made from colorful glass beads and an ornate golden litter stuffed with comfortable goose-down pillows.

Senenmut's guests soon scurried into assigned rooms inside his home. His three-story house also had a basement which could accommodate the overflow of visitors and luggage, especially the four porters, the crying goats, and the honking geese.

The mysterious Mongolian stayed on the top floor never leaving Hatsu's immediate vicinity while the towering Nubian soldiers alternated guard duty outside beneath the portico.

Senenmut gave instructions to his cook. "You must twist their necks and prepare them for dinner tonight. I cannot stand that constant honking! Remember to prepare food for our travel to Giza. I understand the future pharaoh of Egypt wants to see the pyramids. We will be there for several days so you must make sure you prepare enough food for all of us." In minutes the incessant honking that emanated from the basement quickly came to an end.

Nakt, the cook, looked quizzically at his master when he heard the term "pharaoh." However, he knew better than to question Senenmut, for he knew the man was honorable and, unquestionably, a seeker of truth.

That night, a gentle breeze blew through the pergola on the upper room, cooling off Senenmut and his guests. They sat around the table beneath the arbor and dined on simple fare of roasted geese stuffed with garlic and leeks, fried bolti fish, wheat cakes and beer. Princess Hatsu watched the setting sun fall behind the blackened silhouettes of the three largest pyramids that stood boldly on the desert horizon in the far distance.

The pyramids at Giza never change. Ra had set, outlining them with an amazing red-orange aura. The Giza Plateau was also known as the Place of the Sunrise and the Sunset. However, every glimpse was like seeing the pyramids for the first time. Dusk began to soften the hard-edge stone vista. Darkness fell over Heliopolis like a billowing black cape.

After the guest had settled into their quarters, Sitre-Re and her father, Senenmut, stood on the upper room and surveyed the stretches of scorched, white sands on the western side of the Nile. Then they studied the flat, thatched rooftops of the squatty, mud-brick homes of Heliopolis. High above the streets they followed a sprinkling of port workers who were walking through the maize of alleyways heading toward their humble dwellings positioned behind crumbling temples.

Sitre-Re looked up at Senenmut with pleading eyes. "Father, Hatsu is a very headstrong young girl. She is adventurous . . . a great thinker far beyond her nine years. She seeks knowledge. She wants to know the Secrets of the Ages. Curiosity brews within her like steam trapped beneath a ceramic lid. Please, you must help to enrich her mind. She wants to know what life was like before the earth split like a broken cake."

While Sitre-Re and Senenmut privately conversed, Kahn kept his cautious eyes on the princess. But also, at the same time, Kahn kept his lusting eyes on Sitre-Re.

Ramah drew glyphs on papyrus, documenting the events of the day.

Hatsu noticed her guard's intense interest in Sitre-Re and secretly planned a diversionary tactic where she would cleverly trick man's weakness to work in her interest.

She began to entertain her plans for the nights she would have to slip unnoticed from her apartment because clandestine training sessions planned with Aneer would begin soon after she returned to the Place of the Palaces.

A cunning smile pressed Hatsu's lips as she closed her eyes to sleep.

During the night, the wind blew and smoothed the blanched sands of the Giza Plateau for the first footsteps of the future queen and one day, pharaoh, the lovely Princess Hatshepsut Makare Khenemetamen.

While the princess slept, the moon rose on the eastern horizon and made its journey across the glittering, star-studded sky. Hatsu dreamed about a man who one day would build her a temple that would rival the strength and beauty of the pyramids of Giza.

The Giza Plateau

THE FOLLOWING MORNING the royal entourage began their adventure. Four of Senenmut's finest Arabian horses and two of his finely-crafted chariots occupied the upper deck of the royal vessel. The cabs of his chariots included suspension benches. Not having to stand for hours, his passengers could sit comfortably on seats of woven papyrus fibers. He never expected the future pharaoh of Egypt would be riding in his improved, personal chariot, which he had designed for his own personal comfort.

The captain and his crew demonstrated and harmonized their skills as the vessel quickly left the port of Heliopolis. Small fishing boats made of tightly woven reeds and Nile feluccas outfitted with lanteen sails moved aside for the royal ship as it made its way across the river. On the western side of the Nile, the ship carefully eased into a large slip with the bow, as always, facing east when at rest.

All of those aboard were absorbed in Hatchepsut's first royal expedition. Wanting to learn more about their ancient past, they happily followed the princess when she stepped onto the western shore.

With the Arabians now harnessed and hitched to the chariots, the entourage gathered their personal items and boarded the cabs. The four porters quickly lifted the eloquent litter upon their shoulders and carried the empty, pillow-puffed lounge to the site of the pyramids. It was most important that the royal princess must have a comfortable bed to sleep. A goat was tied by a rope to the waist of one of the porters. They would follow the chariot and walk across the windswept sands of Giza.

Hatsu liked and admired Senenmut. He honored her wishes and responded happily and intelligently to her many questions. With the deftness of a natural diplomat, he made her feel like a very important adult even though she was only nine.

Senenmut sat next to her in the chariot and pointed to the remnants of a previous civilization. He identified scattered pieces of the past that dotted the light-colored landscape that she might not have otherwise seen. When Senenmut spoke, each stone relic and broken shard of pottery seemed to come alive. A weathered portal became an entrance to an ancient world, one that had been destroyed and lost when foreign invaders had out-maneuvered a past Egyptian administration. "Those disgusting foreign interlopers!" blasted Senenmut.

Then he pointed to a swelling in the sand slightly north of the largest pyramid. "There is a Great Sphinx resting beneath these sands. One has to wonder about the secrets that are hidden beneath the wheels of our chariots. Oral tradition says that the Sphinx was built by the great Pharaoh Khafre to watch over the pyramids. Others say it was built thousands of years before he ever lived." Senenmut pointed to the Khufu's Pyramid. "This one is the largest one. It is thought the clustering of these impressive pyramids meant these powerfully political factions were united under one god, the great god of Ra."

Their chariots rolled over the ground swell of sand. A top portion of the Sphinx was all that protruded from the tight grip of the earth. Throughout the ages small representations of the Great Sphinx had been recreated by stonecutters. These granite protectors were placed at the entrance hall to many temples and lined either side of esplanades leading to holy places.

As the four Arabian horses pulled their heavily-laden chariots across the desert plateau, the pyramids grew in grandeur. At the base of the glorious pyramid of Khufu, the chariots came to a stop. Hatsu quickly stepped down from the cab, looked up at the pyramid, and had a great intake of breath.

Senenmut gazed upon the gigantic structure with profound reverence. The awe expressed in their faces impacted those who stood around him. Hatsu looked up at the mountain of stone, and then looked back at Senenmut. Displaying the same boldness of the colossal structure before her, she emphatically stated: "What I want, Senenmut, is to have a mighty sovereignty as magnificent and powerful as these massive pieces of engineering!"

Senenmut's wise and honest eyes studied the firm resolve of Hatsu, and he carefully answered, "Then, princess, you must desire it with all your heart, all your might, and your entire mind. Absolute desire, my glorious princess, will become the power, the inner strength, behind your will. Without desire, one can only hope for mediocrity, or worse, nothing. So hold in your mind the things you most desire, and then affirm it in your heart. Desire is the magic secret to obtaining what you want."

Hatsu looked up at Senenmut. Her eyes were as clear as the broad blue sky that canopied the warm, windswept sands. "I have desire, Senenmut! It comes from my great-grandfather, Ahmose, and my great parentage! Their blood flows within my veins! Total desire is seated firmly within my heart! Desire is alive inside every organ in my chest! I have desire; through and through!"

Senenmut admired her grit. He understood and accepted, long before anyone else, the boldness of her amazing strength of character and her undeniable resolve. "If you wish, I will help hone and polish this raging desire that dwells within your heart, Princess Hatshepsut. Tonight, after we dine, I suggest you sleep inside the Pharaoh Khufu's chamber. Then you will become cojoined and united with the spirit of the great pharaoh, whose *ka* (spirit) resides within his wondrous tomb." Senenmut knelt down and once again kissed her sandaled feet. "I am at your service," he whispered.

Taking their cue, the staff quickly dropped to their knees and paid their reverence to the princess.

That night, a long, eerie shadow stretched across the sand as the full moon rose above the horizon on the eastern side of Khufu's Pyramid.

Inside the Pyramid of Khufu

"SLEEP *INSIDE* THE pyramid, Father?"

"Did you not ask me to enrich her mind, Sitre-Re? This is the best way! She must do it!"

"But, Father, if danger befalls her we are responsible! Pharaoh Tuthmosis will have all of our heads!"

"Sitre-Re, my daughter, reason with your heart! No one else will be in there with her except the spirit of Khufu! His *ka* will protect her! If she is seeking wisdom, power, and protection, then she must do it! Khufu's spirit will allow her royal wishes to be fulfilled! Have faith! She is a full royal, a descendant of ancient gods."

Senenmut stared into the eyes of his daughter and demanded, "Now, Sitre-Re, bring her to me!"

Sitre-Re walked up the steep, squared-stone tunnel, holding a flaming torch above her head. Ghostly shadows reflected off the glyph-painted walls as she made her way up the slope to the southeastern side of the pyramid. The outside portico was flanked by a gallery of many columns with the center opened to the sky. She stepped onto the granite stone floor and walked toward the princess. Hatsu was sitting with the others around a brazier dining on fried fish, goat cheese, wheat bread, dates, and beer.

Sitre-Re knelt to her knees and said, "Senenmut wishes you to come with me. He strongly suggests that you spend the night inside Khufu's chamber. According to my father, if you seek the power and protection of this great pharaoh, then this is the only pathway to truth."

The flame from the torch cast flickering shadows across Sitre-Re's anxious face.

"I agree with your father. I want to do this, Sitre-Re! I am ready. Lead me to Khufu's chamber."

Like two brown beetles, Kahn's eyes burrowed into Hatsu's eyes. "You must not go there without me! Pharaoh Tuthmosis has entrusted me to be your shield and protector! Your father has so ordered! I must stay with you!"

The two Nubian bodyguards said, "We must go too! We cannot let you out of our sight!"

Ramah stood up and announced, "I must be with you to record this profound event!" As if saluting his leather satchel, Ramah gripped his hands around his rolled papyrus, quill feathers, and ink jar. "I, too, must always be at your service, your gracious princess!" His heart thumped with desire for the beautiful princess. But he knew his place. *I am only a scribe to her and nothing more,* he reminded himself.

The four porters jumped up and, in a blink, had the lounge propped upon their shoulders. "We will carry your litter! You must not sleep on a stone floor!"

"And we too, have to be there for you, Princess Hatsu. You cannot prepare yourself for sleep unless we help with your wig and garments."

"Yes, yes, that is so!" chimed all of Hatsu's attendants.

Nakt, the cook, jumped to his feet. "Food! Food! You must have something to eat! I will be there for Your Highness when you awake to the morning light." Nakt hurriedly began filling his arms with his home-brewed beer, wine, and food. "I will follow! I, Nakt, will feed you good! Yes! Yes!"

Princess Hatsu and her entourage followed Sitre-Re and her flaming torch. They puffed for breath through the long stone hall that sloped down to the burial chamber that held the tomb of Khufu. The shadows and reflections created by the flame from the torch, danced, and bopped on the walls while Hatsu and her attendants carefully made their way down the low-hanging, narrow maze of stone.

Because of thieves, it had been necessary to move the sarcophagus to a safer location. His body was now resting in the subterranean burial chamber. However, in the very near future, his sarcophagus would be shipped up the Nile to the Valley of the Kings for protection against tomb robbers. The preservation of the ancient remains of the royals was vital to their after life.

Senenmut stood in the dark and watched the flock of people following in the wake of the flaming torch. "All wanted to be here, Father. They would not stay in the mortuary temple inside the great pylon."

The sea of eyes that surrounded Hatsu trembled in fear and awe inside the darkened, massive crypt. They could sense the omnipotence of the structure that spread its weighty massiveness above them! Each member of Hatsu's staff stood at solemn attention awaiting her smallest command.

Senenmut held out his hand to Hatsu. "It is only you that I want. This journey is one that you and you alone must make. I will help you attain your confidence and prepare you for this night's passage. Please give me your hand, princess."

Senenmut took the torch from Sitre-Re. "Hatsu and I will leave you here. Together, she and I will enter the royal chamber of Khufu. But Hatsu alone will ride the night sky with the *ka* of the great pharaoh."

However, in order to ease the earnest concerns of Hatsu's attendants, Senenmut allowed the determined Kahn to stay.

With his arms folded across his chest, Kahn would wait through the night outside the closed chamber door. Without asking any questions, Kahn would sit next to Senenmut through the night. His Mongolian eyes would adjust to the dark. He would rely on his upbringing and focus his attention on the mysteries of the dark. Kahn's mission was to scrutinize the blackness of the hall and watch for any hint of movement.

Inside the chamber, Senenmut clamped a light on a bracket that hung on one of the glyph-painted walls. Before he left her alone his honest and alert eyes looked into hers and said, "You must listen carefully to the advice of the spirit of Khufu. He so admires your courage and respects your royal blood. Now, you must lie atop his sarcophagus and read the glyphs of his amazing story. When the light source dims, you must close your eyes. At that time, Khufu will take you by the hand and lead you through time and space. You must not show weakness or become frightened! Then, my princess, you will be given secrets that you so desire!"

Senenmut stepped out of the room and closed the door. He propped his back against the door and was determined to protect her from anything or anyone going in or coming out. Between Senenmut and Kahn, Hatsu's physical safety was in good, strong hands!

A Night of Remote Viewing

A SMALL AND FRAGILE female child trembled inside the cold, stone fortress. She reclined upon the granite sarcophagus of Khufu that stood boldly in the center of the subterranean chamber. The flame of the torch provided just enough light to read the glyphs that adorned the walls and ceiling. Hatsu's eyes followed the storybook mural. It featured a handsome, majestic figure who dominated the brightly colored glyphs that artfully graced the surfaces above her. It was clearly being repainted but the part that was renovated was stunning.

Gradually the light began to flicker to a flimsy glow. It sizzled and then died ushering in complete darkness. As Senenmut suggested, Hatsu closed her eyes. Time could not be felt within the depths of the crypt. Suddenly she was in a universal force absent of time, space, past or future. Everything was in the now. It was as if every skin cell on her body was in a complete state of suspension. She couldn't tell if she had been there for one hour, one day, one week, or one month. Suddenly, she felt a slight warming beneath her. The granite bed began to vibrate. *I will not show weakness or become frightened,* she thought to herself.

Soon she began to feel a pressure of warmth clutching her right hand. She felt her body lifting upward. Her eyes were wide open and still contemplating the ceiling glyphs. She anticipated her body would soon press against the upper limits of the chamber. She was in absolute darkness.

Suddenly, in the blackness within the depths of the pyramid, a booming voice spoke these words: "Do not be afraid, for there is nothing to hinder your journey." The voice was both commanding and comforting. "Come . . . and I will show you the realm of things that shames the heart of man!"

Hatsu's eyes widened. Beside her was an amazing apparition that the people of Earth could not see. Hatsu sadly realized that all eyes, ears, and hearts were essentially blind to truth.

"Are you the Pharaoh Khufu?" Hatsu asked.

The voice answered like a wind rushing across a vast and mighty land. "I am the one who knows all things. Come. Take a journey with me across this realm."

Together, Hatsu and this mystical Knowing Spirit ascended like falcons through the block of stones that shaped the pyramid, above the alluvial waters of the Nile and soared toward the ever-present cluster of indestructible stars. The life force of the massive oceans sparkled with brilliance while Hatsu ascended higher above the horizon. The blue sky was clear and the views of the earth revealed vast amounts of shimmering water and patches of green and brown. She spotted a dry riverbed where the Nile had in the remote past flowed through the Sahara region that once emptied into the great Atlantic waters.

The earth looked like a swirling, round, glass jewel! Then her eyes focused on the three large pyramids visible from space. The vision of them expressed a sacred geometry known only to chief builders. She blinked and then immediately was gazing into the sky above the Giza Plateau. It was obvious; the pyramids were aligned with stars that were positioned directly above them. These stars held wonderful secrets that would someday be revealed. They were known as the indestructible stars!

A mighty voice thundered across the night sky. "Humans labor under an extreme disadvantage. Dark forces rule the hearts of many." The declaration of words sounded purposeful and ominous and resonated with a hint of warning.

"What is this extreme disadvantage that we labor under? These dark forces?" asked Hatsu.

"Watch, and I will show you." The voice bellowed like the swirling winds of a sandstorm.

In a blink of an eye, she returned inside the darkened walls of the Great Pyramid. A clear viewing began to slowly materialize before her. A scene of a secretive operation began to take place before her eyes. She stood in the midst of semi-nomadic men belonging to the Hyksos people plundering through the burial chambers of long dead pharaohs. She watched while they gripped their obsidian blades ripping through the painstakingly wrapped linens, yanking off jewels and amulets. She viewed the robbers carrying arm-loads of gold and gem-studded jewelry. After their plundering, they ran from the burial chambers, across desert sands, and headed straight for the Nile.

One Hyksos leader stood at the bow of the barge, clutching scrolls under his arms. Hatsu's eyes made out the headings, *The Book of the Dead and the Book of Rossio*–books that contained incantations and a magical alphabet to access heavenly beings for personal power! Hundreds of other scrolls, stored in jar vessels, rolled violently across the deck when the ship entered the north-bound current.

She continued to remotely view the shameful truth. Waiting at the docks of Giza, other barges, camouflaged to look like wheat transports, disappeared up the Rhacotis artery of the delta heading north toward the Mediterranean Sea.

One ship transported a golden barque that contained a small compact device used for calculating the motion of the stars and planets. It was based on the Sothic cycle of the three-hundred-and-sixty-five-day Egyptian calendar. This device included instructional plates consisting of 2,000 icons that could be used by anyone who had possession of it, providing they could crack the code. The Egyptian High Priest and their personal astronomers used it with reliability for hundreds of years for astrological purposes identifying the dates of their annual religious events and adjusting their calendars using the solar cycles. It had many astrological uses–when to plant, when to sow, when to store wheat, when to expect the inundation, the birth of kings, the actual date of volcanic eruptions, and the exact date of great waves, and many other things.

This sacred machine was thought to embody the earthly version of Amun-Ra and was kept inside this sacred barque. It was used to mesmerize and bring fear and wonder to the masses. In past times it had been paraded throughout the streets of Heliopolis.

This relic represented Egypt's god Amun and this sacred loss was devastating to the priests of Egypt. Hatshepsut could see her grandfather, Ahmose, then a young prince, demanding his army to chase down the Hyksos. She heard her grandfather's voice yelling out these words to his army of mercenaries, "They are stealing Egypt's most important symbol! They are stealing Egypt's god! These evil tomb robbers have also stripped the gold from the remains of our mighty royals. Our heritage is quickly disappearing down the Nile!"

These barges, that carried the stolen holy artifact and Egyptian gold, were swift beyond any navigator's understanding and sailed on the withdrawing waters of the great wave to an island called Crete.

Hatsu's eyes viewed this remote island of "Kriti" and watched the Hyksosian thieves leaving the decks of the vessels with their arms weighted down with gold. They ran across high ground, then approached an entrance to a cave. A painting of a bull marked the entrance to the underground. She watched in astonishment as the thieves choked through the labyrinth of halls located deep within the earth. There they melted down the Egyptian jewelry, transforming the liquid gold into items depicting their own hasty departure. By doing so the gold would now have the seal of the new owner and could never be traced back to the Egyptians. Hatsu remotely viewed a most degrading moment in the history of the Hyksos people and the saddest moment in the history of the Egyptians.

Intuitively Hatsu realized that her mother knew about the stolen gold, the books containing heavenly access, and the contents of the golden barque. Hatsu's thoughts churned. *So this is why Mother bares so much anger! She privately mourns the loss of Egypt's inheritance and the daring act of the Hyksos stealing our god! But worse, for Mother, the chimerical veil has been lifted.*

Suddenly, she saw a man known as the Desert Prince directing hordes of people through the Sea of Reeds. That group was spiriting out of Egypt fine filigree gold that had been chiseled and pulled off the altars of Heliopolis temples.

Appalled at what she was witnessing, Hatsu whispered to herself, "I am viewing the past and the future. I see greed! And it causes one to steal! Sadly, it is deception that drives the hearts of men! The Hyksosian and other people have stolen our gold and robbed us of our inheritance. Is this the horrible disadvantage that shames the heart? Surely it must be!"

The voice articulated with divine authority. "There are other things that are much more contemptible than these dark forces of thieving greed. Brace yourself for the ultimate and greatest lie that has propelled and will continue to propel the human race." The voice paused, then continued, "Man has always been impressed with the power of unseen forces and has endeavored to harness and shape these forces into gods . . . gods that would offer a shield of protection and save them from harm. The veil of these complex gods will set nations against nations, resulting in death and destruction, muddling truth."

Hatsu yelled in desperation, "Truth? What is truth?"

The voice answered, "That which is not perceived and that which is obvious. Look for the thing you cannot see and things that stand before you like granite stone. Hatshepsut, you must seek that which is unknown to you! Seek and ye shall find, and the answers shall be given unto you!"

Hatsu stiffened. "I shall seek that which is unknown and unfamiliar. I will look for truth that exists beyond my eyes but yet stands boldly before me."

She was surrounded in darkness. Her heart raced like a cat in the grip of a deadly viper. She could actually hear a heart thumping. But was it hers? Perhaps it was someone else's heart, or thousands of other hearts struggling to beat for one last breath? Then she heard the clear voice of a man speaking in straightforward words.

He was known as the master. She heard the desperate declarations of his voice, "It is not what you put into your mouth that defiles the man. It is the words that he speaks that defiles the man. No good tree produces bad fruit. No bad tree produces good fruit." Then, she viewed this man hurling tables across a temple floor.

The voice of the young man suddenly came to an end like a sharp cycle slashing shafts of early wheat.

"Who is this man . . . this Master? His words seem sincere!" Hatshepsut questions drifted like a disappearing fragrance in the darkness.

"I do not understand this riddle! I do not comprehend what my eyes are viewing!"

The thundering voice answered, "Be still! You must continue to watch the evolution of humans! It is a slow and pitiful story of man's inhumanity to man."

A moment passed, then she found herself standing in the middle of a battlefield. She felt the thin, sharp ends of green obsidian blades and smelted bronze sword tips piercing her body. She felt the shattering thud of a mace as it crashed against her skull. She could see and feel the final thoughts of men, women, and children as they were being thrust through by the artful product of the sword maker. Then she saw children running along a thin tongue of sand innocently clutching small red crosses. Sluggish from hunger, thirst, and the relentless heat of the scorching sun, those misinformed, blameless crusader children running headlong into the awaiting daggers and long-bladed swords would be hushed to future ears!

As if riding the head of a sandstorm, Hatsu was hurled into another world. There she viewed dome-shaped brick buildings heaped with lifeless bodies burning and smoldering like rubbish. She smelled the stench of burning flesh and saw large metal-shaped beetles pushing charred bones through garbage-strewn streets. Then, she watched oblong-shaped chariots fly through the air, destroying buildings that were higher than the pyramids, crumbling the towers to dust. Then she saw clear blue sky turning black like pot ash, blotting out the healing powers of Ra and the glistening waters turning to oil.

Seeing the extensive destruction of the planet and the evil pillars of deception that have gravely harmed civilizations of the past and the future she asked, "What am I to do with these evil visions? These are secrets that I wish I did not know. What is truth? Where can I find truth?" Hatsu paused, "I did not see my future. Will I become a ruler? Will I ever become pharaoh?"

"Foremost of all noble women, when you confirm your leadership, show your people that all life on earth is infinitely precious. You live in an orderly universe. It is rational and based on reason. It is predictable. The cycles are constant. Your universe is in perfect balance. Egypt is nothing without order. Order is logos. Logos is balance. Logos is everything."

Then the voice began to speak with tenderness. "Now I will show you the things that gladden the human heart." A sudden rush of wind and then the rhythmic sound of a beating heart filled the darkness that surrounded Hatsu.

She heard the thumping heart of an infant. Before her eyes she saw herself as an embryo, then as a newborn being cradled in the arms of her mother. She saw herself as the bride of Tuthmosis II and then as an adult woman, standing on the bow of her royal super ship. She was wearing the full pharaoh's crown of Upper and Lower Egypt complete with the golden beard. Surrounding her on the deck of her royal barge were beautiful items from many countries, trees of a certain variety, crates of scrolls filled with knowledge from every port in the kingdom and an unspeakable relic that had been spirited out of Egypt during the mass departure of the Hyksos. The relic which had once had the protection inside the reredos of a Heliopolis temple was destined to be returned to Egypt, and Hatshepsut was the one to do it.

The voice sounded like a horn. "Trust your allies and be cautious of your thin blooded line! You are safe along the southern waters of the Nile. Build your heritage in Egypt! Use stones to speak your words. You are Khenemetamen Hatshepsut, she whom Amun embraces, and foremost of noble women."

Hatsu whispered, "I knew it would happen. Thank you! I have desire! And I am obsessed to seek truth for Egypt."

The voice responded like thunder cracking across the heavenly sky. "You must have more than desire! If humans intend to survive, they will need wisdom! Desire is the steam that propels your will. But first, Hatshepsut, you must discover your world! Through discovery, you will attain knowledge! Through knowledge you will obtain truth! And through truth, you will obtain wisdom! And when you obtain wisdom, you will know love! Love, my young Hatshepsut, is the secret that dispels the dark forces of man. To become a great leader, these are the things you must remember . . . you must be wise . . . you must be wise . . . you must be wise." The voice faded into silence.

That night the sky goddess, Nut, spread her celestial wings over her husband Geb (earth) and gave birth to the new dawn. Then, spoken in a hush of a whisper, Hatsu heard these words, "Every living creature wants to live one more day." Then like a rush of wind she heard, "Logos was. Logos is. Logos will be. Logos creates everything."

The next morning the sound of the heavy stone chamber door grazed across the limestone floor. A fresh supply of air channeled through the maize of halls and rushed into the burial chamber. Senenmut walked toward the sarcophagus and studied her serene, natural beauty. Her eyes, still closed to sleep, Senenmut noticed something else. Poised, yet still in slumber, she seemed to claim a certain air of confidence; she even appeared to look older. "Ahh, the precocious, dear child has indeed become enlightened!"

Sitre-Re and the lesser servants surrounded the sarcophagus. "Father, should we wake her? I am surprised that the sound of the door did not stir her."

Slowly Hatsu' eyes fluttered open. Her morning voice at first sounded frail, but in a manner of certainty she stated, "I know what I must do now, and I shall do it with purpose! I shall honor all people and open my borders to peace. I shall travel and discover the realities of my world, and I will become well informed. I will become tutored and educated in the cultures of the surrounding regions of Egypt. As long as the water of the Nile flows and Ra shines over Egypt, I shall feed all nations, for I am Hatshepsut, soon to be the Nile Queen and future pharaoh of all of Egypt's territories." A knowing look calmed her face and a beautiful and confident smile pressed her full lips. "I am hungry. Someone milk the goat!"

Since her attendants and guards loved and revered her, they all bowed and were joyful for their princess. One attendant quickly jumped to her feet and ran up the ramp to the pylon outside.

"Nakt! Our future pharaoh is hungry! The goat! The goat! You must milk the goat!"

Sorting Out the Riddle

THE EARLY MORNING Ra spread its healing rays above the expansive Giza Plateau.

Tied to a hitching post, in the shade of Khufu's great pyramid, four Arabian horses whinnied in the background. Hatsu and her entourage sat upon a blanket and waited for Nakt to serve up his wheat beer, warm goat milk, bread, and salted fish. He handed the first bowl of milk to Hatsu, then to Senenmut and the rest of the royal retinue. No one dared to question Hatsu about her personal experience inside the pyramid. Everyone hoped that she would express something about the experience she had within the tomb. One never questions a royal. One waits and listens and then calmly and politely reacts with reverence.

Nakt excitedly lifted his cup toward the sun, "Ah, the god of crops is present in our beer and milk! Drink and eat of the blessing from our good earth, Geb!"

They feasted on fried, salted bolti fish, braised geese, dates, figs, olives, and feta cheese. All were famished from a night of worry and wonder. Then Nakt made another blessing. "Tonight, we will eat fresh brazed goat for our supper! Yes?" He lifted his last swig of milk toward the she goat that was now crying sounds of distress. Nakt's proud smile exposed his crowded teeth. Then with one large gulp, he upended his cup of milk.

Hatsu looked at Senenmut. "You cannot let Nakt kill the goat! It was whispered to me in a very clear voice that every living thing wants to live one more day! I cannot let him kill that goat!"

Senenmut questioned, "You heard a voice . . . telling you what?" His eyes were alert with wonder.

Hatsu countered in a whisper, "Yes, a voice said every living thing wants to live one more day, and I must honor that!"

Senenmut's intuitive eyes brightened. His voice was full of insight. "Yes, yes, I see . . . I know!" Then Senenmut looked at his cook and said, "Nakt, you must not kill that goat! I forbid it! We will eat dates and figs and, of course, more beer and more milk. The goat shall live one more day, of course one more day after that, and one more day after that . . . and so on and so on!" Senenmut saluted the goat. "The she-goat will live a long, happy life." Senenmut looked at Hatsu. "You think the voice will be pleased?"

"Oh yes, very pleased!" answered Hatsu.

"Did you forget to tell me something, Sitre-Re?" Hatsu asked while carefully examining the hieroglyphics inside the Great Pyramid.

"What is it that you ask of me, princess?"

"Come here and look!" Princess Hatsu pointed out glyphs to Sitre-Re. "It read that Senenmut, the most venerable architect, dedicated labor to this magnificent renovation project of Khufu's personal tomb." Hatsu looked at Sitre-Re. "Did your father repair Khufu's tomb?"

"My father is very experienced building many things, whether they are weapons, chariots, portals, or buildings. My father has an eye for understanding symmetry, proportion, and balance. He possesses divine secrets! He was asked to design more secure doors to Khufu's many chambers, ones that would be strong enough to discourage thieves. After the renovation program of Khufu's tomb was completed, he felt that there were no more worthwhile projects to devote his life to. So he has all but abandoned the living. I tell him he is too young to retire and to be contemplating his life in the hereafter. He solemnly yearns to walk among his gardens in the land of paradise. He has a life-time agreement with the administration to service the portals of the pyramids. From time to time he brings his foreman with him just to service the granite doors and make certain that they are safe and sound. So yes, my princess, this is my father's work." Sitre-Re touched the portals and smoothed her hands over the painted glyphs.

"Where is Senenmut?" Hatsu looked at Sitre-Re with a very serious expression. "I must speak to him this very hour!"

"He is in another chamber inside the pyramid. He is with his trusted friend and architect, Ineni, a man who my father respects. Together they are checking the other chamber doors. It will take me a while to locate and return with him."

"I will wait inside the entrance to the pylon gateway. Tell Senenmut that I have a commission for him. I have decided to ask your father to build my mortuary temple. I have already selected the location. I trust him and only him. Yes, he is far too young to sit around and await his death! He has yet to complete his masterpiece . . . my mortuary temple, for which he will be remembered for all time!"

A blanket was spread beneath the shade of the pylon. One of the porters who had milked the goats filled each goblet. Ramah sat in a corner drawing glyphs and hieratic capturing Hatsu as she delicately sipped milk from a gem-studded goblet. The mighty Kahn stood strong, like one of the many columns that supported Khufu's temple pylon. His arms were folded across his chest, protectively watching Hatsu. The charioteers were grooming the Arabian horses in the shade of the pyramid. Nakt held up a bowl of oats for the horses to eat. The rest of the porters swept the sand from the stones, trying to provide clean surroundings for their princess. The lesser female attendants moved with keen practice, flounced and primped the hair and tunic of their royal charge.

From the depths of the subterranean chamber, Senenmut ran up the steep ramp, through the rock-hewn corridor and out to the mortuary entrance and toward the blanket near the pylon. Ineni trailed closely behind fully expecting to swoop up Senenmut from a swooning heap.

Out of breath, Senenmut fell to his knees in front of Hatsu and touched his forehead to the ground. His hands were clasped in gratefulness and his tears dropped onto the stone floor. "Dear princess, you will give my life purpose. From now on everyday my life will have splendid meaning. I thought I had reached my greatest achievement with my work on Khufu's chamber. To my dismay, I was only allowed to repair! But now, I am free! Free to build and erect your temple using the building secrets of the ancients! It is for you that I will build my finest triumph. I will build you the most splendid temple, one that will endure forever! Great god of Ra, I am free!"

Hatsu touched his artistic hands and said, "I trust you with my temple, Senenmut. Because you allowed me to stay inside Khufu's chamber, I was allowed to see my future. The better part of living is in the planning of it. And together, we shall plan our future!"

Senenmut looked up at Princess Hatsu and whispered, "Our mutual destiny awaits us, my beloved princess and future pharaoh queen."

Ra traveled across the sky and was positioned directly overhead. Its healing rays shone over the Great Pyramid and the cluster of royals as they dined beneath the shade of the pylon while Ramah recorded what he saw.

Ineni left the royals and rode his horse back to his home town of Memphis. The once beautiful city was legend to have been built by Menes, the first king that united Egypt. He built his administrative capital at this location to best service Upper and Lower Egypt. But through the years, the stately buildings had collapsed into disrepair through the tooling of time and plunder.

Sitting high on his Arabian steed, Ineni directed it toward an impressive large, mud-brick building. He yelled to his workers, "Senenmut and the future pharaoh of Egypt will soon be here! Turn off the fires! Princess Hatshepsut, wants to inspect the foundry!"

This facility designed the chariotry used in the service of pharaonic military. Shields and body armor, knives, swords, and all martial weapons of war were forged from the heat that plumed from the furnaces of the Memphis arsenal.

Hundreds of men scurried here and there picking up discarded scraps of iron. "Open the flues and air out the building!" yelled a worker as he inspected every section of the factory floor for any hidden piece of shards of metal.

Later that day the royal retinue headed toward the arsenal, a short distance from the Sphinx. It was the location of an enormous metal foundry that forged metals for the Tuthmosis administration and building projects.

Senenmut turned to the royal princess. "Before you step down from the cab, let me alert the foremen and workers of the foundry that you are here to inspect. I have ordered Ineni to ask the workers to stop the fires and blowers. It is very hot inside."

Senenmut was greeted by the workers with the greatest respect. The entire workforce lined up in parallel human columns guiding the royals toward the entrance. When Princess Hatsu and her entourage walked toward the foundry, all of the personnel immediately went to their knees and pressed their foreheads on the hot sand.

Ineni knelt just inside the factory and held out his hand to the princess. "Your Royal Highness, this foundry will become the smelting place where your dreams, your needs, and your ideas will be forged and wrought with fire. We are here at your service to mold, pound, and design anything that you wish. Please, enter the Memphis Arsenal and Refinery."

Hatsu stepped inside the factory. The interior was still hot from the snuffed fires and the air was smoky and smelled metallic-like. All the workers scurried back to their places inside the building. Exhibiting stalls displayed military items one after another. The plant produced thousands of stone maces, penetrating axes, flexible body armor, shields of all shapes, curved sickles designed after wheat thrashers, pikes, composite bows, and swords of all shapes and sizes. Each metal artist held up his specialty and stood proudly behind his booth. She listened with patience as each artisan energetically expressed the love for his craft.

"Your Highness. I am Kep, the greatest armor maker in our kingdom! It is I who can outfit you with the strongest of military chest-plates. My metal is the hardest but also the lightest. I have a secret design process that will not burden your body. Here!" The artisan handed a sample breastplate to the princess. "You must hold it in order to believe my words. Touch! Feel!" His eyes were alert and bright and constant as the North Star. So confident was his voice, without a doubt he could have commanded the desert winds to change their course. Kep's eyes locked onto Hatsu like a sea eagle that had spotted a fish.

In a protective manner, Kahn moved up close to Hatsu and took the breastplate from her hands and returned it to the vendor. Kahn's intimidating stare and huge biceps broke the gaze of the young metal worker.

"I shall remember you when I need my armor," Hatsu said to the metallurgist. The fact that he had not shown the slightest objection to designing armor for a girl impressed her greatly. She studied Kep's deep, dark eyes.

"Remember, I am Kep, and I am at your royal service." He bowed.

Further down the aisle Hatsu heard, "I am Nob. I am the greatest pike-maker on earth. My points are the sharpest and designed to rip open the enemy when extracted from the victim." He held one in his hands and pointed out the two sickle-shaped claws on each side of the point. "When using my pike, the victim will suffer from the entrance wound and the exit wound, leaving him gutted like a fish."

Hatsu stared at the point of the pike. The pike maker had many propped behind him on a rack. "Did I tell you they are as light as a feather? Would you like to hold one?"

"Yes!" replied the princess.

Nob lifted one from the rack and placed it in her hands. Hatsu remembered what the voice told her as she felt the weight of the eighteen-foot pike. *Every living thing wants to live one more day,* which, right now, surely includes her! She lifted one of the pikes. "It is light, even for me!"

Without hesitation she demanded, "I will order twenty for my ship!"

"Oh yes, your royal princess. I will have them delivered to the Giza Port immediately. They will await you at your vessel. Thank you, thank you, your gracious princess." He bowed many times.

Hatsu returned to Kep, the metallurgist, and said, "As for your craft, I will give my measurements to Senenmut and you can design my chest plate. On it you will emboss, Pharaoh Queen of the Nile."

Kep was so smitten with the honor of designing her armor that he almost swooned. *Pharaoh? She did say pharaoh,* he thought to himself. He steadied himself as his eyes stared, as if in a spell, at the boldness of the young princess.

Further down the aisle, she walked admiring the ornately carved, ivory-handled weapons.

"Your young Highness, my name is Set, and I have here, displayed before you, the sharpest of blades. They are so sharp that your enemy won't even feel his stab wound. Your victim will be smiling at you as he stumbles to the floor. His death will be a mystery even to him!" Set picked up a small green obsidian blade with an ivory-carved handle. "This, my young princess, I give to you as a token of my loyalty to you and your future administration." He picked up another blade and continued, "This, my royal one, is a blend of the purest of metals. Look . . . see . . . the edge of the blade is as thin as a hair."

Hatsu said, "Then I will order six of the sharpest blades for my bodyguards." She pointed to the six blades of her choice. After analyzing her recent experience inside the pyramid she again realized that "every living thing that wanted to live one more day" indeed included her.

"Oh, thank you, royal highness! I will have them delivered to your vessel immediately. Please remember my name, young princess. I am Set, the sword maker!" He bowed and did not rise until she had walked further down the aisle.

She turned back to take another look at Set's exhibit. Upon his table, were displayed the most splendid knives and swords. Each was complete with its own decorative sheath. Their handles were inlayed with lapis, ivory, and gold, and the craftsmanship was truly brilliant.

"Oh, and I will also take this one." She pointed to one with a golden crocodile etched and painted on its leather covering.

"Oh yes, your royal princess. You have chosen my favorite of all of my creations! It is yours." He bowed most humbly.

Hatshepsut said to her entourage, "Even in peace time, Egypt must never become complacent about their military armaments."

They all agreed, "Yes, your majesty!"

The Upper Room

MILD BREEZES FLOATED in the heights of Heliopolis, cooling off Senenmut's guest. They all sat beneath the stars at a table heaped with an elaborate array of assorted vegetables, fruits, and cheese.

On the way home from their travels to the site of the Pyramids, Nakt the cook, quickly paid a short visit to one of his adoring, lady friends where he implored upon her generosity to bake one of her specialty wheat cakes.

"You mean my cake will be eaten by a royal?" was her answer. She then went straight to her brazier room and began rolling out the dough. She filled it with honey, figs, dates, nuts, and citron. She folded up the dough-filled pastry, then placed it inside the oven. She checked the level of her water clock, and when it had dropped to a quantified measure, she pulled it from the fire, wrapped it in linen, and brought it to the home of Senenmut. She sat the warm, honey cake on the table with other mouthwatering delights.

Nakt broke off a piece and handed it to Hatsu. She bit into it and savored its sweetness. She pursed her lips and said, "Mmmm . . . life is short. It is like lightening streaking across the night sky, so we must remember to eat the sweets first!" Hatsu's joking advice to the others brought laughter and chatter to those sitting around the table. But Hatsu seriously thought about her remote viewing . . . the lessons of the night before. She remembered the fear in the eyes of the young children as they rushed headlong into long pikes. Deep in thought, she pondered to herself, *what land and time was I viewing?*

Hatsu had never been told about that particular incident and wondered if Iy, her temple instructor, had overlooked an important historical manuscript. She also considered the fact that it may not, as yet, have happened. After all, she did see futuristic mechanisms that operated on their own–mechanisms clearly representing the realities of another time and place. *Could the lands to the north have mechanisms that operate on their own?*

While she ate she could hear the sounds of thankful cries wailing up from the basement as the she-goats cried like frighten but grateful children.

Hatsu sat quietly thinking about the recent events. Her eyes were downcast, and serious thoughts rambled inside her head while the others laughed and told amusing stories.

"Hatshepsut, are you thinking about your future?" Senenmut asked.

"No, I am thinking about the past." Hatsu looked up at her gracious host and with beseeching eyes asked, "Tell me about the time before the earth fractured like a broken cake?"

Senenmut looked at Hatsu. "We must move into the house where we can have privacy. This is privileged information and must remain a secret."

Senenmut led her away from the party and directed her to sit at an ebony table covered with scrolls. "I am a collector of ancient wisdom and sacred designs. He unrolled a papyrus scroll and secured the ends." It was a map of the African continent. He drew a line with his finger along a dry riverbed across the desert, which led out to the Atlantic Ocean. "This used to be the Nile River."

Hatsu's eyes were full of wonder. "How could that be? The Nile has always flowed north."

"Always?" He flashed a look that showed a look of "perhaps not" then placed a scarab on the table. It was the size of his hand, translucent and yellowish green in color.

Hatsu stared at the stone, picked it up, and scrutinized the markings. "To our people the scarab beetle represents resurrection. It symbolizes good fortune! But I have never seen this type of stone before. From what mine was this extracted?"

"It was not extracted from a mine," answered Senenmut.

Hatsu gave him a quizzical look. “Then where did it come from?”

“It came from the stars, but I carved it into a beetle.”

Hatsu had a great intake of breath. Her brown eyes widened. She was speechless.

Senenmut continued, “It is recorded on scrolls that our world went through a disaster, one that reformed the earth. Melting stars from the heavens collided with Earth causing it to erupt from within. The impact was so forceful that the Nile River changed its course. There is a saying that the Nile will always find its way. After this cataclysmic event, the Nile forged northward. Now it empties into the closed sea.”

“The earth shattered like a broken cake and the western desert was covered with stones that fell from the sky. They glistened on the horizon in the light of Ra and in the light of the moon. Many sought to own a piece believing it was a bit of heaven and would surely bring them luck. I have asked Kep to encircle it with gold so it can be worn around the neck.”

“I imagine it would feel good to wear a bit of heaven around your neck,” Hatshepsut said as she stroked the stone scarab. “When Kep completes the circlet, you must tell me what it feels like.”

“Oh, you will know, my dear princess and future pharaoh,” he said with a smile and a respectful bow.

Hatsu looked up and with yearning eyes asked, “What was it like when women were deities and ruled equally with men?”

“Ah, the Anunnaki.”

“The Anunnaki?” asked Hatsu.

“Those who from the heavens came!” He paused and added, “Some call them the Nephilim, a pre flood-hybrid race.” He chuckled then continued, “Ah, my beautiful young lady, would you like to hear the greatest secret of all?”

“Oh yes, I love secrets,” answered Hatsu, “and I know secrets are supposed to remain confidential, and I promise I will keep it forever!”

Senenmut looked into the eyes of the royal princess and said, "Women have and always will be deities. It is recorded on scrolls hidden deep within the earth that all beings have blood heritage of star gods. Our ancestors of long ago came from the stars. Not only are you an earthly princess, but you are also a true heavenly goddess but until now you just didn't know it."

"Imagine!" Hatsu smiled, looked at Senenmut and asked, "If these scrolls are hidden deep within the earth, then how do you know about them?"

"Oral teaching of sacrosanct scribes. You see, the pyramids have long held secrets, and because of my profession, I have had access to them. I have spent many years reading the glyphs of chroniclers. Many appear on the tomb wall of the royals. Some scribes, chroniclers, and a few artists have reported that sacred and divine geometry was written down by a man named Enahk (Enoch) and that he stored it in a vast underground temple. Some say that the pyramids were built to store the knowledge of our world. It was a great repository that was designed to preserve the information for future civilization.

"It is thought that this privileged knowledge explains the secrets of our civilization. More than one copy was made of these secret scrolls. Some were spirited out of Egypt to be placed into the hands of sacred keepers."

Senenmut looked at Hatsu and with a serious stare said, "We must search the four corners of our kingdom and bring all the knowledge of the ancients back to our temples."

Hatsu's eyes widened, and she took in an insightful breath of air.

Senenmut carefully unrolled a scroll fragment called the Book of Enahk. "Some of the meaning is shrouded in obscurity, but much of the fragment deals with 'the elect one who should sit upon the throne of glory and dwell in the midst of them,' and has references to 'heavenly angels who are dwelling among us.'"

Senenmut flattened out the scroll with his hand and muttered, "According to this line it reveals an angel, Urial, which means 'god is my light.' Urial guided Enahk through the stars and explained all about the power of heaven and how he could access these powers for building. This scroll also refers to another one called the Book of Heavenly Luminaries. This book reveals star passages and suggests how our monuments should correspond with the coordinates of the stars."

Hatsu inhaled deeply. "There are so many secrets that I should know! Not only do I have the blood heritage of great warrior kings, I am a star goddess . . . and a descendant of heavenly beings!" Hatsu looked up at Senenmut. "My vision is that of a bird. You have brought clarity to the things that I must do."

A look of curiosity shaded her face. "Where is this vast underground temple? Why don't we search for it? Shouldn't we know these secrets that have been denied our civilization in order for Egypt to prosper?"

Senenmut reached out and said, "Give me your right hand." Hatsu placed hers into his. He looked into her astute, brown eyes. "You are a most remarkable young woman. I am holding the right hand of Egypt's future, but there are some secrets that should remain hidden. To know everything would destroy the spirit of curiosity and adventure. As long as there are stars in the heavens, humankind will always have something to discover. Sadly, human civilization can exist in ignorance and can prosper even without the knowledge of these secrets. But there will always be humans who will desire to know more. That is why we have the wise men of Egypt, and you, of course."

Senenmut looked at the rolled fragment of Enahk's book and said, "Perhaps these words should remain secret, and should be 'shut up until the end of time'. Apocalyptic words always find a way into sacrosanct hands."

"Do you think Enahk's temple will ever be discovered?"

Senenmut looked at Hatsu with enlightened eyes. "One day . . . yes."

"Well, then in the future, while we are searching for Enahk's temple, if you are looking for a place to hide this scroll, perhaps you should design a secret storehouse inside my mortuary temple, the one that you will build for me someday."

Senenmut looked at Hatsu and said, "Absolutely, my heavenly angel . . . absolutely."

Throughout the evening Ramah kept his eyes on the princess, and with the hieratic script, he drew the night's proceedings on papyrus. The mighty Kahn kept a protective eye on Hatsu while also keeping a lustful eye on Sitre-Re, the handmaiden. Hatsu observed the timid eyes of Sitre-Re, shyly averting Kahn's stare.

Senenmut whispered to Hatsu, "I will journey to the beautiful Southern City after I receive your final sanction. There I will build you the most inspirational building that the eyes have ever seen."

Hatsu looked up at Senenmut. Her eyes widened with anticipation. But a question lingered in her head. "You know where these secret scrolls are buried, don't you?"

Senenmut looked at Hatsu with trusting eyes and whispered, "I have an idea."

Hatsu quietly uttered, "Hmm . . . I bet they are hidden beneath the Sphinx and that is the reason it is allowed to remain buried beneath the desert sands. There are other hidden places, Senenmut. There is a place deep within the earth in the northlands. It is a maze. It harbors much gold. Gold stolen from Egypt!" Hatsu looked up at Senenmut. "But I don't know if it has already happened or if it is going to happen in the future. I saw visions when I slept inside the pyramid."

"Did your vision reveal who these people were?" Senenmut stared into the eyes of Hatsu and waited for an answer.

"They worshiped the bull."

Ra fell slowly in the west. The goddess Nut (sky) spread her celestial wings over her husband, Geb (earth), as the eternal Ra sunk behind the Giza Plateau. A blazing orange sky glowed like smoldering flames behind the pyramids while Hatsu and Senenmut privately calculated the prospects of their future.

Ramah drew what he saw.

Returning Home

THE CAPTAIN HELD the hand of the princess as she stepped onto the super ship. When she was safely upon the deck, he bowed before her and said, "Your comfort is my only desire, your royal princess."

"Thank you, Captain," Hatsu answered with a smile, then glanced back at her entourage.

Sitre-Re looked squarely into the eyes of the captain. "We have a few extra things that will be accompanying us on our return voyage." She turned and faced the ladder and watched the two she-goats stepping across the flat timber floor that connected the vessel with the dock. Each of the members of the royal entourage carried a live honking goose beneath their arms while four dock workers handled the luggage and the royal litter. "Princess Hatshepsut has acquired a few items of importance that she wishes to bring back to the royal city."

The captain kneeled again at the feet of the princess and said, "Your happiness is my principle purpose, your royal princess. So shall it be." He stood up and ordered the skippers to give the greatest of care to the goats and geese. He shouted, "After all, they are imperial!"

Senenmut and Nakt stood at the end of the dock and waived good-bye to Hatsu and her entourage. The many flags flapped and popped in the wind. He saw his prized chariot strapped to the stern of the imperial deck. Senenmut was proud to give the young princess his finest chariot, the type where she could ride and sit with comfort.

Hatsu looked back at Senenmut. Her eyes held an expression of love and triumph. Her lips pressed an unforgettable smile. It was hard for him to interpret the look on her face. Yet it was directed at him. Deep inside he was looking forward to receiving her formal request that would someday place him as her chief architect within her royal administration.

They watched the captain and oarsmen direct the large vessel across the port. It turned south, splicing into the blue waters of the Nile. Hatsu turned and waved again. The mighty Kahn stood close to his charge. His well-defined arms folded proudly across his chest. A man of few words, Kahn nodded in respect to Senenmut and Nakt who were standing on the pier.

The sails blossomed as the northeasterly winds propelled the ornate barge southward back to the Southern City. Crowds along the port and riverbanks knelt as the vessel floated past them. Children threw flowers into the Nile and sang songs of joy, begging for Princess Hatshepsut to return.

Hatsu gazed in admiration at the ancient pyramids on the western plateau. She thought about the Great Sphinx and hoped someday a team of men would release it from the smothering sands.

She studied the withering city on the eastern side. For centuries, Heliopolis had been the religious center and once sparkled with elegant temple structures. Now abandoned, the temples stood like bleached bones in the fading distance. The holy places had been cannibalized for their remarkable engravings, columns, and pylons and shipped up the Nile to the new city.

The great Southern City was currently Egypt's new religious center. The citizens were dedicated to supporting Thebes's impressive holy temples. Maintaining their splendor was now Egypt's principle purpose. The temple priests were mighty in words and possessed wonderful powers of magic–magic that could be employed for good as well as for harm. The magnitude of the temple priests had solidified their iron grip on the vulnerable citizens of Egypt and possessed a treasury of gold that almost rivaled, in some years, even that of Pharaoh Tuthmosis. This was a detail that would never go unnoticed by Hatsu.

She stood on the bow of her vessel and pondered the words of her mother. Her mind began to anticipate her next venture . . . her private meetings with Aneer.

I will subdue the golden crocodile, and *even the high priests of the temples will revere me. I will make sure that young temple priest, Hapuseneb, watches me while I hold power over the crocodile! If priests must deceive, then so shall I!* A confident smile pressed her lips. A demure wind blew through her thin tunic causing it to lift in the breeze. Her legs were beginning to show a burst of growth and would soon develop her thighs.

Ramah captured the exquisite scene with picture glyphs. It depicted Hatsu standing on the bow of the royal vessel as she held onto one of the blades that she had purchased at the Memphis arsenal. Ramah studied the young princess and was perplexed that he could not draw the thoughts that dwelled inside the beautiful head of the future pharaoh. But he drew her with all the love in his heart.

Port of Luxor

IT HAD BEEN fourteen days since his circumcision, and now Tuthmosis II only felt a slight twinge of pain to his dynastic member. Together he and the young priest, Hapuseneb, stood on the docks of Luxor and watched the royal ship gliding into its assigned slip. They observed Hatsu standing at the bow.

She stood as straight as the thin, deadly pikes that were propped and roped to the masthead. She looked down at her future husband and then at the young priest who no doubt would be assigned to their administration. *I shall sway him to my side,* then she gave a cunning and wily smile to Hapuseneb.

The princess was adorned in a jubilee tunic of blue fabric trimmed with golden beads. The wind pressed the garment against her slim body and revealed a stunning specter of her budding shape. She looked down at her half brother and the adolescent, ram-blowing priest. Bursts of orange and pink blazed across the afternoon sky, silhouetting her imperial radiance. With a confident voice she yelled down to Tuthmosis, "It is good to see you, Brother. Are you feeling better?" Then she looked over at the young priest. "And it is good to see you too, Hapuseneb."

For the first time in his life, Tuthmosis felt a slight pang of jealousy. He moaned in a low voice intended for Hapuseneb's ear, "It is she who is being tutored in the world of commercialization while I sit alone in the temple listening to finger-symbols!"

Hapuseneb leaned closer to Tuthmosis and whispered, "She is only a girl child. Don't show your frailty in front of her. Your father allowed her to have an experience, an opportunity to see boring wheat fields while you, my friend, were becoming a man."

Tuthmosis tried to smile through his tensed lips and whispered to Hapuseneb, "She looks different . . . like secrets are smoldering inside her head." He walked toward Hatsu, took her hand, and helped her down the passageway. With a puzzled look he gazed at his half sister. "There is something different about you" was all he could say. Then he helped her into the awaiting litter.

Hatsu and her attendant sat in the royal litter chatting about the expedition. She leaned over and whispered to Sitre-Re, "The mighty Kahn has eyes for you."

Sitre-Re blushed and giggled behind her cupped hand, then let out a timid, "Oh my!" She studied the well-built guard, then quickly glanced away, trying hard to smother a smile.

A flock of Theban citizens formed behind the royals and followed the entourage back to the walled city. Enamored by the princess, the bustling crowd quickly lost interest in the young Tuthmosis. He had been inadvertently plunged into the crowd of the jubilant citizens. The ecstatic crowd sang songs of praise waving palm leafs in the air as the young Tuthmosis struggled to extricate himself from the knotting cluster of citizens.

The lion-adorned gates opened, welcoming the royal litter while the crowds dutifully remained outside the gate. Clutched in the swarm of the multitudes was a very angry young Tuthmosis. He watched the gates close before him. *I will be king pharaoh and Hatsu will be my chief wife. I will have many wives,* he thought while a scowl formed on his lips. Tuthmosis pounded on the wooden portals. "Open in the name of your future pharaoh!"

Hatsu's Visit with Aneer

KAHN WATCHED HATSU from the shadows of acacia trees. His sharp eyes gazed in curiosity as his royal charge stood respectfully in front of the crocodile trainer. He was standing too far away to hear the conversation.

"I want you to have it, Aneer. The artist at the royal arsenal painted a golden crocodile on the sheath. It is for you."

The trainer looked at the gift and drew the knife from the sheath. Beads of sweat formed across his forehead and temples. "It is beautiful!"

The young student looked up at the teacher and asked, "I am ready, Aneer. When can I begin training?"

"These lessons must be done in secrecy, your majesty. You must remember if your father finds out that I am teaching you the tricks of subduing a crocodile, he will have me tortured and killed!"

"Aneer, I will defend you! And if he tries, you must trust that I will stay his hand! I am the most royal of my father's children. After I subdue the croc, I know my father will admire my strategy. Do not worry. He will not find out until after the event. The pharaoh admires and understands valor. I will appeal to his manhood.

He will be proud of me! Don't worry, Aneer, my ancestral gods will favor me." She lifted her hands to Ra and breathed a prayer.

Ra shone its brightness over the olive skin of the young princess, spreading its healing warmth across her shoulders and cheeks. She completed her appeal, then looked up at Aneer and waited for him to speak.

Aneer stared almost trance-like at the delicate carving on the ivory handle. He kept his eyes locked onto the painted crocodile and the jeweled handle. "We must do this while the citizens sleep. Meet me here when the moon begins to drop in the west. I will teach you the skills that you will need."

Hatsu thanked the trainer. "I shall be here when the moon is level with the western (Venus) star." She hurriedly took a less traveled route back to her apartment within the temple complex. *I must deceive! It will be difficult getting out of my apartment without Sitre-Re or Kahn seeing me.* She studied the narrow alleyway and examined the small window set high in the wall-face, the same window that opened to her private bedroom. *I will need enough lead so that I can hoist up the interior wall to the window and then down the exterior wall. I will leave it dangling in order to reenter my quarters. I will find a way to meet with Aneer tonight and no one will stop me!*

Kahn Dines with Sitre-Re

"WHY DON'T WE invite Kahn to dine with us tonight?" Hatsu smiled cunningly and waited for Sitre-Re to answer.

"Princess! Although he is your guard he is but a commoner! An Asiatic! We cannot have him communing with you at the same table! Your Majesty, I must remind you, he is your protector, not your dinner guest."

"Nonsense, Sitre-Re! If I am to bond with my Egypt, then I must absorb all that I can about its inhabitants. I will expect him to be our dinner guest tonight. You, Kahn, and I will dine in front of the fountain. Now, let us begin the preparations. These are the things that I want on our table tonight–Leeks swimming in garlic sauce, trays of oysters from the blue waters of the Nile, fried bolti fish, honey cakes, and lots of wine."

"Lots of wine?" Sitre-Re stared at Princess Hatsu. Her eyes blinked in awe. She was speechless. "Uh . . . my, my . . . why yes, Your Majesty . . . but . . ."

"But what, Sitre-Re?"

"Meat, Your Highness. Asiatics like their meat."

"Oh yes, so then serve him rolled peacock's tongue soaked in mint." *It is said to be a delicacy for the loins,* she thought. *I hope it works!*

Sitre-Re turned and walked swiftly to the door. She opened it and stepped out to the hypostyle. She looked at the guard who was standing like an unwavering pillar. Her eyes fell on his shapely torso, then she quietly uttered, "The Princess . . . uh . . . Egypt's future Pharaoh . . . well . . . you see . . . she wishes you to dine with us tonight."

Hatsu had asked three female musicians to play until the moon fell behind the Valley of the Kings. She had requested them to begin the evening with lively melodies, gradually changing the tempo to soft sensuous music. The night breezes flowed through the high windows of the apartment and swirled around the spicy aroma of Ethiopian incense.

Sitre-Re was a virgin, but she would not be for long. Hatsu had skillfully engineered the romantic evening for her two unsuspecting attendants. She wanted them elsewhere in motion so she could sneak out of her quarters. Tonight she had an appointment with Aneer, and she intended to keep it.

Sitre-Re's inebriated eyes studied her guest. *His muscles beneath his smooth coppery skin are sturdy and strong. He is like a fighting bull exploding with testosterone, when competing for a mate.*

Although Kahn wasn't competing, he did want that pretty maiden seated before him. His black eyes were like the darkness that was falling across the city of Thebes.

Sitre-Re, drunk with wine, put her hands on his forearms and quietly said, "She was too tired to finish her supper. She is a delicate child who needs her rest. Did you see her yawning earlier?"

Kahn smiled with anticipation. His lips had become the gateway for the succulent foods that was artfully laid out before him, but his eyes were devouring Sitre-Re inch by inch. He was not accustomed to smiling, but his Mongolian eyes took in the spectrum of the lovely eighteen-year-old royal handmaiden and anticipated greater things beyond the table. He smiled at Sitre-Re through his confident eyes as he tilted a golden goblet to his lips.

"Is she asleep?" he asked.

"Fast asleep, like a baby in a cradle," Sitre-Re whispered.

"Come here, my lovely maiden, and lay with me."

The three musicians could be heard outside the apartment door. Their plucking had become less lively and now flowed to a syncopated beat. One of the musicians accompanied the harpist and drummer with a high octave flute. The sounds pushed and pulled sultry notes through the cricket-filled night air.

Sitre-Re and Kahn embraced in each other's arms while the moon journeyed across the sky.

In the meantime, Hatsu had eased out of bed and tiptoed toward Sitre-Re's room. Nothing could interrupt the goings on in Sitre-Re's bed, short of an earthquake. It was time to go.

Hatsu placed a knife inside her tunic and tied a long skein of silk yarn to her bed leg. She threw the opposite end of the rope out the window. It tumbled down the outside wall and made a slight thumping sound which blended with the sounds emanating from Sitre-Re's room. She stood upon a stuffed pillow and pulled herself toward the high window then squeezed through the small opening. The musicians' songs could be heard in the background, and the crickets rubbed their hind legs together, making their ancient nightly clatter.

She gripped the skein of fabric and quickly lowered herself to the stone floor below. *Women must be clever.* She remembered the words of her mother.

Within the temple complex Hatsu ran like a gazelle on a stone pathway. It led to a side entrance where two massive pylons supported a red granite beam. The doorway to the Temple of Amun was dark and shadowy. *I will be strong!* she thought to herself as she scrambled inside the weakly lit holy place.

A torch shone through the hall of pillars. She could hear the musicians but soon their sound became muffled when she scurried past the brightly colored columns that led to the solaria. Afraid to be seen by those strolling about the temple complex, Hatsu dashed beneath the shadows of the acacia and date trees that grew in abundance to the south of the sparring lake that was fed by the Nile. Her heart raced like a hound on a hunt.

Out of breath, she softly walked toward the golden crocodile's exhibition. She looked down and peered at the stock-still reptile then whispered, "Aneer! Aneer! I am here for my lesson!"

Flaming torches tied to ground-supported pikes threw leaping shadows across the crescent-shaped arena. The weary crocodile trainer ambled from an adjoining mud-block dwelling. Freshly worried lines were etched between his eyebrows, and sweat dripped from his temples. His arms went up in adoration, then he fell to his knees. "Princess and future pharaoh queen of Upper and Lower Egypt, I am at your humble service. Tonight you will begin your elementary lesson on how to subdue the golden crocodile. But first we must honor the god of Sobek."

Hatsu looked down at the kneeling trainer and with self-assured tenacity said, "Let's begin, Aneer. I am as eager as a hungry lioness."

Aneer's face displayed a look of controlled fear and confidence. His thoughts rambled. *I am dead either way. If I don't train her, she could order my death. If I train her and Tuthmosis finds out, he will slice off my head!* He placed an amulet representing Sobek, the god of protection around Hatsu's neck. He whispered, "This will give you safety." He took her hand and walked to the divided section of the crocodile pens.

The moon's brilliance sparkled on the Nile waters. A warm breeze blew across the enclosed arena and stirred the crowns of the trees. A few of the crocodiles moved their positions, but the golden one lay motionless.

Aneer spoke softly. "Do not be fooled by his inaction. He knows everything that is going on around him. He can push off with his back feet and lung ten feet in a blink of an eye and run faster than you can run. He is a clever crocodile."

"We're a good match . . . you see . . . because I am a clever girl."

Aneer looked at his young, confident student. "Tonight we shall begin our first lesson on subduing the golden crocodile." He reached down and slipped his hand inside a leather bag, then brought his hand up through the opening. A small crocodile wiggled inside Aneer's clutching grip. "You must hold it and get the feel of his skin. You must learn all there is to know if you desire to subdue the golden croc." Aneer placed the young crocodile in Hatsu's awaiting hands.

"Is it a girl or boy?" Hatsu asked.

"Oh, my exalted royal one, it is too early to tell. You will get to know your crocodilian god from the size of this tiny baby to the golden one lying there on the banks of the arena." Aneer looked at his student. "Do you know why we venerate the crocodile, my royal student?"

"Not really, but I do pray to Sobek the crocodilian god. Every night I pray to him to give me power and strength!"

Aneer was excited to impart his knowledge to the most royal contender and said, "They have survived many glacial extremes and survived for millions of years. Most importantly the blood of the crocodile will cure infections. Their blood has magical powers that grants them many years. From time to time I injure my skin from neglectful or from being overly confident while training with the crocs. I always extract a small amount of their blood and smear it onto my cut. It aids in healing."

"I have never heard of such amazing information. Shouldn't that be on file in the great hall of records?" Hatsu asked.

"It is, along with many other remedies. The high priest keeps records and files it inside the repository of knowledge."

The night was filled with the most intense training. Hatsu touched the dried out skull of a long dead croc and felt the sixty-six conical jagged teeth. Aneer said, "A croc can learn hand and foot signals from its trainer. They can recognize their own name and can chase and stop on command. They open their mouth wide to Ra in order to warm their body." Aneer showed Hatsu where the muscles were attached to the jaw bone. "And this is what gives the reptile such strength used to kill and rip their prey."

"Do you have a name for this little one?" asked Hatsu.

"Well, no, not yet," answered Aneer.

Hatsu looked up at her trainer and declared, "Then we shall call him, Turtle."

Aneer looked somewhat amused. "That is a splendid name because he eats plenty of them." He laughed. "But you should be ever-vigilant in knowing the true nature of your 'Little Turtle.'" Aneer exhaled an exhausted breath. "Never forget his sixty-six teeth. They bite and rip like a lion, scissoring off chunks of meat."

Thirty-six moon phases of training sessions followed with each month being more rigorous than the one before until finally Hatsu had mastered the art of subduing the crocodile. The occasion would soon present itself for her to prove her strength of will, which would follow the wedding ceremony. The royals loved to celebrate, and Hatsu had a special event planned. But first it was time to unite in marriage with her brother, Tuthmosis II.

The Marriage of Hatsu and Tuthmosis II

Hatsu, Age Fourteen

SITRE-RE SMILED, LOOKED at her charge, and asked, "Hatsu, why did you choose Nekheb for your breathing ceremony?"

"In our archives I discovered that an influential family who had supported my grandfather's military forces once lived at Nekheb. This family's abiding support altered the course of Egypt's history. With their military reinforcements, my grandfather, Ahmose, who at the time was just a young prince, was able to kick out the Hyksos and retake the throne of Egypt. So you see, Sitre-Re, Nekheb holds special powers for me. Someday just like my grandfather and father, I will become pharaoh."

Hatsu looked up from the horse-drawn chariot and spotted her brother. "I am marking time, and I must do this for my Egypt."

Sitre-Re held the trembling hand of the young princess. "Remember, my dear Hatsu, you must find balance in your world. When he comes to you at night, remember he is your husband and you are his chief wife. You must submit."

"Submit? Oh, that my heart was filled with love for him. Life for me would be heavenly. Sadly, I do not hunger for his presence." In an inaudible whisper she continued, "My heart loves another."

Hatsu looked at the ship and the awaiting retinue of servants. She spotted her future husband standing proudly on the bow. She faked a smile and whispered a prayer to the goddess of Shai and the goddess Ma'at. *Oh goddesses, since you have chosen my destiny, help me to always choose the pathway that will enable Egypt to flourish and that I may always find a balance in my world. Make me a servant to my people, and when it becomes my time for the weighing of the heart, be ever forgiving and merciful.* She took a deep breath, then proceeded to walk closer to the ship. Sitre-Re held firmly onto Hatsu's hand.

Kahn followed his royal charge with the utmost heed and discretion. His steps were silent, and his hands clutched the obsidian stars within the folds of his cotton tunic.

"Here comes my little turtle. We shall be married tomorrow!"

Hatsu yelled back, "I am not the turtle that you think I am." In a much lower voice she said . . . "and someday soon I will prove it to you."

Sitre-Re squeezed Hatsu's hand harder. "Balance, my dear princess. Unfortunately, love has nothing to do with this marriage to your brother. Some records reveal that rarely does love play a part in royal weddings. It is all about royal blood-born heirs. Do not believe the glyphs on the temple walls."

Sitre-Re's kind eyes looked at Hatsu. "Someday you will find real love . . . you will find it outside the confines of your sovereign world, and it will be the kind of love that melts your heart and scrambles your thoughts. Right now, though, you must marry for the sake of Egypt. Let us board your vessel. You must go now and become chief wife to Tuthmosis II, your half brother, who is soon to be your husband."

Hatsu leaned closer to Sitre-Re and whispered, "Yes, first I will become chief wife, and then I will become pharaoh of Upper and Lower Egypt." She smiled, then scampered up the ramp and confidently walked toward the bow to face her destiny. "I have already found it, Sitre-Re!"

Her handmaiden followed protectively and with questioning eyes asked, "Found what, Princess?"

Hatsu looked at Sitre-Re and said, “Love! I have found it beyond the walls of my sovereign world.”

Sitre-Re looked at Hatsu and thought, *the child’s heart must be rent asunder with the thought of becoming chief wife. Whoever has she met beyond the walls of her sovereign world? I bet it is her scribe.*

The wind pressed against Hatsu’s thin white tunic. No longer was she a little girl. She had turned into a beautiful young woman who had the will of a fighting crocodile.

The super ship floated southward into Upper Egypt. High craggy cliffs lined both sides of the valley while sea eagles followed in the wake of the royal ship. Ptah had dutifully planned the ceremony at a certain location requested by the princess. There were other spots along the Nile that he thought was by far more fitting for the ceremony. He kept thinking, *Nekheb, why Nekheb?* (Present day El-Kab.)

The Breathing Ceremony

ONLY FIVE MEMBERS of the ceremony disembarked the super ship and walked up rocky steps that led to a picturesque waterfall. Blue skies seemed within touching reach and delicate pink-tinged clouds brushed through the air like long, wispy feathers.

The ritual would be conducted by the high priest, Ptah, and his son, Hapuseneb, the young priest in training.

Priest Ptah and Hapuseneb chanted incantations, rubbing essential oils on the forearms of the young couple. A long decorative sash was draped around the couple's arms signifying they were now unified as one.

Ptah whispered these words to young Tuthmosis. Now you must say, "I, Tuthmosis II, am the son of the great pharaoh. Silver and gold shall fill my lap. Thou shalt be my chief wife. I will be thou husband. Like a fruit garden I will give thee offspring." Tuthmosis repeated Ptah's words.

Then Ptah looked at Hatshepsut and said, "Repeat these words: I will deliver thee a continuation of my royal blood, and my ancestors will protect and claim our children a heritage for Egypt."

After the officiating words were spoken, Tuthmosis II and Hatsu remained alone on the cliff for a while. The "breathing ceremony" was personal and confidential. No one else was allowed to witness this singular moment.

As for Kahn, he was hidden behind an outcrop of rocks and was no more than a few feet away during the entire ceremony. He was Hatsu's protector, and Tuthmosis the Great laid down the command to always protect his daughter, and protect her he would.

Knowing the commitment of this single instant, Hatsu drew in a breath of confidence. She stared into the distance to the right of her half brother, now her husband. She gazed into a vast unknown and a revelation of her true love began to fill her heart.

Alone on the cliff, Hatsu and Tuthmosis II could see the Nile below and to the east could see desert that stretched toward the Red Sea.

Gray and white sea eagles dipped and swayed, shrieking their ancient sounds. The young couple prepared to kiss. Tuthmosis held Hatsu in his arms and forced open her mouth with his lips. "You will breath into me, my little turtle."

Hatsu closed her eyes and inwardly cringed. *Dear Ma-at, give me balance . . . dear Sobek, give me protection . . . dear Thoth, give me wisdom.* The vision of Senenmut calmed her mind. She submitted, then opened her mouth and breathed the breath of the mighty ancients into Tuthmosis II. *I must do this for my Egypt,* she thought.

Surprise for the Royals

Several Months after the Breathing Ceremony

HUNDREDS OF DELICATELY rolled papyrus scrolls tied with vermilion-colored string were distributed throughout the Amelu section of Thebes. Royals and visiting crowned heads were invited to attend an exciting event at the Golden Crocodile Arena the first night of the full moon.

Another timely dynamic that would add to the importance of the event was the heralding of the star, Sopdet, the western star that announced the annual flooding. The alluvial waters brought minerals to the crop fields.

Egypt's agrarian economy was the power behind the pharaonic leaders, and if the Nile failed to flood, then the citizens looked toward their pharaoh. On the hushed lips of all the citizens were the words, "Is Ra unhappy with our leader?"

Thankfully, Sopdet was shining brightly, and the Nile began to spill over the Black Lands rushing with great force like a charging lion after its prey.

Thebes was aflutter with this special invitation circulating within the great city. Tuthmosis I had been cavorting with one of his lesser wives, but now his eyes were watching her hands untie the red string. She straightened the papyrus. She began reading the contents aloud while reclining next to him on his royal bed. Her excited eyes sparkled with joy as she read the glyphs out loud. "It is in three days time, my lord. A celebration will be held at the Golden Crocodile Arena, starting when the afternoon sun falls behind the Valley of the Kings. It is signed only by Hatshepsut, the chief wife of Tuthmosis II . . . This is from your daughter, my lord." The lesser wife bit her sensual lips and smiled, then handed the invitation to her lord and lover.

Pharaoh looked at the papyrus. Searching for some clue as to the celebration he laughed. "Ha! Of course! It is the beautiful Feast of the Valley! What a clever girl my royal daughter! She has chosen to hold it inside the Crocodile Arena. A brilliant change! I shall be there in front. I do not want to miss a thing! I shall even drink a goblet of crocodile blood and toast the golden croc. I shall pray to him for protection and a long life. Ah . . . yes my daughter . . . she is brilliant!"

The lesser wife of Tuthmosis I clapped her hands with joy, then reached down and kissed her master on the lips.

Chief wife Ahmose sat quietly, facing her board game. She opened hers and studied the scroll. Her eyes were blurry and could not focus. She handed it to her handmaiden and ordered, "Read this thing!"

In another part of the temple complex, Pharaoh's young teenage son, Tuthmosis II, read his invitation. "She is treating me as if I were a mere royal! I will soon become the official pharaoh!" He scrutinized his invitation and compared it to his concubine's papyrus. "Mine is the same as yours! Why is she keeping me in the dark about her plans? This event is in three days!" He stared at the papyrus as if it might reveal magical powers. "I will go to Hatsu's apartment and find out what this is about!"

Tuthmosis II waved the papyrus in Hatsu's face. "I will soon be pharaoh! You must include me in your festival plans!"

Hatsu looked at her husband-brother with annoyance and said, "Oh, you know how you love surprises, my husband. I cannot tell you everything. Just be there." Hatsu stared at him with a serene smile on her lips, then said, "Now go back to your concubine and conc!"

Stellar Day at the Arena

ON THE DAY of the event, the arena was cordoned off and lined with red and yellow flags. The entire Crocodile Arena staff, including Aneer, was fully prepared to either have hosted the most important event in the history of Egypt or subjected to a bunch of immediate beheadings–one being his own. If things did not go as planned, Aneer's beheading would be officiated by Tuthmosis I, Tuthmosis II, the High Priest Ptah, and any other important administrative official that might demand his death as well as his cohorts'.

Aneer's wife had already sought refuge in a reed felucca and was hundreds of miles south of Thebes. *He is a mad man! I am sure I am a widow by now,* were the words that rolled around in her head. *I have to get as far away from the royals as possible. I am certain the authorities are after me too.* The winds inflated the sails and pushed her southward while her small boat braved the northbound current.

Aneer had been up all night praying for Sobek to protect Hatsu in her bold and daring attempt to capture the citizen's confidence. The sun continued its journey across the sky and fell behind the Valley of the Kings. The torches were lit and the arena shone like the light of Amun-Ra.

Musicians began their compositions, combining the harpists and flutes. Dancing girls moved in rhythm to the music. Trays of delicate sweet morsels were passed around, and beer and wine flowed faster than the inundation that was roaring past them.

The event attracted every royal in Thebes, including the reclusive chief wife. She took her seat on the left side of her ailing husband, Tuthmosis I. Mutnofre and Pharaoh's other lesser wives were seated in the shadows with the other royal concubines, and Sitre-Re sat with her sister servants. A section was prepared for the high priest, Ptah. Hapuseneb, Ptah's son, sat next to his father but kept his eyes on his young friend, Tuthmosis.

A disgruntled Tuthmosis II sat to the right of his father. "I cannot keep my wife-sister in line. I have no idea where she is? She is a rebel, that one."

Tuthmosis I chuckled and scanned the crowd for his daughter and her protector, Kahn. "She is somewhere orchestrating this event. Allow her some slack, dear boy. Knowing my Hatsu, I am sure she has some grand performance prepared for us." He chuckled and gulped his beer.

Tuthmosis II shrugged his shoulders. "It is her duty to take her place next to me." He looked back at the section of concubinas and winked at Isis, his chief concubine.

The arena was designed to accommodate one thousand people. The din of laughter and excited chatter roared across the complex. The music came to an end and the dancers backed off the portable stage that had been erected just for this special occasion. Aneer walked confidently to the middle of the arena. His heart thumped like a beating drum, and his blood flowed through his body faster than a shooting star could fall from the sky. Sweat trickled from his temples.

In a loud voice, he yelled, "She comes to you in beauty! He comes to you in power! Her will is stronger than the granite blocks at Giza! The one who comes to you today will subdue the golden crocodile!"

The crowd roared with amusement and were somewhat confused about the gender of this mysterious entertainer. Aneer's use of the pronoun, she and he, was confusing to the crowd. The audience figured Aneer must have had too much beer.

The stage hands removed the portable scaffold revealing the golden crocodile that had been lurking beneath the platform.

Quickly, Aneer began to coax the crocodile out of the water. It slithered through the pond, climbed to the water's edge, then relaxed along the bank. Aneer looked up and watched the determined bold steps of the approaching and mysterious young royal.

The colorful ceremonial attire worn by the young entertainer was designed to deliberately confuse the crowd. The headdress was cropped suggesting a young male. The tunic was bound tightly across the chest and the loin cloth was the usual male tunic style.

The crowd hushed. *Who was this boy?* The royal family sat silently at the front of the crowd. They imagined that he must be a child of one of the concubines or perhaps a secret son of Ptah. Aneer called him a "royal." The crowd was fascinated, confused, and full of anticipation.

Aneer draped a Sobek talisman around the neck of the brave young performer, then backed away and knew that his moments on earth were numbered. He took a deep breath and thought, *When they find out who she is, I am dead. I hope the officials never find my poor wife. They will have her head too.* He kept a steady gaze on the young brave royal.

The delicate voice yelled, "I am looking for Turtle! Does anyone know where Turtle is?" The golden crocodile moved upward along the bank and headed directly toward the young trainer.

The voice sure sounded familiar to the young, soon-to-be pharaoh. His eyes stared down at the youthful entertainer.

"Oh, there you are, my little Turtle." The young trainer motioned to the crocodile with subtle hand movements, then slowly bent down.

The crowd stood up in disbelief. Tuthmosis II thought he recognized that voice. *Could it be? No . . . it is but a mere child down there! A boy at that!*

In one sure-footed, well-trained motion, Hatsu grabbed the tail and flipped the four hundred pound croc onto its back.

Training for this single moment had taken more than thirty-six full moons. Aneer had actually seen her perform this act many times. Never-the-less, he still trembled like a fragile butterfly captured inside the whirl of a desert wind. *She did it!* He watched his student performing a superhuman feat especially for a girl so young and so delicate.

Aneer panted like a gazelle running from the jaws of a crocodile while he watched with eagle eyes a performance that would sadly be erased from the records of Egyptian history.

There was a great intake of breath from the assembled. A hush hovered over the crowd. The only other sound was the ancient clatter of the crickets and a calming voice that asked, "Are you my little Turtle? Shuu! It is time for a good night kiss." Hatsu leaned down and kissed the under throat of the crocodile, then laid her delicate body belly-to-belly upon the dangerous reptile.

The crowd roared with exhilaration. They were absolutely stunned at the valor of one so small. *Who was this entertainer?*

Wine was spilling from the tipping goblets of the royals, and beer was dribbling from the gaping mouths of the shocked crowned heads of Egypt.

Hatsu jumped up and back-stepped away from the croc. She snapped off her tunic, then pulled off her headdress. Her youthful breast pressed beneath her thin under garment. Her long hair spilled out, and the throng of royals and guests were amazed. The crowd went wild! Is it a girl or is it a boy? It was Hatshepsut, chief wife of Tuthmosis II.

The musicians resumed their music. The nearly nude dancers returned to their seductive dance with delicate finger symbols, and the acrobats tumbled and flipped. It was the grandest circus ever seen. Never had the royal house and elite citizens witnessed such a spectacular act that included an imperial member. Administrative scribes were busy drawing glyphs including Ramah whose heart pounded like a drum while he drew exactly what his eyes were seeing.

Hatsu backed away from the reptile and ran toward her husband. People in the arena tried to touch her shoulder for good fortune. Tuthmosis II stood wide-eyed. With his mouth aghast he yelled, "Hatsu, it is you!"

Hatsu looked at her husband and boldly whispered in his ear, "Call me Turtle one more time, and you will be swimming with the golden croc." She turned and pointed to the golden reptile now making his way back to the water.

The young Tuthmosis yelled, "You can't talk to me like this! You are talking to the future pharaoh!"

Hatshepsut looked at her brother-husband and yelled, "Ah, but you are staring at Egypt's future pharaoh!"

Tuthmosis II ran to Aneer and yelled, "I'll have your damn head for this! You have aided her in making me look like a weakling!"

Aneer's thoughts screamed, *You are a weakling!* But at the same time Aneer's eyes widened with fear. His muscular legs trembled and began to weaken. He dropped to his knees. "She insisted on learning this skillful art. She would have ordered my head if I had refused her wishes. Either way I am doomed to be a dead man." Accepting his fate, Aneer bent over and touched his head to the ground and said, "I am prepared to die."

The young Tuthmosis pulled out his sword and pointed it at Aneer's neck. He lifted his blade and just as he was ready to thrust downward, Hatsu jumped onto Aneer's back and laid her head on top of his neck. "Great god of Sobek! Hear my cry!" Hatsu looked up at her husband and yelled, "You will have to kill me first! I am the most royal of the ancients! If you spoil a hair on my head or Aneer's, you and your descendants will forever be cursed!"

Stunned by her valor and terrified at the possibility of an eternal curse, her husband stepped back and retreated to the section where the concubines were seated.

Isis, his preferred one, strained to see the commotion and finally spotted her young lover running up the steps. She batted her coal-lined eyes. "I declare, this has been a stellar day at the arena, my lord. Would you like another goblet of wine?"

She offered him the drink, but he flung it to the ground. He grabbed her hand and yelled, "Come with me, and make me feel like a man as only you know how to do!"

Hatsu got up and brushed the sand from her trainer's head. His body still trembled from the drama. His voice quavered and whispered into her ear, "Thank you . . . thank you . . . most noble of all women, chief wife and someday, pharaoh of Upper and Lower Egypt. You spared my life. I praise you for your bravery."

Hatsu looked up at him and said, "Aneer, it is you that have spared my life. Because of your patience and training, you have helped secure my heritage. You have helped me look mighty in the eyes of our citizens. You will always have my respect and honor. Ask me for anything, and your wish will be granted."

In disbelief he looked at her wide-eyed. "My wife has left me and is headed south somewhere along the Nile. I fear that I have lost her forever. She was quite certain that I would be killed for this. Her last words were, 'I would rather think that you are alive than to know that you are dead.' I want her back." His tears spilled out and dripped down his sunburned cheeks.

Hatsu assured the king of the crocodiles, "I will issue an official bulla tomorrow to be distributed throughout all of Egypt. Trust me, you will have your wife back in due time." Hatsu looked at Aneer with new-found respect. "By the way, you are quite an entertainer!"

After the evening's events, the ailing pharaoh walked over to his daughter. With a stern look he said, "I don't think I can survive another stunt like this." Then a smile pressed his lips. "You have the bravery of your ancestors. Too bad you were not born a boy."

"Ah . . . but, Father, I rather enjoy being a woman. I know in my heart that I was born to be an agent for change. Someday I will lead Egypt as mightily as any strong military man. Time is a revealer of all things. I know this to be true."

Her father looked at his royal daughter and said, "Yes, I do believe you will. By the way, where is Kahn, your protector?"

"Before your eyes, Father."

"I do not see him."

"Look at the acacia tree."

Tuthmosis I stared at the tree and realized Kahn had been there all along. He had painted himself to blend with the bark and branches. Kahn's eyes had been watching steadfastly over Hatsu throughout the entire event. He had been only a few feet from the show with the obsidian stars in his hands that he would have discharged them into the croc if it had been necessary.

"You mean he knew about this?"

"Of course, Father. I have his trust. He is my protector! He knows my every move."

"Give me a goblet of crocodile blood!" ordered Tuthmosis. "I want to live a long life and witness more of my daughter's bravery!"

Hatshepsut had instructed the royal scribes to spend the entire night preparing the bullas for distribution.

The next day hundreds of official papyri scrolls were issued to the four corners of the lands of Egypt. It read:

This is an official bulla from the House of Tuthmosis, Egypt's Most Esteemed Woman.

Aneer, the newly honored officer of entertainment to the royal family, formerly the crocodile instructor of Thebes, needs his wife to return to him immediately. He misses her. A heap of gold will be the reward for anyone returning her in fitting health.

From the royal granddaughter of the ancients, most royal daughter of Tuthmosis I, chief executor and principal wife to Tuthmosis II, Egypt's illustrious future,

Queen Hatshepsut Makare Khenemetamen.

Ahmose Visits Her Husband

RARE WERE THE times the chief wife, Ahmose, visited her husband's apartment. Hearing the whispers that he had taken a turn for the worse, caused a stir of concern. *After all I am his wife,* she thought, as a small envoy of attendants surrounded her in the forecourt while she waited to be announced.

A Nubian attendant stood like an ebony statue. Head bowed, he said, "You are splendor in this place, chief wife of our great Tuthmosis. Pharaoh anticipates your presence. Please walk this way."

Ahmose stood at the entrance of the private quarters of the ailing king. She walked past the golden inlayed chairs, past the copper tray of nuts and honey cakes, and past the temple cat curled at the foot of his bed. She looked down at a very sickly man.

Pharaoh looked up and gestured for her to sit. "I am a far cry from Egypt's military conqueror. Here I lie, a wounded champion too weak to enjoy my conquests."

Ahmose eased her small frame alongside her husband. She selected a fig from a tray of sweets. "Your exploits as a military king are extraordinary. You have seized the gold mines of Nubia. You have enlarged the borders of Egypt. You have opened up the Valley of the Kings and Queens. Oh, my lord, you are leaving your heritage in Egypt."

Tuthmosis sighed. "I have left everything but a full-royal male."

"Oh, but you do have a true full royal, my husband."

Together, they both whispered, "Hatshepsut." Their eyes locked and a certain knowing settled inside their hearts.

Wife of Aneer Returned

FOR WEEKS ON end following the official bulla, hundreds of feluccas flooded the port at Thebes. It would take only minutes for the boat owners to dock and scurry along the crowded streets, pushing their way to the temple complex.

"This woman claims to be the wife of Aneer! I have found her, and now I am returning her to the esteemed officer of entertainment." Bowing humbly, each man pushed their willing captive in front of an official with hopeful expectations of receiving a reward of gold.

Because the bulla had generated such a flurry of excitement, a special court had to be arranged to accommodate the flood of people. Only Aneer could pick the right woman as his true wife. Every day, Aneer sat next to an administrative official saying, "No, not this one. Not this one either. She is young enough to be my granddaughter. How young is this one . . . four?" Or "This woman is dead and just doesn't know it yet. Look at her. She is one of the ancients! She is old enough to be my great-great-great-grandmother!"

However, during this intense time of daily interviews, from time to time a beautiful woman would be presented to Aneer, and he would ask, "Clearly you are not my wife, but do you have a talent?"

"Oh yes, sire. I can dance. Rejal is my name." Or Aneer would hear "I can sing . . . I can play the harp . . . I can play the flute . . . I am a gymnast." These daily appointments had successfully turned into auditioning for the entertainment committee.

As a result some of the best talents had been delivered quite by accident filling Hatshepsut's administration with the most highly trained female entertainers in all of Egypt's history.

However, after several months, a woman who had been desperately on the run, at last stepped forward. "It is I, my dear husband. I have returned. Thankfully I see you are still wearing your head."

Aneer's world quickly resumed to an orderly fashion and the two continued their lives together. They were offered an apartment within the temple complex, and soon, Aneer was handed a list of special celebrations where he immediately began planning the entertainment for the long list of annual events. The royals loved to be entertained, and Aneer was the man for this job.

Sending Young Tuthmosis In Search for Gold

"HE FEELS HE has to prove himself to the citizens. His valor has plunged to great depths since the Feast of the Valley. He still suffers from Hatsu's dance with the crocodile, so I told him the best way to bring valor to Egypt and be admired by the citizens is to descend to the depths of the desert and bring up gold. So, can Egypt's diviners suggest a possible new site, one that has never been plundered?" Tuthmosis searched the eyes of his chief advisor for advice and waited for him to reply.

"My king, it is told to me by our official diviners that their sticks were trembling in the region of the eastern desert between the Nile and the Red Sea. It is a place near Ikoptos, Ombos, and Apollinopolis Magna. It is diviner's opinion that at that these sites much gold will be found."

"Good. I will send my son there. Make provision for an army to accompany him. He will leave tomorrow. He needs to descend inside the earth in order to rise up in valor."

The Young Student

HATSU TOOK ADVANTAGE of her husband's absence and set a new plan in motion. From the time Hatsu was four she had been schooled in the domestic arts and religion. It was in her fourteenth year that she began her military and geographical studies. After Hatsu's husband left for his pursuit of a new country, Hatsu threw herself into researching every battle, strategies of war, tools of weaponry, customs of other countries, and their tenets of beliefs.

She poured over manuscripts and scribal paintings, drawings of seaports and geographical descriptions of the Nile, the Red Sea, the closed sea (Mediterranean Basin) and the Great Ocean to the West, land masses as they related to the seas, and major water and land trade routes.

On this day there were many manuscripts twelve inches wide and some thirty feet long unrolled across the temple floor. She crawled from one manuscript to another absorbing every morsel she could like a starving lion in a drought infested land.

Her instructor, Iy, who was also the temple archivist, had unrolled many scrolls for their studies. "Now, explain this one to me, Iy, and do not leave out even the smallest detail. You must tell me everything there is to know about this land . . . all about their minerals, jewels, gold, their proximity to navigable waters . . . the language they speak . . . animals in their kingdom, their culture, religious tenets . . . everything!"

Iy looked into the eyes of Hatshepsut, and asked, "Religious tenets?" His eyes searched around the temple like a lion peering through tall grass. His voice was barely audible.

Iy whispered to Hatshepsut, "Every nation has their magic men . . . their Magi . . . their wise men. Every nation has their collection of sacred writings . . . and every nation has their god! Humanity would prosper if these writings of collected godly wisdom could be organized inside one official storehouse where we could all share in the knowledge of wise minds."

Hatsu remembered Senenmut had said the same thing years earlier.

Iy unrolled and pressed the scroll flat. He pointed to a position on the map. "I hear there is such a place. This one is particularly interesting, most noble of women." Iy pointed to an island surrounded by water. "Ahh, yes, this one is known as the sacred lake. It is known as . . ." He looked around to make sure no one except Hatsu was listening and then Iy whispered, "God's Land. It is rumored that many scrolls are stored in the depth of this island–scrolls that contain the wisdom of the ages and relics too complex for the human mind."

Hatsu touched the map and whispered to Iy, "Someday we will go there. This I know is my destiny, and I must fulfill it. I will bring you with me and together we will return with the secrets for our Theban temples. I will conduct an expedition to this land. So what kinds of holy items can one find on this island . . . this place called God's Land?"

Iy's voice sounded like the rush of a wind. "Oh, many things. It is recorded in ancient scrolls that Pharaoh Sahure who lived a thousand years ago sent an expedition to God's Land where ships returned with heaps of myrrh and electrum."

"Electrum, huh?"

"Yes, it is an alloy of gold and silver and has the power to turn darkness into light."

"Iy, we must capture the market for electrum! Most of our artisans have to take a psychotropic drug in order to work within the darkness. It is an offering that is given to them by the priest. The House of Tuthmosis has to pay the high priest much gold in order for them to release this drug for the underground stone masons and artists."

"You will find many items in God's Land. It is rumored that this sacred temple has scrolls on mathematics, an exposé explaining the mysteries of the universe, medicine, alchemy, judicial law and many more items of value. It is said that a very rare book called the Book of Enahk (Enoch) is hidden inside this temple in the deep. This book was written by a very wise man. It is said that it holds strange mysteries."

Hatsu's eyes grew large. "The name of the man was Enahk?" Her eyes narrowed, and her voice reduced to a whisper. "I saw fragments of this book several years ago."

"Most honorable woman, where did you see these fragments? Where are they today?" Iy was rapturous with joy. His eyes were wide with anticipation.

Not willing to give up her source or better yet choosing to protect her source, Hatsu answered, "I had a chance encounter with the owner of these relics, but now they are in a temple buried deep beneath the desert sands." *I had to tell him something. I wonder what Senenmut has done with these fragments?* she thought, then said, "I will try to get them for you, but you must swear to protect them with your life."

"My purpose is that of a sacrosanct custodian of truth. You can trust me, most noble of women."

Together Iy and Hatshepsut poured over maps that showed ancient water and land routes that branched along the Nile, south of Thebes. They studied the routes from the Red Sea leading from the Gulf of Aden across the Big Sea to the land of India. "Someday I will go on a quest for knowledge. I will organize an expedition to God's Land and acquire the sacred information that is stored within this island temple. I will go to Ta Netjer and bring back wisdom for our temples."

Iy pointed to a specific place on the map. He lowered his voice to a whisper. "It is reported a talking relic is hidden inside an underground temple. Oral teachings say this unspeakable thing contains the secrets of our genesis and can reveal the future of our civilization. It has the capability to increase our knowledge. Once it belonged to our temples. My grandfather told me our wise men of Egypt were able to hear it speak. It was a repository containing our past. If we do not know from whence we came, we will never know who we are or where we are going as a developing civilization." Iy breathed deeply, then exhaled, "Our session should never be uttered to anyone! This expedition will be an enormous contribution to Egypt . . . a noble cause, most noble of women. To bring back this relic would bring remarkable power to Egypt. What do you think?" Iy looked intently at Hatshepsut.

"A talking relic? *It sounds like the thing that was spirited out of Egypt when the Hyksos plundered our sacred temples.*" Hatsu suddenly remembered her remote viewing experience. *I have seen it, and I know what to look for.*

A faraway look settled in her eyes. She spoke in a whisper, "I must lead an expedition to find these scrolls and historic relics. I will be remembered for bringing back Egypt's memory." Hatshepsut lifted her hands to the sky as a promise to Iy and the sun god, Ra.

From that moment on, Hatshepsut immersed herself in the study of temple scrolls with Thebes's most trusted archivist and overseer of sacred temple records searching for the unspeakable . . . the truth.

But shadowed inside the temple, behind a wall of stored scrolls, Ptah and his son watched Hatshepsut and Iy. "This is uncommon! This is unusual activity for a woman! True, she is a successor of the greats, but why does she feel that it is necessary to become privy to administrative matters? She is studying affair that should be assigned only to her husband who one day will become pharaoh."

Hapuseneb looked at his father. Covering his mouth with his hand, he whispered, "The young girl once told me she has been in here studying sacred geometry."

"Sacred geometry? That is elite, only for architects! She is going far beyond her abilities! Who does she think she is? I have never known a woman to aspire to such lengths! Sacred geometry? It is not something a chief wife needs to know."

Ptah's eyes widened, then shifted from side to side. "I do hope she has not decided to delve into our realm of knowledge. Priestly magic are matters that only belongs to the priesthood!"

Hapuseneb whispered, "It is rumored that she is planning a major building project. I guess she wants to understand mathematical ratios, proportions as it relates to the heavens and nature's designs. It is reported that she has memorized the golden ratio to its thousandth power! She claims the numbers are predictable and not random as they seem to appear. It starts . . . uh . . . three point one four one five nine etc., etc., etc.!"

Ptah furrowed his brow. "No one can do that! Hundredth, maybe!"

Hapuseneb paused to catch his breath. "She is becoming too informed, Father. We should do something that will slow her progress in these matters. She must not overshadow her husband . . . or us! I fear that she might encroach into our priestly realm. We must show her that we are in touch with mystical powers, powers that are greater than anything. That should slow down her unquenchable thirst for knowledge."

A Memo to Hatshepsut

READING ALOUD FROM an ostraca, a small piece of pottery no larger than her hand, Hatsu read the following glyphs:

"We will be honored by your presence to enjoy a private showing by Hapuseneb, our young priest of Thebes. You will marvel at the impossible. Miracles of indefinable words will commence the night of the next full moon, to be held inside the Great Temple of Amun at the highpoint of the full moon."

. . . A Week Passed

The full moon was directly over head, casting its radiance over the town of Thebes.

Hatsu stood at the temple entrance with her exclusive entourage positioned around her and waited for the signal. The mighty Kahn, Sitre-Re, Aneer, and her mother, Ahmose, were invited to join the viewing of this miraculous show.

Ahmose leaned toward Hatsu and whispered, "If it defies logic, it involves trickery."

"Yes, Mother," Hatsu answered.

"Do not drink anything. It will dull your thinking," instructed Ahmose.

"Yes, Mother."

"If Ptah insists that you drink, then spit it on the floor."

"Yes, Mother."

Faint footfalls could be heard in the recesses of the dark temple. Soon they became louder, then they suddenly stopped.

Ptah walked from the shadows and appeared before them with a confident expression on his face. His robe was shrouded around his head and fell to the floor like a dune of black silica. In a grim voice he said, "It pleases me to see that you have accepted our invitation. You must come in and gather before the altar." He held up a lantern and motioned for them to enter.

They followed Ptah down the dark hypostyle, passing the many brightly colored columns. Temple cats meowed in the shadows creating a sense of eternal mystery.

The interior was dim. Contained within the temple walls was a coldness that was generated by the stone walls and something else that was indefinable. A single flicker glowed from an oil lamp positioned atop the reredos. Ptah blew out the flame of his hand-held lantern.

The private audience could barely make out the outline of a pitcher and silver goblets. Ahmose bumped Hatsu's arm in a gesture of, "I told you so."

Ptah said, "Before you witness the miracle that you are about to witness, I must insist that you enjoy the fruit of the vine. In doing so, you will cleanse your heart from all malefactions. That way you can prepare your heart and eyes for the miracle of all miracles."

A fragrance of lotus attar and burning timbers permeated the dark temple. Each were handed a goblet filled with a drink made from wine.

Ptah lifted his goblet and said, "Repeat after me. I shall drink the fruit of this wine."

A chorus of, "I shall drink the fruit of this wine," could be heard inside the dark temple.

Ptah instructed, "It will cleanse my heart from all malefactions."

They repeated, "It will cleanse my heart from all malefactions."

Ptah tipped his goblet and supped, instructing the others to do the same.

Ptah praised the benefits of the drink by adding, "From birth to tomb this vital drink is atonement for any bad deeds."

Ahmose rolled her eyes in a gesture of boredom and thought about her own tomb. *I should visit the Valley of the Queens and check on the progress of my burial chamber. It has been months since I have shown respect to the tomb builders.* She leaned closer to Hatsu and whispered. "All this fluff about the afterlife means nothing to me. After my death, my skin will shrink like a drum cover and eventually turn into a pile of dust." She reached into her sleeve and pulled out a rolled up lotus leaf and pressed it beneath her tongue. In her mind she entertained the ivory chips on her board game and planned the moves she would make when she returned to her apartment. Her glassy eyes stared into the darkness and waited for the so-called miracle.

The wine had an immediate affect on the spectators. They began to feel its warm, calming, hallucinogenic effect.

Hatsu did what her mother had whispered to her moments earlier. She took her goblet and quietly spilled hers onto the floor. *I don't want this drink to dull my thinking.*

Ptah's drink was a secret formulation. His contained a psychotropic blend that gave him night vision because he would surely need it for what he was about to do.

The other goblets contained a blend of poppy seed, wine, and attar from a night shade plant. It was formulated to be potent enough to make them susceptible, no matter how unsuccessful or successful this "miracle" might be.

Almost immediately, Ptah's eyes began to adjust to the darkness. He hurriedly ran across the altar and reached up for the two black streamers dangling from the rafters wrapping them around his hands. He looked up and called out for his son, the young priest, Hapuseneb.

A high-pitched meow pierced the darkness. Seconds later Hatsu felt the warm fur of a temple cat rubbing against her ankles. Moments later she sensed there were a number of cats gathering around her feet licking up her spilled intoxicating drink.

Hatsu looked up and could barely make out Ptah holding onto two black straps that were dangling from the darkness of the ceiling. Soon they began to tighten.

Hapuseneb hated this miracle. He always feared that his father would accidentally cause him to fatally fall from the rafters. He straddled the cedar rafter and hung onto dear life. He waited for his cue.

In a loud booming voice Ptah uttered a few words that possessed power, then said, "It is time, oh young priest of Thebes, to begin your descent upon the royals standing here in this Great Temple of Amun. Show your powers!"

Even though Ptah and Hapuseneb had performed this "miracle" many times before, the young priest shook with fear. He slowly calculated his moves like a spider spinning his web in the wind. He lowered himself and dangled from the rafters, swaying quicker than he liked. All of the rafter acts he had preformed were executed in the dark.

Ptah yelled out in his priestly voice, "God of Amun-Ra said, let there be light!"

There was a tightly secured leather vest supporting Hapuseneb, which was wrapped around his torso. In his hand he clutched a crystal tube about four inches long. Inside the tube was vinegar. A metal rod fixed at one end of the tube was connected to a hardened piece of tree sap floating inside the vinegar. Sometimes this unusual stone sap was worn as a jewel by the royals. Little did the common masses know, including some of the royals, that this amber stone had the properties to hold an unspeakable charge.

Hapuseneb responded to the thunderous sound of his father's voice and shook the vile. It began to faintly glow like the sun rising above the eastern horizon.

Ptah slowly lowered his son from the rafters. Hapuseneb, suspended above the altar of the temple, began to swing from one side to the other. He placed the vile inside his robe, illuminating the space around his heart. The light glowed then abruptly dropped about five feet. A sudden intake of breath could be heard in the darkness.

To the ones viewing from below, all they could see was a faint glow illuminating a figure that appeared to be flying in the air. They were so looped from the wine drink that the black straps holding Hapuseneb were completely invisible to their eyes.

But not Hatsu's eyes. She saw it all! The black straps looped over the rafters, while Ptah held onto the other ends. And if he lost his grip, Hapuseneb would surely fall to his death. The glowing light, though, was a mystery. *I wonder if it is electrum. I know how that trick is performed.*

There was a sense of urgency in Ptah's voice. "Ahhh! That is it! This declares the end of the miracle! You must go now!"

Ptah did not offer assistance with an oil lamp for them to use to exit the dark temple, but they finally made their way out after bumping into some of the pillars. Behind them in the darkness they heard a quick "zip" and "thump" sound followed by a painful cry.

Kahn, Aneer, and Sitre-Re had taken the drink, and at the end of the miracle session, were absolutely convinced Hapuseneb had flown through the night air and that his heart was emblazoned by the rays of Ra.

Somewhat disoriented and still dizzy from the drugs, they left the temple and walked back to their respective apartments. Kahn, knowledgeable about the malevolence of man, was astounded at what he had just witnessed. He and Sitre-Re chatted. Occasionally, Aneer chimed in too. "It was amazing! I am flabbergasted at that miracle! Wow! It was better than any one of my crocodile tricks!"

As they walked Hatsu whispered into the ear of her mother. "I see why it is necessary to allow the priest to have influence over the masses. Just listen to them, Mother. They have been wooed. Hapuseneb was not flying. I could see the straps holding him up, and Ptah was the counter weight and that light source, I bet, was electrum."

Ahmose looked at Hatsu through her drug-induced eyes and said, "I did not see the black straps because I also took the drink. I do so enjoy my wine. But you, my intelligent full-royal, let the cats lick up your share. It is good that you understand these things. The knowledge you have learned here tonight will help you bargain with the priest. Remember their coffers are filled to the brim with gold. Only speak of this event to the priest because from time to time you may need to notch them down to size. Do not let their administrative forces trample you down. You must allow these so-called miracles to exist. You see, the priest helps the masses behave." Ahmose placed a rolled lotus leaf in her cheek, then sighed deeply. "My limbs feel weak. I must sleep."

Hatsu kissed Ahmose on the lips. She cupped her mother's face between her hands and whispered, "Mother, you are going to have a beautiful existence in the afterlife, and your face will not wither to dust. The god Anubis will make sure you last forever." She chuckled. "Get some sleep, and I will see you tomorrow. I bid you good night."

A peculiar looked washed across Ahmose's pale face. "You are Egypt's best choice, my beautiful daughter. Your ascendancy is quite possible."

Hatshepsut's smiling lips pressed against her mother's cheek and whispered, "I know this, Mother."

Back at the Temple

PTAH CONTINUED TO wrap his bleeding hands with narrow strips of linen, and Hapuseneb listened to the ongoing ranting of his father. "You must not eat so much! It was all I could do to hold you up! You are getting fat on figs! I nearly dropped you! Look at this! You almost ripped my hands off!"

"I have grown, Father, since the last time we did this. I am now twenty-four moons heavier. I can't stop eating for the benefit of this trick. We must have a meeting with the alchemist and see if he can build a lifting machine, one that can accommodate my weight, now and in the future. Then, I can eat all the figs that I want!"

Controlling light was practiced exclusively for the high priest at Dandera, located about an hour's boat ride from the royal city. At Dandera, a temple was employed exclusively for the purpose of astounding a great number of Nile travelers. Beneath this temple were many secret rooms reserved for different alchemy experiments. The mystery of light was exclusive to the temple priest. It was a miracle that gave them power and respect.

Like most amazing miracles, these methods of performances and contraptions were often seized or purchased and became top secret used only by the high priest. For any invention that could astound the masses, the priests were willing to pay large amounts of money for a spectacular act. In many cases the inventor was inducted into the service of temple life enjoying the benefits of the upper crust of society and doing what he loved . . . fabricating deceptions! The most amazing of these temple deceptions was a statue that cried. Putting the fear of god into temple goers was the first aim. Guilt was the second.

In the future the temples of Egypt would become a warren of disappearing exits, lifting machines, and traps of consequences . . . and some quite deadly. Egyptian builders who were used in the sphere of controlling the soul were clever at creating magic. They were masters of illusion.

A Queen Sleeps

IN THE EARLY hours, before Ra rose above the eastern horizon, the temple complex awoke to a calamitous sound. Roaming the halls were the clatters of sandaled feet thundering like a herd of rumbling horses.

Administrative officials were roused from their sleep. Attendants pounded on doors and a chorus of women shrilled a high-pitched trill with their tongues. The sound pierced the stillness of the night.

Hatshepsut awoke to the sound of tongue warbling approaching from the far end of the royal complex. Her eyes opened. She hopped from her bed and ran to the arms of Sitre-Re.

"That sound is a heralding of dread. Someone has died!" She buried her head in Sitre-Re's breast. "Please say it isn't so!"

Sitre-Re tried to sooth Hatsu, "I do not know what has happened, but we will know soon." She rocked the chief wife like a handmaiden holding an infant. "Be calm, my child. Soon the news will come. Be strong. You are the future of Egypt."

Hatsu screamed, "Oh, Ma'at! Help me be strong to the words I am about to hear!"

The mighty Kahn darted through the dwelling, checking every high window in the apartment before he opened the door. A group of tearful women were bowed with their foreheads touching the floor and slapping their backs with papyrus reeds. They moaned the words, "Ahmose is dead! Our glorious queen is dead!" Heads prostrate to the floor, they continued slapping the stick against their backs, wailing sentiments of sadness.

"The news is about your mother. She is . . . she is . . ." Sitre-Re bit her bottom lip.

Hatsu sat up like a young lotus blossom. "I know. I know." She stood up as ridged as an obelisk. Tears slipped down her cheeks. "I must go to her." She walked purposefully from her apartment and headed straight to Queen Ahmose's private quarters.

The young princess yelled, "Sitre-Re, alert my father that my mother sleeps with the ancients!" Hatsu rushed down the corridor with the mighty Kahn at her heels.

Tuthmosis Given a Gift

A YOUNG NUBIAN GIRL nervously waited beneath the portico outside the king's bedroom. She was shrouded with colorful linen. Her hair was braided with multiple plaits that fell across her shoulders and back. Each braid was cinched with gold balls and clinked at the slightest movement of her head. Gold bracelets adorned her arms and wrists. She shook with fear while listening to the conversation between the two men.

A councilman stood beside the bed of the great pharaoh. His shaved head was covered with the typical headdress of an administrator. He looked at Tuthmosis and said, "I know you are still grieving for your chief wife, Ahmose, but life still possesses a bountiful amount of joys, my lord."

Tuthmosis studied the back of his hands as if to affirm that he was still among the living. "Death comes so suddenly, without even as much as a courteous warning! Thanks be to the god of Anubis that her tomb is finished. By the time her embalming is completed, her eternal resting place will welcome her. I hear the workers in the Valley of the Queens are planning a grand illusion for her interment. It is so secret that even I have not been briefed."

"Ah, mighty one, you must not worry about trivial things. Her body is being preserved by Egypt's finest embalmers, and her interment will be overseen by the cleverest of inventors and alchemists. I hear a most wretched death will befall any intruder who might attempt to defile her tomb. Trust me and be assured that no one will ever be able to disturb her rest." The councilman bowed in a show of dutiful respect and continued with his purposeful visit.

He took in a deep breath and exhaled with a smile. "Your Highness, I have come to deliver a gift to you in your most solemn days. I have brought you a girl who will help you resume your joyful life, a girl you can add to your harem of concubines. She has been delivered to you as a gift from a Nubian lord. News of the death of Queen Ahmose pushed up the Nile like a sorrowful wind. In light of your recent sadness, the Nubian crown head wishes you to accept into the House of Tuthmosis, this young and very beautiful Nazli. She will enlarge your staff of concubines and return happiness to your broken heart." He turned to the door and shouted, "Come Nazli!"

Eyes wide with fright, the young Nubian girl stepped toward the overseer.

"I shall reveal this marvelous gift that comes from one of your political admirers." The councilman unwound the colorful linen from the brown body of the frightened girl. Her nude skin glistened with exotic oils.

"Your Magnificence, she is like the night sky that floats above our beautiful city. And her eyes resemble the winking stars that guide our wisest men across the desert sands. Look upon her face and take in her sensuous lips of pleasure. She contains the graces of all the gods. She is so beautiful all of your royal women will want to look just like her."

The council man brushed his plump fingers along the young girl's high cheeks. He slid his palms across her budding chest and said, "Look upon her bosom. She is a flower yet to bloom."

The pharaoh answered, "Yes, she is beautiful." He folded his arms across his chest and studied her like a jackal eyeing a lion's kill. "Leave her with me. I will try her out."

"Ahh, majestic one, you will be pleased with her, I can promise . . . uh . . . at least, I was told that she was trained to be a pleaser, Your Highness." A nervous tic appeared across the councilman's upper lip. He feared that the pharaoh might assume that he had tried her first. "I shall send a note of thanks to your patron for their generous contribution to the House of Tuthmosis."

With renewed vigor Tuthmosis ordered, "Councilman, bring her to me!" He smiled while he watched his latest contribution bashfully approach his bed.

"Hum, indeed, you are beautiful, my little Nazli," Tuthmosis said excitedly.

Valley of the Queens

TUTHMOSIS STARED AT the Valley of the Kings. *I wish it wasn't so far from the Nile's western edge,* he thought. He looked south along the rocky cliffs. The Valley of the Queens was a high ridgeline south of the kings' burial chambers. He walked across the wooden planks onto the western shore of the Nile, easing himself into the shaded litter.

The city of Deir El-Medina was positioned between the two burial valleys. There he would meet his architect. The entourage began the long walk across the plains. The pharaoh, not feeling well in recent days, stretched out on his royal litter. The canopy shaded the rays of Ra. He was surrounded by an elite group of military archers.

"These solemn trips to your world are becoming far too frequent. Sadness has entered my royal house. My two sons rest in your mountains of sorrow, and now my chief wife. I will be next, and Egypt will soon be inheriting a half-royal, and he is leaving soon to command a mission to a small mineral rich country. What would happen to my Egypt if his blood is spilled on the desert? My daughter, Hatshepsut, keeps delaying children. Our royal blood is disappearing like the dried up waters of a *wadi*."

"Pharaoh, you have plenty of women in your court. Should your fears prove true, you can select any one of your consorts to produce an heir for Egypt's future. You are still a robust man."

Tuthmosis lamented, "Ah, but it is too late. Besides, the heir would not be a pure prince. I only have one full royal left who is a female!"

The architect answered with tense compassion, "Or, well then . . . you can . . . well . . . you can always . . . you know, sow the seed with Hatshepsut." The architect coughed nervously. "It has been done many times. Your most honored king, it is highly acceptable. Remember, royal blood is imperial blood."

Tuthmosis held up his hand in a gesture to "stop." "That has crossed my mind, and I may have to resort to it." Tuthmosis cradled his face in hands. "You are a good man for listening to my woes. Now take me to Ahmose's tomb. How long will it take your stonecutters and artisans to complete her sarcophagus?"

"We have been working on it for quite a while. The paintings on her walls have been completed for a long time. Her sarcophagus is finished except for the golden paintings on the cover. It can be done in plenty of time for her entombment. I have been informed that her body is being prepared for the final process. I am certain her sarcophagus will be completed in time, and just to make sure, I have put my extra workers on the task. I can assure you, we will work overtime."

Tuthmosis answered, "Good. Her unexpected death has brought about disorder in the temple. I will leave everything in your hands."

Tuthmosis folded his arms across his chest and straightened his golden beard. A look of dismay rested on his brow. "Now, I would like you to tell me about this thing called the golden ratio. How far can you recite the number?"

The architect looked at Tuthmosis and smiled. "So you are interested in the most sacred number, pi? It is the ratio of a circumference to its diameter. It is a profound number! Some say it is perfection, and in its inscription lays the secret of the universe. Some say it is a code for perfection on earth. That is why it is considered sacred. It was also a necessary number to know during the construction of the pyramids. It is thought that a man named Enahk who lived thousands of years ago was given this heavenly number. It is suggested that he might have assisted in the building of the great pyramid. No one knows how far out the digits can be proven. It is eternal, I think."

The architect chuckled. "I do not know where the number ends. But I can only recite it to the third seven." The architect rubbed his chin and said, "Let's see . . . 3.141592653589793238462643383279502884197 . . . That is about as far as I can recite by memory, but I used to know it to its hundredth digit. I can honestly say that once you begin to investigate further into pi, it will beguile you like a moth being drawn to light. Nobody knows more about pi than I do."

The architect stood up and said, "If it pleases you, oh king, we should be on our way because after we leave Queen Ahmose's tomb, we shall travel to yours. It will thrill your heart to see the paintings on your walls."

Tuthmosis stumbled along the dark passageway leading into Queen Ahmose's secret burial chamber. During his trek, he remembered the whispers circulating around the temple complex that Hatsu could count up to one thousand digits of pi. He kept the secret in his heart because hearing that news could possibly put his architect into a spin.

Gossip among the stonecutters and artisans was as welcomed as a bath after a sandstorm. The catacombs of the queens were filled with whispers and laughter. The whole town of Deir El-Medina was energized with the news about the young chief wife's cleverness. Whispers about Hatshepsut shot through the dusty streets faster than an arrow could be flung from a composite bow.

"She is more skillful than a lion outsmarting its prey. She is sharper than a copper chisel. She is stronger than a dolomite hammer. She thinks faster than a speeding chariot. She is brighter than the North Star."

But the one statement that pierced the man's heart was the gossip that found its way straight into the chief architect's ear. "Did you hear that she can count to the one thousandth digit of pi?"

News for Tuthmosis I

TROUBLED BY THE latest news, Tuthmosis I ranted like an enraged elephant. He paced back and forth inside his gold-speckled apartment.

"What am I to do? I am still reeling from Ahmose's death, now my chief architect has dropped dead! My tomb is only half completed! What if I should die before I find someone to finish it? One leg will be ensconced in my sarcophagus and the other will lie out in the chamber! Great god of Amun-Ra, what am I to do?" The disturbed and now reclusive pharaoh sat in misery over the recent turn of events.

Nazli heard a knock and ran to the door. She opened it and immediately dropped to her knees and touched her head to the floor. "Most honored Hatshepsut . . . your father is despondent over the news of his chief architect, and he still mourns for his chief wife, Ahmose. Woe is me. I cannot seem to ease his broken heart."

Hatsu stood boldly at the door. "I know . . . I also mourn for my mother. Nazli, I have just heard about his architect. You must tell him my news is important. I have information that will make him very happy. Announce me at once!"

Nazli returned to the devastated man's bedside. "Oh great mighty king, your daughter is asking to speak to you."

Tuthmosis I gave an incredulous look at Nazli. "Is she going to tell me she wants to dance with a lion? I can't take much more of her wild antics! I was hoping that the prospects of marriage would settle her wild, impulsive nature and make her fertile as the Nile soil!"

"Do you feel up to seeing her? Should I bid her off, oh majestic one?"

Tuthmosis flung himself back onto his plush pile of pillows and began his usual fervent prayer, "Oh god of Bes, have mercy on me and give my Hatsu many children. Children that will quiet the powerful will that moves within her like a raging bull." He sighed heavily, "Yes, yes bring her in." He closed his eyes and tried to brace himself for her next grand stunt and the problem of his half-built tomb.

Hatsu's sandaled feet stepped quickly across the stone floor, then she stopped beside his bed.

He opened his eyes. It had been several months since he had seen her and for a moment did not recognize the breathtaking woman standing next to his bed. "My daughter, what has happened to you? Where is the child that I used to know?"

"Father, it is me, the same girl. I am a season older."

"How old are you now?"

"Father, I will soon be in my fifteenth year. Are you pleased?"

"Yes, and . . . and you are most beautiful! How does it feel to be Egypt's great future?"

Hatsu looked down at her ailing father. "My husband treats me well enough. I am involved with the duties of my role as Egypt's future pha . . . uh . . . I mean queen. I am speaking with the wisest of philosophers, and I'm learning the water tributaries within and without Egypt's realm. The wisdom of Amun-Ra lives within me and is giving me many tasks to do for Egypt, but the duty that Amun-Ra has conveyed to me is the one that I believe to be the most important at this moment in time . . . to build for Egypt. I am saddened to hear about the news of your architect. However, I do have information that will gladden your heart!"

Tuthmosis looked up at his daughter. "I am sick. My architect has just dropped dead. I have just lost my chief wife. My tomb is incomplete. My bones are hanging on my skin like old bark sloughing from the branches of a spindly tree, and you have news that will gladden my heart? Are you planning to dance with a charging elephant?"

Hatsu stood like a divine living sculpture, bold and proud, with a most serene smile pressing her lips. She leaned down and whispered into the ear of her father, "His name is Ineni, and he is considered to be a most gifted architect in all of Lower Egypt. He understands sacred geometry and is the best friend and loyal partner to another great architect who is equally gifted. I have asked Ineni's friend, Senenmut, to design my own tomb. I have kept in contact with both of them since my trip to Heliopolis. Shall I send for them, Father?"

Tuthmosis reached out for Hatsu. "I feel Ra's hands stretching down from heaven, giving you his divine touch. I see a light above your head. Indeed, you have the radiance of wisdom within you. Yes, yes, please send for Ineni at once, also this man . . . the other architect, Senenmut. When Ineni completes mine, Senenmut can begin yours. Thank you, my royal and most enlightened daughter."

Hatsu held up a finger as if to say "stop." "My father, it is my wish that the two projects, your tomb and my temple, be constructed at the same time. Remember, these two architects are equally gifted, and they do not lean on each other for council. I am a little less than half way through my years, and it will take many more years to complete mine. My temple must commence immediately. I am beginning to feel the weight of time."

"You're how old, Hatsu?"

"I am approaching my fifteenth year, Father."

Tuthmosis eyes looked at his daughter. "You are convincing." He reached out for her hand and squeezed it. He whispered so only Hatsu could hear, "You are much wiser than I. In your delicately fragile body there is strength. Within my strong bones there is weakness. You always make me think. Of course, they will be built simultaneously."

Color returned almost immediately to the premature ageing face of Tuthmosis I. A surge of strength gushed through him like a mighty windstorm. He sat upright, raised his arms high, and with upturned palms declared, "Oh, how I love building projects. These architects will leave our heritage in Thebes. My name will not be lost in the sands of time. My bones will not be plundered like the others. I hear that sacred geometry is within the design of the Great Pyramid at Giza. Oh, god of Heliopolis, I have not forgotten you . . . great sun god Ra, I am a happy man! Great god of Amun, hear my praise! Oh . . . and, of course, great god of Sobek, please protect me!" He fell back onto his plush pillows and winked at Hatsu. He chuckled and added, "There is a rumor within the temple that you can count by heart the golden ratio all the way to one thousand. Is that true?"

Hatsu turned back and smiled, "Ha-ha, temple gossip is often enhanced, my father."

Nazli followed Hatsu to the door and knelt at her feet. "Thank you, most noble of women; you have brought color back to your father's cheeks. Thank you." She dropped to her knees and kissed the feet of Egypt's new queen.

"Rise, Nazli. It is only you that can bring life back to his ailing bones. Go now and embrace my father."

"I shall!" Nazli ran back to the bedside of her master. She crawled next to him and cuddled like a silk worm devouring mulberry leaves. "May I embrace you, my lord?"

"Great god of Amun-Ra, give me many more years to enjoy this bountiful earthly feast! Come here, my beautiful girl! You are a boost to my ailing bones."

In a prayerful chant the desperate pharaoh prayed to the god of fertility, "Bes, I pray to you! Bring Egypt a boy child through my royal daughter! I guess it would help if her husband slept in Hatsu's bed instead of the beds of his concubines."

He rolled over and embraced his newest and very young concubine, Nazli. He stared into her innocent eyes and said, "You are such a tantalizing treat in my sorrow."

The great king breathed the breath of the ancients into his youngest and most beautiful concubine.

Hatsu Learns the Art of Dance

THE DANCE COACH held up her hand to the musician. "Quiet!"

The flutist stopped her playing.

Rejal instructed, "You must remember, foremost of royal ladies, no matter what others may say, it is the eyes and the hips that are the most seductive parts of a woman's anatomy. I am told by my patrons and visiting royals that the eyes are like a hypnotic drug. You must use them to your advantage. While you are dancing for a special guest, use the muscles of your lower lids and raise them ever so slightly . . . like this. See, how it changes the manner of your gaze? You are now giving him the 'come hither' look. And believe me! Men love it! And while you have his attention, turn your hips this way and that way. Fast! Shimmy like this." Rejal laughed and rapidly shook her shoulders and hips.

She slowed and continued, "Now, you must string your veil across your nose and secure the ties within your wig. Your veil must not become dislodged during your swirling movement of the dance or your intended will lose the power of your intentions." Rejal showed by lifting the upper layers of braids of her wig.

"The only time your face veil should be untied is when you are ready to breathe into your lover. Clearly, that will be after the dance is finished and when you are ready to recline with him upon your lounge.

"But before that special moment you must disappear behind a partition and have your wig removed. He must not see this. Your natural hair must be smoothed with a comb. It must be sweet smelling. Your personal attendants must be swift as a flickering fire fly, because your lover is ready for you, and you mustn't make him wait. During the time of your brief absence, hand him a tray of rolled peacock's tongue and oysters. It will ready him for cavorting beneath the linens. Hold your breath while your attendants are pampering your hair, and by the time you must catch your breath, you should be ready to flee to the arms of your lover."

Hatsu listened like an archer receiving orders from a military general.

"Now let's go over the arm movements, once again. Remember your wrist and the delicate flipping motions. Never drop the veil. Keep it firmly pinched between your thumb and pointer finger. Let us return to the art of dance."

Rejal clapped her hands and looked at the musician.

The flutist resumed her playing.

Hatsu followed Rejal's instructions, imitating every sensual gesture, hip movements, and using the muscles of her lower lids to entice her intended, which happened to be at every session, a vase full of sacred white lotus flowers.

Off to Stake His Claim

FOLLOWING IN THE path of the young pharaoh-in-training, the large Egyptian army clanked southward along the Avenue of the Sphinxes. While the army boarded the ships, the citizens of Thebes crowded the port and watched with pride. On the lips of the Thebans were comments such as these: "There he goes . . . just like his father . . . off to push further the borders of Egypt. He is trying to be like the great one. He is in search of another gold mine for Egypt. He will need to secure more slaves for the gold shafts."

After several days of ship travel, Egypt's army disembarked and marched westward across the desert. Their purpose was to claim this small country for their minerals, but among their spoils they would capture and return with robust men to power the production for their massive building projects.

At that moment, the young Tuthmosis did not have minerals or spoils of war on his mind. He yelled to one of his bowman, "It is said that my wife is learning the art of seduction. It is I who will reap the rewards. Upon my triumphant return, she will seduce me with her charms. Ha, ha."

Hatsu Sends for Senenmut and Ineni

Heliopolis

SENENMUT RECOGNIZED THE golden seal. He read her name aloud, **"Hatshepsut, chief wife, Egypt's great future!"** Somehow, this scroll seemed different from the others–more important, more official. He slid the red ribbon off the scroll and plucked the seals from the tightly rolled edges and mumbled the letter to himself–H ~ T (House of Tuthmosis). He quickly unrolled the papyrus and read:

"Throughout the past five years I have kept you informed about the demands of my role as chief wife. In my previous letters I have mentioned the need for a chief architect and that the day would surely come when I would call for you to join my administration. Circumstances now require the need for you to include your friend, loyal advisor, and architect, Ineni, to join you in serving Egypt, the land of my beautiful citizens, and any other important craftsmen that will complete your assemblage. My father's chief architect died suddenly, and now my father, pharaoh, desperately needs Ineni to resume the work on his own tomb. Also it is time that I should begin the planning for mine of which I obviously will entrust only to you. My dear Senenmut, the time has come for our destinies to finally, at last, be joined. Thebes is urgently seeking two of the best architects in all the land, and I am desperately seeking you. Also, I want to learn about the many mysteries you hold in your heart. It is time for you to use your sacred geometry. Please come to me."

Alone on the upper roof of his home, he yelled. "Alas, I am free! I can fly like an eagle! Great god Amun-Ra, I have put my trust in you! Great gods of Heliopolis, do not forget me! I must leave your beautiful city. It is you, great one, which has given me the crafts to use for Egypt and our future pharaoh. I am being called to Thebes, and I must go!"

He clutched the scroll and descended his steps faster than a stone could drop from ceiling to floor. He yanked open his door and ran down the sandy street, yelling at the top of his lungs, "Ineni! The letter . . . It has finally arrived! We are free! Our hearts can soar!"

Senenmut and Ineni Come to the Place of the Palaces

THE ROYALS SAT upon their gilded thrones and were carried along the passageway leading to the port. These thrones were made of zebrawood and covered with gold, inlayed with mother-of-pearl and various jewels mined from the far reaches of the empire.

Temple slaves gently lowered the sovereigns onto the hardened clay platform of the greeting center that overlooked the harbor. The royals waited for the ship to dock. Imperial visitors, upon seeing the royals seated upon their thrones, were immediately struck by the splendor and remained in a state of awe throughout their visit to the Southern City.

Followed by a long line of administrative officials, scribes, servants, and archers, the envoy of royals positioned themselves around the platform. Scribes took their places in their assigned corner. Ramah sat next to his father and together they readied their quills, ink, and papyrus. The mighty Kahn watched with the keen eye of an eagle.

Colorful drawings outlined with permanent ink covered the floor of the dais. Painted by clay artists, the designs reflected the social character of Thebes. The images featured pictures of brown boats, blue and red fish, golden crocodiles, black and tan-colored dancing girls, goblets of red beer, and yellow wheat stalks.

Beneath a canopy made of fresh green palms supported by four tall muscular Nubians, the royals sipped wine from crystalline goblets and munched on dates and figs that were stuffed with a minced nut mixture. They watched the young harbor boys catching the heavy papyrus ropes that were being tossed toward the docks.

In the absence of Tuthmosis II, his father, the great Tuthmosis I, was seated upon his ornate throne marked with the seal, HT (House of Tuthmosis.) Ahmose's throne was now being occupied by Hatsu who was seated to the right of her father. Sitre-Re sat dutifully within whispering distance of Egypt's chief wife, the beautiful Hatshepsut.

The sun cast splintered light across the faces of the royals. They watched a smattering of harbor boys diving into the port waters. Retrieving silver coins that were being thrown from the decks of docking ships was a pastime for the local boys. The children dove for the silver that streaked through the Nile water, bringing them up moments later, clamped firmly between their teeth. They were entertaining the royal family and loved every menacing moment of it.

Lurking beneath the waters was one of their most respected and feared gods. One of the divers failed to surface. However, that did not dull the remaining diver's excitement because they were making in one afternoon the equivalent of three years of sweaty field labor.

Hatsu noticed, though. She had counted the divers and realized one was missing. She clutched the amulet that Aneer had placed around her neck and prayed to the god of Sobek, *"Make his way trouble-free through the weighing of the heart. May all the waters in his part of paradise be filled with bolti fish and sweet-smelling lotus. Oh yes, and may there be beautiful girls waiting to please his every need."*

The thought of seeing Senenmut reframed her momentary sadness as she watched the ship gliding ever closer to the dock. Powered by hundreds of oarsmen, they put a drag on the oars easing it to a stop.

The younger Tuthmosis was not in Thebes. He was still fuming from the crocodile episode, so he had assumed his father's army and was leading a military campaign into a small mineral rich country that he planned to conquer for Egypt. He was expected to return months later with a rehabilitated valor, slaves, minerals, and a newly claimed realm.

Hatsu looked at Sitre-Re and smiled, "Are you happy that you will be seeing your father at last?"

"Oh yes, most honored woman. I look forward to the times we can all dine together beneath the portico." Sitre-Re looked at Hatsu, and with a probing look asked, "And you, Hatsu, are you excited to see my father, as well?" Her look was humorously perceptive.

The golden collar circling Hatsu's neck shone with exquisite green emeralds and red rubies mined from the many countries conquered by Egypt. Her eyes were steadfastly watching every member of the ship's crew and passengers exiting down the ramp. She spotted Senenmut and thought, *When the sun shines on his dark hair, it takes on the color of an afternoon sunset.*

Her eyes sparkled like the jewels set in her collar. She hung on Sitre-Re's question, then whispered into her ear, "I have dreamed of Senenmut while in my brother's bed. Senenmut is ever-present in my heart, and I speak his name many times throughout the day." Her eyes kept a steady gaze on the two architects that were now being escorted down the ramp and toward the dais.

Her heart pounded like a baker thumping her bread from a pot. *I must sit and stand straight like an obelisk! Divine Hathor, give Senenmut the desires of the heart equal to mine! Ma'at, give me balance in all things! I beseech all my gods to support my wishes! Ancient fathers of my blood, guide my steps to the throne.*

Royal officials and servants met the two architects and their entourage. Senenmut and Ineni led the troupe down the wooden ramp followed by Nakt, the cook; Set, the sword maker; Kep, the producer of armor, and several apprentice stonecutters who were identified by their leather aprons. Following the men was a long line of goats, sacked squawking geese, and a heap of bundled leaks, Senenmut's favorite food. They were greeted by administrative officials at the base of the ramp while the royal family waited for the two architects to be ushered to the dais to be officially accepted into the administration of the House of Tuthmosis.

Hatshepsut watched in anticipation as the entourage walked toward them. Her impulse was to jump up and run toward Senenmut, but alas, she had to be patient and "royal like" and remain seated like a budding lotus on her throne.

Six years had passed since she had last seen him. From the distance she could judge the years had been good to Senenmut, leaving him with only a slight graying around his temples. He was very alert, observing his surroundings. She could tell his eyes were searching for the little girl that he once knew. His steps were sober and proud. He reverently bowed as he approached the dais.

Both architects were gifted with a golden collar before stepping onto the platform. Both men bowed, touching their foreheads to the floor. With downcast eyes, the highly regarded master architects approached the royals. Ineni was guided before the throne of Tuthmosis I, while Senenmut remained at the edge of the dais.

Tuthmosis spoke first, "My chief architect is resting from life. Unfortunately, he left my tomb unfinished. It will be you, Chief Ineni, which will take the reins of responsibility to complete my eternal resting place. Do you accept this duty that I place before you?"

Ineni answered, "I am humbled before you, oh mighty one. I will be privileged to walk in the steps of your late chief architect. I will finalize your tomb with great pride and reverence honoring his exact plans for your eternal resting place."

"Arise my chief architect, Ineni, and accept this ring of gold. Press my seal for any request that you may need to complete my tomb."

Ineni looked at the seal. It was clearly Tuthmosis I, Egypt's great warrior king, standing in the cab of a chariot, the horse stampeding the body of an enemy.

Ineni stepped backward and thanked His Most Royal. Rubbing the ring with pride, he left the dais, head lowered, and back-stepping toward the entrance. Then patiently he waited for his friend, Senenmut, to complete his audience with the daughter of Tuthmosis I, the young and very beautiful, Queen Hatshepsut.

Senenmut stepped across the platform with his head bowed. He knelt in reverence before the young queen.

Sitre-Re watched her father's respect for the young chief wife, wondering when she would have the opportunity to privately welcome him to the Beautiful City. Alas, she exercised her restraint and considered her position. *First things first. My father must show duty to the queen of Egypt, my glorious charge.*

Hatsu looked at the bowed figure before her. Protocol prevented Senenmut from gazing upon the queen's face while she was seated on her throne, so he focused on her sandaled feet and waited for her to speak.

Hatsu leaned closer to the bowed head of Senenmut. In a breathless voice she whispered exclusively into Senenmut's ear, "My will is stronger than ever. I will become Egypt's pharaoh queen. The very thought of you being near me brings joy to my heart. I have no fear of the future because you will be my sturdy rock, my chief advisor and chief architect of my mortuary temple. Do you, Senenmut, accept this much honored position in my administration?" Hatsu's heart pounded faster than the day she subdued the golden crocodile. She waited for a response.

Senenmut answered, "I do accept this honored position, most royal of women, Egypt's greatest future. I will build you a splendid eternal home that will survive even the grandest of temples. Nowhere on earth before your golden presence has there been or will there ever be a more beautiful temple than the one I will build for you." He then kissed her feet, lifted his palms, but kept his head bowed.

"Arise, Senenmut, and take this ring. Use it as a royal seal for the requisitions for any and all material to complete my grand temple."

Senenmut took the ring, placed it on his finger, and kissed the seal.

Hatsu whispered so only his ears could hear, "You can gaze upon me tonight beneath the glow of the full moon."

He stood up, kept his head bowed, then back-stepped across the floor. Senenmut struggled with the temptation of stealing a glimpse of the now mature and beautiful Hatshepsut. In recent years, her beauty had become reputed throughout the Egyptian Empire.

A triumphant smile pressed Hatsu's lips as she watched the valued entourage of men exiting the dais.

Ramah recorded in glyphs the scene at the dais. He could sense the admiration Hatshepsut had for Senenmut. In the scribe's heart was a tinge of sadness.

The line of royals began their march back to the temple complex when shouts from the fringes of her many admirers caught the attention of Hatshepsut.

"Magnificent queen! Look what I have for you!" a young voice shouted from the crowd.

Hatshepsut demanded that the litter bearers stop. "See what that child wants!"

The young water-logged missing diver lifted his hands to the queen. "For you, my magnificent queen! Hapi, our Nile god, wants you to have this." Inside the palms of his hands was an oyster that contained a pearl as large as the eye of a crocodile.

"Hapi, the god of the Nile, wishes you to have this gift from his waters!"

Hatsu had a great intake of breath, "You're alive! Oh, it's a black pearl! It's beautiful! You risked your life for me!"

"Oh no, magnificent queen, Hapi gave me breath for you!" Still dripping wet from the water, the young diver, Nunzi, pulled the pearl from the oyster's grip and placed it in the queen's hand. He bowed, back-stepped away from the queen, then ran back to the port, quickly blending among the crowd.

"Find that "pearl boy" and bring him to my apartment tomorrow at the high point of the sun. I must thank him properly!" Her orders carried the weight of an official bulla.

These words erupted from the throat of one servant, "Stop that pearl boy!"

In the meantime, a minister of protocol guided the two architects and their associates of craftsmen to a royal suite that was used for visiting dignitaries.

An oil lamp stood behind an alabaster clock. A soft glow shone through the transparent stone revealing the gradually dropping waterline. "When the water reaches this mark, I will return for you and your staff. A private celebration of your arrival will take place in the solaria. You will be the most honored guests." The minister of protocol bowed, then closed the door.

Patiently the men listened for the fading footsteps, and when they could no longer hear his steps, Senenmut yelled, "Great god of Amun-Ra! God of Heliopolis! We are alive in the most glorious time and place in Egypt!"

The assembly of elite craftsmen lifted their wine-filled goblets and toasted their good fortune. Senenmut's eyes, dark and knowing, looked at Ineni, Nakt, and his elite group of artisans. He raised his goblet and said, "Men, let us lift our chalices to the god of sacred design. We are on the forefront of change. Let us toast Egypt's future female pharaoh, Queen Hatshepsut. Her temple will usher in a new dawn. We will revolutionize the concept of perfection in the people's mind. Hatshepsut's temple will make the pyramids look like crumbling piles of stones. Here's to change! It shall be called Djeser Dejeseru, the most magnificent of the magnificent. Because of this glorious woman, Hatshepsut, Egypt will not lose her memory."

Beneath the Stars

HATSU HAD LISTED all the requirements for the evening, and Aneer orchestrated the program down to the very last detail. He was behind the scene, demanding perfection with every facet of the night's entertainment.

Two nearly nude female court musicians stood beside the pool's edge playing their high-pitched flutes. Their sultry music could be heard throughout the temple complex. They dipped and swayed their bodies with the beat of the music while they entertained the selected guests.

Senenmut spotted a barge floating across the sacred lake. Positioned on the bow, a harpist plucked her stringed instrument, and the soft sound of her music could be heard in the distance.

Clashing blends of aromas swirled around the night air. Fried clams, bolti fish, lobster, and crabs simmered in garlic sauce. The smell of date nut bread drizzled with cinnamon from Madagascar mixed with local honey enticed the appetites of the dining guest. Clusters of sacred blue lotuses were artfully arranged in crystal vases and copper urns, creating a garden-like atmosphere beneath the stars while, at the same time, emitting scents of hypnotic hallucinogens in the air.

Privatized dining areas were separated by gossamer drapes, but the front of each one opened to the lake. Suspended between stone columns, these thin drapes sparkled with golden rings making faint jingling sounds when spread open upon entering, or leaving. Tightly woven, intricately designed carpets covered the stone floors and were topped with purple and red-colored pillows. Oil lamps covered with hollowed crystal bulbs, carefully positioned away from the drapes, emitted a soft light through the thin sheers, blurring images slightly.

Senenmut, Ineni and their supporting associates, dined separately within their own personal cubicle. Each man had been offered a personal lady attendant to be used for the desires of the night. Senenmut declined the offer, politely motioning to his personal "offered courtesan" to leave. He had but one person in mind for his companion for the evening. Through the thin drapes Senenmut could hear the giggles and whispers of the others and was hoping that Hatsu would appear soon.

The small barge continued to make its way toward the solaria's border. On the bow of the approaching barge stood the court harpist plucking her stringed instrument with syncopated rhythm, joining in unison with the music of the flutists. As it glided closer to the solaria, the music became louder, and began to slow to a sexy syncopated beat.

Alone inside his private booth, Senenmut reclined on one of the pillows and kept his eyes fixed on the barge. *She is inside the vessel, coming for me. I know it!*

Sipping wine from a golden goblet, he focused on the scene before him. His thoughts remembered the time Hatsu, then a child princess, stood on the bow of the royal ship and waved good-bye to him, the day she left Heliopolis. He remembered her strong will, a trait otherwise absent in the female consciousness in these modern times. Not so with Hatsu. She possessed a knowing of her future, a mere girl child claiming her heritage in Egypt. *How bold,* he thought as he imagined what she must look like now.

Today, he kissed her feet, but he was forbidden to look upon her face, although he knew he would definitely look upon her face tonight. His heart pounded like a stone hammer. The barge docked and the harpist lifted her small harp and carried it across the flat timbers joining the other musicians who were standing beside the water's edge.

The golden rings jingled from a southern breeze that blew through the drapes.

The three musicians moved closer toward the private cubicle where Senenmut reclined. Suddenly a company of nine belly dancers ran across the solaria, spacing themselves in front of the barge. In unison they danced to the rhythm of the music.

The belly dancers began a theatrical version of Egypt's social dance. They tipped their hips in unison to one side then another, while using their arms to express the sentiments of the song. This indigenous dance of Upper Egypt consisted of gyrations of hip-swiveling movements. The use of a long veil, representing flowing femininity, was used to create added exotic mystery. A small covering draped across their noses allowed only the eyes to express their longings.

Each dancer kept her seductive eyes on the men inside each cubicle. The dancer in the center kept her eyes confidently fixed on Senenmut. With every beat of the music, her movements captivated his emotions, promising him anticipation of unspeakable joys. The middle dancer moved closer to Senenmut until her thin skirt and long flowing veil touched his face when she twirled and bumped her hips to the sound of the music.

This dancer is mesmerizing me. She is using her art to seduce me! I must be strong! When will Hatsu come for me! Has she sent this dancer for my unlimited pleasure? Protocol is eluding me! Great gods of Egypt . . . Help me!

The music became more intense. The rhythm of the melody pulsed through his body and inwardly he reacted to the alluring movements of the young dancer.

In one flowing movement, the dancer lowered her long veil throwing it over Senenmut's head nestling it around his back. Keeping the shroud pinched between her thumbs and the other fingers, she guided her selected guest to stand up and follow. She back-stepped across the solaria and kept her alluring eyes on Senenmut.

He was enveloped within the clutches of her veil and could not resist her charm. He stared into her black eyes that spoke volumes of desire while being guided across the flat timbers that led to the interior of the barge.

Nunzi Visits the Queen

"WHEW! THE CHILD must not enter the queen's quarters, smelling like fish guts!"

Sitre-Re ordered the boy to stand in the anteroom. "Don't move! You must let the women clean you before your appointment with the queen."

The attendants fussed and giggled while they pampered the boy for presentation. After they were finished, Sitre-Re leaned down and sniffed the boy. Pleased with the outcome, she pulled the drapes back and entered the queen's apartment. "I have the young pearl boy. He is ready for you now."

"Ahhh, my young pearl boy," Hatshepsut said with a smile, lifting her hands in a welcoming gesture. "Please come here."

Pearl boy walked toward her, then knelt. He stared at the floor. In an amateurish voice he said, "My name is Nunzi. I bring fish to the dealers. I am nothing to you . . . really, but you wish to see me?"

The young queen tilted her head and scrutinized her visitor. "Oh, I don't know about that. You do mean something to me. You have proven yourself even when it was not required. You actually placed yourself in double danger. You almost drowned, and you could have been eaten by a crocodile! So, the reason I have asked you to come is this. I would like you to work for me as my annunciator . . . my personal messenger."

Nunzi's eyes equaled the size of the pearl he plucked from the Nile. "How can I please you, my queen?"

"I need you to transfer messages back and forth across the Nile. Can you handle a felucca?"

"Yes, of course, I was born on the floor of a felucca! I am eight years old, most noble of women."

Hatshepsut laughed. "Good, I will make sure you have your very own. Now sit over here. You must always wear this." She placed a golden ring on his finger that had the initials "HT" and placed a golden collar around his neck. "You must show this when you enter the temple complex. Now you and I will talk about the things I want you to do."

Nunzi said with a readied voice, "Noblest of women, I am at your service."

Ineni Assumes the Completion of Tomb

IN THE DAYS to come, Ineni assumed the completion of pharaoh's burial tomb. He studied the construction manuscripts drawn on papyrus. Because of shock and sadness, the workforce had temporarily suspended their duties but trickled back one by one to listen to their new master, the new architect hired by their great king.

Ineni stood in front of the tomb workers and praised the effort of his masterful predecessor. He instilled in them a sense of loyalty for their previous task master whose body was now being prepared by the embalmers.

Ineni shouted in a commanding voice to the stonecutters and artisans. "Now you must show your allegiance to me. After all you are building your great pharaoh's tomb. Lord Tuthmosis will be visiting on a regular basis, so we must show him the respect that he deserves. Remember, he is Amun-Ra's earthly representative, and when our great pharaoh dies, he will become a god, and when that day comes, you can trouble him for your request for many blessings."

The little pep talk infused the hundreds of workers with vigor, especially the last part about troubling him for requests. Within hours, the tomb was filled with rock, dust, and sweat. The workers became inured with their duties, all becoming like swirling bees resuming the work on their pharaoh's tomb.

Tuthmosis I Dies

Six Months Later

DARKNESS CAME TO the Royal City. Flames flickered from the metal sconces braced along the limestone walls. Flecks of gold dust powered the walkway.

Ptah and Hapuseneb knocked on the sculpted entranceway. Kahn opened the door, stepped back, and allowed the two priests to enter. They delivered the somber message to Kahn. "This news will break her heart. I will fetch her, so you can inform her of this sad news."

The priest watched Kahn leave the room and waited for him to return.

Moments later, Hatshepsut entered the room where the priests stood. She looked into their cheerless eyes and sensed the gravity of their visit. Her heart thumped to a mournful beat while she waited in fear of the news. *Sadness is visiting my doorstep once again.* She immediately thought of her father and froze in fear.

Ptah's voice whispered, "Your father's breathing is labored. His time draws nigh, and he is calling your name."

Hatsu leaned on the arm of her trusted handmaiden, and together they quickly walked the dimming halls toward her father's apartment. A flurry of priest, concubines, and servants crowded the lavished residence of Tuthmosis the Great.

Hatsu spotted Nazli pressing tightly against the dying king, trying desperately to bring warmth to his icy body. A temple cat had curled into a gray furry ball onto the heaving chest of the great king. The king's smoothed hands were folded like marble stones across his chest.

Nazli's tears had washed away the black mascara-lines around her eyes. She looked up at Hatshepsut and said, "Foremost of noble women, he has been asking for you."

Hatsu noticed that Nazli was showing evidence of morning sickness. Nazli gripped her mouth in a gesture that was familiar to Hatsu. Her eyes followed Nazli and observed a slight swelling of her stomach. *She is pregnant.*

Hatsu sat on the bed next to her father and reached out for his hand. She observed that his skin was a ghastly shade of blue. The dying warrior's eyes were fixed on a vague spot beyond the painted stars that studded the ceiling above his bed. His soft voice uttered a whisper, "I can see the beautiful wheat fields and the pools of clear blue water."

His head turned to Hatshepsut. "Come closer, my royal daughter. I must say to you (cough . . . cough) that I leave this world with a troubled heart." A grimace veiled his face, and his voice became a whisper. "You are to possess my apartment immediately." His voice began to falter, but after a few failed attempts, he regained his strength and whispered into Hatsu's ear, "Your brother . . . your husband cannot fulfill the great throne. He is an ineffectual boy. You, my dear Hatsu, possess the wisdom that must rule my precious Egypt!" Tuthmosis exerted his body's last ounce of energy. He turned his head to those surrounding his bed, and with a stronger voice he declared, "This daughter of mine, Khnumet-Amen Hatshepsut, my darling Hatsu, I have appointed her as my successor upon my throne . . . she shall direct the people in every sphere of the palace. It is she indeed who shall lead you. Obey her words, unite yourselves at her command." He turned his head toward his daughter and uttered these desperate words, "Promise me!"

Hatsu leaned down and whispered into the dying ear of the once mighty Pharaoh Tuthmosis the Great. "Father, I will continue your powerful reign. I will trade peacefully beyond our borders. Egypt will feed even her enemies. I will bring enlightenment to our temples of learning and bring together the lost secrets of the past. I will dress proudly in your garments and speak clear words of wisdom. It is my destiny to rule. This I know for when I was a mere child, while inside the Great Pyramid of Giza, the spirit of Khufu gave me his promise that I would someday rule. So, my dear father, go peacefully toward the wheat fields, the pools of fresh blue water. Walk through the beautiful gardens of Amun, and enter your paradise with the knowledge that Egypt will prosper under my rule. I am certain that you will face a serene voyage through the weighing of the heart."

Tuthmosis exhaled a satisfying sigh. He looked into his daughter's eyes and motioned with his bony finger for her to lean closer. He whispered into her ear. "Remember to use speaking stones to rule your citizens. They will believe what you say if they see the words written in stone. Remember, my daughter, the word creates everything. Remember that, will you?"

"Yes, Father."

He coughed a bit, then cleared his throat. He whispered, "Gold is beneath my feet, and Sothis is above my head. My dear Hatsu, for me gold has no value in the stars." Then he slipped his hand beneath the sheets and handed Hatsu a metal key. Frantically, his dying eyes searched the painted star-studded ceiling for the indestructible stars. His eyes widened with a look of amazement, and in a frail voice said to Ptah, "Fix me. I am ready. Slowly his eyelids closed."

Hatshepsut kissed her father's arms that lay across his chest. Then she placed his royal scepter in his right hand. In a flash, an empty but proud ethereal expression settled across his face.

A blaze of light beamed through the high clearstory window and illuminated the somber and crowded room. The temple cat jumped up and with its nose, touched the lips of the dead pharaoh as if it were drawing out the last breath from the great warrior king. The cat let out a pathetic meow and sprung from the chest of the dead man. Like an arrow flying from a bow, the temple cat darted from the crowded room and disappeared in the shadows.

Nazli began a more pitiful wail of sorrow, kissing and clinging to the dead pharaoh's body. Hatshepsut gently pulled Nazli away, trying her best to comfort her father's favorite and most loyal, and youngest concubine . . . a young pregnant concubine.

A steadfast Mutnofre stood firm. On her face was an ever-so-demure smile. She did not like the declaration Tuthmosis had made about Hatshepsut assuming power. *I will find a way for my son to rule.* She picked up her tray of half-eaten honey cakes she had prepared for the pharaoh and held them like a servant holding an ordinary tray of sweets. *I will take these back to my apartment and feed them to the rats.*

Ptah and Hapuseneb immediately began their rituals, starting with earnest prayers to Anubis, the god of embalming. This prayer would assure that the body of the great king would be supervised by the skilled hands of the embalmers. The two priests prayed the traditional murmurings from the Book of the Dead. They sprinkled the corpse with frankincense, touched the king's forehead with oil of myrrh, and placed his body on a litter, slowly draping the cotton sheet over his head and body.

An ever-so-slight smile pressed Mutnofre's lips while she watched the body of the dead king being taken from his gold-glittered apartment. *My son will rule, and I will make sure of that.*

An entourage of military, priests, and family members began their somber walk through the temple complex in the early morning light. They passed through sun-kissed gardens, and crossed over foot bridges that spanned decorative pools studded with white and blue lotus. They walked through brightly colored halls and pillar supported temples. They walked along the Avenue of the Sphinxes and turned right onto Canopus.

Trailing the entourage, the pharaoh's royal concubines chanted a chorus of tongue trilling and weeping. They reached down and scooped up the garden soil, sprinkled it around their heads, and pulled at their hair. The royal clatter woke up the temple complex to the sad event.

The *ka* of the great Pharaoh Tuthmosis I left his human body and began his journey across the field of flowers. Then his spirit flew toward the indestructible stars. His *ka* slipped through the invisible dimension that separated his earthly life and his afterlife. He carried with him charms and chants to be spoken in the presence of Ma'at where his heart would be weighed against a feather. His journey into paradise would not be obstructed by Ammit, the destroyer, but instead his heart would be found to weigh no more or no less than the feather in Ma'at's crown . . . a perfect balance for the easy access into paradise.

Throughout the walk to the embalmers, Sitre-Re held onto the saddened Hatshepsut. With each step she encouraged her cheerless charge. "You must be strong in spite of your grief. You must show confidence with each step from this time forward. You are the foremost of noble women, the direct descendant of Egypt's greatest pharaohs. Your father's ka now dwells among the greats."

Sitre-Re stopped, looked straight into the eyes of Hatshepsut, and spoke these clear words, "Know your father is now a god, and someday you will be among them. You must learn to radiate joy through your tears because soon enough your beautiful smile will be chiseled in stone."

When the great pharaoh was given over to the embalmers, his brain was quickly emptied from his head through his nasal cavity and discarded. The brain had no function in paradise. Four internal organs–the stomach, the lungs, the intestines and the liver–were soaked in baking soda and salt, then stored in separate canopic jars. His heart was removed and encrusted with baking soda and salt and repacked inside his chest cavity. The heart was the organ that held the prized wisdom of the gods. Natron powder was packed inside and around his body, and for forty days, Tuthmosis would dry and then be transferred to Wabet.

Wabet was the House of Purification where every appendage would be wrapped until his entire body was swathed in the finest of linen and placed inside his sarcophagus. Finally he would be entombed in his eternal resting place, his secret sepulcher inside the Valley of the Kings.

Hatsu examined the curious gift that her father had entrusted to her. She knew it was a key but a key to what? She returned to her father's apartment where the teary-eyed Nazli met her with slavish attention.

"What is to become of me? My lord is dead." Nazli's forehead was pressed on the stone floor at the feet of the most noble of women.

"I appreciate your favored arts of seduction, Nazli. You are finely tuned for the pleasures of a deserving man." In a quiet voice Hatshepsut reassured Nazli, "For now I will bring you under my supervision. But I sense that you are carrying the seed of my father."

"Yes, noblest of women. I have peed on wheat kernels, and they have opened quickly. I will hide within the shadows of your city if that pleases you, my queen."

"You deserve to be treated like royalty, Nazli. After all, you are carrying the blood of the ancients. In time, I will gift you to a worthy man that will treat you with kindness. However, now I want you to show me the door this metal shaft will open."

Hatsu held out the gift her father had entrusted to her. It was a rod about the length of an adult hand designed with a number of knobs at each end.

Nazli reached up for the key and sobbed with gratefulness. "Yes, I know exactly where it must go." She walked purposefully across the room and quickly locked the chamber door. Then she began pressing against the bed, pushing it across the floor. She rolled up the carpet, lifted an inlayed metal latch, and opened a door hatch. She held an oil lamp high in the air and began descending down a set of stairs that led to a secret chamber. Nazli directed Hatsu to insert the metal shaft into one of many holes in the wall. She inserted it and turned it seven revolutions. The sound of a "click" filled the small anteroom, and suddenly, a section of the wall began to move.

Nazli lifted the lamp, shining the light into the secret chamber. Many times she had been seduced atop blocks of gold by her great king. It was a memory she would secretly keep inside her heart.

Hatshepsut's eyes grew large. As far as her eyes could see, the subterranean room glistened with gold and silver. She whispered her father's dying words, "Gold has no value in the stars." *So this is why he wanted me to take possession of his apartment.*

In the dead of night, Hatshepsut took ownership of her father's royal house. She ordered the possessions of Sitre-Re, Kahn, and Nazli, including her own, to be moved in bit by bit until every last speck of property was resting on top of her father's reservoir of gold.

Nazli kept her small room beside the antechamber. The seed inside her grew like a blossom does into fruit.

Thebes was in a royal crisis. The death of Tuthmosis the Great was kept quiet until his throne could be officially filled.

The Hyksos' invasion years earlier left a bad taste in the consciousness of Egyptian citizens. They were hypersensitive to leaders from other countries rushing in and taking over the administration during an unguarded throne. So the order of business was to keep the death of the great Tuthmosis hushed until a successor could be crowned.

A frantic Tuthmosis II screamed, "Father was clearly delusional when he declared Hatshepsut his successor! If he was thinking with his heart, he would have never agreed to this outrageous idea. It could never be! I am his rightful successor. I have been training for years! I, Tuthmosis II, am his only living son! The people would never accept a female for their leader. For Amun-Ra's sake, a male god would never allow such a thing! Look at her–she has breasts . . . a clear sign of weakness! My father was uttering senseless babble on his death-bed!"

The young Tuthmosis argued with Ptah until his face turned purple. "Besides, Hatshepsut and I have an agreement. She said she would give up her entitlement if she could move into her father's apartment! So, I agreed!"

Ptah and Hapuseneb listened. They looked at each other, remembering the last decree of the dying pharaoh, then out of desperation uttered, "So be it!"

Several days following the death of Tuthmosis the Great, his son, the young Tuthmosis II, was quickly crowned the new pharaoh of Egypt. The coronation was hastily planned with little regard for detail, and because of the quickness of the coronation, it was not well attended.

But Mutnofre was there, enjoying the pomp and splendor of the procession. With immense pride, she observed her son walking proudly toward the reredos inside Amun's temple.

Overwhelmed with pride, Mutnofre was gleeful as the two priests placed the crown that represented Upper and Lower Egypt on her son's head. She glanced over at Hatshepsut and smiled evilly.

Hapuseneb, the newly assigned administration's priest, smiled at Tuthmosis II. Hapuseneb said, "Now, and forever more, your throne name will be known as Akheperenre, Great is the form of Ra." He whispered something into the ear of Tuthmosis that only the young pharaoh could hear, "But you will always be my childhood friend, Tuttie."

Throughout the ceremony, Hatshepsut silently prayed to Ma'at. *Help me! This is not the way it is supposed to be. I should be pharaoh. My father made a declaration on his deathbed and the priests heard it! As a child while inside the Great Pyramid, I saw myself as the pharaoh. I will not be denied!* Hatshepsut gazed at the arrogant Mutnofre and did not allow her personal disappointment to show. *I will get my wish. I will become pharaoh.* She forged a regal smile while watching her husband being crowned.

Although Hatsu's eyes were dark and empty as a dried up well throughout the celebration, the gears inside her head were turning like a newly invented temple machine. *I have my father's gold* was the thought that made her feel tall like a granite obelisk glistening in the sun.

Shortly after the death of Tuthmosis the Great, Tuthmosis II ascended in royalty to pharaoh of Upper and Lower Egypt. It was necessary for him to gain the confidence of his citizens, so he left on a military assignment and would be absent for several months. He was checking on the productivity of Egypt's gold mines south of the Southern City. Nubia was in rebellion, and the young Tuthmosis II was going to snuff it.

Hatsu Tells Secret to Sitre-Re

"WILL YOU MISS your husband, Hatsu?"

Sitre-Re massaged essential oils into Hatsu's hair and waited for her to answer.

Hatsu took a deep breath. "I will share with you my tale of woe. During the royal course of marriage preparations, his teachers, both female and male, bestowed upon him all the elements of the pleasures of marriage. They instructed him that it was the male who was the one to be coddled and pampered. When I refuse to submit 'the courtesan way,' he becomes violent."

Hatsu caught her breath and continued, "So, the night before he left for Nubia, I stood before my brother and cried out, 'Am I to do all the work? Am I but a concubine to you? It is time for you to pleasure me! After all, I am more divine than you, my Brother.' And so he ran from my apartment whining like a hurt child. I am sure he ran to the house of his chief concubine to find bliss because I have seen Isis within the royal complex, and she is fattening up like a heifer."

Hatsu sobbed in the arms of her handmaiden. "I simply do not love him! He is such an awkward brutish boy! Woe to my sad, sad heart!"

Sitre-Re stopped combing Hatsu's hair for a moment and poured bittersweet liquor into a crystal bowl. "Drink! This will help you with your emotions. You will find someone to love. I am sure of it! Someday a man will love you and show you the greatest of delights."

Hatsu sipped from the bowl and looked up. Her eyes blinked as if in a daze. "I have found love, Sitre-Re. This night I vow to tell you the man who knows the pleasures for which I desire. I love your father, Senenmut." Hatsu's lustful eyes sparkled like the dazzling stars that glittered above the royal city.

Sitre-Re's eyes widened. "Whoa! Be still my heart! My father?"

Hatsu whispered, "Yes, Sitre-Re. I have loved him for years, and I always will."

Husband Returns

Several Months Later

THE TUTHMOSIS II returned from a region south of the Southern City of Thebes. Colorful flags representing the newly acquired regions flashed on the bow of the royal ship.

The young pharaoh stood at the bow of the ship decorated in his army regalia and searched the harbor crowd for his sister-wife. He did not see her, but he did spot his chief concubine, Isis. Her arms were waving in the air, and she was yelling, "I have wonderful news for you, Tuthmosis! I am with child, and it is yours . . . and guess what? It is due any day now!"

Mutnofre gave her son a long penetrating look. "I pray the god of Seth smothers the breath of this child. Your firstborn should be a royal child! You must impregnate Hatshepsut. Tuthmosis, pay heed! You must have a son with your chief wife! She possesses the blood most royal! Egypt's citizens will demand it, and the gods will demand it!"

"Mother, I cannot persuade her! It is hard to get her to submit to my will! I think she practices magic. Seems I always fall asleep before she is ready to receive me. Then when I awake she is gone! She is crafty, that one!"

"Then you must take her! And this is how you will do it."

That same night young Tuthmosis II stood at the door of Hatsu's royal apartment. He was dressed in his semi formal regalia. On his head he wore the golden pharaoh cap that represented the House of Tuthmosis.

"I have delicious wine I brought back from Kush. Drink with me. I need to talk with you about administrative matters."

His request was legitimate, so Hatsu invited him in. She turned to Kahn and Sitre-Re and said, "Leave us in private. You are dismissed for the evening."

"We will check on Nazli. She is nearing her time."

"Good. Go check on her. She told me today pains were gripping her groin. Besides, it is time my brother and I unite our powers and discuss the future of our precious Egypt."

Young Tuthmosis poured her a goblet of wine and soon Hatshepsut began to swoon.

The young pharaoh whispered in her ear, "Sadly I have to use a potion to get you to submit to your duties. You know that we must produce a child for Egypt's future. So relax and breathe into me the breath of the mighty ancients."

For a few moments, Hatshepsut tried to wiggle out of her half brother's grip, but her arms became too weak. She began to yell, but her yells were obscured by Nazli's wailing out in pain several rooms away. Unable to move, Hatsu prayed to the goddess Ma'at for justice and balance, to Sobek for protection, and finally to Osiris to stop fertility in the union with her brother.

During this activity, the young Tuthmosis practically squeezed the life from his helpless wife trying to capture her breath. He pressed his hands around her throat, released and waited for her to catch her breath. When she coughed for air, he hovered above her and huffed in her royal breath. The third time he tried

Hatshepsut did not respond. This provoked his anger and began to strike her in the face. But soon his fury turned to fear. *Did I just kill her?*

Tuthmosis gazed in dread at Hatshepsut's seemingly lifeless body. For a moment he thought the potion his mother concocted might have killed her . . . or maybe he had choked her too hard while she was drugged. "Great god of Amun-Ra! I didn't mean to do this unspeakable thing!"

He dashed from the room and barged into the apartment of his chief concubine. "Isis, Hatshepsut looks dead! She is limp like a dying lotus. What am I to do?"

Isis held her infant son and patted his back.

"Did you capture her breath?"

"Yes, but what am I to do?"

"You must do nothing. You have captured the breath of the mighty ancients. I can become chief wife and life will be blissful for us. After all isn't this what you secretly wanted?"

"No! If my hands brought death to her, then I will bring the wrath of all the gods and all the ancients against me! I will have destroyed my heritage! I will be a walking target for the angry spirits of her ancestors! After all they are gods now, and they have godly powers! My woe cannot be measured!"

Isis cared less about Hatshepsut's wellbeing and said, "Have a goblet of wine. This will make all the angry spirits go away." She offered him the wine. "Come here, my lord, and let me ease your troubled heart."

She handed her infant to her handmaiden, "Take him. My love needs me."

She lifted her arms to Tuthmosis and said, "Now give me some of that royal breath."

Tuthmosis lay in bed and trembled like a dying fish gasping for air. Nothing Isis did could ease his frightened heart nor gladden his dynastic member.

Hatshepsut Runs to Senenmut

IT BECAME EVIDENT after Hatshepsut awoke from her ordeal that her husband-brother/pharaoh abused her in a violent way. She coughed and held her throat. Blood oozed from her lips. *I must seek protection in case he comes back to finish me. I have always been a threat to him.* She yelled for Sitre-Re and Kahn, but they were with Nazli, and she was in the throes of childbirth.

Senenmut opened his door. Hatshepsut stood before him disheveled, bleeding, and bruised. She let out a long sigh and whimpered, "Trouble dwells beneath our sheets. He demands a royal child. He is artless in the ways of love. His sexual capers have left me terrified. He hurt me. He drugged me, and it is quite evident that he was violent. Look, I am undone. Tonight he came to me using the guise of discussing administrative matters. He left me like this."

Senenmut could not believe his eyes. "You look as if you are going to swoon. Come to me." Senenmut lifted her in his arms and brought her to his bed.

Senenmut whispered, "You will be safe with me. You will not be harmed here."

Since his arrival at Thebes, Senenmut had imagined her in his bed. But not like this. Immediately, he began swabbing her face with an unguent that he and his stonecutters used for wounds. His dark eyes looked closely at her deep olive skin. "You should not have to subject yourself to this another night. If this is his way, then his concubines should become his battlefield, not you, my glorious queen."

Hatshepsut's voice was frail, almost a whisper, "Yes, but he wants a royal child. Royal children brings valor . . ." Hatsu's voice trailed off and soon sleep came to the young chief wife of Egypt.

Darkness fell over Thebes, and the stars sparkled like gems. Nut, the sky-goddess, began to stretch her long arms over Geb.

Senenmut put his protective arm around Hatshepsut and gave comfort to her.
The cries of an infant could be heard filling the night air inside the royal complex.

In the middle of the night Kahn and Sitre-Re ran to Senenmut's doorway.

"Father, she asked us to leave. She said she needed to plan administrative decisions for Egypt. We were several rooms away assisting in the delivery of Nazli's son, and when we returned to the royal suite and saw blood, we knew something terrible had happened. We know Tuthmosis hurt her. So we came here. Is she OK?"

"Yes, she is sleeping now. Tuthmosis did hurt her. He was forceful, claiming it was his right to produce a royal child."

The mighty Kahn hung his head. "I failed at my job, chief architect, and I have brought shame to the royal house as well as my own heart."

"Father, I have brought shame to my heart, too. How can we make amends?"

"Go back to her royal suite and purify it. I will bring her back when she is strong."

Sitre-Re handed her the wheat seeds. "Pee on them, and if after three days they have not germinated, then you are not with child."

After three days Hatshepsut looked at the wheat kernels. She screamed, "Praise to you Amun-Ra! Praise to you goddess, Ma'at! Praise to you Sobek!" She rejoiced and immediately began preparations for an evening with Senenmut. She engaged the expertise of Aneer to plan the evening, which included food preparations, dancers, and musicians at the peak of their artistic development, mood lighting, sweet-smelling timbers, lotus, and all to be done inside Hatshepsut's barge in the middle of the sacred lake.

After the bruising had diminished, Sitre-Re dressed the chief wife in a sheer straight sleeveless caftan. She held up a golden vest that had been designed by Kep to fit the shape of Hatshepsut's upper body. Sitre-Re strapped it on with flaxen thread. Hair attendants braided Hatshepsut's hair and wove in blue sapphires, rare red pearls, and green emeralds. Her leather sandals were adorned with lapis and pearls. The jewelry attendant placed golden earrings on her queen's ears. She adorned her royal charge with armlets and bracelets formed with golden filigree and placed rings on her fingers and toes.

A makeup artist drew on the black coal lines around her eyes and painted diamond dust on her lids. Cerulean dust was artfully painted between her brows and lids. He painted her lips with a henna stain and brushed a dusting of diamond powder across her lower lip.

Hatshepsut smiled, thinking about her plans for the evening. The headdress was placed upon her head.

Sitre-Re and the attendants stepped back and admired the beauty of their queen.

The heaviness of the golden vest slowed her steps as she walked toward her awaiting litter. *Tonight, I will have him.*

Tonight, They Love

THE BARGE WAS decorated with blue and white lotus. Oil lamps made of alabaster were positioned here and there. A harpist plucked her instrument. The silver-pronged trays were heaped with oysters and lobster, and wine was plentiful.

Sounding somewhere between an order and a plea, she uttered, "I need you tonight."

Senenmut's strong arms reached out for Hatsu and enveloped her slender frame like northeasterly winds sliding across the desert sands. His powerful hands slid beneath her garment touching her warm skin. Beguiled by his appeal, Hatsu was utterly captured like a helpless animal inside a whirlwind. Unable to move, she quivered at his touch. She thought, *I must remember to breathe or else I will die! I am the Nile, and he will sail my waters. I have waited for him to be a part of my life for so long!*

Senenmut whispered into her ear, "You are like a delicate lotus opening its petals to the early morning rays. You are a goddess, a member of the heavenly realm. I am only a grain of sand upon the earth. You are an indestructible star, and I am the dust beneath your feet." Senenmut looked at the reclining queen before him. "I never expected love to come my way. Why me, Hatshepsut?"

She looked up adoringly at Senenmut. "Breathe into me, Senenmut. The force that flows within you I want to flow within me. I want to rest next to your brilliant mind that understands the mysteries of sacred geometry. I trust only you to calculate the exact accuracy that will build our breathtaking temple. You are the only man who understands my emotions, the only man who can pluck the desires from my heart. I need the strength that flows within you. I need you, my dear Senenmut. I have loved you since Heliopolis, the moment my eyes looked into yours. I have always loved you, and I always will. I shall whither like a dying vine if you turn me away. Breathe into me the sacredness that only your spirit possesses."

Senenmut pulled her close. A timeless gaze locked into her eyes. He softly spoke, "I wish for the same. You empower me, my love. Never will I turn you away, my dear Hatshepsut. I will love you and bring you the happiness that you wish for and deserve. Together we will unlock this portal that separates our worlds."

Their bodies tightly pressed, and his arms enveloped Hatsu like the winds that swept the dunes of the desert. Senenmut exhaled into her mouth, and she breathed into him the breath of the mighty ancients.

Later that night . . .

"The ankh is said to be the representation of the exact location of where life first began." Senenmut handed her the golden amulet. "I want you to have it. I commissioned Kep, the metal artist, to make this for you. Kep was overjoyed when I told him that he would be making it for you."

Hatsu held the ankh in her palm and squeezed it and placed it against her cheek. "Oh, my love, I shall wear it every day."

Senenmut lifted her chin with his hand and gazed into her eyes. "It is said that the shape of the ankh holds many secrets."

"You know I love secrets. Do tell me about them."

Hatsu looked into Senenmut's eyes. "And tell me where the exact location of creation began."

Senenmut held up the ankh. He touched the left part. "This side of the circle represents the Euphrates River." Then he touched the right part, and said, "And this side of the circle represents the Tigris River. This line represents the Pishon River where the gold for this ankh was found. The other line represents the Gihon River, and the stem represents the headwaters of the four rivers. It is said that Ra looked down and marked it with his fluids to celebrate the birth of life. He brought forth the flowing of life into the headwaters. This stylization represents the creation of eternal life–eternal life that I wish to spend with you, that is if you desire it."

With adoring eyes, Hatsu looked up at Senenmut, "I will cherish this gift forever, and yes, our spirits will dwell in the most magnificent temple in paradise, which you will build for my eternal rest. And, of course, my dear Senenmut, you will be there with me. How could I possibly live without you?"

Senenmut's eyes looked at the reclining body of the young queen. *Do I dare trust my ears? Did she just say our spirits will dwell together in the temple?* "Ah, my dear beautiful Hatshepsut, you give me powerful wings–wings that will enable me to build a universe solely for your pleasure." He leaned down and breathed into Hatsu, and she returned the breath of the ancient gods into his mouth. Senenmut held her close and kissed her lips. He took the ankh, placed it around her neck, then pressed his body against her slender frame.

Later that night, after Hatshepsut returned to her apartment, she admired the golden amulet. She held it in the palm of her hand and contemplated the shape. A scheming look washed across her face and thought, *In my perfect kingdom, when my brother is dead, I shall become pharaoh. Then I shall send my thin-blooded nephew, Tuthmosis III, to mine for gold when he reaches his twelfth year. Running my precious Egypt is far too important to leave in the hands of a child from an ill-bred, crude concubine and her inept supporters. I will make sure he grows to become a man beneath the hot sands where he will surely become fevered by gold.* "Per stirpes," she said out loud, "I will place him in charge of the scorching gold mines while I run my Egypt."

She touched the section that represented the land around the Pishon River. *I will send him to a land faraway, perhaps even land surrounding the Pishon, where he will discover gold. I have seen the addictive obsession of gold hunters. The search for gold will be his seductress, and you, my precious golden ankh, will keep him away from Egypt for many, many years.* She held up the amulet, kissed it, and fell back onto her pillows. It glistened like the light of day, even in the dark.

Tuthmosis Proves His Valor

SEVERAL WEEKS LATER, Tuthmosis II led his army south into the Kingdom of Nubia. He was astounded at the beauty of the buildings and the many pyramids that dotted the horizon. The young Pharaoh sauntered his horse around the pillars inside the largest palace in the desert kingdom. His horse reared up on his hind legs and whinnied. Tuthmosis II yelled, "These Kushite . . . these Nubians are trying to imitate our palaces. They must be siphoning gold from our mines! I will take down the royal family and his minions! I will force my will upon this entire city!"

A tight squad of Egyptian military wrestled the Kushite royals to the floor. Tuthmosis jumped off his horse, walked toward the subdued family, and yelled, "It has come to my attention that you are hoarding gold that rightfully belongs to the Royal House of Tuthmosis! I will crush this entire city like worms beneath my feet! I will lay carnage throughout this entire region."

Pharaoh's foot pressed against the neck of the Kushite patriarch. His soldiers held down the rest of the royal Kushite royals. "However, I will safeguard one person in your family . . . your firstborn." The pharaoh gave a sardonic smile to the choking man. Then in the blink of an eye Tuthmosis used his penetrating axe in a swift and concise way. Chaos rained down and bled through every edifice inside this gold-rich realm.

After the bloody melee, Tuthmosis II looked down at the youngest surviving royal. "So, if you want to live, show me where your family has hidden the siphoned gold."

Before he left, he lit up the bodies of the Kushite family and the flume of wind carried the stench of burning flesh for miles.

The preening pharaoh sat tall upon his horse and entered the gates of the royal Place of the Palaces.

Bound with papyrus rope, the humiliated young Kushite captive stumbled behind Tuthmosis's horse. He was in shock after witnessing the assassination and burning of his entire family. While entering through the gates of the Southern City, the battered boy cried out loud to anyone who could hear, "I am alone! And I am a stranger in this strange land!"

The Kingdom of Kush quickly withered and died like a flower in need of water. Egyptian workers took over the gold mines, and now Tuthmosis II was in charge.

The new pharaoh forced the young Kushite royal to become one of his personal slaves.

Being the same age as the pharaoh, bitterness swelled in his heart like poison gas spewing from the earth. *I will destroy him, and no one will ever know! I will rise up and declare my own heritage in my own land.*

Within months, Tuthmosis II engaged in another battle, this time with the desert Bedouins in Palestine. After returning from this campaign, Tuthmosis was home several days and suddenly became deathly sick.

Whispers whirled within the royal complex. "Shuu, we must be quiet about this because foreigners ever-ready to invade, might devour Egypt's throne yet again. Our pharaoh has been so malevolent in his ways. Our goddess Ma'at must not be pleased with his administration. She has made him weak with fever. Perhaps Mut, the divine consort of Amun the patron god of our city, is not pleased with his treatment of his chief wife. I hope it is not a deadly curse. Perhaps we should call for his chief wife."

Tuthmosis II Dies

ISIS HELD ONTO her son and bounced him on her knee. Tears rolled down her cheeks sometimes splashing onto the shorn head of her toddler. She looked at the sick pharaoh and whispered, "Our son needs to claim your birth name. If you don't recover from your sickness it ought to be our son that should inherit your throne. But if you don't give him your name, his heritage will suffer."

The ailing pharaoh looked at his scribe and said, "My chief wife . . . Ptah . . . Hapuseneb, and my mother should be here." He sighed. "They must be present. I feel my hour is near."

His chambermaid constantly dabbed the sweat from his brow and shorn head and placed crushed coriander seeds beneath his arm pits to treat his fever.

Queen Hatshepsut entered the apartment of her sick husband. Ramah, Hatshepsut's personal scribe, followed closely and sat beside another scribe.

The last time she had seen her husband was the night he tricked her with tainted wine. She held her head high and showed no pity for his weakened condition. She looked at the scene and studied her surroundings. It was obvious to the others that Hatshepsut was pregnant.

"Sit here, Your Highness." A servant guided her to a golden laminated chair that was nestled close to the pharaoh's bed.

Hatshepsut stiffened at the sight of Isis and her baby boy. But in spite of her disfavor of her husband's concubine and their thin-blooded offspring, she showed Isis a courteous nod. Hatshepsut was angrier about the appalling measures her brother-husband had been using toward the neighboring kingdoms. *Surely Ma'at was getting her revenge.* "You are not well, I see. What can I do to make you less anxious, my husband?"

A surprised pharaoh coughed, then said, "I see Bes, our god of children, has blessed you." His face lit up with pride. "It gives me pleasure to look upon you, my little turtle." He grinned, "Mother will be thrilled to know I have a full royal."

"Husband, I will forgive you for calling me your little turtle, considering your color today is that of a blooming cotton field."

Pharaoh looked up and noticed Hapuseneb entering the room. A slight wave of his hand directed the high priest to step closer to the bed. Immediately, Hapuseneb fell to his knees and began to weep.

"Oh, Tuttie . . . I mean, pharaoh, it displeases me to see you like a weakened bird. Please get better, my friend . . . I mean, pharaoh."

Hatshepsut watched the display of sadness, and at the same time her eyes glanced at Isis and watched the concubine gritting her teeth in anger. Clearly, Isis was mad. The blubbering display coming from the young priest and the fact that Hatshepsut was now carrying a baby that contained more royal blood than her boy was causing Isis to squirm like a captured badger.

In the corner of the room, a Kushite slave bowed his head in mocked reverence. He was not displaying slavish sorrow regarding the mourning going on inside the royal bed chambers, but instead his memory was replaying the day his entire family had been murdered . . . murdered by the pharaoh who ironically was now preparing to accept his very own death.

A spiteful look gathered on the slave's face. His curved lips pursed in anger; a tear slid down his black cheeks. Fists clenched, his tongue slid across his lips as if enjoying the sweet taste of revenge. His eyes focused on the stone floor. *One day I will return to my land.*

Hatshepsut noticed the nervous look on the face of the Kushite slave. She was astute to the quiet drama going on within the room. She had heard about the treatment of the slave boy's people. *I will give Nazli and her newborn to this slave boy. I will send them back to their desert land and give them enough gold to reclaim their lives. Nazli will be carrying the seed of a great pharaoh.* She stared at the toddler in the arms of Isis. *I will send this thin-blooded toddler to a gold mine deep in the earth when he is eight. I will direct my destiny, and I will become pharaoh.* A knowing smile pressed her lips.

Ptah and Mutnofre walked into the chambers. Mutnofre immediately began to wail. She began pulling at her hair and scratching in torment at her neck as if trying to stop the words welling up inside her throat. It was to no avail.

She finally screamed, "Someone has poisoned him!" Between cries she examined the color of his skin expecting it to turn blue. The only thing her examination revealed were patches of white skin evident on his neck and forearms. But that had been there since he had been a child. She thought, *There must be some other kind of poison used on him. I will go to Lata. She knows all about the necessary arts.*

In a weakened voice the young pharaoh whispered, "Mother, my ka is still with me!" He turned his head toward Hatshepsut and said, "Look, Mother, cast your eyes upon my chief wife! Hatshepsut, my little turtle, is carrying my baby."

Isis bounced her baby on her lap like she was attending a Feast of the Valley celebration. The small child giggled, and everyone in the room watched the antics of the toddler. Sadly the child shared the same skin blemish as his father, genetic bumps on the back of his neck, and white scabs on both forearms. Isis whispered into his tiny ear loud enough so all could hear, "My plump little pomegranate, maybe you will be given your father's birth name, Tuthmosis III."

Mutnofre looked closely at Hatshepsut and was baffled beyond words. "You're with child?" A show of reverence washed over her face as she said, "Most noble of women, you are carrying my son's child." She remembered the evening she concocted the powerful wine mixture for her son. *My potion must have worked!*

Mutnofre put her hands over her mouth to cover her large grin and to stifle any more accusations that might suggest someone had poisoned her son. She immediately realized that the turn of events surely firmed up her heritage in Egypt. *Either child, the one bouncing on the concubine's lap or the one being carried in Hatshepsut's womb, would make that as certain as the sunrise.* She clasped her hands and uttered in amazement, "My son is the father of a pure prince . . . or princess."

Hatshepsut returned a modest nod to Mutnofre, but her thoughts spun faster than a desert sandstorm. *No one will ever find out the true father of my child.*

Hatshepsut looked at the sick royal and reached over to touch his hand, "So my husband, it is obvious you are hotter than a cook's brazier. Why did you seek my council?"

"Now that you are with child, it does change my intentions. I would like Ptah and Hapuseneb to hear my request before I enter into paradise."

"My husband, you are too young to leave your earthly throne!"

The sick youth nodded his head in agreement but continued, "Since you are carrying the blood even more royal if you have a boy, then your son . . . our son shall have my throne name, Akheperenre, Great is the Form of Ra. But if you have a girl, then this bouncy little boy (he pointed to the toddler on Isis's lap) shall carry my name."

Balance in all things! She thought then said with an ever-so-demure smile on her lips, "My husband, if the latter comes to be, then I shall be co-regent for Tuthmosis III until he is ready to take the throne." She offered a compassionate smile to her dying husband, then a curt look at his concubine. But in her heart were the intentions, *I have the royal blood of my ancestors, and I will declare myself pharaoh.*

"Did you hear that, Ptah, Hapuseneb, and scribe? If my chief wife doesn't have a son, then she will stand in as regent until this boy is ready to be king."

"We understand, pharaoh."

Ramah sat quietly in the corner. With the quill feather in his hand, he wrote the agreement with hieratic glyphs. He looked at Hatshepsut and felt that he would never enjoy a pleasurable moment with her other than merely documenting her life, especially now that she is pregnant.

Within two days, Tuthmosis II died, and his chief wife took power. The royal city was immediately informed that the royal throne was filled by god's only living daughter, Hatshepsut.

The citizens were awed.

Body Prepared for Burial

FOR SEVERAL MONTHS the young Tuthmosis II's internal organs were soaked in a salt and baking soda mixture then placed in canopic jars. His heart was wrapped in linen and repacked inside his chest cavity.

The embalmers bound each toe, then each foot, wrapping both legs up to the thighs. Each finger was bound with the finest of linen, with the left arm placed ceremoniously across his chest. Resin made of oil, honey, and wax saturated the linen after it was tightly secured around his abdomen, neck, and head.

After mummification was completed, one of the embalmers said, "His body is ready. He ruled for three years and now he is in paradise to be united with the other gods." Tuthmosis II was lowered into the golden sarcophagus, and the lid was secured in place.

The canopic jars rested nearby, awaiting the royal escort across the Nile to the Valley of the Kings. There the organs would be buried with the sarcophagus inside his royal tomb.

Senenmut had been busy orchestrating the burial chambers of Tuthmosis II and was told by Hatshepsut that this took precedence over her temple.

The night descended over the beautiful Southern City. The stars dimmed like the jewels that were embedded between the resin-soaked wrappings of the dead pharaoh.

Within months of her husband's death, Hatshepsut began her building campaign. She ordered an elite group of stone masons to create monuments for the Karnak complex. Two one-hundred-foot-tall obelisks each weighing 450 tons were erected to the sun god, Ra. In the years to come, Hatshepsut would insist they be sheathed by electrum. They shone like Ra and could be seen for miles by day, and by night the glow brought light to the royal complex.

BIRTH OF NEFERURE

THE CITIZENS WERE still adjusting to the death of their pharaoh, but their hearts were soon lifted with the news of Hatshepsut's infant daughter. Gossip about the newborn was rampant and flew across the Southern City like a sea eagle plunging for a fish. On the lips of the citizens were sayings like these:

"Isn't it a shame the child was born after her father's death?"

"Ah, but do not worry. Her mother, the supreme regent for baby Tuthmosis III, is more courageous than any man on the frontline of battle. Some even say she is a man."

"She is a rebel. That is what she . . . or he is! How could she be a man having just given birth to a girl child?"

"Fool, when you're a god, I guess you can do anything!"

"Is she a man-woman? I've never heard of such a thing!"

"Fool, what I mean is that she can conduct the administration with man-like confidence. But I do hear she is a direct descendant of Ra."

"I hear her chief architect brings flowers every day and while he is there, he attends to the infant as if he were a chambermaid."

"And I hear the infant has hair the color of a sunset."

"Oh my, could it be?"

"Praise be to Amun-Ra!"

Hatshepsut Becomes Pharaoh

Four years after the Death of Tuthmosis II

ROYAL MILITARY GUARDS surrounded the golden chariot that carried Egypt's soon-to-be-crowned pharaoh of Upper and Lower Egypt. Her daughter, five-year-old Neferure sat beside her. Sitre-Re, her handmaiden, was seated on the other side. They were carried along the avenue with military protection. The chariot wheels crushed the palm-covered stone road.

Charioteers held the reins of Arabian steeds that transported Egypt's best bowmen. The archer's strong hands clenched composite bows while their fingers gripped the pulled arrows. The slightest threat would release one hundred fifty pounds of draw power and discharge arrows with deadly force.

At a certain point, Hatshepsut, her daughter, and Sitre-Re were transported from the chariot to a golden barque supported on the shoulders of strong and devoted Nubian carriers. Kahn walked beside the queen's barque and kept his hands on his deadly metal discs.

Pike throwers lined both sides of the royal entourage and tapped, in unison, the pike handles on the stone street.

Hatshepsut stood up while Neferure and Sitre-Re remained seated. "Desire has immense power, Sitre-Re."

"I never doubted your desire for a moment, Your Highness. Desire has shaped your smiling lips and rooted determination inside your heart since you were a child. Your godly ancestors are smiling with happiness. Your brothers are running through the wheat fields of paradise. Your mother and father are singing songs of praise for you today. And your husband-brother . . . well he collapsed in the face of your power."

Hatshepsut reached for Sitre-Re's hand and said, "I have you to thank for many things. It was your suggestion for me to meet your father that put me on the road to my fate. His insistence that I sleep inside the Great Pyramid sealed my destiny. Senenmut has helped me to keep my strong will alive and burning like the sun."

The citizens were awed at the sight of their regent, soon to be pharaoh. She stood unwavering like a perfect granite obelisk. Her head was covered with the traditional pharaoh's *nemes* head cloth with the sacred cobra. Onyx lines were drawn over, and beneath her eyes and her lids were highlighted with cobalt blue talc. The official golden beard, worn by her predecessors, was hooked onto her ears. Her womanly frame was hidden beneath the golden vestments. It covered her upper body and made her look like a military king on review.

The feelings the royalty and citizens had for her were mystified at their own behavior when catching a glimpse of Hatshepsut, in her male regalia, being carried through the palm-covered streets. The citizens breathed in the air that surrounded her, hoping to capture her royal and godly breath.

When she paraded through the avenues wearing her golden vestments, the hearts of the women were actually love-struck by her manly appeal. When spotted in her gossamer gowns, the hearts of the men thumped with affection. She was a mystery of disguise that captured the hearts and minds of her subjects. She was a rebel on the pharaonic stage of the Egyptian Empire.

Hatshepsut stood tall inside the gold-covered barque. The royal entourage walked through the Temple of Amun to the reredos. All eyes were on her . . . especially Senenmut's eyes.

Hapuseneb, now the high priest of Hatshepsut's administration, spoke with confidence. "At this coronation, Hatshepsut has decided to terminate being regent to the six-year-old Tuthmosis III and declare herself pharaoh."

Hapuseneb's voice bellowed through the pillared temple. "From now on Hatshepsut will be known as Horus Powerful of Kas, Two Ladies Flourishing of Years, Female Horus of Fine Gold, and Divine of Diadems, Pharaoh King of Upper and Lower Egypt, Ma'atkare, Living Daughter of Ra, Khenmet-Amen Hatshepsut. It is through this ceremony the future of Egypt will be secured and provide unity throughout the realm." Then Hapuseneb's voice became louder, "Our enemies camped outside our kingdom will know that strength binds the borders of Egypt like a wall of impenetrable granite."

Hapuseneb handed the golden staff to Hatshepsut and turned his palms toward her and said, "You are now our king, our leader, our ruler, highest of men . . . Most noble of women . . . You are pharaoh, Hatshepsut, Egypt's glorious one."

Ramah sat in the place set aside for scribes and encircled her unique group of names, finishing by writing the forth name (throne name), then her nomen (birth name), and finally encircling them all with a shenu. He looked at her, and his heart pounded with affection. Every mark was drawn with love.

Later that night when the ceremony ended, the mighty Kahn and an elite group of archers walked her back to the royal apartment. Inside her royal apartment, Senenmut rested on a chaise. She walked over to him and removed her nemes. She untied the golden beard. She unclenched the gold vestment. She removed the golden collar and slid the bracelets from her arms. Her eyes did not avert one second from his gaze.

"Come, lay with me, my beautiful pharaoh." Senenmut reached for her hand.

She stepped closer, leaned over, and said, "Thank you for believing in me."

He pulled her close and handed her the yellow-green stone beetle she had seen when she had visited Heliopolis.

"You were a child when you first held this. Do you remember?"

"Of course, I do. It is the stone that fell from the stars."

Hatshepsut kissed it, then placed it on Senenmut's chest. She removed her thin tunic then lowered her body onto her lover.

"You are my star goddess," he whispered in her ear.

"And you are mine," she answered.

Construction Continues On Hatshepsut's Temple

THOUSANDS OF WORKERS were dedicated to their pharaoh. With great love they worked tirelessly to please. They shipped granite and marble from the Aswan quarry to the foundation site.

Deir El-Bahri was swarming with activity. Hundreds of stonecutters outfitted with leather aprons and gauze nose protectors angled their chisels, cutting the limestone and granite into long smooth blocks and pillars. They were obsessed in creating the smoothest stone surface for their pharaoh. They called it the Perfect Ashlar. A haze of dust hovered like a cloud above the temple site. Beer was offered to the workers beneath the hot summer sun.

Senenmut sat alone beneath the shade of a tarpaulin and studied a very secretive ancient scroll. He moved his fingers over the characters and traced the o's and connecting dashes. The intersecting lines and the spacing of the circles was secret information that had been used by sacrosanct masons for thousands of years. A secret collection of three hundred scrolls revealed that certain structures could be viewed from the stars. Among these monuments built around the world were the Giza Pyramids–a massive stone circle located on the 51st parallel and colossal buildings of the Great Pangaean land mass now lost beneath the waters located beyond the sunset.

Senenmut summoned for heavenly assistance. Quietly, he uttered this incantation, "Ras El-Fajhmat, the father source of all knowledge, the transmitter of consciousness, I need your helping hands upon this temple. Father, send me your angels of knowledge." Senenmut continued uttering the name of a guardian of the sky, "Abufihamat . . . Abufihamat . . . father of understanding assists my hands to express perfection. Honor my attempts with the source of all knowledge."

He held a feather stylus in his right hand, dipped it in the ink well, placed it on the papyrus, then watched the point of the feather magically draw o's and lines in a marvel only he could feel. It was a formula that would embody Hatshepsut's temple. A sense of weightlessness took over his arm as if someone or an invisible force was controlling the sharp pointed instrument.

He decoded this highly guarded information that had been used with reliability by specialized craftsmen. It was a heavenly code that only a few select builders would ever be privy to.

His heart began to beat faster than usual. He had invoked this help only one other time while living in Heliopolis, but he trusted its faithfulness with all his heart. After obtaining the formula, Senenmut stared down at the building site. Slowly, a completed image of the temple began to form. At the same time while he was watching the three-dimensional image materialize at the building site, Senenmut recreated it on papyrus.

After Senenmut established the extremely secretive plans, he rolled up the Rahzzio scroll, the one that Enahk had scribed while in the heavenly realm. He tied it with a purple ribbon, dropped it into the leather tube, then placed it inside a cedar chest. He looked at the building site and burned the finished image into his imagination and then sipped his beer.

In the distance, riding toward his workplace, a young annunciator hopped off his donkey, dropped to his knees, and lifted his palms to the heavens. "I am Nunzi, and I am humbled in your presence."

Senenmut always enjoyed seeing Nunzi. "Young man, what do you have for me today?"

"Magnificent chief architect, I have for you a message of great importance. It is from the most noble of women, our pharaoh queen, majestic leader of all of the lands that Egypt controls."

"Well, my esteemed annunciator, don't kneel there like a granite stone! Rise up like an obelisk and give me the message."

Nunzi shot up like a grasshopper and handed him the scroll.

Senenmut unrolled the papyrus and read silently to himself. "My dear Senenmut, tomorrow I will journey across the Nile and bring you a most delicious dinner. We will sup on the overlook, and there you will discuss the plans for the temple that you are building for future eyes to see."

The next day a warm wind was blowing across the Southern City when the royal chariots and the assigned military archers rolled through the industrious town of Deir El-Medina. Hatshepsut and her personal protector passed through the main section that serviced the construction workers. Living in this labor village were families of tomb builders, artisans, stonecutters, tool makers, bakers, cooks, and distillers of beer and wine.

Deir El-Medina had a brewery in constant operation all through the day and night as well as ovens that produced hundreds of loaves of bread a day. The bakers used wild airborne yeast that produced large puffy loaves of coarse grained bread that sometimes contained a fair amount of gritty sand. Desert winds raged across the village, infiltrating every aspect of the villager's home, including their stored grains. Besides cooking ovens, there were huge ceramic ovens that fired cups, jars, and tile products.

In the distance, Hatshepsut could see tomb workers walking the paths that snaked up the cliffs. Wearing only a cotton loin cloth and covered by a thick leather apron, their purpose was to complete the chambers for the royal family in the Valley of the Kings and the Valley of the Queens that lay beyond the rock face.

A group of giddy teenage girls approached the chariots. They bowed and said, "We have goat cheese and bread if you are hungry." The royal entourage stopped for a minute and tasted their offering, then continued on their journey up the cliff.

They passed by a smaller building site located at the extreme north end of the village. A group of builders were busy constructing a pergola on the third level of the three-storied house of limestone. It was being built for Senenmut and his very important guest. It was scheduled to be completed within two full moons. It was designed after the exact dimensions of the house he left in Heliopolis. He also kept a suite in the royal complex on the eastern side of the Nile.

They passed a separate quarry where hundreds of artisans were sculpting many images of Hatshepsut from large granite stones. She remembered the words of Sitre-Re: "*Someday your beautiful smile will be chiseled in stone.*"

The small entourage came to a stop on the plateau above and to the north of the temple site. She looked down and observed the three landings had been smoothed and the limestone terraces had been laid and polished. The porticoes were being artfully chiseled and smoothed. A few had been smoothed and fixed into place.

Senenmut greeted her with a smile. She was radiant. Her head jewels shone in the sun and jingled with the slightest movement. He admired her budding body beneath the thin colorful garment. He offered his hands and assisted her from the chariot.

"Come, my beautiful lady, and see the final plans for the temple. Come and take a seat beneath the tarpaulin."

Senenmut lifted the lid of cedar box and pulled out the scroll. "My queen, you have given me wings." He held up the rolled papyrus to align with the construction site.

Together they stood on a cliff to the north of El-Bahri, looking down onto the unfinished temple. "I wanted you to see it from heaven's view. Then Senenmut unrolled his drawings. This will be the temple when finished."

Hatsu looked at the drawing and at the same time drew in a great intake of breath. "It is beautiful! I am without words! It is completely different from the monument of my ancestor."

"It will take at least ten more years until completion unless we can redirect the Nile by constructing a canal."

"Redirect the Nile?"

Senenmut lifted his arms toward the section in front of the king's tombs. "We have to calculate the inundation of the Nile. Records show that the Nile does not encroach this far from the western shores. So we will need to construct a canal for the building materials. It will be easier to cut a channel so the barges can float the blocks of marble to the site. You might even want to consider allowing the waterway to become a permanent fixture. It will eliminate the overland travel and unite heaven and earth at the foot of your temple."

Hatsu had a hint of worry on her face. "I cannot believe the planning and preparations this project will involve. We will need thousands of workers for this. Thanks be to Amun-Ra my father left me a legacy of peace, so I simply have to conscript the workers from the army."

Senenmut looked at Hatshepsut. "You are overwhelmed, my beautiful pharaoh. You can ponder this tomorrow and the days after. There is no reason for you to tremble. This is why I am here. I will carry your burdens. I will be your rock."

"There is no time for me to ponder this, Senenmut. You must do what is necessary and put a quick end to any other projects and immediately bring your workers together to complete this temple. I am humbled by the certainty of death and our brief time on earth. It is as swift as lightening flashing across a darkened sky. I still mourn the death of my parents. There is only a generation to leave ones heritage in Egypt. I trust your knowledge. I simply hope you and I can live to its completion. Besides, I would love to enjoy the fruits of your labor while still in this life. Speaking of fruit, let us dine. We have a table prepared for us. Then we shall talk about our temple."

Senenmut looked into the eyes of Hatshepsut. His thoughts raced. *Did she say our temple? Surely she did.* He picked up a pomegranate, broke it open, put the fruit to her lips, and spilled the seeds into her mouth. She rolled the tart seeds across her tongue, then swallowed. Her dark alluring eyes looked into his and whispered, "As long as you are my rock, I shall not tremble."

Senenmut reached up and untied the rope that held the rolled sides of the tarp. The rest of the entourage gathered together beneath another tarpaulin a distance from Senenmut's headquarters. The flaps to Senenmut's tent flipped down and blotted out the blinding afternoon sun. The floor of his private office was covered with colorful woven tapestry and filled with the most splendid comforts. He poured wine from an urn into a silver goblet and handed it to Hatshepsut.

Senenmut looked into her eyes and lifted her chin with his hand, "Let us drink to your eternal home."

"Our eternal home," corrected Hatshepsut.

Senenmut reached out and pulled Hatshepsut close. The sun's rays were bright and pierced the valley with eternal warmth. Long shadows stretched across the valley floor that extended from the temple terraces.

After they loved, Senenmut informed Hatshepsut the messages he had instructed the artisans:

"I have instructed the painter to draw the words of Khnum to speak these words on your temple wall, the divine potter who sculpted the forms of the gods: 'I will make you to be the first of all living creatures. You will rise as king of Upper and Lower Egypt, as your father Amun, who loves you, did ordain.'"

"I will also ask the painter to write down in words your divine claim of a direct lineage of Amun-Ra. These will be the words I will instruct him to draw on the walls of your tomb: 'Amun who took the form of the noble King Tuthmosis and found the queen sleeping in her room. When the pleasant aroma that proceeded from him announced his presence, she awoke. He gave her his heart and showed himself in his godlike splendors. When he approached the queen, she wept for joy at his strength and beauty, and he gave her his love.'"

Senenmut held the hand of his love and continued, "Let me also suggest this, my beautiful pharaoh. Knowing that citizens can be controlled by words, let me order some of my stone workers to chisel and distribute a list of commandments. These stone sculptures will clearly state the things that one should not do that could interfere with their eternal fields of wheat. If they violate rules, then they will suffer a curse. Let me instruct my masons to list commandments to inform the people of peaceful living. These can be strategically positioned so they could be seen upon entering Egypt's boundaries by waterway, trade routes, and upon entering every port and city within your rule."

Hatshepsut agreed, and within weeks, these stone tablets began to appear throughout the kingdom. Every citizen of Egypt saw the commandments that Pharaoh Hatshepsut had set along the Nile for sea travelers and every citizen within Egypt's realm. By reading her stone mandates, the people knew what to love, what to hate, what to fear, and how to behave. Peace ruled because words were written clearly in glyphs.

These words created blind obedience, and during Hatshepsut's time in power, there was peace.

Hatshepsut Talks to Senenmut

HATSHEPSUT HELD NEFERURE on her lap and kept her entertained with a string of jewels.

"I will leave you in charge of my chief duties. I will bestow upon you the title of chief advisor and you can administer from the west bank and continue your supervision of our temple. I trust no one else but you, Senenmut. You have acquired much favor with the citizens and have enormous respect of the royal house. I shouldn't be gone for more than three moons." She looked up at her lover with yearning eyes, awaiting his response.

"Hatshepsut, I can surely do what you ask, but I do not know if I can be without you for that long." He tightened his embrace and kissed the palms of her hands.

"You will be ever-present in my thoughts throughout my journey of trials and joys. I must do this for my Egypt. Without your assistance, this expedition to Punt would not be possible." Hatshepsut kissed her chief architect. "Now I have something else I want to ask of you."

"Yes, my love, you may ask anything of me."

She whispered, "I want you to take charge of Neferure. Teach her the things that you know. After your days at the construction site, I want you to spend time training her in the knowledge that you know, especially the wonders of sacred geometry and all about the pre-flood race."

Senenmut looked at Hatshepsut and asked, "Shall I tell her how much I love her mother?" Senenmut kissed the cheek of Neferure.

Hatshepsut looked into the eyes of her lover. "With your new title everything will make sense to the royal family and the citizens when they see Neferure in your presence."

"You can trust me, my love. I will take good care of Neferure." He picked up the child and walked to his desk. He held up a level and said, "This, my little Neferure, is a level that is used for determining how straight a thing is. You must remember that everything you learn in geometry can be applied to your personal life. So with this instrument we must remember this will help you to be on the level with your people."

Hatshepsut smiled and said, "You take care of my daughter, and I will take care of yours."

Rebel Pharaoh Hatshepsup Unveiled

Part II

Expedition into the Sacred Land of TA Netjer (God's Land) The Land of Punt

THE SHIP EASED away from the port. Hatshepsut stood on the bow of the ship and fixed her eyes on Senenmut and Neferure. The summer sun shone healing rays over the expedition.

Appearing like a granite obelisk, Senenmut stood tall on the dock and watched her as she waved to him from the stern of the royal ship. He raised one palm, then tenderly touched his heart. He held little Neferure in his other arm.

"Your mother is on a quest, my little princess, so it will be just you and me for the next three months."

Citizens crowded around the harbor and began running along the banks waving palms and singing songs of joy. The ship slowly eased away from the dock.

The royal ship displayed colorful flags representing all the territories ruled by Egypt. Hundreds of deadly pikes were tied to the mast head. The tips glistened in the sun. Hundreds of soldiers stood at attention on the deck of the super ship. Their breast plates shone in the morning sun.

The Egyptians absorbed many of the cultural symbols of their neighboring realm, and the slanted cross was one of them. It was an ancient Kush symbol for eternal luck. Since Egypt's religious beliefs were rooted in the eternal, this cross was boldly displayed on both sides of the bow.

The hot winds were lively with force and pushed the royal ship southward up the Nile. Ecstatic with excitement, the passengers mingled on the broad deck and chatted about the long-awaited expedition. Strong oarsmen, ship hands, litter bearers, many archers, one dedicated archivist, one loyal scribe, one devoted guardian, one dutiful handmaiden, a multitude of servants, and several cooks, were selected to accompany Hatshepsut on this voyage.

The journey to Punt (God's Land) was an epic event that would astound crown heads across the known world. Hatshepsut's covert purpose that motivated this voyage was to return with scrolls and any other sacred relic that would enlighten the temples. Under her rule, Egypt would become the repository for all of the knowledge in the known world.

However, the overt and celebrated purpose was to return with a bountiful amount of items that would seduce the eyes of the citizens–incense, jewels, intricately sculptured items carved from stone and marble. They were expected to bring back woods of every kind–teak, ebony, ivory, cinnamon wood, khesyt wood, and mahogany. Hatshepsut wanted to bring back animals to amuse her citizens. Among them would be monkeys, baboons, and dogs. Prized among these items would be soil and rooted fauna from all lands and ports of call, most importantly, myrrh trees that perfumed the air.

It was decided by the captain and his navigation team that to access god's mysterious land by way of the Nile was out of the question. Too many dangerous cataracts, submerged volcanic rocks, and violent current from rapids made the approach impossible. So based on ancient and present day reliable records, their plan was to travel south on the Nile to an overland corridor that led to the Red Sea.

They sailed southward on the Nile to a port that was located a hundred and fifty miles south of the Southern City. The expedition disembarked, then traveled by foot across a land passage that connected commerce from the Nile to the Red Sea. The expedition proceeded eastward using Arabian horse-drawn chariots, carrier donkeys, and elephants. The expedition finally reunited at the Red Sea Trading Port of Berenike.

A convoy of five smaller ships waited for the royal explorers to arrive. The plan for these ships was to network along the eastern coast of Sudan, Eritrea, Ethiopia, and Somalia.

In time, some of Egypt's subsequent trading ships would cross the great ocean to India's western coast, returning with the monsoon winds powering their lanteen sails. These future trading expeditions would return through the narrow channel that led back to the port of Berenike overflowing with exotic incense, spices, hand-carved furniture, teak wood, woven carpets, fabric as light as air, jewels, and pounded silver vases.

But this expedition was unique. It followed the western edge of Africa and tracked an ancient journal to a remote island. The most important possessions that returned with Hatshepsut's expedition were sacred scrolls for the temples and an unspeakable relic that would, in time, be hidden from history.

Submerged beneath the water passage along the Red Sea were many dangerous coral reefs. The ships that entered the channel were smaller transports navigated by skillful captains who could maneuver their craft through the narrow and dangerous passage of Man-dab Eye.

The five ships sailed in and out of the many ports of Eritrea, making contact with the local officials. At every port, Hatshepsut steadily asked to speak to the wisest Magi of their province.

It was at the port of Djibouti that a man named Nehsi told her that there was a very wise man that lived inland, but his temple was surrounded by a deep and treacherous lake. His words sounded like the threat of a distant thunder when he calmly said, "Inside his temple is a sacred relic, but first, in order to cross this lake, it will be necessary to travel across a hot and torturous terrain. If you choose to take this journey, your most honored pharaoh, I am the only one who can take you there."

Hatshepsut was not threatened by the demanding journey. She stared at the bowed head of the tracker and said, "A prize so wonderful will never grow feet and come to me, so I must make the journey no matter the risk. Fear is only a thought, and thoughts are things that I can control. After all I have my protector with me." She looked up and gave a slight nod to the mighty Kahn.

Nehsi stood firm before the pharaoh queen. He wore a long white robe and a Chambia knife saddled in front of his waist belt. The decorative handle of the knife was more important than the blade because it identified his region of the Shebian Kingdom he called home. He was a tall, swarthy, dark-skinned man. His head wrapped with linen, and his eyes were black as the night sky. "I am your tracker, mighty pharaoh, and I will lead you to the Land of Punt."

So it was decided. Since everyone on board the royal ship pledged their service to this mission, they would champion their pharaoh without question because pleasing Egypt's most noble of women was their sole purpose for living. Besides, they all wanted to be in her service when they traveled to their afterlife.

The expedition disembarked at the Port of Djibouti where they began their journey on land. Nehsi, the tracker, led the entourage, sitting atop his trained elephant. "Let us begin!" he yelled.

Their passage followed, for a while, a part of the Great Rift along the East African coast. The many archers took their positions on either side of the litter bearers that carried Hatshepsut and Sitre-Re. The mighty Kahn directly followed on foot, never being at more than an arm's length from Hatshepsut at anytime. A reserve of litter bearers followed and took turns placing themselves beneath the weight of the carriage every mile. Their transition was so practiced and smooth that Hatshepsut never felt the changing of the carriers. When not bearing the weight of the carriage, these men gripped their threatening sharp-pointed pikes.

Nehsi, the tracker, yelled to the entourage, "We will begin the journey through the Danakil Depression. We will passage through a region of salt flats. Be vigilant to keep the line tight throughout the rest of the day!"

The travelers were careful to form a tight line, and at the same time, they kept a strong hold on their payloads. The landscape changed from high crowning ranges stretching into a deep, broad depression intermittently peaking with volcanic like craters. The ground for a while was brown in color but changed to a pure white surface of solid salt. The entourage inhaled the salty air which caused them to daydream of clear spring water.

The Hatshepsut and her entourage passed through the Bahr al Assal Valley. They traveled across the salty shore of Lake Assal. The lake was the lowest point in Africa and saltier than the Salt Sea. There was no eatable vegetation–only bright, crystalline salt. And there was a hot, blinding sun.

Iy, the archivist, and Ramah, the scribe, walked side by side. Iy chatted with enthusiasm but with cautiousness, "It is rumored this unspeakable relic warms the hand. One can see the future and the past and can communicate with you through thoughts." It was obvious Iy was excited by the possibility of decoding this object. Because of the glare of the sun, they all kept his eyes lowered to the heel of the ones in front.

Ramah had no idea what this "unspeakable" item could be and was eager to know more about it in the days ahead. He would surely be drawing this object. Making certain the cork was tight, he touched his ink container. He didn't want the hot temperature to dry up his cache of ink. He watched, with great concern, the litter that carried the pharaoh.

Every step descended the travelers to the lowest point of the ravine. Beneath the salt floor one could see the green, steaming hot water sloshing only a few inches below the level of the crystal clear salt crust. The travelers were hesitant to continue their journey across the salt flat because the foundation seemed too thin to withstand the weight of the pack animals and travelers. Fear could be seen in the eyes of the litter bearers, but Nehsi, the guide, reassured them, "It is strong like rock. Do not fear! I have taken many packed elephants and asses across this same path!"

"Come, we must continue the expedition." But then he stopped, turned around, and with a stern warning said, "But you must be sure you do not venture from the trail."

Hatsu was uncomfortable inside the litter. The heat was torturous. She had never experienced temperature like this, and for a period of time, she felt nauseated. She thought of Neferure and Senenmut and wondered what they were doing. She found the thought of them calming. Ra aimed his rays over the ravine, bringing such a wave of stifling heat that Hatsu considered, for a while, dismissing this part of the expedition. *Is Ra warning me to abandon my efforts to search for these unspeakable secrets? Perhaps I should return home to the favored city of god Amun.*

She removed her headdress and jeweled collar and eventually slipped off her cotton tunic and sash. Sitre-Re placed a feathered fan across Hatsu's breast and made an effort to be humorous, "You must not charm the gods lest they might steal you away to their sett (den.)"

Every breath was like breathing in the heat of fire. Ra traveled across the sky, lowered his blinding brilliance in the west, and slowly disappeared behind the ridge. The travelers set up their camp on a hardened edge of the flats where the waters beneath the salt floor gurgled precariously. The night offered a much needed respite for the hot, thirsty, and weary travelers.

After the camp was settled, Nehsi took his walking stick that was hewn from the hazel tree and waved it in front of a large outcrop of rock. He whacked the stone with the dowsing rod, and within minutes a stream of fresh water began to trickle down the stone wall and into a natural rock basin. "Don't be afraid. It is not salty. You may drink it and fill your water sacks."

Nehsi was a diviner with his hazel rod and could always find water in the desert. Sometimes he might have to dig for six feet, but water always lurked beneath his feet. After the travelers drank their fill and topped off their water carriers, they settled into their mats and closed their eyes to sleep.

The moon traveled across the sky, and Nut, the sky goddess, stretched her long arms over Geb, the earth god, and the travelers slept.

The next day Nehsi led them across the western end of the salt plateau. Occasionally, one of the members of the entourage would stoop to pick up a halite crystal that had been formed by a dab of mud. That spark of mud was enveloped within the crystal which marked it a wonder in the eyes of the travelers. At the end of the day, each exceptional item found was drawn onto papyrus by Ramah.

For the next two weeks they walked through the rugged highlands of forested mountain ridges, eventually reaching a small village of Bahar Dar located at the southern rim of a large lake. A line of reed boats were pulled onto the shore; each one was equipped for fishing.

Wise men from various kingdoms visited with reliability. But no one of such royalty had recently visited their humble fishing village, and the news spread to the community faster than an eagle could fly.

The local women donned their tribal regalia. They stood at the entrance of the village dressed in their colorful long dresses with rounded collars and short domed hats waiting with arms filled with baskets of fruits and exotic flowers. They greeted the expedition with happy grins.

Later in the day, the women of the village put together a simple meal of Azifa, a lentil salad, beans, and Injarah. Injarah bread was dense and hardy made from the teff grain grown in the Ethiopian highlands. The grain was so tiny it could easily slip through the bakers fingers. For the night's entertainment, a group of village children sang songs and clapped their hands with joy for the pharaoh queen and her royal ministrants.

After their dinner, Nehsi instructed the entourage, "I can only make one trip each day. The first group will start out tomorrow at first light, which will include the most noble of women, her hand-maiden, her protector, the archivist, and scribe. The following day I will return for the second group, and we will resume the morning after."

The travelers listened to the instruction of the tracker. It had taken twenty-one days of treacherous foot travel from the port to the small village. Too tired to move, they fell upon their bed mats and closed their eyes to a much needed sleep.

SOUTHERN RIM OF SACRED LAKE

THE NEXT MORNING Hatsu awoke thinking about Senenmut and Neferure. Her heart ached for them. She opened the drapes of her private litter and watched Ra ascend his splendor across the eastern slope. A streak of heat lightening blazed across the sky, followed by a gentle rumbling of thunder.

The early morning sun, although common and unfailing, was for her always a marvel to see. Her sun-god nurtured all things. It brought life to the seedlings. It reached down and touched the earth with miraculous rays of power. Without Ra life would cease. She remembers Iy schooling her about the time when ice covered the planet and Ra's hands could not touch the earth.

Suddenly, to Hatsu's amazement, a baboon reached into the litter and pulled out her headdress. He placed it upon his head and began jumping up and down making screeching noises and preening his face in a display of mockery. The locals were horrified and immediately began chasing the baboon.

Hatsu had seen paintings of baboons but until now had never encountered one in real life. She jumped from her litter and began trailing the animal around the small village. The mighty Kahn took off chasing Hatsu and the baboon. After quite an effort Kahn finally caught the black hairy rascal and pried the wig from its small hand.

"Don't harm him!" Hatsu cried. "He's so cute! I want to bring him back with me."

At first the villagers were horrified that their pet had intruded into pharaoh's private chamber, but were relieved when they saw her laughing and pleading with her protector not to harm it. They were enchanted with the most noble of women and were honored that she wanted to return to her palace with one of their backwater baboons.

After the excitement was over Nehsi began to unfurl the sail and readied one of the larger boats. Sitre-Re had been up for a while organizing Hatsu's personal makeup box and garments. The others were sitting around a ground fire, heating up water for arrack, a bitter drink made from fermented grain. A large bowl full of Injarah bread rested near the fire. They chatted and laughed about the baboon prancing around with the royal headdress.

A sudden breeze jerked the sail and turned the boat onto its side. Nehsi stood on the shore and studied the lake. The surface of the water began to ripple.

"We must go now!" insisted Nehsi.

Crossing the Lake to God's Land

TRAVELING INTO AN unknown sacred land was for Hatsu the most spine-tingling event that she would ever experience in her lifetime. Her first expedition to Heliopolis when she was eight rooted this desire to search for hidden secrets.

Seated inside the boat Hatshepsut looked across the lake and could feel a cold wind drifting in the air.

Her heart thumped fast and her blood coursed through her like it did when she was a child. An eerie mist began to form just above the surface of the water. Nehsi warned the passengers to sit firmly in their seats while his wise eyes squinted and surveyed the lake.

Several minutes into the crossing, the wind began to push and pull at the water's surface. Its power rolled the reed boat forward, then backward. The tightly woven papyrus reeds began to squeak and moan causing a sense of fear and helplessness among the passengers. The rain and spray plummeted with a fury, creating a gray opaqueness upon the lake. In a short period of time water began to fill the floor of the boat covering the feet of the drenched passengers.

Hatshepsut and the other held onto anything that was woven into the framework of the boat and rode the movement of the water. Stern faced and quiet, Nehsi offered no words of comfort to his passengers. He just gripped the oars tighter and plowed through the looming waves. A pharaoh and her ministrants were in his care. He had traveled through hot terrains, across perilous mountain peaks, and traversed the most threatening situations. Like any other day he would command his reed boat across the threatening waves. The boat lurched forward, then backward, and tipped from side to side. Water sprayed with a fury across the prow.

The mighty Kahn balanced himself forward, wrapped one arm around Hatsu, and held firmly onto the side of the boat. Hatshepsut did not cry out in fear, but instead to those in the boat she assured, "Amun-Ra is testing our will! We are on a noble expedition for our temples. He is testing our devotion. He will not deny our desires!"

A watery wall crashed and spilled over the passengers. Finally, in desperation Sitre-Re yelled, "Oh Amun-Ra! Will you allow Egypt's future to perish in the headwaters of the Nile? Send us Hapi to calm the water of your holy lake. Show us your mercy!" She reached out of the boat and brought the lake water to her mouth and kissed it. Exhausted by fear she finished her prayer, "Hapi, show mercy to our great leader of Egypt."

At the next beat of the heart the lake waters began to calm. Ra burned his brilliance through the gray mist and soon the fog lifted. The rains suddenly stopped and before their eyes emerging into view was something beautiful. Nehsi smiled and pointed to a lush green island that materialized from the mist. "There! Pwenet! Punt . . . God's Land! We will be there soon!"

The sandy shore of the water-bound island was a welcoming sight to the travelers. Nehsi began to coil the sail and with his oar steered the boat to the water's edge. A large woman, clad in colorful attire walked toward the boat. Nehsi smiled, and with liveliness in his voice, he announced, "Queen Ati, I have brought to you Egypt's pharaoh. Like you, she is also a great woman of nobility. I bring you, Pharaoh Hatshepsut. She seeks the wisdom of the mighty ancients."

Before the deadly crossing had a chance to be reconciled in her mind, Hatsu stared amazingly at the queen of Punt. At first glance Hatsu was astounded at Queen Ati's ripples of fat but was quickly impressed with her jovial presence. Hatsu kept a smile on her lips and nodded in agreement about seeking ancient knowledge.

Queen Ati instantly was impressed to have a woman seeker visit her on her private island. "Bring her to me, and we shall speak of ancient scrolls and many things."

"Thank you, Queen Ati." Hatshepsut bowed humbly to the queen of God's Land. Then the queen of Punt bowed to her visitor, Pharaoh Hatshepsut.

Queen Ati and her servants led the visiting delegation to an underground passage that led to separate rock hewn cells. In minutes, each visitor was given a tray heaped with exotic fruits and delicate cakes that melted on the tongue.

Ribbons of a sweet-smelling fragrance drifted in the air.

Attentive to their queen, the servants listened as she spoke, "I know the crossing was difficult, so after the noblest lady relaxes, bring her to the auditory. I will speak to her about the hall of records."

"Yes, mighty queen."

God's Land

THE MOUTH OF the cave was small, almost indistinct and hidden behind a cluster of flora. The stone passage coiled through the mountain and opened into a large room. Oil lamps were placed around the auditory, illuminating the natural rock-hewn room. The thick fragrance of frankincense drifted in the air.

Beneath a ceiling of rock the two great women sat together, discussing the agreement. Ramah positioned himself within listening distance of the two nobles. He wrote down their conversation and drew a picture of the two extraordinary women working out the details of their trading contract. Oil lamps filled the banquet hall projecting shifting shapes across the walls.

"There are many things on Pwenet that must remain here but others items we are willing to trade." Queen Ati and Pharaoh Queen Hatshepsut munched on delicate morsels of fish eggs, figs, a fluffy white fruit pudding, goat cheese, bread, and wine.

"I have heard about the beauty of your palaces and the awesome wonders designed by your artisans." With a look of wanderlust in her eyes, Queen Ati took a bite of bread and cheese and said, "Perhaps someday King Parahu and I will travel there." But a look of doubt soon shadowed her eyes. "Ahh, but I don't think he will ever leave his home. Besides, the king is not well. He dwells in the hall of records day and night, afraid to leave his sacred scrolls for even a second. He hungers for knowledge. He reads day and night until he finally collapses with exhaustion. He sleeps for days, then he awakes and has a good meal. Then the cycle continues."

Queen Ati sighed, "I have never been off this island. It has been a duty for our time to protect these sacred scrolls and, uh, that other items, too. We have no heir, and now that we are getting old, I would like to see the beautiful sights along the Nile River that I have heard so much about." Queen Ati wiped the bread crumbs from her hands. "I shall show you our treasures when you are ready." She then reached for a bowl of fluffy white pudding. "This fruit grows in abundance on our island to which I am hopelessly addicted." Queen Ati pushed the bowl toward Queen Hatshepsut. "You must try it."

"Your most honored queen, you and King Parahu would be most welcomed in my city." Hatshepsut took a bite of goat cheese and grain bread, then reached for the fluffy white pudding. "I shall like to see the scrolls when we are finished. Iy, my archivist, and Ramah, my scribe, would like to join us if you will allow it. You see, my real purpose for this expedition is to acquire knowledge for our temples. But to please the lavish needs of my people I must return with items that will also dazzle their eyes."

Queen Ati's eyes blinked hard when she heard the words "dazzle their eyes." She reached out and touched Hatshepsut's hand. "Your journey to God's Land will please both your temples and your people. Let us take a walk. We shall bring along your archivist and your scribe."

Queen Ati uttered something in a language unknown to Hatshepsut. Within seconds, two Ethiopian attendants appeared before their sovereign. Queen Ati said, "We will descend to the underworld with the most noble Hatshepsut, her archivist, and her scribe. Bring us the light." The queen looked at Hatshepsut and said, "Your personal handmaiden and your guard will stay behind. It is not necessary for them to join us."

Hatshepsut chuckled and quietly said to Queen Ati, "It is just as well. My handmaiden and my personal guard are lovers, and I suspect they are enjoying the company of each other right now."

Queen Ati informed her guest, "Many years ago, sacrosanct secret keepers hand-chiseled the stairs and walls from rock. It will take us many steps before we reach the floor of the grotto."

Queen Ati instructed her servants, "Keep the lights focused so that our feet won't falter."

The Ethiopian attendants led them down the craggy spiral steps. Hatshepsut braced her hand along the rock face and could feel moisture trickling down the walls. The deeper they stepped beneath the ground the cooler the air became. The carriers held the luminaries high, which flooded the pitch black cavern with light. Finally, at the base, the group walked toward an arched door that was made from acacia wood. While the two slaves fumbled with the latch, the royal guests stepped back and waited for it to open.

Then Queen Ati stepped inside the room and said, "King Parahu will not leave this place. He worships every scroll inside the great hall. He claims we possess the oldest and most complete records on earth."

THE HALL OF RECORDS

AT FIRST GLANCE the hall was dark. The smell of ancient wisdom hurled toward Hatshepsut like a hypnotic breeze. It tantalized her desire even more to uncover secrets of the past. She noticed a dim light radiating from the vast underground hall which seemed to illuminate from the rear of the repository. The air was cold and moist, and a constant dripping sound threatened the dimly lit grotto.

The interest that fueled her expedition lured her closer to the scrolls. She touched the quadrilateral cubicles with reverence and embraced the ancient skins with tenderness. She opened all of her senses and breathed in the smell of hide and ink.

Noticing her interest, the attendants lifted their oil lamps casting light on the rolled up papyrus and lamb skin documents, shining light onto the many cubicles that held the following books:

The Books of War; Books of Love; Books of Hate; Books of Enahk and the Heavenly Luminaries; Books of Splendor; Books of Angels; Books of Numbers and Mathematics; Books of Alchemy: Transmuting the Formula for Electrum; Book of Promise; Book of Persuasions; Book of Letters; Book of Throwing and Ending Curses; The Book of Incantations; Book of Laws; Books of Creation; Books of Stars; The Book of Unveiling of Heavenly Secrets of Panspermia so on and so forth.

Hatshepsut took in a great intake of breath and sighed, "I want to breathe in everything. I want to know the thoughts of these great thinkers and to know the wisdom that fueled their civilizations. I want to know the secrets that powered their thrones." The scrolls held her spellbound. Unable to move, she thought, *I must have these scrolls.*

Queen Ati called out in the dark underground repository, "Parahu! Parahu! We are entering the Hall of Records! I am bringing with me the Pharaoh Queen, Hatshepsut, Great Ruler of Egypt, her personal scribe, Ramah, and Iy, the sacrosanct archivist."

Queen Ati turned to her guests. With both a concerned and an anguished look in her eyes she said, "My husband is in his late years, and his entire life he has been a protector to these scrolls. Because of his age and his illness he knows his duty to these scrolls is coming to an end. He is saddened about the finality of life and has a knowing of his own death. He feels life's energy slipping away. Both of our children are dead, and Parahu knows I cannot accept the responsibility to become the keeper of records. I am not well. Woe be to the future of these scrolls and to the other items in our safekeeping. There is no one else in Punt that has the understanding, dedication, and sufficient wealth to protect them." Queen Ati appealed to Hatshepsut with yearning eyes.

Hatsu looked compassionately at the queen of Punt. She mentally prayed to Ma'at for the weighing of scales and for the right words to impress the queen. "Noble Queen Ati, at the great Southern City our temples are considered to be the most splendid of holy places and, surely, the sturdiest of engineering. These temples are shrines to all the gods for the benefit of enlightenment and illumination to humanity. I and my capable entourage will be grateful to you if you and the king will allow us to have the honor of receiving these scrolls and the other divine items of importance so they can be secured inside our great temples. Your collection will be transferred into responsible hands and treated with utmost reverence."

Queen Ati's face revealed a most grateful and happy expression. "Parahu! Parahu! We are coming back to see you!" Queen Ati repeated her words about every fifty feet until finally reaching the end of the great hall of records. Her steps became slow and cautious.

"Parahu! We have a wonderful guest! The most noble of women! The one you have been expecting!"

He's been expecting me? Hatshepsut thought.

A light source emanated from an alcove on the right side of the hall that reflected onto the wall in front of them. The light flickered. They looked around the corner and saw a figure sitting at a table. His back was to his visitors.

On this table, rested before the man, was an oil lamp. In front of the lamp rested a scroll that had been unrolled and secured by crystal weights.

His words came out like a slow moving vessel traveling against the current. "Please . . . come . . . in."

Queen Ati stood beside the seated man and said, "My husband, my king . . . I have brought you pharaoh queen of the Nile, the most noble of women of Thebes and all of Egypt's boundaries, Pharaoh Hatshepsut. She is on an expedition, a quest for the most splendid reason. My husband and lordship of Punt, her quest is for knowledge. She wants to bring wisdom to her temples. Her temples are large, safe, and soundly engineered." She waited for an answer and then added, "I have brought you food, my dear king."

The old man slowly stood and turned. Although he did not practice Egyptian ways, out of respect, he extended his arms toward Hatshepsut with his fingers high and palms facing her. She did the same, and their palms touched.

He looked at her with knowing eyes and said slowly and clearly, "I . . . have waited . . . for you. Many years . . . I knew . . . you would come. Please . . . sit . . . and the others, too."

Hatshepsut looked up at King Parahu. Her eyes were wide with wonder. "How did you know I would come?"

His answer sounded like a blustery wind mixed with happiness and regret. "I! . . . know! . . . e-v-e-r-y-t-h-i-n-g!" He cradled his head in his hands. "It is a woeful burden to know all things."

King Parahu's eyes looked at Hatshepsut and said, "You descend from the mighty ancients . . . Your father . . . was Tuthmosis I, a great military leader . . . His life was cut down like young wheat . . . Duty dictated that you marry your half brother . . . and Ahmose . . . your mother who sleeps . . . enjoyed the leaves . . . of the sacred flower which dimmed her world . . . There are children of your blood . . . who play together . . . in the wheat fields of paradise . . . and . . . there is a man . . . Senenmut . . . whose love for you . . . will bring lasting beauty to the lands of Egypt. His gift is greater than silver and gold . . . Because of his love . . . you will endure throughout time . . . A young royal struggles in the deep . . . You are loved by all who surrounds you . . . all but one . . . A northern king is jealous of a modern temple . . . He will want one of his own . . . Beware of . . . god's divine nectar . . . can be a potion of death."

For a moment Hatshepsut was speechless. *He talked of things only I could know. My mother and her weakness for lotus leaves; my two brothers whose spirits roam the fields of wheat; my father who died before his time; my nephew who dwells deep within the shafts of gold. God's nectar can be a potion of death . . . what can that mean? I came here to find the ancient secrets, and he gives me a personal examination of my life. But how does he know these things? It is a riddle that I must solve.*

Hatshepsut blinked as if being awakened from a dream. "King Parahu, you do know everything. How do you do it?"

Parahu's answer sounded almost like an apology. "I . . . I can . . . see."

"You're a seer? A prophet? A wise man?" Hatshepsut questioned.

"I cannot do it alone, though . . . I need the help of the . . . unspeakable object." The king looked at his wife as if waiting for an authorization from her.

Queen Ati looked at him and said, "Go ahead and tell her. Show her."

Hatshepsut glanced at her scribe, then her archivist, and then she gave a questioning stare at the queen and king of Punt. "Would you show me how you see these things?"

Parahu stood up and said, "Please. You must follow me."

They left the alcove and journeyed through a warren of hand-chiseled tunnels turning right and left. Water dripped from the low craggy ceiling and pooled along the floor and disappeared into a hidden underground stream. One attendant led the group through the tunnel, and the other one followed holding their lights so the group would not falter. The light shimmered across the wet rock walls along the passageway to the room that held the unspeakable object.

The Unspeakable Object

THE ATTENDANTS LIFTED the lid from the ornate golden box.

King Parahu closed his eyes and draped a shroud over the glowing object. He reached down and lifted the relic from the carrier and placed it on a nearby table.

Hatshepsut, Ramah, and Iy were mesmerized watching King Parahu move the shrouded relic. A faint glow emanated through the covering. "What is it?" Hatshepsut asked.

"It was brought to my island . . . years ago. My father and his father have protected it. People have died from fright . . . staring at this relic. It has an unexplainable allure. You have to force your attention away from it. I am going to pull off the cover, but you must not look upon it for more than a few blinks of an eye."

Amazingly, as soon as he pulled the cloth from the relic, the brilliance of the thing lit up the room. Hatshepsut was stunned at what she saw. "It shines like Ra!" She blinked, and before she knew it, King Parahu had covered it with the shroud.

"In the brief moment that I looked at it, I felt it was communicating with me!" Hatshepsut could hardly catch her breath and take it all in. "Is it a thinking object? Again, I ask, what is it?"

King Parahu breathed in deeply and chuckled. "It is a profound mystery. It is an unspeakable relic! It knows things! You are right! It did communicate with you. It is mind-boggling! It has powers . . . unspeakable powers!"

Hatshepsut looked at Parahu and asked, "You knew I was coming. Did this unspeakable thing tell you this?"

King Parahu let out a sigh. "Yes, it did. I know my days are numbered, and it is you, the rightful owner, who must now take ownership of this thing of mystery."

Iy stared at the glowing cloth and whispered, "This thing . . . I have heard about it. It was spirited out of Egypt over a hundred years ago when the Hyksos left during the great wave. It is too profound to possess. It has memory, and it knows the future!"

Parahu glared at Hatshepsut. "You, Iy . . . or perhaps your priest, should be the one to safeguard it and the other precious items of value. You can find a secure place in one of your Theban temples. These sacrosanct items must be delivered into the right hands . . . hands that can care for them and keep them safe–hands that will respect their powers."

"You see, Pharaoh Hatshepsut, you are the one who has been found to be trustworthy. This relic has led you here. Now you must seek protection for this and the other sacred items of wisdom."

Hatshepsut wondered what other items King Parahu would reveal to her. *Should something so powerful be held back from the people?* Hatshepsut's thoughts were teeming with questions. Wanting to know more about the shrouded thing was Hatshepsut's main concern. "Please show me its capabilities?" she asked.

Parahu sat in front of the shrouded illuminating relic and placed his forehead against it. He took in a deep breath, exhaled, then asked a question, "Speak to me of your future. Who shall be your next caretaker?"

The glow beneath the cloth began to radiate from white to pink. Parahu's eyes were closed and the room was soundless. "It is telling me a riddle . . . it is saying . . . 'I will dwell inside a temple of red . . . A person on high will be at my head. The earth will shake, and you will return me to a rocky deep.'"

The relic glowed pink in color for a few minutes, then it slowly dimmed. It was as if the item no longer wanted to communicate.

King Parahu lifted his head and looked at Hatshepsut. "It no longer speaks today. It knows its own future . . . and I cannot change the future. So be it." Parahu got up and carried the shrouded relic to its container. He bent to place it inside the barque, and his arms touched the side. The golden box jiggled a brief moment but then it quickly steadied itself.

Hatshepsut noticed it. "The box . . . it is hovering! It is not resting on anything!" She walked toward the box, bent down, and slid her hand beneath it. "This is magic! How can it hover?"

King Parahu laughed. "It is not magic. It is opposing stones that possess repelling energy. These stones do not want to touch. You see . . . the only weight the carriers are burdened with . . . is the weight of the supporting block of stone. They are not burdened with the weight of the golden box plus the relics within. This has been resting here for many years. Who knows how long it has been hovering before it arrived here."

Hatshepsut began to think about the benefits of having such an unspeakable relic and its amazing magical container. *Should I reveal it to the masses? Will it assist in a peaceful rule? I will know what to expect before an event. Perhaps I can even alter the future. Oh, the glory of it all!*

The forthcoming days were spent preparing the sacred cache for travel. Many scrolls were carefully secured inside clay jars, then placed inside boxes of cedar. The unspeakable relic was stored inside the hovering arc and a litter was build to symbolize a boat.

While the inventory was being readied for travel Queen Ati introduced Hatshepsut to a dedicated Ethiopian arborist named Zachiah.

The moment Zachiah stood before Hatshepsut, the young arborist raised her palms in Egyptian reverence to the pharaoh queen. "I have been asked to show you the collection of the fauna that exists in abundance on God's Land."

Hatshepsut gazed at the young girl. "I am impressed. A female arborist! Please show me your trees."

Hatshepsut, her hostess, Queen Ati, and a small entourage followed Zachiah through the lush green garden. Fruits of all kinds hung from the sprawling branches.

Servants pulled fruit and stored them inside hemp bags. Throughout the walk, Zachiah addressed the pharaoh in halting Egyptian language about each fruit and their shelf life after being plucked.

Ra was high in the sky and shone his rays to the earth. A table was set beneath the canopy of sweet-smelling trees. The fruit was cut and the entourage of guests sat beneath the aromatic branches.

"This is why your land is called God's Land. There is a sacred aroma that permeates the air." Hatshepsut inhaled deeply.

Zachiah smiled. Her eyes were dark as the night and shone with confidence. "You are sitting beneath the branches of myrrh trees." She stood up, lifted her hands to the branch above, and then snapped off a twig. "Here, noblest of women," she said and handed the twig to Hatshepsut.

"In Egypt, we treasure these timbers like gold. May I purchase trees for my return home? I would like to plant them at my temple site."

Queen Ati looked at Hatshepsut. "We would be honored for you to take them for your temple. We have thirty-seven ready for travel."

Zachiah kneeled before the two queens and humbly begged, "I grew these trees from young saplings, and I am the only one that can care for them. May I travel back to Egypt with the pharaoh and become the arborist for these trees? I will guard them with my life."

Queen Ati looked down at Zachiah, then turned to Hatshepsut, "She is such a gifted arborist that I am convinced she can coax a flower to grow from a slab of granite."

The two royal women looked at each other and soon Queen Ati agreed.

Leaving Punt

THE DAY CAME when the expedition had to leave the island and return to the beautiful Southern City.

"Someday our kingdom will boast of a strong and clever woman like you. It won't be for another five hundred years, but she will be a stately woman . . . like you, Your Highness . . . a visionary . . . a seeker of wisdom."

"You speak with such a knowing," answered Hatshepsut.

Queen Ati looked eastward across the lake and pondered a future kingdom that someday would produce a strong and very clever woman. "She will come from a Shebian kingdom. She will mesmerize a king and produce a son. She will abandon her kingdom and come here to seek safety." Queen Ati turned and looked toward the mountain. "Her feet will tread upon my footsteps. My country, my Ethiopia, will always be safe grounds for the godly."

"Seek safety for what reason?" Hatshepsut asked.

Queen Ati looked into the eyes of her honored guest and said, "Soon you will know many things. This land will give safe harbor in the times to come." Queen Ati looked at the barque then back at Hatshepsut.

Queen Ati let out a sigh. "Ah yes, what goes around comes around." She watched the attendants carry the golden container onto a reed cargo ship. She scrutinized the carrier's careful steps and their tight hold around the gripping rods. She watched them lowered it onto the deck. The barque hovered rigidly above the stone base.

Hatshepsut turned to King Parahu and asked, "Did you receive this information about this future queen from the crystal relic?" Hatshepsut asked.

"Oh yes, it knows the future and the past. It is making this journey with you because it knows this is the way it is supposed to be, and we must allow it to journey back with you." Then the king advised, "It should always be covered when you are traveling. Brigands will try to steal it for its gold content, ignoring completely the amazing ability of the real prize that rests within."

In the background Hatshepsut watched as the attendants covered the arc with a linen drape.

The king and queen of Punt were saddened to see their guest leave but saddened greater by the realization that their life's purpose was now being carried onto a ship and removed permanently from their day-to-day charge.

"The sacred barque is now in your hands, Pharaoh Queen Hatshepsut. It will dwell inside your temple in the Place of the Palaces."

Beneath the mountain on the Isle of Punt, the lowest level of the repository that once gave shelter to the most important relics and scrolls of all time soon began to flood. Waters from the lake finally stretched the cracks and poured in just as the loaded ship was being pushed away from the shore.

The expedition made their way back across the treacherous forest and grueling hot salt plains. When they arrived in Djibouti, Pharaoh Hatshepsut offered Nehsi the title, "chief tracker for the most noble of women." She urged him to return with the entourage to the royal Southern City for the celebrations. He agreed and proudly acquired the position of chief tracker for the many future expeditions to come. They returned to the ships with all the possessions and made their way back through the narrow passage of Man-dab Eye.

During the voyage to the Port of Berenike, deep within the storage section of the lead ship, Hatshepsut and Iy secretly removed the unspeakable item from the barque. They stole quick glimpses and watched a survey of the future to come.

In the twenty-first year of your reign, on the third month, on a full moon, your sovereign will be seized by a thin-blooded usurper. Royals will be in danger. Seek safety in the southern region of Nekheb.

Hatshepsut became fatigued and realized her life was being manipulated by an entity unknown to her. Perhaps it was Ra. Perhaps the gods were manipulating events for their pleasure.

She quietly spoke to Iy in the ship's cargo hold. "I know what I must do . . . what I must eventually plan for regarding my destiny."

On the way back to the Nile, she asked Sitre-Re to call for Ramah the scribe.

"Come closer, Ramah. I have a request." She whispered into his ear, "Before we board the royal ship that awaits us on the Nile, I would like you to go to the family that supported my grandfather in his quest to rid Egypt of those interlopers, the Hyksos. The descendants of this mighty family that helped my grandfather still reside in the same location near the spot of the breathing ceremony. I would like for you, Ramah, to remove yourself from this expedition until you can complete my request. You are to hand them this note and these gifts. The ship will not sail until you return." A look of knowing and consent glazed across the pharaoh's face. "My future safety depends of it."

He bowed with respect and said, "Your wish is my command."

Hatshepsut Unveiled

Part III

Return Trip from Punt

Temple Construction

RA SPREAD HIS amber glow across the sacred white cliffs of the Valley of the Kings. Hatshepsut's Temple, still in a state of completion, stood boldly in front of the grooved rock wall that housed the mighty warrior kings.

Senenmut had engineered most of the temple masterpiece by using the stone quarried on site. He ordered large boulders to be cut and hewn to represent perfection by using privileged sacred geometry only privy to a few chosen men. Senenmut instructed hundreds of stonecutters to shear the extracted area to look as if it had been weathered by the tooling of time. Just beneath the grooved cliff rock the artisans chiseled a relief that represented Hatshepsut's daily life of a splendid royal. These dedicated workers suspended themselves by reed ropes and chiseled the freeze to shape a ghostly appearance of her royal life. The relief hovered like a stone cloud above the top terrace of the temple.

Senenmut wanted the rocky background to appear like water cascading over the mountain edge, the groove marks forming into the limestone relief depicting her administrative life as the rock face magically melted into Hatshepsut's perfect geometric temple.

He designed it to look as if nature had hewn the crevices, man had formed the relief, and Amun-Ra himself had created the temple. It was a combination of nature and the divine in perfect harmony, proving that in nature perfection can be born from disorder.

But time and the tooling of wind would erode, confirming that nothing stays the same, and time, the destroyer of all things, would reshape the artfully chiseled marks from the rock face and other parts of the temple. But for now the devoted work force chiseled, cut, smoothed, and painted glorious pictures depicting life of Hatshepsut's administration on the walls and pillars above and below the expansive three-tiered portico.

The super ship floated northward along the Nile toward the temple-filled Southern City. The Phoenix date palms lined both sides of the Nile and fluttered their crowns in the brilliant morning sunshine. Masses of citizens ran along both sides of the Nile following the super ship, waving palms leaves and sacred blue and white lotus flowers scenting all of Thebes.

Women citizens trilled their tongues in joyful chorus. The ecstatic citizens crowded on the eastern and western borders of the Nile and waited for the ship to dock and the envoy of travelers to disembark.

Hatshepsut excited beyond words instructed, "I want the sacred barque to lead the procession. My litter will follow."

Important clay jars rested beside Iy and had been in his charge since leaving Punt. He assured Hatshepsut, "I will oversee the safety and make sure they will be locked safely inside the Temple of Amun." He sat next to the unspeakable relic and kept his hands on the cloth covering. The entourage was lining up within the ship.

Admiring the vista from her private quarters, Hatshepsut stared at her shining white temple positioned in front of the Valley of the Kings. She could hardly wait for the ceremony to end so she could fall into Senenmut's arms. *Tomorrow Senenmut will show me all the things that he and his stone masons have built in my absence. I wonder what Senenmut has taught our daughter. I wonder if I will recognize her after being gone for a year.* Hatshepsut's mind was full of anticipations. A smile settled on her freshly cleaned face as she prepared herself for the full ceremonial dress.

She sat on her throne amid a flurry of attendants who began primping her with all the celebration and pageantry that was expected for her royal homecoming. A male cosmetic artist carefully drew on the traditional coal black eyeliner across the lids of Hatshepsut's eyes. A male clothier helped with the time-honored pharaoh's golden vestment. He fitted it over her transparent calasiris (tunic) tightening it so that her torso looked manly. He hooked on the traditional golden beard drawing the strings over her ears and tying them behind her neck. A female wig attendant placed a lapis and gold Nemes crown on the pharaoh's head and carefully threaded her hair through colorful glass straws. Maidens rubbed her arms with essential oils from the Isle of Punt containing the attar from the sacred white lotus. The perfume attendant rubbed Sitre-Re's golden lotion on the pharaoh's arms, neck, and feet.

Hatshepsut's transformation was magical.

When she displayed the pharaoh's traditional regalia, the citizens were awed by the illusion that transformed her into a shimmering golden statue. Men looked upon her and swore the image before them was that of a man. Women looked upon her and immediately fell deeply in love. Almost everyone worshiped her.

Sitre-Re ran down the hallway to the stern of the super ship and entered her suite. "Beautiful pharaoh, the city is brimming with joy and exaltation. They are waiting for you."

"Yes, I can see them. My people are loyal, and indeed, they are anxious to know about all the wonderful things we have brought back for them to behold."

Sitre-Re reached out and said, "Please take my hand, and I will assist you to the shore. You and the sacred barque will be leading the procession to your amazing temple. I know your heart is pounding like a drum."

The pageant began at the imperial suite located at the end of the long hallway inside the super ship. Hatshepsut and Iy walked down the ship's hallway behind the barque that held the ancient relics. Musicians lined up behind the pharaoh and shrilled their high-pitched mizmar instruments that sounded like a million screeching seagulls while the nearly nude female flutists filtered into the procession. They proceeded down the hall, through the luxurious lounging room, across the one-hundred-foot deck and down the platform to the docks.

Golden covered litters awaited along the Nile's edge. Hatshepsut and the members of the expedition were lined up inside their assigned litter. They were lifted quickly upon the strong shoulders of burly Nubians. One by one they began their long walk across the plains to her temple.

Egypt's holy barque containing a precious ancient relic led the procession. It was carried on the shoulders of six strong Nubians who walked beneath a protective canopy that was supported by eight foot soldiers. Hundreds of charioteers carrying the best archers rolled beside the pageantry. The movement of the prancing horses kicked up sand and created a flume of dust that drifted above the procession.

In her absence Senenmut had ordered an open air platform to be erected for the purpose of grandstanding Her Majesty and the assorted items traded at all of the ports-of-call. Senenmut realized he had limited time to build this dais so he instructed his masons to cut red quartzite from the quarry of Djebel Akhmar, known as the mountain of red stone and ordered the blocks shipped to the Place of the Palaces on a barge.

From the docks, he supervised the transportation of these red stones onto a flatbed cedar transport outfitted with dolomite stone wheels. They were then hauled by a team of oxen across the plain all the way to Hatshepsut's mortuary temple. These red stones were erected at the base of the ramp . . . a fitting dais to greet her people who one day would flock to her temple and come to solicit her in her afterlife.

But at Hatshepsut's request much later in her reign, this platform would eventually be moved piece by piece inside the protective walls of the royal complex. Walls and a roof would be added and the red chapel would become the future sanctuary for housing the original barque of Amun-Ra and the unspeakable item it contained. But for now the red floor rested in radiant splendor at the base of the bottom ramp resembling a red carpet that rose in shocking splendor above the white sands.

The barque now leading the procession was home again. The red open-aired dais glowed beneath the afternoon sun . . . waiting the footsteps of Pharaoh Hatshepsut and the unspeakable relic.

The citizens were unaware that their barque had ever been stolen. To them the one parading toward Hatshepsut's temple was a beautiful gift given to the expedition and no doubt contained something wondrous. The onlookers were impressed that another empire honored a god that might even resemble their own.

The stolen barque was a cleverly concealed secret known only to a few men, a privileged honor shared only by a thin line of high priest. Ptah and Hapuseneb knew that the original barque and its wondrous contents were home again.

One hundred years ago after the plunder, the priests were so horrified about the unforgivable robbery of Egypt that they quickly ordered an exact replica to be fashioned so the Egyptian people would have an object to venerate. The high priest understood the citizens needed to be awed into submission by a relic that embodied Ra. Having a god to fear was a necessary thing but a god who would also show them mercy was a powerful thing for any kingdom.

During Hatshepsut's stay in Punt, it was pointed out by King Parahu that the gold crafters of the Hyksos had altered the original lid of Amun-Ra. Egyptian designers placed their goddess Ma'at at the four corners of the sacred container in order to protect its contents. But sacrosanct goldsmiths of the Hyksos tribe had etched the original design beneath the newer lid; the four winged creatures that Egyptian artisans had once spread their wings at the four corners were reduced to two larger winged creatures that now rested on the top at each end of the lid. Their wings spread forth touching the other as if to protect the place their god sat while offering mercy to the citizens.

Egypt had a history of being plundered. Gold and their holiest of objects were the driving force for looters. Since the Hyksos had ruled Egypt for a hundred years, when fleeing their shattered stronghold they were convinced the barque of Amun-Ra would bring power to their people.

After all, while ruling Egypt, the Hyksos had worshiped it for a hundred years and felt it was theirs to seize. These ever-vigilant usurpers . . . Egypt's in-house enemy . . . had taken with them Egypt's most elemental secret–the barque of Amun-Ra, later altered and given a slightly different name.

It was the flawed thinking of the Hyksos that the powers of the barque could benefit their nation. These same powers that were summoned up by the Egyptian high priests with reliability could not be understood by the Hyksosian leaders no matter how hard they tried.

Sadly, after many unsuccessful years, the Hyksosian leaders were not given the power they expected but instead they slowly became bewildered by its contents. After many years of rootless travels and constantly being refused a place of refuge, they began to fear the very thing they had stolen. No city wanted this stolen relic or the ones who were linked to the sins against Egypt to enter their city because they feared retribution. So the Hyksosian nation began to rebel.

It came to be that every city knew in advance when the Hyksosian dispersion was advancing toward their city walls. The reputation of the relic was proclaimed like scattering birds heralding a coming storm.

That which could not be understood was always feared. At one time only Egyptian priests could understand the unspeakable power of the sacred relic, and the priests who understood it had died with the knowledge of how to use the mysterious relic.

After years of disorder and fearing vengeance on their own people, the Hyksosian leaders spirited away the barque to the Land of Punt, a secret safe haven known only to a few. Sacrosanct keepers of knowledge received all kind of sacred items and stored them in their facility. The Egyptian barque had been in God's Land (Punt) for over eighty years, and now it was being returned to its rightful owners.

King Parahu was the last in the line of keepers, and he had a knowing of his demise, so the guardianship of the sacred items was rightfully the responsibility of the Egyptian temples.

Egypt's history ofbeing subjected to plundering made the citizens hypercautious, and for now, the blazing red granite dais represented the initial steps that would unknowingly welcome home the authentic barque of Amun-Ra.

Second in line was Hatshepsut's gold-studded litter, followed by her personal attendants. The remaining envoy consisted of a choice sampling of every item that was obtained during the expedition. The rest of the objects remained secured inside the ship's hold.

From a distance her temple seemed weightless and airy but strangely fixed solidly to the earth. The red stone platform was positioned between two obelisks located at the base of the ramp that connected the expansive temple terraces. Ceremonial flags staked along the pathway popped in the wind. Date nut palm, sycamore, and fig trees adorned both sides of the lower level ramp. Thousands of flashing red lily plants decorated the perimeter of all three terraces. Sphinxes lined the lush green gardens.

Aneer had carefully orchestrated a group of musicians, acrobats, dancing girls, and singers to entertain the eminent pharaoh and her returning ambassadors. The troupe of entertainers waited with nervous energy and smiled in awe at the approaching envoy. Every movement was choreographed on queue. The dancers and tumblers' nearly nude bodies shone with essential oils beneath the sun's rays.

The ship's chefs had prepared large trays of sweet delicacies for the royal palates. Chefs assigned to the royal complex crossed the Nile in feluccas holding silver pronged trays heaped with mouthwatering delights.

Among the returning envoy was a girl named Zachiah, an Ethiopian arborist. This young girl had left her family and willingly joined the envoy. She would be received into the administration of the pharaoh queen. Zachiah was dedicated to the pharaoh and accompanied the thirty-seven prized frankincense trees. She would plant them at the temple site, promised to care and attend to them with devotion throughout the rest of her lifetime. These prized trees were among the most dazzling items transported from Punt.

Each tree was carried on wheeled litters and pulled across the plains to the temple site. Full of pride, the arborist stood next to the largest tree leading her display and held onto the fragrant branches. She stood proudly within the procession of travelers who were making their way to Hatshepsut's temple.

Zachiah was tall and thin with an unforgettable delicate face. Her cheekbones sloped upward and blended into her hairline while her intelligent eyes focused on the temple in the distance. The branches of the trees waft their fragrance in the Nile air and generated awe in the heart of the onlookers. Zachiah was joyful. She looked at the back of the royal barque and thought; *I will sleep near my precious trees. I will water them and prune them with the utmost care, bundle the twigs, and present them to the pharaoh. I will protect these trees for the pleasure of Egypt's people.*

Senenmut watched the entourage approaching the temple. He walked proudly across the third and highest level of his impressive structure. He stopped and watched the royal litter that carried his lover. He could see the sparkling jewels and colorful glass straws dangling from her hair. He looked down at the platform admiring the finished construction, smiled, and thought, *She will love our mortuary temple.*

He began his walk across the highest terrace. His chest thumped like a rock-splitter hitting its mark. He thirsted for her like a dying man in the scorching desert. His arms palpitated for her embrace. He longed to hold her in his arms and breathe into her the breath of his love.

The entourage approached the red dais at the base of the rising monumental avenue leading up to the first courtyard. Hatshepsut passed the granite sphinxes, the surrounding gardens, and flapping flags. Her heart thumped like a musician's drum. She watched her lover descend from the third terrace.

Her golden vestment warmed against her breast beneath the heat of summer and shimmered in the sun. Her blue tunic lifted and pressed against her legs at the whim of the wind. Her tunic, headdress, and golden beard were weighty on her small frame. The litter bearers lowered the royal litter. Her jewel-like eyes summoned Senenmut.

He was dressed in the ceremonial apron. His hair pulled back and tied at the nape of his neck. He wore the traditional head gear fitting of royalty, and his golden collar sparkled with inlayed jewels.

Senenmut's steps drew closer to the pharaoh, then he knelt before her.

Ramah was within hearing distance to the spoken words of the beautiful pharaoh. He recorded precisely what his ears heard.

Hatshepsut pressed her hand upon the head of her chief architect and whispered, "My true confidant. Oh, how I have missed you whose utterances I so rely."

Part IV

INRI

By Fire Nature Is Renewed Whole

Summary of Pharaoh's Administrative Life and the Passing of Time

IN THE DAYS of Pharaoh Hatshepsut during her peaceful twenty-one years in power she enlarged the borders of Egypt . . . not by war but by commercialization. The Egyptian Kingdom swelled with knowledge from every corner of the world. Scrolls of every subject brought from every port were available to the citizens. The temples became the repository for knowledge. Ships sailed across the big waters and returned with information that would stun the keepers of knowledge. The kingdom of Egypt grew in wisdom under Hatshepsut's rule. In her world, wars were not fought. She empowered the economy with goods of all kinds from Egypt's enemy in exchange for golden wheat.

She closely united herself with the deity of Amun-Ra. She endorsed a rebirth of respect for all gods within the Egyptian realm. She remembered the words her father drilled into her head when she was a child: *The word creates everything–all that we love, all that we hate, and all that we believe. It is the totality of being. Nothing exists before it has been uttered in a clear voice.*

During her rule the "stone scribes" that Senenmut ordered for her kingdom imprinted with official commands were efficient tools. The words spoke clearly the law for the realm and ushered in a sense of order to her kingdom. These stone scribes held the dos and don'ts for conducting oneself when entering Egypt's territories. Some were shaped like scribes, others like lions, and some in the image of herself. On these stones that expressed her laws ended with these words, "My command stands firm like the mountains." All of her commands impressed the citizens.

Hapi, the Nile god, was so pleased with Pharaoh Hatshepsut that the Sopdet star brightly shone, alerting the citizens to the precise hour when to expect annual inundation. Great were the annual Feast of the Valley celebrations during her time in power.

Personal joy and sadness flooded her life like the roaring of rolling waves and the retreating of tides. Her most joyful times were the occasions enveloped within her lover's arms and the product of his love for her–yes, the ever splendid mortuary temple. But there was something else Senenmut gave her that no one in her administration would ever realize–their daughter, Neferure, who was born shortly after the death of Tuthmosis II.

Neferure grew in knowledge under the brilliant tutelage of Senenmut and Pharaoh Hatshepsut. Aggressive training in the administrative policies began during her eighth year and continued until Hatshepsut felt Neferure was steeped in the skills required for leadership.

Praise Celebration at the Temple

"MY CHILD, I am feeling the weight of time and you must leave your heritage upon this land. So tonight you will stand beside me inside the barque and wave to the citizens you soon will inherit. The Feast of the Valley will soon begin, and I will announce my intentions."

"It's so heavy, Mother. Can't my vestments be made from a lighter material? I feel so weighty."

"Gold is the metal of the gods. It is made by gods and for gods and for the royals and their administrations. Gold will give you power. It is the light of the world. It has the power to transcend all female characteristics. You must learn to be like a man, Neferure! The citizens will not accept you if you show weakness. Power up to your responsibilities! After all, you are the earthly representative of gods, my dear child."

Hatshepsut looked at the chief metallurgist and ordered, "Kep, you must tighten Neferure's chest vestment. Make her look manlier."

Beneath the weight of the golden chest gear, head dresses, and traditional golden beard, the gender of the two women was barely discernible. They stepped onto the royal barque and began their journey down the Avenue of the Sphinxes.

They stepped aboard the royal vessel and sailed across the Nile. They were carried across the plains to Hatshepsut's completed mortuary temple where Senenmut awaited.

The citizens applauded the royals with song and praise, but the pharaoh's world would soon meet a sorrowful end . . . an end that she knew one day would surely come. She pressed a smile on her lips in an effort to disregard her destiny.

Years earlier she had seen a glimpse of "twenty-one years into the future," and now the days were unfolding.

Hatshepsut reflected on the similarity of Neferure and Senenmut. No one had ever mentioned, even in jest, that Neferure bore the likeness of the famed royal architect.

Hatshepsut held the hand of Neferure and said, "I am so proud of you, my daughter. You are Egypt's future. Follow in my steps, Neferure, and you will make an excellent pharaoh."

"Will I be marrying my half brother?" Neferure's eyes rolled in disgust.

"If you married Tuthmosis III before I transferred my power to you, my darling daughter, he would only make you his chief wife. It is even possible that your lesser brother may have even met a woman near the site of our gold mines. It is rumored she is his concubine and has already given him a son. He could bring her here to reclaim his throne, and you my dear would be shunt aside as a lesser wife. You don't want that, do you? Neferure, you are enlightened and have reached the age to manage . . . to lead the citizens of Egypt. You have been groomed for this, Neferure. Do not fear. Your thin-blooded brother is overseeing gold mines, and while he is away, I will crown you pharaoh. Remember, you are the one with more royal blood, and because of that, you must be crowned first. Aneer is planning your celebration to take place in three months."

"Who will father my children?"

"There are ways to inform the citizens about the deification of your children."

"How is that, Mother?"

Hatshepsut smiled. "Come, my child." She led Neferure up the temple steps and walked toward a beautiful illustrated mural. She looked up and pointed to a carved mural inside the portico on a temple wall beneath the towering columns. She lifted her arm and pointed to the words and hieroglyphs.

"Remember, the word creates everything. These are the words: 'Amun-Ra walked to Ahmose's bed and appeared in the form of Tuthmosis I (my father). God Amun awakened Ahmose with pleasant fragrance of myrrh. God Amun placed the ankh, the symbol of life, to her nose. Ahmose (my mother) breathed in the sweet smell of life and behold, I was conceived.'"

Hatshepsut reminded Neferure of the power of words. "You may have to marry him, one of your lesser half brothers or cousins, but you can find love outside the realm of your royal marriage. No one needs to know. There are secrets that operate in every administration, some even in plain sight and others so secret they will never be known."

"Neferure, remember, as pharaoh you can bestow a crown upon your husband. In our modern world, it takes two clever crown heads to carry out such authority. One pharaoh cannot be on the battling field and check on the gold mines, granaries, and cotton fields at the same time. It is difficult to govern this vast kingdom on your own. It is good to be married to or have a lover that can assist you in all facets of your universe."

Hatshepsut was thinking about her relationship with Senenmut of whom so much she relied and how he was able to govern while she was on the expedition. She also thought about many secret scrolls and the unspeakable item that rested inside the secret chambers beneath the Temple of Amun.

Neferure listened to the clear words of her mother.

Senenmut walked toward the two women. "Ah, there are my two beautiful royals! Come! We will begin the Feast of the Valley beneath the portico. My honorable pharaoh, give me your hand, and I will lead you to your table. Nakt has prepared a bountiful table for your royal palates."

Senenmut then looked proudly at Neferure. "And give me yours too, Neferure. You remind me of your beautiful mother. Come, let us celebrate."

Hatshepsut gave her daughter an admiring glance. "And you remind me of your handsome father," she said quietly as the breath of a butterfly. A demure smile pressed her lips. Her eyes gazed at Senenmuṭ in adoration. The three walked up the center steps.

The pharaoh was dressed in military regalia complete with the golden braided beard. Her hair was covered by the traditional head dress, topped with the golden uraeus crown. A thin blue floor-length tunic flowed beneath the golden vestment and slid softly against her legs. Her delicate ivory-inlayed sandals stepped across the floor of the third terrace.

Senenmut, now in his sixties, still possessed a stone hewn physique. His auburn hair was graying along the temples. He wore a duel crown of chief advisor and chief architect. His golden collar shone like the sun. He was adored by the citizens and was admired and treated with awe and respect just like a pharaoh.

Aneer had planned the Feast of the Valley to be celebrated at Hatshepsut's completed temple site. Hundreds of citizens lounged around beneath the lush green temple gardens, eating delicacies offered from the silver trays. Zachiah had pruned the fragrant trees and had bowls of burning timbers on every table. The fragrance from the trees and the smoldering timbers scented the air.

The hearts of the audience were joyful, anticipating an epic Valley celebration. Aneer started the show with a troupe of dancing baboons, continuing with the most extraordinary display of artful gymnasts and seductive dancers ending with the blasting sounds of the mizmar and the rhythmic tunes of the harp.

CHANGE FOR EGYPT

CHANGE WAS INEVITABLE for peaceful Egypt. Egypt's youth began to trumpet their disfavor like young raging elephants in musk season. "Egypt should go back to the old ways. We need a male pharaoh, one who can triumph over these damn invading Asiatics. The speaking stones and their curses can no longer subdue the citizens and hold back these intruders," were the words on the lips of many citizens.

Rumors spread that the crown heads of Egypt were in possession of something great and wondrous. Stories about the amazing relic and the many scrolls that unlocked the heavens were stored inside the southern temples that were now used as scriptoriums. The tantalizing news sailed across the Mediterranean and entered the ears of the countries of the north. Was this the same unspeakable relic that frightened the people years earlier? It was rumored that the Egyptian priest knew how to make the amazing relic bring power to their kingdom. To obtain such a powerful item was every ruler's dream. Egypt was a storehouse of knowledge and enticing secrets. To the eyes of northern kings, Egypt was beguiling.

It had been over a century since the Hyksos had been expelled from Egypt, and now unwanted intruders began to pour back into the powerful kingdom from every country. It was the mysteries of the southern temples and the unearthly relic and heavenly scrolls that held magnetic allure. Even the lowliest of citizens were allowed to enter the scriptoriums and read the scrolls.

Toward the end of Hatshepsut's rule the air within the royal complex began to reek with jealousy and distrust. Loyalties began to shift with the slightest gust of the wind. Politics in the royal temple began to turn into a delicate confidence game.

Whispered among the many temple priests and their powerful influence were these words, "She is allowing the citizens to become knowledgeable in all things. We must redirect the power back to our elite men."

Mutnofre, bitter with age, whispered to her daughter-in-law, "Isis it is time your son takes his rightful place in this administration. It is rumored that our illustrious pharaoh is considering handing over the crown to Neferure."

Mutnofre looked at Isis through squinted eyes. "Your son has always expressed a sense of worthlessness and nothingness. I wonder if Hatshepsut put a curse on him when he was a child. It is possible that she ordered the demon, Irritum, to enter his body when he was a toddler. I will remove all worthless demons from your son so he can navigate himself back to his rightful heritage. I will remove this curse, but he must return to the royal city, and he must come to me."

"How can I inform him? My son is far away in the east. He is deep in the earth overseeing the gold mines."

"Daughter-in-law, leave it to me. I will get word to my grandson."

Within days an elite squad of soldiers who supported Tuthmosis III hurried in their horse-drawn chariots across the eastern plains east of the Southern City.

Tuthmosis III Notified

THROUGH THE YEARS Hatshepsut did encourage young Tuthmosis III to become informed about all the administrative duties of the royal house. Accepting his role as the chief gold overseer was among the most important of his obligations and oddly the only one that interested him. Fortunately, having him away from the temple complex would make him inaccessible to temple gossip and the jealousies that muddied up the administration.

Tuthmosis III grew up under the tutelage of the temple priests and the military and was now living in a desert facility west of the Red Sea overseeing gold mines.

Within days a royal entourage who supported the young Tuthmosis III presented him with shocking news.

"Your aunt is going to crown Neferure and bestow upon her the title of pharaoh. It should be you, my lord."

The young prince drew in a deep breath. He looked at his attendants and said, "It will take me several days to reach the Southern City. Ready me for travel."

Within the hour, chariots rolled with a purpose heading westward across the desert to the Southern City, with Tuthmosis at the lead. Soon the city favored by

Amun-Ra would be inundated with hundreds of three-men chariots filled with the drivers, archers, and followers of Egypt's would-be king.

The gates opened wide for Tuthmosis III, his many followers, hundreds of chariots and exhausted horses.

Tuthmosis III Speaks to Hatshepsut

SITRE-RE ENTERED THE throne room. She shuffled quickly across the stone floor, past the ornate tables decorated with silver-pronged platters. She walked up to the banquet of fruits and picked up a handful of mulberries recently picked from a mulberry tree that was a gift from a king far to the east. She gave an offering of berries to the pharaoh, then said, "Your nephew is back, most noble of women, and he insists on speaking with you."

Pharaoh Hatshepsut reached for the mulberries and said, "Usher him in." Her face showed the weathering of time but was washed with a sense of knowing. Her eyes did not sparkle with youth but shone like timeless diamonds containing the wisdom of the ages.

Tuthmosis III walked toward Pharaoh Hatshepsut. His eyes stared at her like an eagle spotting its prey. Without displaying the usual protocol, he stood as rigid as a cobra ready to strike. No longer a thin and spindly child, his muscles were chiseled by the brutal working conditions deep inside the mines.

He looked at Hatshepsut and coolly said, "You have stolen my headship . . . my throne. When I was ten years old, you had me delivered to the inferno of a gold mine. You fully expected me to smother and die like a cooked scorpion. You have separated me from my inheritance, my people, and my throne. I have come to reclaim my heritage."

Hatshepsut looked calmly into the eyes of Tuthmosis III. She coolly stroked the golden beard attached to her chin, drew in a long breath, and said, "You are a thin-blooded royal. I am a full-blooded royal. My grandfather kicked out the Hyksos, which was no easy task when he had to build his own army from regions outside our city. My father was a gallant general and married my mother, the blood sister of Pharaoh Amenhotep. Breathing her breath gave my father godly status. You are the child of a concubine, a lowly one at that."

She smiled cunningly and continued, "Nephew, my decisions are based solely on benefiting our Egypt. You know you are illegitimate in the eyes of the citizens. You were born to a lesser concubine. Egypt's leadership must have one who possesses a high level of royal blood. Historically, royal blood supersedes even the most extraordinary qualification for a leader of Upper and Lower Egypt. It is evident our citizens will accept a female. After all they have been ruled by one for twenty-one years. My daughter has the blood most royal, and it will be Neferure that I will crown the next pharaoh." Then Hatshepsut gave her nephew a skeptical look, "Perhaps you two will marry."

Tuthmosis III looked at his aunt and for a second felt like striking her, but fear from her wrath stayed his hands. Hate for her coursed through every vein inside his body. The fire in his eyes nearly took the breath out of Hatshepsut. He yelled, "I will assemble my own army. I will become pharaoh! I will reclaim my throne." His eyes burrowed into Hatshepsut like dolomite spikes. He huffed, "You sent me to the mines so that I would die beneath the sand, didn't you?"

Hatshepsut looked at him and with quiet self-confidence she answered, "If I wanted you dead, I would have hired an assassin to take you out years ago. Stop and think with your heart. I have given you the greatest of opportunities. You have had the best military schooling. It appears your spirit has been smelted beneath the sands . . . smelted with bronze to make you strong. Your temper will serve you greater than the gold you have been mining. It is necessary for you to develop your best before you can wear a crown."

"But you said you are crowning Neferure!"

"You must realize, my dear nephew, if the citizens will accept a female pharaoh then it is probable they will also accept an administration run equally by wife and husband. When you are leading your army into the far reaches of your kingdom or checking on your gold mines, your wife will be taking care of business in the beautiful Southern City, the Place of the Palaces. In these modern times our vast kingdom and our daunting administrative duties require co-rule, an equitable balance that would gain the consent of goddess Ma'at. I have relied on Ma'at for all of my decisions."

Tuthmosis stared at his aunt. A look of assurance washed across his face. "I will become pharaoh. I will become mighty in the eyes of the citizens, and I will become the ruler of Ma'at."

Hatshepsut looked disbelievingly at her nephew. "We cannot rule our gods! Our gods rule us!"

Tuthmosis stared at Hatshepsut and said in a whisper only meant for her, "Watch me!" Tuthmosis then smiled in the face of Hatshepsut, but inwardly he cursed her.

Tuthmosis left his aunt's royal apartment. He visited his mother, Isis. From there he visited his grandmother, Mutnofre. It was inside Mutnofre's apartment he endured a ritual that gave him a conquering spirit, one that would dominate all of his future decisions. Mutnofre rubbed her grandson with holy oil and said, "You must feel power on your skin." She also ordered Irritum to leave her grandson's body. Exhausted from the ordeal, he later returned to his army of men and planned his takeover. He looked at his assassins and said, "First, you must kill Senenmut."

Tuthmosis III Plans His Takeover

"HE MUST BE eliminated. It is he that she so heavily relies."

The young Tuthmosis III looked at the assassins and with clenched teeth said, "We must chop the head off the snake."

The messenger answered, "If you don't mind me saying, Neferure must be eliminated as well, and soon, that is, if you plan to take full control of Egypt, my young lord."

Tuthmosis spoke with the boldness of a king, "Arrange it and be swift."

Hatshepsut's Plan

HATSHEPSUT CALLED OUT for Kahn. "You must bring Nunzi to me. I have an important request that I must ask of him."

Nunzi, the royal annunciator, stood before his pharaoh. No longer the timid little pearl boy, he now stood tall and proud, nearing his thirties. "Ask anything of me, Your Greatness. I am at your command."

The pharaoh asked, "How well can you navigate your felucca going against the flow of the Nile?"

"You are asking me to sail south?"

"Yes."

With cool confidence Nunzi answered, "Your Greatness, I can sail over anything, rocks if I have to. I know the Nile. I was born on it."

"Good! Prepare your felucca to sail tomorrow morning and say nothing about this to anyone. I and seven other passengers will be in your safekeeping."

"Your Greatness, I can be at the port before Ra has a chance to shine his rays above the horizon. Simply say the time, and I will be there for you and the others."

Nunzi disappeared down the hall of the royal palace. He hurried past the Temple of Amun, out the heavy double doors that protected the royal family and ran down the long Avenue of the Sphinxes and out the city gates. He did not know where he was going, but he knew one thing. He was in charge of a great mission for Pharaoh Hatshepsut.

Hatshepsut Warns Senenmut

STILL EXISTING IN Nekheb were the descendants of the wealthy family that once gave military assistance to her great-grandfather. All through the years, Hatshepsut kept a secret dossier on the family and their whereabouts, maintaining a clandestine relationship with the family. She knew that the day would come when their protection once again would be needed.

"We must prepare to leave in the morning. I know what my future brings. I have seen it! The unspeakable relic, 'the wonder maker,' warned me years ago on the return trip from Punt. It told me I would have twenty-one years of reign and that my rule would be seized by a thin-blooded line. It is he, my nephew, and today he visited me. I must flee to Nekheb, the land that will give me shelter! If I don't, he will order my death. Doubting my memory, I visited Iy, our archivist. Today we sat before the unspeakable thing and it reaffirmed everything. My death, and our daughter's death as well as yours are being plotted right now. I have the ability to alter our fates. So that is why we must flee! It must be tomorrow morning before Ra reaches the horizon."

Hatshepsut took in a breath and shook her head, exhaling these words, "I can't believe I have not paid more attention to this dreadful thing that has haunted my thoughts and hovered above me daily like a miasma. I have been a prisoner of my own ambitions. I can only pray to the god of Baphomet to give me wisdom and to goddess Ma'at to keep me balanced."

Senenmut studied Hatshepsut in disbelief. He though, *Once a tightly woven rope, she is unraveling before my eyes. She seems to have been besieged by a sense of helplessness. Only one other time she came to me in distress.*

Instinctively, he knew her plea was heartfelt. He embraced her and said, "I have always loved you, Hatshepsut, and I always will. I'll be waiting for you at the port before Ra has a chance to raise his arms to the sky."

Tuthmosis had instructed the assassins to kill Senenmut. However, the hired killers' strategy was to satisfy the need of their leader . . . to eliminate the chief advisor to Pharaoh Hatshepsut. These assassins knew of a great king from the north lands that was searching for an illustrious builder, one who knew sacred building techniques. To assassinate a treasury of intellect, such a talented article of trade would be the actions of a fool. Senenmut's craft was worth his weight in gold-weight that could rival the wealth of a well-outfitted army.

These assassins planned their attack that night. They were as quiet as the breath of a stalking lion.

An unanticipated thing happened. Unable to sleep, Zachiah, the much revered temple arborist decided to stroll along the second terrace and observe her beautiful myrrh trees in the moonlight. She spotted several men carrying a rolled carpet from the home of the famous architect. It seemed odd to her that Senenmut would have his carpet removed in the middle of the night. Something about the mysterious event didn't seem right.

A select group of masons, the "servants of Truth Square" banged on Senenmut's door. These elite stone masons had prearranged an early meeting with him before first light to discuss plans for additional work to be added to Hatshepsut's temple.

The door was ajar. They yelled out his name but no one answered, so they pushed on the door and it opened. They called out his name and walked up the stairs to his apartment. They did not find him there. His prized cedar chest of building secrets were missing. The well-ordered home was disheveled. Further investigation revealed Senenmut's personal cook, Nakt, laid dead in his bed with his throat slashed like a slaughtered goat.

Zachiah's home was located next door to the architect's home and within the hour she could hear the murmuring and buzzing of anguished voices.

"His cook, Nakt, has been slaughtered! Senenmut is nowhere to be found! We must warn the pharaoh!" were the desperate yells that echoed throughout the town of Deir El-Medina.

Zachiah followed the envoy of masons and journeyed across the plains to the Nile. Feluccas filled up with desperate workers and crossed the water and hurried to inform the pharaoh.

The entire working community of Deir el-Medina began an extensive search for their chief architect, Senenmut, but they could not fine him anywhere.

Tuthmosis III Informed

STANDING BEFORE THE young prince, one of the assassins said, "We entered his house when we knew he was asleep. It is done, your majesty."

"Why did you not bring his remains to me?"

"You did not ask for his remains. His body has already been consumed by crocodiles, your majesty. We stood there and watched as their deadly aim ripped him apart. It was done quickly, my lord. So, there is nothing left."

"Just as well. Go! You will be paid handsomely!"

The real story of Senenmut's disappearance was never revealed in hieratic script or hieroglyphs. His disappearance was a mystery to the ancient Egyptian world.

Senenmut had a knowing of heavenly building secrets and the assassins knew it. To them he was as valuable as a salt mine, a gold mine and a silver mine. Senenmut was tied up like a captured slave. They stashed him beneath the planks of a cargo ship. His ankles and hands were bound by rope, his mouth stuffed with cotton and fixed with papyrus straps. His cedar box that was filled with treasured scrolls was positioned on the floor above him. Any noise he made blended with the squeaking and moaning of the ship.

One of the brothers of the assassin said laughingly to a collaborator, "We shall be richer than the wealthiest merchant. We could even establish our own army."

Beneath the planks of the ship Senenmut could hear the words of his captors. He knew the ship was headed to a destination north of Egypt, and he knew he would be forced to become an architect to a northern king. He could hear his captors debate his new name. No longer could he answer to Senenmut.

The pressure and weight of the wooden timbers pressed against his body. He could smell the cedar chest that rested inches above him. His eyes closed, and his heart pounded like a dolomite hammer.

These thoughts would keep the greatest architect's heart beating. *I will die a stranger in a strange land, and I will never again see Hatshepsut, my beautiful love and our beautiful daughter, Neferure. My heart will always carry the greatest love. It was love that created your temple. Love formed every angle, every pillar, and every terrace. Love for you, my Hatshepsut, carved every stone.*

Wrapped like a butterfly inside a dark cocoon, the most famous architect in the Egyptian world laid imprisoned beneath the planks.

LEAVING THE PLACE OF THE PALACES

RA HAD NOT yet raised his arms above the horizon. The port was lit with lamps. Flames flickered in the darkness. Nunzi busied himself packing the felucca with royal items handed to him by the pharaoh.

Appearing like a common citizen Hatshepsut stood on the dock where Nunzi had his felucca moored. She stared over the Nile and watched the early commercial ships sailing in and out of the port. She waited for Senenmut and watched for his boat. He promised to meet her and sail to Nekheb, a place where they could seek protection.

In the distance an overloaded felucca sailed toward the port. A group of men piled out and hurried toward the gates of the royal city.

Zachiah followed behind the worried stonecutters. They quickly revealed their golden collars to the gatekeepers and immediately were admitted into the city. But in a fortunate moment before Zachiah had a chance to reach the city gates she glanced toward the group of commoners standing on the dock.

The flame from a nearby lamp shone on the most recognizable face in the beautiful Southern City. Hatshepsut looked at the temple arborist. Their anxious eyes met. Zachiah made her way toward the pharaoh.

The look on Zachiah's face was revealing. Hatshepsut held her hands to her heart.

"Tell me. Where is Senenmut?"

Zachiah's heart thumped like a drum while she told her story. "Tonight I could not sleep. I was walking among the trees on the second terrace of your temple, and I spotted men carrying a rug from the home of the famous architect. A short time ago Senenmut's cook was found dead, his throat slashed. My heart tells me Senenmut was spirited out of Thebes hidden within a rug. I fear he has been seized."

Surrounding the pharaoh was Kahn, Neferure, Sitre-Re, and Ramah. They crowded closer to Hatshepsut and held her arms to prevent her from swooning. In the darkness Hatshepsut's face paled like the moon shining down on the beautiful Southern City.

Neferure seemed wobbly and displayed a dimming sense of what was going on. She held her stomach and slurred these words, "I must sit down. The thought of fleeing my beautiful city is making me sick."

Nunzi heard the murmurings and offered a hand to Neferure and the pharaoh. He helped them inside the felucca. Kahn looked at Hatshepsut and said in halted Egyptian, "I need to take care of a matter. I will return before Ra reaches the horizon. Do not leave without me!"

While they piled into the felucca, Kahn slipped back into the royal city and headed straight to Mutnofre's apartment. He was crafty in the ways of breaching private dwellings. He slipped through a high window and quietly lowered himself into her gold-speckled room. He walked toward her bed and put his strong hands around her neck. Her eyes popped opened and the last thing she saw was Hatshepsut's bodyguard. The mighty Kahn whispered to her, "You will never kill again."

He left her apartment as quietly as he entered, but this time through her heavy door. He ran like a lion in pursuit of its prey down the Avenue of the Sphinxes and exited the city gate. Quickly he made his way to the port where the pharaoh and her envoy waited.

Hatshepsut cried out, "Zachiah will be coming with us. I know what my nephew will do. The "wonder maker" revealed it to me. He will destroy my beautiful temple and the entire temple staff. I will not let him destroy me or any of you. I hope

Senenmut will one day return to me. He will know where to find me. Now, we must go."

Within days of arriving at Nekheb, Neferure fell ill and died. Moments before her death, her skin tinged a curious shade of blue. Not even a whisper of a good-bye could escape her lips before she closed her eyes to death.

These sad words were spoken by Hatshepsut: "Bury my daughter at the site of my breathing ceremony where her ka can soar above the cliffs and observe the pink clouds that spans the Nile and the Red Sea. Sadly, like my brothers, Neferure never had a chance to leave her heritage in Egypt."

Epilogue

FINALLY THE DAY came. The precise moment that Tuthmosis III felt the weight of the crown being placed on his head, the firmament shook like a helpless goat struggling inside the mouth of a crocodile. Within seconds hordes of Nile rats darted to and fro looking for stable ground. The high-pitched sound of temple cats mewed louder than the desert cats that prowled the sandy dunes. Horses broke loose and ran from the rising waters.

The skies darkened. Potash billowed and spun around like a cloud of locust. The Nile valley flooded with water surging across the black land faster than an eagle could fly. This was not the annual inundation but something different . . . something that made hearts tremble. The water was rushing south and roiling against the Nile's natural northern flow. The closed sea (Mediterranean) had channel through the delta and rushed up the Nile like a band of raging wild elephants.

Once again the historical memory of the citizens was alerted to the all familiar terrifying incident. The psyche of the citizens was always mentally rehearsing for the worst of times. The survival motto was to remember that much is needed to be accomplished during bleak days of uncertainty. When the fear of stealing no longer disciplined ones behavior, the real plan, the survival plan, was always put into action. Fear tempts the most steadfast. Desperate people are always willing to challenge the fury of the gods. Each person had declared that which he or she would steal for their own future survival.

The loyal servants to the royals knew exactly where the jewels were hidden and the gold was kept. The sacrosanct scribes, pure priests, and ordinary citizens were known to brazenly plunder riches in a moment's notice if they truly thought the end was near.

In the memory and the oral teachings of the citizens of the beautiful Southern City the skies mimicked the atmospheric conditions like the days when the Hyksos ran from the temples of Egypt.

People hurried toward the boats with their arms loaded with goods. The river was overrun with north-bound and south-bound feluccas. Large transports were confiscated and sailed by hysterical citizens.

Iy, the archivist, managed to gather up the most important scrolls and ran to one of the larger transports. He stood on the bow, embracing sacred scrolls beneath his robes.

In years to come, after Iy's death, these sacred scrolls eventually were given to sophists, the sacred keepers of unspeakable secrets, who would fiercely protect these ancient writings.

In the future, a certain cedar box containing heavenly geometry scribed in the Book of Enahk (Enoch) would be destined for the eyes of a glorious king. This future king, yet to be born, would study this book, learn from it, and use the instructions to build a great temple in a future city in lands north of Egypt.

This great king's wise thinking would spring from careful reading, absorbing the heavenly teachings that the angels once revealed to Enoch–the same one once held by the hands of Senenmut.

Sadly, far into the unimaginable future, these heavenly secrets would be deemed apocryphal. Some burned and some buried and lost to civilization.

Tuthmosis III rose from the shadow of Hatshepsut's reign. He feared the "backward water" was an omen from the gods.

Tuthmosis III stood in front of his army and yelled, "I order you to scratch her face from all of her murals, sculptures, and crack the uraeus and golden beard from every stone image that represents her. This will insure she will have no life in paradise! Destroying her murals and sculptures will destroy her heritage! And you . . . my newly acquired citizens . . . will lose the memory of her!"

He caught his breath and continued. "These are 'divine orders' from your pharaoh, and I know these orders will please all the gods. I will clean the slate and begin my own building campaign! Amun-Ra loves war, and I will become his earthly champion! I will become a brilliant warrior and break the will of Egypt's enemy. Furthermore, I will no longer allow the citizens to access the scriptoriums. From now on knowledge will be viewed only by a select few. I, Tuthmosis III, will start a society of secret keepers!"

He lifted up the "wonder maker," a strange combination of crystal and an alien metal box that seemed to possess an unusual kind of force. "I will personally bury this thing that she brought back from Punt." He wrapped a cloth around it, put it on the floor of his chariot, then picked up his son, Amenhotep II, a lad born of a concubine. He held him up for all to see and yelled, "Amenhotep II, my son, you will follow in my steps!" He secured his child in his arms and ordered his charioteer to snap the reins of the horses. He rolled away from his army and yelled, "I order you to destroy! Destroy!"

Hatshepsut lived out her last days with a broken heart. With each passing year sadness from the loss of her daughter and lover devoured her heart like a venomous serpent. She reminded her loyal friends, "Once I stood tall like a strong obelisk, but now I am broken and fractured never again to be raised, and never again will I feel the power of the sun."

In her solemn final days her closest friends surrounded her: Sitre-Re, her devoted handmaiden; the mighty Kahn, her protector; Ramah, her loyal scribe who secretly loved her to her last breath; Nunzi, her faithful courier; and lastly, Zachiah, who devotedly kept Hatshepsut's room filled with fragrance of frankincense and myrrh.

In her forty-seventh year the most noblest of women closed her eyes beneath a full moon that shone brightly over Nekheb. Her ka soared across her once beautiful mortuary temple that now revealed broken images of her face. She sensed the presence of her life guide, the knowing presence that once spoke to her during the visit inside the pyramid when she was a child. She relived the night of remote viewing and remembered the things that gladdened the human heart.

She followed a bright light that beckoned her like a magnet. In the distance glowing figures stood with outstretched arms. Her heart pounded like a drum as she stepped into the light.

The once beautiful pharaoh died a recluse in the peaceful little town of Nekheb, which eventually would become known as the Place of the Lady of Punt.

In the hours before Ra raised his arms above the horizon, just before Hatshepsut threw her last breath, she looked into the eyes of her scribe. Her voice was weak. Her breathing was labored. "You have brought honor to my life, Ramah, my dear friend. I will see you in paradise. Tell Nunzi to inform the House of Purification that I am ready. I must be fixed for burial."

Ramah waited for her eyes to close. When she took her last breath, Ramah did something that he had always wanted to do. He leaned down and kissed her lips and drew into his lungs the last remaining breath of the most noble of women.

Truth is words diluted to its basic form. The truth of Hatshepsut's story is revealed within these pages. Although her story is a book of fiction it is based on facts.

According to *Ramah, the loyal scribe to the most noble of women, the beautiful Pharaoh Hatshepsut Makare Khenemetamen.*
Pilak (the end)

Rebel Pharaoh

List of true historical characters

Hatshepsut Makare Khenemtamen, most noblest of women, also known as Hatsu
Senenmut–Chief advisor and chief architect of Hatshepsut's mortuary temple
Tuthmosis I–Hatshepsut's father
Tuthmosis II–Half brother and also royal husband to Hatshepsut
Tuthmosis III–Known as Hatshepsut's nephew/stepson
(Hatshepsut became his regent)
Sitre-Re–Hatshepsut's chief maidservant and confidant
Aahmes–Hatshepsut's mother also known as Ahmose
Neferure–Hatshepsut's daughter
Mutnofre–Chief concubine to Tuthmosis I and mother of Tuthmosis II
Isis–Chief concubine to Tuthmosis II and mother of Tuthmosis III
Ptah–High priest
Hapuseneb–Young priest and son of Ptah
Ineni–Replacement architect for Tuthmosis I
Nehsi–Personal tracker for the Punt expedition
Queen Ati–Queen of Punt
King Parahu–King of Punt
Amenhotep II–Son of Tuthmosis III

LIST OF LITERARY CREATIONS:

Ramah–Hatshepsut's personal scribe

Kahn–Hatshepsut's personal protector

Iy–Chief archivist

Nazli–A young Nubian concubine and a gift to Tuthmosis I after Ahmose dies

Pearl Boy also called Nunzi–Personal messenger to Hatshepsut

Aneer–Crocodile trainer and entertainer during Hatshepsut's administration

Nakt–Personal chef for Senenmut

Keph–Personal handmaiden to Tuthmosis II

Rejal–Belly dance instructor to women of the royal temple

Kep–Maker of golden chest armor for Hatshepsut

Nob–Pike maker

Set–Maker of obsidian blades and metallurgist

Zachiah–Arborist from Land of Punt and supplier of frankincense for Hatshepsut

Lata–Bee keeper and alchemist for the "necessary arts."

Other Books by Charlotte Kramer

(Fictional stories based on fact)

Holy Murder; The Death of Hypatia of Alexandria

It was in the illustrious city of Alexandria that the celebrated beauty Hypatia, a fifth century "renaissance" woman lived her brief but brilliant life as a professor of philosophy, mathematics, chemistry, and astronomy. Bishop Cyril despised Hypatia and ordered her brutal death. Cyril attempted to erase her name from history by ordering his army to destroy her manuscripts and inventions. Her trusted scribe and lover, Ramas, however hid some of her secret scrolls in the ancient city of Petra.

The New Landers; An Early American Novel

In 1788, a poor Scottish family crosses the Atlantic Ocean in a leaky ship in search of a better life. The new lands of America offer them a promise. The McKinnon's dream, to prosper like nobles, withers to the realities of surviving the wild woods of Rockingham, North Carolina.

Birthing at sea, a wounded deck hand plummeting overboard in the midst of a hurricane reveals a grueling shipboard voyage. The Philadelphia Wagon Road becomes the backbone of their adventurous and harrowing travels. They meet up with the true character of the Cherokee Indians, a hungry bear and a ruthless encounter with the infamous Paxton Boys.

Slave issues, gossip, local feuds, the great awakening and a home invasion were misfortunes they faced in the backwoods of Rockingham, North Carolina.

The Journey of Bridge Boy; Along the Cherokee Trail of Tears

A near drowning puts the rebellious young Jim McKinnon into a coma. Transported into the past, he travels with the Cherokee during their winter exodus across deadly mountain ridges and snow storms. Jim's face-to-face confrontations with Andrew Jackson reveal concealed, carefully protected historical secrets.

Lightning Source UK Ltd.
Milton Keynes UK
UKHW012203060622
404004UK00001B/322